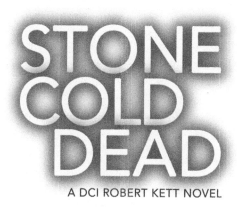

STONE COLD DEAD

A DCI ROBERT KETT NOVEL

ALEX SMITH

RELENTLESS
MEDIA

STONE COLD DEAD
Published Worldwide by Relentless Media.
This edition published in 2021.

ISBN 978-1-913877-05-7

Edited by Hanna Elizabeth

www.alexsmithbooks.com
relentless.media

ALSO BY ALEX SMITH

For Gran.
We miss you.

PROLOGUE

Friday

"I'll kill you, squirrel dick, and don't think that's an exaggeration."

If Chase Masefield's jaw had dropped any further it would have unhinged entirely and clattered to the floor. The young man stood there for a moment, his cheeks blazing, looking for all intents and purposes like a post box. Across the room, Mr Skinner smiled. It wasn't a kind smile, not one bit. He was a big man, well into his late forties even though his daughter was just seventeen, the same age as Chase. What little was left of his hair was plastered over the sweaty dome of his enormous head, and his face seemed to glow, as if all the brandy he'd drunk that evening had ignited inside him. He patted the formidable gun safe he'd just locked and slid the keys into his pocket.

"Uh..." Chase said. "I beg your pardon?"

The big man didn't reply, he simply studied Chase with an expression that the boy couldn't place. It wasn't kind, but there was something else there, something that put him on edge, something almost predatory. He'd only met Lauren's dad a handful of times, usually at school pick-up, but tonight was the first time he'd been properly introduced, and the first time they'd been left alone together. He hoped there wouldn't be another, especially after the stories that people shared at school about the gym that Mr Skinner kept in his garden, the people he invited there.

The *things* he did.

Still, putting up with him was a small price to pay for dating his daughter.

"Chase?" came a voice, and he spluttered out a breath he hadn't even realised he was holding.

"In here," he squeaked.

Somebody laughed from behind the closed door of the large utility room and a second later it opened, Lauren's smile beaming through. She took one look at Chase and burst into golden laughter, the same laughter he thought perhaps he was falling in love with—not that he had any intention of mentioning that tonight, or indeed *ever* if her dad had anything to do with it. Lauren was undeniably beautiful. His mum said she reminded her of a young Audrey Hepburn. Chase didn't know who that was. All he did know was that she made his legs weak.

"Oh god," she went on, looking from him to her father and back again. "Don't tell me you two are conspiring."

"I thought I'd show him the guns," said Mr Skinner—his name was Greg, but he hadn't invited Chase to call him that. "Thought a city boy like him would want to see them."

They had been downright terrifying. Three shotguns of various sizes, all stinking of oil and smoke. Mr Skinner had taken one out and made no small show of demonstrating how well he knew how to use it, and how well he knew where to aim it if he needed to safeguard his daughter's honour.

"He's hardly a city boy, dad," Lauren said, tutting. "He lives on the other side of the village."

"The Dereham side," Mr Skinner said. "They're as good as city folk to me."

"Are you going to stand in that room all night or are we going for a walk?" shouted Lauren's mum from somewhere in the house. There was a flurry of footsteps and Matilda Skinner—*Tilly*, she had insisted—appeared next to her daughter, wrapping a knitted scarf around her head. She was a short woman, her face and body like some half-formed lump of clay, but she had the sweetest eyes and the kindest voice. How she'd ended up with a bully like her husband was anybody's guess.

Chase wondered if she knew about the stories too, the rumours.

"Dad was just showing Chase the guns," groaned Lauren, as if she'd been in this situation a hundred times before.

"Always the guns," said Tilly, shaking her head in mock disapproval. "Greg, it's not like you even use them anymore. When was the last time you took them outside?"

Mr Skinner shrugged, his grey eyes locked on Chase.

"You never know when you might have to shoot some vermin," he said, that same smile crawling onto his lips.

"Uh..." said Chase, feeling like the floor was opening up to swallow him and kind of hoping it would.

"Oh dad, shut up," said Lauren, stomping into the room and grabbing Chase's arm a little harder than she needed to. He was all too happy to follow her out of the airless space, into their enormous farmhouse kitchen where an AGA the size of his car was doing a grand job of keeping the chill out of the air. "Just ignore him," Lauren said, kissing him on the cheek and making his freshly shaven face sting. "He does this to all the boys."

"All of them?" Chase said, feeling his heart clatter down past another couple of ribs. Lauren tutted again, letting go of him.

"You know what I mean. Are you ready?"

"For what?" Chase asked, feeling like he might be close to vomiting. Mr Skinner had poured him a brandy at dinner and teased him relentlessly until he'd knocked back the whole thing, and now everything seemed to be swimming.

"A walk," Lauren said, looking at him like he'd just sprouted horns. "Earth to Chase, are you still with us?"

"Yeah," he said, snapping his head away when she reached for his face. Lauren frowned—one of anger rather than confusion—and Chase instantly regretted it. He was well aware of the fact that he was batting *way* above his league—Lauren Skinner was the belle of the ball at school, beautiful and smart and destined for great things. Even his own mum had reminded him of this when he'd announced who he was dating, warning him to stay away to avoid the inevitable disappointment. He reached for her but this time she pulled away, marching across the kitchen.

"You're blowing it," said Mr Skinner, his mouth too close to his ear. The big man put a hand on his shoulder and let it drop down to the small of his back where it sat until Chase moved away, his skin crawling. He had to force himself not to break into a run as he entered the grand, flag-stone-clad hall. Compared to the kitchen it was positively Arctic in here.

"Are we bringing the dog?" Tilly asked as she followed him out of the kitchen.

"It's too cold, Mama," said Lauren, her coat so puffy that

she could barely see over it to work on the zip. "Little Alfred will freeze."

"It's little Chase I'm worried about," said Tilly, but there was no malice in her words. She handed him his coat from the rack, buttoning it up for him before offering a dimpled smile. "It's hardly thick enough, Chase, you'll catch your death out there if you're not careful."

"Give him a hat," said Lauren.

"It's fine," said Chase. "I don—"

"A hat, good thinking," Tilly rode over him, plucking one from a basket on the sideboard.

"I'm fine, honestly."

"Take the hat," said Lauren.

"The hat," Tilly added, thrusting it at him. It was a shade of neon pink that had no right to exist.

"I'm used to the cold," he said.

"Take the bloody hat," growled Mr Skinner, and there was no doubt that it was an order. Chase grabbed the hat and pulled it over the curls he'd spent an hour trying to tame before he'd left home. Lauren's dad laughed. "You look like a tit."

"Greg!" Tilly said.

"I think you look lovely," Lauren said, everything apparently forgiven. She ran a hand down the front of his coat, gazing up at him with an expression that could have melted every bone in his body. Well, every bone except *one*. "It'll keep those lips warm too."

"Uh..." said Chase, looking across the hallway to where the red-faced Mr Skinner was attempting to shoot daggers out of his eyes right into Chase's heart. He was tapping his pocket, the keys for the gun safe sounding an alarm.

"Right," Tilly said, pushing past the two of them and opening the front door. "Brace yourselves!"

The cold entered the house like a blade, scalpel-sharp and lethal. For a moment, the four of them looked into the pitch-black night, listening to the artillery fire of the gusting wind.

"Gosh," said Tilly. "Picked up a bit, hasn't it?"

"Can't we stay here, Mama?" Lauren said.

"But it's tradition," Tilly answered, pouting as if she was the child. "Friday roast and a walk in the woods, whatever the weather. Come on, darling, we won't go far."

"Chase?" Lauren said, looking at him as if he had any say in the matter at all.

"It will be nice to get out?" he said, more question than statement. He glanced at Tilly and she nodded her approval, which seemed to take some of the chill out of the air. At least he was getting on the good side of one of her parents tonight. And it wasn't a lie, right now he'd do pretty much anything to get out of the house, out of the stifling heat and away from Mr Skinner's obsessive attention.

"Come on then," Mr Skinner said, lifting a torch from the telephone table. He brushed past Chase even though he didn't need to, forcing him to take a step back. Then he pulled a flat cap over his bulging head and stepped into the night, the wind almost ripping his Barbour jacket clean off his body. Chase willed him to disappear altogether, prayed for him to be blown right out of existence, but he simply put his head down and stomped away from the house.

"Do you think we need an umbrella?" Chase asked.

"No umbrellas," Mr Skinner yelled back.

Mrs Skinner shrugged apologetically, smiling at Chase as she pulled the hat down over his forehead.

"He's not the ogre he makes himself out to be," she said. "He's popular with the young men in the village. He trains half of them in his gym, you know? He'll come around. Maybe he'll train you too."

Christ no, he thought.

Tilly marched out of the house and Lauren took Chase's hand, leading him through the door. The night had lost its mind, howling and roaring like a madman. Fingers of wind tugged at his coat, teased his hat, stole the air from his lungs when he tried to breathe. The weather had been bad in the three weeks since New Year, but tonight it was wild, and it sought to do them harm.

Not that the Skinner family seemed to care. Mr Skinner was already a shadow, eclipsing the light from the torch as he pounded his way down the track. His wife tottered after him, both hands planted on top of her head in an effort to save her scarf. The Skinner house sat right on the eastern edge of Lesser Lyng, edged by fields to the south and woodland to the east. Chase had been in and out of the forests here a hundred times but rarely since he was a kid, and never on a night like this. The way the trees swayed and thrashed reminded him of the times he'd had the bonnet of his Mark II open, an engine of cogs and pistons that would crush and dismember them in an instant if they strayed too close.

And yet stray too close is exactly what Mr Skinner did. He swung right, the torchlight setting fire to Chase's retinas as he aimed it back, like an interrogator's lamp.

"This way," he roared as he entered the woods, whistling so loud that even the wind couldn't mute it.

"Dad, no!" Lauren shouted, Chase's arm clamped in both of hers. "Let's just go up the road a bit, it's bloody freezing."

Her pleas fell on deaf ears as the woods gulped her father into its gaping throat.

"He can be such a *dick*," she said. "Sorry, Chase."

The fact that she was apologising to him made him feel a little better. Perhaps he could use that guilt to levy a kiss before he headed home, or something more. That's what his friend Jonah always told him, that guilty girls put out. Then he glanced down at Lauren and decided he didn't want her to feel guilty, or sorry, or anything bad. He pulled his arm free and wrapped it around her shoulder, shielding her from the worst of the wind.

"Where's he going?" he asked.

"God knows," she said. "He just likes to make things difficult."

Tilly beetled into the woods after her husband, illuminated by a memory of torchlight. Chase thought he saw her glance back but he couldn't be sure. Above him, the trees swayed back and forth, something mechanical in the creaking, clacking sound of them, and he felt the first of the rain hit his cheek.

"Come on, dad, it's gonna chuck it down," Lauren said, and the night howled back as if in outrage. There was no reply and she grunted with angry resignation. "Oh for fuck's sake, let's get it over with."

She upped her pace, the two of them hunkered into each other as they cut down the path into the woods. The trees did their best to stop them but once he was past their blind reach Chase found that it was quieter in here, the storm locked outside the wind-stripped canopies. It was more open than he'd been expecting, Mr Skinner clearly visible ahead as he strode ever onwards. Chase took a step and a bony root caught his shoe, making him stagger.

"Sorry," Lauren said again when he'd recovered.

"It's fine," he replied, laughing before he even knew he was doing it. "Wasn't quite what I expected, you know?"

"Freezing your arse off in the woods?" Lauren replied, smiling up at him. "Aren't all your dates like this?"

What dates? he almost replied, before realising that this confession probably wouldn't win him much street cred.

"Only the good ones," he said. "This is nice, though. Can't think of any other place your dad would let me put my arm around you."

"He's been giving you a hard time?" she asked.

"I think he said he was going to kill me," Chase replied, keeping his voice low. "I'm also pretty sure he called me squirrel dick."

This time Lauren's laughter was like a pheasant's call, and even the woods seemed stunned by it.

"I've heard him say worse," she said. "Way worse."

"And I don't," Chase added.

"Don't what?"

"Have a squirrel's dick," he said, leaning in.

The look she gave him—*prove it*—made the night feel like it was burning.

"Oi! I'm talking to you."

Mr Skinner had come to a stop ahead, glaring back. Tilly stood by his side, her arm looped through his, her teeth chattering.

"I'm sorry," Chase said. "I didn't hear you."

"Yeah," said Lauren's dad, his eyes dark. "Hard to pay attention when all your blood is in your—"

Tilly gave him a solid elbow in the ribs and he growled into silence. He sniffed, glancing past the trees to where a solid curtain of rain was now falling.

"Go get us some umbrellas," he said, shining the torch in Chase's face again.

He blinked away the imprint of his own retinas, staring at the ground.

"I thought you—"

"Go on now," Mr Skinner barked. "And hurry back."

Chase nodded, turning slowly so that he didn't have to take his arm from around Lauren's shoulders.

"Just you, son," Mr Skinner said. "Don't think I'm letting you two out of my sight."

He was about to protest but Lauren wriggled free, smudging a hand over her wet brow. She looked mightily pissed off, although Chase didn't know if it was with him or her dad.

"Just do it," she said. "The only way to get this over with is to do what he says."

"Door's open," Tilly called out, a shiver in her voice. "Sorry Chase, you'll find your way okay?"

Chase nodded, staring back the way they'd come and seeing nothing but dark.

"He does this to everyone," Lauren said. "He's just... I don't know. It's just his way of showing you who's boss. He doesn't mean anything by it."

"Sure," Chase muttered. "I left my phone in the house, can I borrow yours? For the light?"

Lauren frowned like he'd asked the stupidest question in the world. She pointed down the path.

"It's like two minutes that way."

"Right," snapped Chase, walking away and wondering whether he should just keep walking, climb into his knackered little Golf and go home.

Yeah, sure, and waste your one and only chance with Lauren Skinner.

He'd taken a dozen steps before the night moved in, the woods so dark it was like somebody had put a bag over his head. He wanted to look back to make sure he wasn't alone but he knew if he did that he'd see Mr Skinner's grinning face and he didn't want to give the man the satisfaction. Instead, he fumbled forwards, testing the ground with each step to make sure he didn't piss over. Another dozen steps and he'd lost the path, or perhaps the trees had simply got up and moved. He put his hands out in front of him to feel the way and couldn't see them there, his blind eyes full of rainwater, his ears full of wind.

"Fuck," he said, rubbing his face. "Fuck fuck fu—"

A light ahead, just a glimmer, as faint as the will-o'-the-wisps his mum had always told him stories about. Chase was almost crying as he staggered towards it, his hands stinging from the whipping branches. He pushed out of the forest fifty yards or so from the path they'd used to enter it, feeling the same sense of shifting dread as when he swam in the sea and the water carried him south—as if the woods too had tides. The light was from the Skinner house, every window blazing, golden. He didn't think he'd ever been so happy to see a building in his life and he set off, his foot dropping into a ditch and something popping inside his bad knee.

"Fuck!" he said again, limping and hopping and somehow ending up on all fours. His fingers sank into something soft, something *putrid*. He pushed himself up, sniffing his hand and almost throwing up Tilly's roast duck.

It was the last straw. Fuck Mr Skinner. Fuck Tilly. And fuck Lauren too. She hadn't even warned him about this evening, not even a hint. She could go—

Something cracked in the woods, right behind him, a branch underfoot. And Chase felt it like a kick to the stomach, a feeling, an instinct, some animal part of him that screamed a warning.

Run.

Because there was another noise too, a sound that rose

over the wind, relentless, unmistakeable. Something moving.

Something *running*.

Thudthudthudthudthudthud.

He looked back, and even in the dark he saw it, a *deeper* darkness that exploded from the trees.

"Fu—"

A limb that seemed too long, that swept down and cracked into the side of his head so hard that he felt his conscious mind leave his body, felt it cartwheel up into the shaking trees, into the gasping wind, up and up and up—

And then pain, pain the likes of which he didn't think possible. He opened his mouth to scream only to choke on his own spit, each hacking cough detonating inside his skull like an explosion. He was sitting, a wall or something against his back, but when he lifted his hands to protect himself from another attack he found he couldn't. His first thought was paralysis, that he'd been struck hard enough to snap his neck. But then he tried to move his hands again and felt the rope that bound his wrists.

What the fuck? he tried to say, the words trapped in his head by the endless rush of agony. Was there a sound behind the wet pounding of his pulse? Drums, maybe? Beating out a rhythm like thunder. He looked down, seeing nothing but the dark, fearing blindness until he breathed out and felt the heat of it against his own mouth.

There was something over his face.

"Hello?" he said, his jaw working the word like it would work a piece of toffee. "What the fuck?"

He flexed his arms. They were definitely tied behind his back—not rope but wire, he could feel the sharpness of it, the wetness where blood had already spilled. He tugged and tugged but it only brought pain, and something worse, *terror*. It swelled from his gut like a wave, so dark and so loud that he couldn't breathe.

Somebody had done this to him. Somebody had attacked him.

He must have passed out because he would have felt himself being tied up. How long had he been out? Lauren and her family had only been a short walk away, surely they would have heard something?

"Help!" he said, hearing his words muffled against whatever sat over his face.

Nothing, just the laughter of the wind and that same pounding, pulsing, deafening agony.

"Lauren?" he shouted, and he was on the verge of calling for her dad when he wondered if Mr Skinner had done this to him, if he'd followed him through the night and clubbed him.

You never know when you might have to shoot some vermin.

"I won't say anything," he sniffed. "Just let me go."

Nobody replied but he felt the wall behind him shift—a sudden blast of cold against his back. It wasn't a wall at all, he realised. Somebody had been *sitting* there, their body pressed against his.

"Please," he said again, crying now, suddenly seven years old. "My mum, she'll be wondering where I am. My brother."

A breath in his ear and the darkness over his face shifted, something burning into his eyes. He squirmed, blinking until the brightness made sense—a bonfire, the hiss of rain as it was swallowed by the flames. The world had been cut in two and Chase understood that he was wearing a mask of some kind, eyeholes cut into it. He was still in the woods, in a small clearing, the grinning night craning past the trees as if to gloat at his captivity. Those same drums beat, like a giant metronome.

"Please," he said again, shaking his head and surrendering himself to the sobs.

The man who stood behind him was speaking—no, he was *singing*—tuneless and guttural. The words rose and fell, broken by the wind.

"Here's your chance, take it or leave it, lambs to the slaughter or you're in the shit, in the shit."

"Please," Chase said. "Please. I'm scared."

Branches cracked underfoot as the man walked into the centre of the clearing, a figure made monstrous by the flames. When Chase saw that he wore only underwear he started to groan—a noise that pushed up from inside him like it was being born.

Then he saw what the man was holding and the noise died in his throat.

There was a scythe in his right hand, the blade full of firelight and the shaft dragging along the ground.

"When it's your turn don't fight it, don't flee," sang the man, lifting his arms as if embracing the night, the scythe rattling. *"Give yourself up for them, for me."*

The wind roared and the trees clapped their branches in lunatic applause. For a moment, Chase thought he saw figures between the trunks, phantoms of pale cloth who danced to the beat of the drums. Then he blinked and they were gone, devils that melted into the dark.

"Give yourself up for them, for me," the man said, the music gone from his voice.

No, thought Chase.

He closed his eyes and tried to see Lauren there against the dark, tried to see her golden smile—and he saw his mum instead, just as welcome, standing in front of the cornfields in the middle of summer, her face full of laughter.

"I'm sorry, mum," he said, smiling back at her.

"It's okay," he thought he heard her say, but whatever else was in his head was drowned out by the pounding of feet and the grunt of feverish breaths as death rushed towards him.

"I'm sor—"

CHAPTER ONE

Sunday

THE CRIME SCENE WAS A MESS.

Just the way he liked it.

Robbie Kett leaned forward in his chair and studied the room, taking in every detail, every clue. It was hard because his mind was still a chaos of white noise, amplified by the gunshot wound in his chest. He lifted a hand to scratch his beard and even this was enough to set off a depth charge of dull pain in his ribs, as if he'd been shot all over again.

With the pain came the flashback, the way it always did —the crack of Gordon Keefe's assault rifle, the sensation of being kicked by a horse into an endless, ageless darkness that he thought he would never escape. He tried to hide his reaction but there was nothing he could do to stop the sharp intake of breath, the flinch that rattled his chair. He exhaled slowly, counting to three.

"You okay, sir?" asked DC Kate Savage. "You sure you're up for this?"

Kett nodded, breathing in again as slowly as he dared, the pain ebbing but not leaving him.

It *never* left.

Savage studied him from the other side of the table, her face full of sympathy. She was dressed in her civvies, jeans and a black Nike hoodie, because she was technically off duty. One hand played with the lucky silver whistle that hung around her neck, causing phantoms of reflected light to dance over the ceiling. She'd let her pixie cut grow out, her hair longer than Kett had ever seen it. DI Pete Porter sat to her left, his physique barely contained by one of his immaculate Tom Ford suits. He was chewing on something he didn't seem to want to say.

"I'm fine," Kett said, working his tired face into a smile. Even his voice sounded wounded, like it was being dragged through gravel. "I need to finish this."

"We're perfectly capable of solving this one without you," Savage said.

"I'm sure you are. But then I don't get any of the glory. And I know where it happened."

"The study?" said Porter, looking around. "What do you think? My card says the kitchen."

"You're not supposed to tell us, Pete," Savage said.

"Why?" said Porter. "It was definitely the kitchen. She used the rope."

"That's the theory you're going with?" Savage asked.

"Yeah, the rope," he said. "I've got it here."

The big DI laid a card on the table, quite clearly showing a rope. Savage slapped a hand to her head, the sound echoing around Kett's kitchen.

"Pete, seriously? We've been over this a hundred times, you can't just show everyone your cards."

"Why not?" Porter said. "It was obviously that Scarlet woman, in the kitchen, with the rope."

Savage grabbed his hand, twisting it so that she could study the cards he held. Her face creased with disgust.

"*You* have Miss Scarlet," she said. "And the kitchen. And the rope. Bloody hell, Porter, I'm going to ask Clare to bump you back to constable. It's just embarrassing."

Porter looked to Kett for backup but Kett was doing his best not to laugh. He clamped a hand to his chest, feeling the bandages there and knowing what lay beneath them. It had been a month, nearly, since Keefe had shot him, leaving a fragment of the bullet resting against his heart, and every day had been a nightmare. There wasn't a single movement that didn't make him want to scream, and laughter was the worst.

"What?" Porter protested. "It's not my fault this game has ridiculously complicated rules."

"It's *Cluedo*!" said Savage, putting her cards face-down on the table. "It can't get any simpler."

"Stop," Kett said, the laughter a well that was threatening to overflow. "For Christ's sake stop, it's too much."

"Fine," Porter said, pushing himself out of his chair. "You obviously don't need my input. I'll put the kettle on."

"No!" both Kett and Savage shouted together, and this time Kett couldn't hold it anymore. He barked out a laugh, followed by a growl as the fire started spreading in his chest. The pain was so bad it actually set off a ringing alarm in his ears, the world turning black for a handful of heartbeats.

"Can I get you anything?" Savage asked, her voice muffled.

"I'll be okay," Kett said. "Give it a moment."

"You need more than a moment, sir. You look like you're about a hundred years old."

"Thanks," Kett muttered, straightening up. The pain was easing but it had spread around the circumference of his torso, wrapping his spine in barbed wire. He cursed Keefe, then regretted it, because the truth was it could have been so much worse. Keefe had been one of the Force's best sharpshooters and he'd been standing a dozen yards away. The investigation into the case was ongoing—it would *always* be ongoing—but of one thing he was certain: however much of an arsehole Keefe had been, that night he'd made the decision not to murder Kett.

Wound him and leave him in unspeakable agony—it was the only way he could keep his family safe—but not murder.

"You want to keep going?" Savage asked.

He didn't need to reply because the sound of drumming footsteps and squealing laughter rose from outside, followed by a chorus of hoarse barks.

"Oh, sorry," said Savage, standing up. "I'll get Colin. Last thing you want is a fat little rescue dog jumping on your lap."

As if on cue Colin the dog pushed the back door open and scrabbled into the kitchen, her claws slipping on the linoleum and depositing her onto her flank. The Staffordshire Terrier twisted her body until she was on her feet again, her backside moving from side to side, tail thumping when she saw Savage. She gave the DC a look that was one part *I am having so much fun!* to two parts *Those girls are crazy, please help me!*

Savage ducked down and gave the dog a giant hug, grimacing at the sloppy kisses that followed.

"Oh, that's gross, Colin!" she said, laughing. "Go kiss Pete instead."

"Uh, no thanks," Porter said, positioning himself behind

his chair and looking nervously at the little dog. "I only like human kisses."

"Colin!" shouted Evie from the open door. The newly turned four-year-old was wrapped from head to toe in winter gear and mud, her cheeks blazing. She patted her legs. "Come on, girl, we've found another stick."

"Colin!" yelled Moira from outside. "I *uv* you!"

The only daughter who wasn't present was Alice, who still hadn't got over her fear of the stout little rescue dog. She'd been locked in her bedroom for the last couple of hours with Maggie, the chinchilla they'd taken from the man posing as Joseph Bains. The chinchilla wasn't a massive fan of the dog either.

Colin turned in mad circles, foaming at the mouth, her eyes wild.

"I think she's had enough of—" Kett started, but before he could finish the dog was off, bounding through the door into the garden. She was replaced almost immediately by Billie, mummified in her blue duffel coat and a long scarf.

"Phew," she said, leaning on the door frame and offering him a tired smile. Her face had caught the weather and the wind had ransacked her short, honey-coloured hair. She looked beautiful for it, like she'd stepped right out of a Tennyson painting. "I don't know who's got more energy, the kids or the dog."

"Trust me, it's the kids," Savage said. "Colin will sleep for a week after this."

Billie laughed, but it quietened when she saw Kett's expression.

"Bad again?" she asked.

"Only because I was laughing so hard at Pete."

"Easily done," Billie said, smiling. "Maybe we should call it a day?"

"Sure," said Savage, tucking the silver whistle into her hoodie. "But you let us know if you need anything, okay?"

"And pick an easier game next time," Porter added. "I don't know how anyone is supposed to follow those rules."

The DI made sure there was no sign of the dog before stepping out from behind the chair, making it three steps across the kitchen before his phone rang. He pulled it from his pocket, grimacing.

"It's the *other* Colin," he said, answering it. "The hairier one. Hey boss, what's new?"

Even from where he sat Kett could hear Clare's angry voice. Porter nodded as the Superintendent spoke for what had to be two full minutes, then ended the call and turned to the expectant room.

"Body," he said. "Out near Dereham."

"Homicide?" Savage asked.

"Oh yes," Porter said. "And then some. You in, Kate?"

"Like I'd miss it," she replied. She turned to Kett, that look of sympathy back on her face. Nothing to do with the pain, this time, and everything to do with an altogether different kind of loss. "I'm sorry," she said.

Kett felt it too, he felt it in a deeper part of himself than the bullet in his chest. He looked at Billie and she looked back, waiting for something.

A fresh start.

It was what he'd promised her. It was what he was going to give her.

"Good luck," he said to Savage.

"We're going to need it with this one," Porter said. "It's messy."

"You don't need luck," Kett said, trying and failing to stand up. He resigned himself to the chair. "You've got this."

Outside, Evie laughed, the sound quickly turning to a playful scream.

"I'll catch you both later," Billie said, retreating into the garden. "Be safe."

"Yeah, be safe," Kett said when she'd gone. He offered the two coppers a smile. "And remember, I'm right here if you need me."

CHAPTER TWO

THERE WERE FEW PLACES KATE SAVAGE FELT MORE AT home than behind the wheel, and nowhere she felt more in control. Even her little lime green Fiat Punto with its ageing 1.4-litre engine and sticky clutch was a joy to drive, nimble enough to dart in and out of traffic as she made her way across Norwich. *Little Jeff*, she called it, after her granddad, who had always been known as Big Jeff Savage. It wasn't exactly in the same league as the police-issue BMWs and Iron Man-red Audis that she got to drive sometimes, but it was hers, and she loved it. Life was unpredictable, it was chaotic—never more so than working as a police officer—but right now none of that mattered. When she was driving, everything responded to her touch, everything did exactly what it was told.

Especially with *Van Halen* blasting from the speakers.

It took her right back to being a kid on the dodgems in Hemsby, the thrill of moving when everything else felt so hard. She'd spent hours on those little cars, going fast enough to outrun the other drivers, to outrun all the shit from her mum, to outrun all the sadness. She'd always imagined driving them right through the railings and over the dunes, never stopping. On the dodgems, everything had felt *right*, and sitting here now she allowed herself to take a deep, calming, certain breath.

"You need another air freshener," said Porter from the passenger seat. He tapped the one that hung from her rear-view mirror—the ghost of a strawberry-scented jellybean that had died many years ago. "It reeks in here."

In the boot, Colin barked in outrage.

"Yeah, I'm talking about you, dog," Porter said, craning back. "Doesn't your mum ever wash you?"

"He smells fine, sir," Savage said, pumping the brake as the rear end of a bus filled the windscreen. "He probably thinks *you* smell gross."

She tapped the wheel impatiently as they crawled forwards, watching the oncoming traffic in the opposite lane, studying faces, always alert the way her granddad had taught her to be. *Everyone has a secret*, he had told her once, sitting there in his bobby blues. *You just need to learn to read them.*

"Davidoff," said Porter, making a show of sniffing his armpit. "I smell like a king."

"You smell like a *princess*," Savage muttered as the bus finally started moving again. Colin barked her agreement, or perhaps it was a warning, because seconds later a smell rose up that could have come from a barrel-load of rotting fish. Porter clamped one hand to his nose and used the other to jab the button for his window. Nothing happened.

"It's broken," Savage said, winding down her own window and letting in a rush of freezing air that did nothing to chase away the stench.

"What's broken? Your dog's arse?" Porter tested the air and retched. "Jesus, it's so bad. What do you feed her?"

Savage flicked the indicator as she pulled onto the McDonald's roundabout, the wheels whistling as she took the first exit faster than she needed to. Droplets of rain rode in on the wind and by the time she took the next turn on the right—past a long-abandoned police house, of all things—her face was numb. She drove halfway down the quiet street of identical, block-shaped brick buildings before stopping outside her own.

"I'll just be a minute," she said, climbing out of the car.

"Don't lock me in with this godforsaken smell," Porter cried out. "I think she's done another one."

Savage opened the boot, catching Colin like a goalie when the little dog made a break for it. She held her tight, clutching her squirming body as she walked through the gate and down the small set of crumbling concrete steps. Colin licked her face like she was edible, her tongue pleasantly warm against the cold, her breath anything but pleasant.

"What *have* you been eating?" Savage said, fumbling her keys from her pocket, the dog practically riding her shoulder by the time she managed to get the door open. She laughed as she pulled her free, depositing her on the door-mat. Colin galloped up the steps to the first-floor flat and Savage followed her, sniffing her hands as she went. "Maybe you do need a bath, mate."

She refilled the dog's water bowl in the small kitchen, and by the time she'd carried it through to the living room Colin was lying on her bed, her chin resting on a mangled bunny toy. She gazed plaintively at Savage, whining.

"Those Kett girls really did a number on you," she said. "Get some sleep."

Colin yawned a reply and Savage left her to it, washing her hands in the bathroom. She ran to the bedroom and stripped from her off-duty jeans and hoodie, pulling on one of two suits that hung in her wardrobe, and her work boots. There wasn't much she could do about her hair even on a good day, so she smoothed a hand over it as she jogged back down the stairs. Porter was standing outside the car trying to waft the air from his open door and Savage laughed as she got into the driver's seat.

"It's really not that bad," she said. "Aren't you guys trying for a baby? They smell a tonne worse than this."

Porter grimaced as he joined her, shaking rain from his hair. Savage started the engine and put the car in gear.

"Right, guv," she said. "Where's our dead guy?"

SHE'D DRIVEN on the A47 a thousand times, and never for anything good. The last time she'd been out this way she'd been in Joe Bains' bright pink Cinquecento and she'd almost died in it when one of Kett's ghosts had tried to drive her off the road. Fortunately, it wasn't long before Porter pointed to a sign and she pulled off the dual carriageway, heading north. The countryside was barren here, almost black and white, as if the brutal cold had sapped all of the colour from it. The long, straight road was practically abandoned, just the occasional four-by-four passing her, their elderly drivers dismissive to the point where she wondered if they could even see her all the way down here. The car's tinny stereo was on, doing its best to handle Aerosmith's *Sweet Emotion.*

"I can't believe you listen to this shite," Porter said.

"Classic rock? What's wrong with you? It's amazing."

"It's really not."

"What would you listen to, then?"

"Normal music," he said, as if it was the simplest answer in the world. "Smooth—"

"Pete," she interrupted. "If the next word out of your mouth is jazz then I swear I'm stopping the car and leaving you here."

Porter swallowed.

"All I'm going to say is that Kenny G is a god," he said quietly. He stared out of the window for a moment. "There is way too much empty space in Norfolk. Why don't they fill it?"

"With what?" Savage asked. He shrugged.

"People, buildings. *Normal* things."

He had a point. The road went on and on and the view never changed, as if they were stuck in some kind of temporal loop. Overhead the sky was a slab of concrete, too low, heavy with the threat of snow. Even in this vastness of space, Savage was starting to feel claustrophobic. It seemed like an age later that she finally reached a junction.

"Head for Lyng, then Lesser Lyng," Porter said, tapping a finger on his window. She pulled left, accelerating past barren trees and ragged hedgerows, past fields full of crows who soared into the air as the Fiat buzzed past. It might have been the end of the world, she thought, until finally a handful of brave little houses appeared, peeking out from the vegetation. She slowed as they entered the village, but even doing thirty they were out of it in a minute or so, into fields full of doe-eyed cattle.

"I just don't get how anyone can live out here," Porter said, shuddering. "Those cows look evil."

"Yes, cows," Savage said, rolling her eyes. "Nature's most dangerous predators."

She reached a junction and turned left, almost hitting the back of a marked police car parked in a lay-by. She pulled in front of it and cut the engine, letting in the unnerving silence of the day. Ancient trees hugged the side of the road, rendered skeletal by the season—as if this wasn't a woodland but a graveyard.

Although now, of course, it *was* a graveyard.

"Did the Super tell you much?" Savage asked as she opened her door and stepped out. The temperature here felt ten degrees lower than it had in Norwich, the cold cutting through her thin suit jacket and nestling against her bones. She shivered, looking at Porter in his heavy overcoat. He read her mind, pulling it around himself protectively.

"You can have it... if you *really* need it," he said, his words appearing as a cloud of breath.

"I'm fine, Pete," she replied. "Nice to know you're a gentleman, though."

She checked the backseat, finding her black puffer jacket there and throwing it on. It didn't help much but by the time she'd set off, climbing over a small gate and up a shaded path, she'd started to warm up. The naked trees shivered in the wind, their leaves abandoned on the wet ground and halfway to mulch. It had rained heavily in the last week or two and entire sections of the woods were lost, as if the flora here had grown out of the surface of a lake. The smell of rot was almost overbearing. After a few minutes the path had vanished and Savage set off into the woods, grateful for her boots. Porter minced along behind her, doing his best not to dirty his Cleverleys.

"It's the body of a young man," the DI said, finally remembering her question. "Mid-to-late teens. Clare said he was found draped over a boulder, cut up pretty bad."

"A boulder?" Savage said. "Did he fall?"

"Clare didn't think so. There was evidence of some kind of mutilation."

Savage's first thought was animals but she didn't say it. There wouldn't be anything in these woods big enough to pull a body to pieces, alive or dead. Now that she was paying attention, she wasn't sure if there were animals in these woods at all. They were entirely silent, not even the call of a bird to cheer them on their way. Every step she took sounded like a gunshot, like a warning. It made her feel uneasy, because despite the absence of life she felt as if she was being watched—some instinct that made the hair rise on the back of her neck. She stopped, studying the spaces between the trees, listening for anything over the laughter of the wind.

"Keep going," Porter said, squelching past her. "It's over that hill I think."

She followed him, cresting the slope to see that the path dropped into a hollow. Right in the centre, at the lowest point, sat a small, white forensic tent. A handful of figures surrounded it, most dressed in white overalls and looking like worshippers as they stooped and bowed across the uneven ground. The man in the middle was dressed like a priest, his bandaged head bowed. Savage wanted to call out but the words died on her lips. She didn't know why, only there was something about this place that seemed to demand quiet. She had the uncanny feeling that if she made too much noise something here might open its eyes and see her.

"Oi, boss!" yelled Porter, making her jump. She clamped a hand to her chest, watching the big DI as he galumphed down the slope towards Superintendent Colin Clare. Again, that feeling of unease washed through her, the fact that Porter's cannon-shot of a call hadn't sent a single bird clapping from the trees.

The Superintendent turned around and offered a sad

nod of welcome, his hands firmly wedged in the pockets of a chestnut brown overcoat that looked at least three sizes too big for him.

"You took your time," he bellowed back. "Get down here."

Savage didn't want to. There was something about the atmosphere in the hollow that screamed for her to turn back. She took a deep breath of mouldering air then set off after Porter, tripping on roots that rose from the wet earth like bones.

"What do you make of this place?" Clare asked when they'd reached the bottom of the hollow.

"Dirty," grumbled Porter, brushing green stains from his coat.

"I don't like it," Savage said. "Something feels... I don't know, *off*."

"My thoughts exactly," said Clare.

"How're you doing, sir?" Savage asked. Clare cleared his throat, lifting a hand to the bandage on his forehead. The bullet wound he'd received just before Christmas had only been a graze, but it was taking a long time to heal. It was the stab wounds that made the man stand like a lightning-struck tree.

"Tired, grumpy, pissed off with this tossing county and all the tosspots that live here."

"Same as always, then," said Porter.

Savage glanced at the members of the forensic team as they planted their flags in the soil, frowning when she saw that one of them was DI Keith Dunst. He stood in a giant puddle, poking at the water with a gloved hand. She waved to him and he nodded back, his face a mask of misery.

"What are you looking for, sir?"

"Nothing," Dunst called back. "Absolutely bloody nothing. He's just got me in this puddle because he hasn't forgiven me for the whole toast thing back at the hospital."

"Rubbish," growled Clare. "There could be evidence out there. Keep going, Dunst, another hour or so and we'll get you out of those wet clothes into something warm... and *toasty*."

Despite herself, Savage laughed. Dunst flashed a finger at the Super's back—from the hand that still had five of them—and went back to his puddle. Clare managed to suppress a wry smile before gesturing to the tent.

"Are you ready for this?" he asked.

Nobody answered.

"Tough, because he's all yours. And I hope for your sake you didn't eat lunch."

CHAPTER THREE

CLARE WAS RIGHT, LUNCH WOULD HAVE BEEN A BAD idea.

The smell hit Savage as soon as she walked into the tent —still so alien, so unfamiliar, even after all her time on the job, after all those poor souls. Her empty stomach contracted, her face breaking into a sweat despite the freezing air. She felt for the heavy whistle beneath her shirt, touching it and grounding herself.

Only then did she look.

The first thing she noticed wasn't the body but the stone that lay beneath it. It sat in the middle of the tent like some kind of ancient throne, green with algae and dark with blood. It was the size of a small table and there was something about the angular shape of it that made Savage think it couldn't be natural. It didn't belong here, amongst the mud and the twigs.

The boy didn't belong here either, and yet here he was. He lay spreadeagled over the stone like he'd fallen asleep there, his arms out to his sides, frozen not by the cold but by rigor mortis. His head was craned back, revealing the mess of his throat—the dried blood doing nothing to hide the slash wounds. He was naked apart from his underwear—grey Calvin Kleins—and his body was a tapestry of destruction, a map of the horror that had been inflicted on him. Savage counted at least twenty stab wounds, and twice as many contusions.

There was no denying the worst of them, though. His chest had been opened like a gift basket.

And his heart was missing.

"You going to stand there all day, Kate?" Clare said.

Savage manoeuvred herself around the circumference of the tent to let Porter in beside her. He retched, gasped, and retched again.

"Oh god," he said.

"Move up, Pete," Clare said, pushing past him, the back of his hand held to his mouth. The two big men crouched beneath the low roof of the tent, blocking the exit. Savage shuffled around a little further, her foot catching on a root and almost sending her crashing onto the corpse. She grabbed Porter's hand to steady herself, and he must have felt she needed something because he held onto it for a moment, giving her fingers a squeeze before letting go.

"He's currently a John Doe," said Clare. "But I've got a PC *en route* to the house of a woman in Lesser Lyng who claims her seventeen-year-old son hasn't been home for two nights. A kid called Chase Masefield. This poor fellow matches the description to a tee, right up to the *Meet Me at McDonald's* haircut. A jogger found him late this morning." Clare checked his watch. "Going on two hours ago. Emily Franklin is on her way. I don't want anyone to touch him before she gets here."

"A jogger found him?" Savage asked. "Who'd be

running through these woods? It's half-flooded and treacherous as hell."

"Indeed. I think *jogging* might have been a euphemism. For him and for the woman he was with."

"Guess we don't have to ask what killed him," said Porter, leaning over the body to stare into the ruin of the boy's chest. "But it didn't happen here."

He was right. There was blood on the stone, trickles that had made their way from the boy's blackened underside to the hungry earth, but nowhere near enough to have come from a body as butchered as this one.

"He was positioned," Savage said, a thought beetling around the back of her head. "He was killed somewhere else and brought here to have his heart removed. It's like a... like some kind of offering, a sacrifice."

"I've walked the perimeter but I can't see any blood," said Clare.

"The rain could have washed it away," Porter said. "It's been non-stop the last couple of days."

"It's quiet round here, though," Savage said. "Pretty easy to move a body without being seen. Where are we again, sir? We passed through Lyng, didn't we?"

Clare looked at her, nodding.

"This is the border between Lyng and Lesser Lyng, although the latter is actually bigger."

"Lyng," she said, searching her memory and finding it. "This is the Great Stone of Lyng, I'm sure of it."

"The what?" Porter asked.

"My granddad was into this stuff. Before he passed he took me all over the place looking for legends, history. We never came here—he never could have handled the terrain, not with his knees—but I remember him talking about it. Uh..." She clicked her fingers. "It's supposed to have powers or something, bad powers, after a battle was fought here. I can't remember it all, sorry."

"This is a great stone?" Porter asked. "What, like Stonehenge or something?"

He pulled a face, ducking down to get a better look at it.

"It's a bit shit. That thing's in danger of being crushed by a dwarf."

"What?" said Clare. Porter managed a grim smile.

"You know, sir, *Spinal Tap*? The six-inch Stonehenge?"

"What are you going on about, you great dolt?"

Porter shrank back, his cheeks burning. Clare turned to Savage.

"Good work, Kate. If you're right, it makes it all the more likely that this was a ritual killing of some kind. We—"

"It bleeds," said Savage. "I just remembered, that's what granddad told me. If you prick the stone with a pin, it bleeds."

The three of them studied it for a moment, entombed by the silence of the hollow. Porter swallowed noisily, taking a couple of shuffled steps back towards the flap.

"Whoever this was, he didn't make it easy for his victim," Clare said after a moment. "As well as the missing heart and the attack on his throat, the boy has a number of wounds that look like they came from a knife. Stabs and slashes, neck and torso mainly, but several to his wrist. He sustained a severe injury to his hand as well."

Savage had to angle herself around the rock to see that the kid's right hand was a mess of swollen tissue, his little finger bent out at an impossible angle—like he was drinking tea with the Queen. His nails were caked with dirt and dried blood.

"I haven't turned him over but I suspect there will be injuries to his back as well."

"There's something frenzied about it," Savage said. "It's brutal."

"He's filthy too," added Porter. "It looks as though he fought back. His knuckles are grazed like he's punched something."

Savage nodded, turning her attention to the boy's face. She'd heard it said that people looked older in death, that whatever youth or vitality had been there was lost completely. She'd always felt the opposite, that people looked younger when they'd passed over. Especially children. The boy's expression was relaxed, revealing nothing of the agony of his death, and his eyes were thankfully closed. He might have been ten or eleven rather than in his teens. His face was as pale as marble, as if he'd been carved from rock, just like the altar he rested on.

"That's weird," she said, thinking aloud. "His face is spotless. There's not even a drop of blood."

"Somebody cleaned him up, maybe?" said Porter.

"Maybe."

She leant closer, a hand to her mouth as if that might somehow stop the smell of death from finding her. There was a ring of dried blood around his face, hiding in the mess of his curly hair, winding under his chin like the strap of a helmet. Everything beyond that was alabaster white.

"I think his face was covered," she said. "A mask of some kind."

Clare sighed.

"The longer I stand here, the worse this gets," he said. "Masks, sacred stones, missing hearts, I can't remember the last time I saw anything like this."

His phone started to ring—quietly, as if it didn't want to disturb the moment—and he pulled it out of his pocket, staring at the screen for a good few seconds before answering.

"Yes, this is he. Uh-huh. Uh-huh. Well, that's unfortunate news. Send it over just in case, then stand down until a detective gets to you."

He hung up the phone, then hung his head.

"PC says the boy is almost certainly Masefield."

The Super's phone dinged and he looked at the photo on his screen.

"Tossing hell," he said. "Porter, I need you to go and speak to Masefield's parents."

Porter nodded. His sad eyes fell on the boy once more, then he turned and ducked through the tent flap. Clare started to follow, but hesitated.

"Doesn't quite feel the same without Robbie, does it?" he said. "I'd got used to him being here, before he tossed it all up the wall."

"Yes, sir," Savage replied, not quite sure what to say.

"Take some photos before you go, would you, Savage?" Clare said. "I know you'll be careful with them, but if any should accidentally find their way to *former* DCI Kett I wouldn't be too upset."

"Sir?" Savage asked.

Clare exited the tent, batting at the flap with both hands when it stuck to his face. He called back as he went.

"I have a feeling we're going to need all the help we can get with this one."

CHAPTER FOUR

"Goddammit!"

Porter leant against the Incident Response Vehicle and studied his shoes. Not that much was visible past the shell of mud and dried grass. It looked like he'd put his feet through a couple of coconuts, and even when he stamped hard on the tarmac the clay-like dirt didn't show any sign of coming loose. They were George Cleverley Nakagawa Cap-toe Oxfords and they'd cost almost a grand, *on sale*.

He ducked back into the car, looking at the constable who'd driven him here.

"What size are you, mate? Shoes?"

"A nine," the man replied, looking nervously at his feet. "Why, sir?"

"No reason," said Porter, staring forlornly at his own size elevens. "Wait up there, will you?"

He turned to the street, if you could call it that. It was a terrace of small houses positioned on both sides of a narrow road in the middle of Lesser Lyng. They must have been built long before cars tore back and forth because their low front doors opened right into traffic. The driver of the IRV couldn't even leave the car there because there was no room for anything to pass it, and when Porter tapped the roof it rumbled off and vanished around the bend.

"Right," said Porter, popping his lips and trying to steel himself.

This was the worst part of the job by a long stretch. He *hated* it. Telling a parent that their child was dead was like killing them. It was *worse* than that. At least with your own death came peace.

He scanned the dark windows of the Masefield house and realised he was being watched—a pair of ghostly faces trapped behind the glass. One, a teenage lad, stared at him like he was the enemy. The other, presumably his mother, was already sobbing, her breath clouding the window like she was trying to hide from the truth. He sighed, mentally kicking himself. His expression had already told them everything they needed to know.

He walked to the door, waited, and when they didn't open it he rapped twice on the peeling paint. Still nothing. He stepped back, pulling his overcoat around him against the wicked cold, his own clouded breaths escaping into the dark afternoon. The faces in the window had gone.

"Mrs Masefield?" he said, his voice batting back and forth between the buildings. They seemed to be closer together now, as if the street was rallying against him. "It's the police. I'm very sorry but I need to speak with you."

"Piss off," came a cry from inside. "You can just piss off. I don't want to know."

Muffled shouts, and the sound of a bolt being pulled back. The door opened a crack, the boy's face appearing there. He looked even paler in the flesh, almost transparent, and when he opened his mouth to speak, nothing came out. There was no doubt at all that he was the brother of the dead boy in the woods—the same round face, the same curly hair. This one was younger, but even so it gave Porter's heart a mighty kick, as if he was looking at a ghost.

"Blake, don't," shrieked his mother, sobbing now. "Don't let him in."

"Is he okay?" the kid asked. "Have you found Chase?"

His face opened like a flower, full of hope.

"Can we talk inside?" Porter said, and Mrs Masefield's sobs became a wail of desperation.

Beaten, Blake opened the door and stood back. Porter crouched beneath the shoulder-height lintel and when he straightened on the other side he cracked his head on the ceiling. The house was tiny, built for a Hobbit, the corridor narrow and dark and imprisoned by solid beams. He had to blink to make sense of the shadows, seeing a dusty mirror, a coat stand full of expensive North Face puffer jackets, a pile of trainers and at least a dozen photos of a murdered boy fixed to the browning woodchip wallpaper.

Finally, he turned to the mother. She was a tall woman, bird-thin and bent double in the doorway that led to a dingy kitchen. One long arm was wrapped around her stomach as if trying to hold it in, the other braced on the door frame. The noise she was making—half gulping cry, half mourning song—was unbearable, and when Porter looked at the boy to his side he saw that he had his hands over his ears. He was looking at Porter, *begging* him, and there was nothing he could do to make it better.

"I'm really sorry," Porter said. "Is there somewhere for your mother to sit?"

"I don't want to sit," she screamed. "I don't want you here. Why won't you *piss off*?"

The adrenaline in Porter's blood was making his head

fizz, the house too small, too dark. He held up his hands in surrender.

"I know how hard this is, Mrs—"

"Oh, you know, do you?" she shot back, her head snapping like a viper's. "You've lost a child, have you?"

"Mum!" the boy said, his hands still clamped to his head. "Please!"

She seemed to notice her son for the first time, the anger falling from her face as quickly as it had appeared. Her expression crumpled and she held out a hand to the boy, one that she quickly withdrew to her mouth as the sobs started again. She said something that was lost behind her grasping fingers and seemed to curl herself into silence and stillness, like paper in fire. Porter looked at her, then at the young lad, then at the floor.

"I'm truly sorry to have to be the one to tell you, but Chase is dead. We found him in the woods a couple of miles away. He..."

Mrs Masefield walked through the kitchen door and slammed it shut behind her. The boy pulled his hands from his ears and jutted his chin out, his eyes raw.

"Somebody kill him?" he asked.

"Why do you say that?"

The kid shrugged, his eyes darting to the open front door like he wanted to make a run for it.

"Are you his brother?" Porter said. "Blake, right?"

He nodded.

"How old are you?"

"Sixteen in a couple of weeks. Chase was going to take me out in his car, take me into the town, let me go cruising. He..."

He stopped, glancing at the kitchen.

"He's teaching me how to drive. He's good at it, you know? He's careful."

His frown deepened, as if he'd just noticed he was using the wrong tense. His tongue flashed across his dry lips, searching for something. He looked so much like his brother, although from here Porter could tell that Blake's hair had been permed.

"Can I ask you a few questions?" Porter said. "About Chase?"

The kid nodded, looking to the kitchen once again before accepting that he had been abandoned. He pointed past Porter to another low door. Pushing it open with his fingertips, Porter saw a microscopic living room. The smell coming out of it was earthy, dusty. It reminded him of his grandparents' house back in London. He bent down to unlace his shoes.

"Don't bother," said Blake, walking inside, the bare wooden boards creaking beneath him. "Place is a shithole. Mum's always bollocking us for tracking mud in, she won't even notice."

All the same, he kicked off his shoes before ducking beneath the door. He felt like a fairy tale giant here, the ceiling too low for him to stand up straight. The room was yellow with age, the walls unpainted plaster that had started to crumble, braced with a skeleton of beams. An ancient sofa sat to the left of the window, an even older cat fast asleep on it. Blake sat down next to the animal, running a trembling hand down its back. Porter took in the rest of the room, the big TV and the PlayStation beneath it, a pile of games stacked in the corner.

"You play *Call of Duty*?" Porter asked.

"Of course," Blake replied, giving him a quizzical look. "Why?"

"Just wondering. I play too. *Black Ops* mainly."

"Fuck off," Blake said without malice. He was shaking hard, holding it all in, as if acting normal might make it normal. "You prestige?"

"Only a few times," Porter said, smiling. "Ten, to be exact."

"Fuck off!"

"Kids are all playing *Fortnite* now, but I like *CoD*. Helps me relax after work."

Blake sniffed, running the back of his hand over his nose. The cat used its front paws to pull itself onto his lap, curling up there, and he idly tickled the back of its neck.

"Chase and I used to take turns, die and swap out, you know? He was always better than me, quicker. I could never get the sniper kills close range like he could. Bet I could kick your arse, though."

"You'd bet wrong," Porter said. Blake's smile grew for a moment before burning out.

"What do I do with his saves, now?" he asked. "All his weapons?"

"Maybe he'd have wanted you to have them?"

There was no other chair to sit on so Porter knelt on the floor. In the kitchen, Mrs Masefield sounded like she was throwing furniture. He wondered if he should go to her, try to calm her down, but the kid seemed to read his mind, shaking his head.

"Don't. She'll get through it. Mum's got a temper."

"She's never hurt you, though?"

"No," Blake said. "Well, she used to whack our arses if we did wrong by her, and she slapped Chase across the face once for calling her a bitch. Not that he didn't deserve it. But no, she gets angry but she's not angry at us, she's angry at the MS."

"MS?" Porter said. "Multiple Sclerosis?"

"She's had it for years but it's getting worse. Always told me she just needed to hang on until Chase was eighteen, just another year and he could look after me, make sure I was okay."

Porter breathed out slowly.

"What about your dad?"

"What about him?" Blake said with a look that said it all. "Was he killed? My brother?"

"We're investigating it now. I can't tell you much because I don't know much. But yes, I think maybe somebody killed him."

"How?"

Porter didn't answer and Blake bent forwards, practically folding himself in two. The cat slipped off his lap and limped across the bare floor to investigate the newcomer. Porter let it sniff his fingers before running his big hand down the knobbly ridge of its back. It nudged its face into his knuckles and the purr it made seemed ridiculously loud in the small space.

"Do you know where he was two nights ago?" he asked after a moment. "Friday."

"He was out with Lauren, his *girlfriend*." He spat the last word like it had a foul taste. "Was at her house, I think. Mum told you lot this when he didn't come home, on the phone. He went there for dinner and we figured he'd just stayed over, but then he didn't show up yesterday and Lauren didn't know where he was. Mum called you like five times asking you to find him."

"I'm sorry," Porter said. "I'll try to find out what happened. Do you know their address?"

"It's a huge house over the other side of the village, right on the edge. The Sawmill, it's called. I don't have the number or anything. All the kids know it, though."

"Why?"

Blake opened his mouth to reply, then closed it again.

"Why do they know it, Blake?" Porter said.

"Ask him yourself, when you get there. I'm not saying shit."

"Ask who?"

"Mr Skinner, Lauren's dad."

The kid's eyes widened, as if he had just thought of something.

"Do you think *he* did this? Mr Skinner?"

"I don't know anything about him, son," said Porter. "But we're doing everything we can to find out. Can you tell me why you think it, though?"

Blake shook his head, afraid of something. He looked through the door into the dark hallway, sniffing again.

"Then can you tell me if Chase had any enemies? Anyone he owed money to or had a beef with? Anyone new he'd been speaking to at school or online? Any money that seemed to come from nowhere, gifts? Anything like that?"

"Nobody," said Blake. "Everyone loves him."

He glanced at Porter, then up at the TV, his eyes glassy.

"I love him."

Porter pushed himself up, his knees popping. He stood awkwardly for a moment before walking to the boy and placing a hand on his shoulder. He thought Blake might pull away, but instead he leant his head on Porter's hand the same way the cat had, everything inside him shaking. They remained like that for what felt a small eternity before Porter let go and Blake's head dropped. It was such a weird moment that Porter didn't quite know what to make of it.

"If you think of something else, let me know," he said,

pulling a card from his wallet and leaving it on the arm of the sofa. "And if you need anything, anything at all, just call, okay?"

The boy didn't reply. From the kitchen came more sounds of destruction. Porter didn't want to leave, he didn't want Blake to be on his own. But what was he supposed to do? He couldn't exactly bring the kid with him.

"Blake, it does get better. I know it doesn't feel like that now, but I promise you, it gets easier. One minute at a time, one hour at a time, one day at a time."

If the kid heard him he made no show of it. Porter walked into the hallway, leaning against the wall so that he could pull on his shoes. By the time he'd laced them up the noise in the kitchen had stopped, replaced by the sound of Mrs Masefield crying quietly. He half thought about going to her, because at some point they'd need to find out what she knew. But it was better she calmed down—better for her, and better for her son.

Besides, the house seemed to be getting smaller with every second, crushing the air from Porter's chest. He glanced into the living room and thought one more time about bringing Blake with him. Then he opened the door and stepped out into the cold day, alone.

CHAPTER FIVE

"BIT LATE FOR THAT NOW."

Kett heard the crack of the rifle. He felt the impact of the bullet as it thudded into his chest, as it splintered his rib. He fell back into that aching, awful darkness, into death, and he opened his mouth to scream—catching himself just in time because he wasn't standing outside in the dark and the rain with Gordon Keefe. It was the middle of the day and he was at home. He was safe. He was alive.

But the memory had left its mark, the adrenaline tearing his body to pieces, his chest packed full of barbed wire.

It's not real, he told himself. *It can't hurt you.*

Except every time he took a breath, he felt like crying.

He braced his forearms on the kitchen table, trying to stay as still and as calm as possible until the phantom horror had passed. The flashbacks didn't come as often as they had in the days after he'd woken in the hospital—back then they'd been every few minutes, and he'd almost lost his mind to them—but they still hit him like a hammer five or six times a day. It was always sound that sparked them, a thump from a neighbour's house, a bang from a car door closing, a shout from one of the kids that pulled the trigger inside his head and threw him right back to that night. Keefe's face was etched onto the fabric of his retinas, he knew he'd see it for the rest of his life.

At least he had a life, though. It's all that mattered.

The pain was quietening and he turned his attention back to the laptop that sat on the kitchen table. At least a dozen tabs were open on his Chrome browser, all of them related to one word.

Hollenbeck.

It was the single clue given up by the nameless assassin who had disguised himself as Joseph Bains. Both he and his accomplice were rotting in Whitemoor, buried in solitary confinement for their own safety. Because whoever had sent them to kill Kingsley and Bingo and Schofield and *him* would send somebody else to kill them. Whoever they worked for, this was the price of their failure. Neither of them had said a single thing since their capture, just that solitary word spat out by the man moments before Kett had been about to put an iron bar through his head.

Hollenbeck.

Google hadn't offered him much. There were a handful of places in the States, a park and a school in California and a hall in Iowa, not to mention a few famous people, all American. Most were dead, and even those that weren't seemed to have no link to anything useful. The only politician with that name was a congressman in his eighties. Facebook was full of Hollenbecks but none of them stood out.

No, this had to be something else, because whoever the ghost had been talking about was the shadow behind the most brutal crime conspiracy Kett had ever seen, a network of killers and kidnappers who had left hundreds of bloodied victims in their wake. It was the force behind the Pig Man, powerful enough to murder anyone who threatened to give him away.

This is a game to them, the ghost had said. *Because these people are wealthy beyond your wildest dreams, they are powerful, but more than that they are bored. There's nothing more dangerous than that, is there? There's nothing more dangerous than boredom.*

Unless the ghost had been full of shit, of course.

Kett sighed and instantly regretted it when the bullet screamed his name. He put a hand to his bandaged chest, massaging it gently.

Hollenbeck.

"Who the fuck are you?"

He picked up his phone from the table, wondering if anyone had called him back with news about the word. There was only one message there and it was from Savage. There was an image attached but he couldn't make out what it was. Something pink, something red. He unlocked the phone, wincing when he saw what greeted him there.

A dead man.

Very dead.

"What's that, daddy?"

Kett slammed the phone face down on the table as Evie walked into the kitchen. She was holding a cereal bowl in both hands, milk slopping over the sides as she tried to lift it onto the table. She'd left a trail of Cheerios behind her, like Hansel and Gretel.

"Just work," he said. "Nothing interesting. You okay? Did you want to keep any of your cereal in the bowl?"

She shook her head, yawning so hard he heard her jaw pop. Colin the Wonderdog had truly knackered her out, Moira too—he was pretty sure the little one had fallen asleep on the sofa because he hadn't heard her for at least half an hour. It was only just two but it felt much later.

"I don't want any more cereal, I'm full. Can I have some more cake?"

"I thought you were full? Your birthday cake's all gone, sweetie, but there will be more next week."

They were never short of cake in January because all three girls had their birthdays within two weeks of each other. It was a fundamental, catastrophic planning error on his and Billie's part, because after Christmas the whole thing felt like a gauntlet of presents, stress and overeating. At least Alice's was the last, next Thursday, and after that they could go another eleven months without any danger of a fondant icing overdose.

"I'm bored," Evie said.

"Can't you play with your toys upstairs?"

"I can't," she said. "Mr Marshmallow is up there."

"Right," said Kett. "Except you know he's not, because he's not real."

It was a conversation he had with her every day, and every time it felt more infuriating. Evie's obsession with the witch in her wardrobe—and then the witch in her chest of drawers, when Kett had dismantled the wardrobe—had become worse over the last few weeks. In a valiant effort to help, Alice had told Evie that there couldn't be a witch in her chest of drawers because another monster lived there, but this monster was made of marshmallows and sunshine and was very friendly.

For a while it had worked, until their oldest daughter had doubled down on her efforts and drawn Evie a picture of Mr Marshmallow. It was, despite her good intentions and an insane amount of glitter, one of the most terrifying things Kett had ever seen. Evie thought so too, and now refused to go upstairs without somebody with her, and often woke in the night screaming about marshmallows. *And* sunshine.

Given what she'd been through in the last year, Kett didn't exactly blame her for being afraid. Better Mr Marshmallow than a pig-faced man.

"Can you play with me?" she asked.

"I can barely scratch my own bum," he replied. "Sorry, Evie. Soon. Where's mum?"

"Asleep," she said. She stared at her fingers and Kett noticed they were stained with colour.

"What have you been doing?"

"Nothing," she said.

"And Alice?"

"She's upstairs, hiding from the dog."

"The dog's gone."

"Yeah but nobody has told her," Evie said with a wry smile. "Can I have your phone?"

Kett thought of the dead man on the screen and shook his head a little harder than he needed to.

"I'll bring it through in a minute," he said. "Go ask Alice what she wants for dinner, and tell her it's safe to come out of her room."

"Nah," said Evie, spinning on her heels and sloping out the door.

Only when he was sure she'd gone did Kett pick up his phone again, navigating back to his text messages. The corpse was there to meet him, a young man draped over a rock that looked like an altar, in the white church of a forensic tent.

Sorry, Savage had written underneath. *Seventeen-year-old boy, at least twenty stab wounds including the ones to his throat. Heart removed.*

"Shit," said Kett. He zoomed in on the gaping wound in

the kid's chest, the familiar tickle of nausea crawling up from his stomach and settling in the back of his throat. He'd seen a wound like this just a few months ago.

Bad Dog, he thought.

He zoomed out again, looking instead at the boy's face—what little of it was visible from the angle Savage had taken the shot. He looked younger than seventeen, and there was a remarkable serenity in his expression. At the very least, Kett hoped, he'd died before he knew what was happening to him.

As gently as he could, Kett pushed himself to his feet. He needed to cling onto the back of his chair for a minute or two until the world stopped spinning, but despite the fresh onslaught of pain it felt good to be moving. The doctors had told him to stay as active as possible, even if that just meant a walk around the garden once a day. He was grateful for his orders because nothing would stagnate his mind more than the stagnation of his body.

And he was going to need everything his mind had to give him, because something about the picture was familiar, something in the way the boy had been posed, in the total absence of blood on his face.

He'd seen it before.

Nothing to do with Howarth this time. Something else, something he'd seen in a case file.

"But what?" he asked himself, tapping his knuckles on the table.

His head was a mess of white noise, it was impossible to find anything in there. He called Savage's number, counting the rings until it clicked through.

"You get the photos, sir?" Savage asked, breathless. "Sorry, the Super asked me to send them."

"Clare did?"

"Well, not in so many words, but it was a pretty big hint. I think he's spooked, looks like a ritual killing."

"Looks like it," said Kett. "But it might not be. The killer may have posed the kid like that to throw us off the scent."

"He went at him pretty hard," Savage said.

"I saw. You okay?"

"Just walking up a very steep hill," she replied, something cracking beneath her feet. "It sucks out here, too many trees."

"You sound like Porter," Kett said, closing his eyes, seeing the crime scene, wondering why he found himself mourning it. "Anything else of note?"

"No blood on the face, but there's a perfect halo."

"A mask," said Kett, pushing himself away from the table like a leaking boat on deep water, barely making it to the sink.

"That's what we think, but there's no sign of it. Killer moved the victim to the scene. We've found a trail of blood but the rain's been heavy and it dead-ends after a hundred yards. The stone's famous, the Great Stone of Lyng, it's called. Plenty of local folklore."

Something tugged at Kett's mind, a sensation of *déjà vu* that made the world turn even harder.

"Any of this sound familiar?" he asked.

"No," said Savage. "Should it?"

"I don't know. I... It might be nothing. But check the system for missing hearts because it set off an alarm bell in my head."

"Eden Howarth?" she said. "He ate a heart, didn't he?"

"And he's rotting in a secure hospital. It's not him, it's something else."

"I'll check, sir," Savage said. Kett laughed quietly.

"You don't have to call me *sir* any more, Kate."

"Force of habit, *sir*," she said. "Porter just called with the address of the last people to see the victim alive, I'm going to meet him there now. And Robbie, if you don't want any part of this let me know, because I'm happy to leave you out of it."

He opened his mouth to answer but stopped when he heard quiet footsteps from the hall. Billie walked through the kitchen door trying to stifle a giant yawn with both hands. When her arms dropped, he noticed that her face was covered in felt-tip.

"I'd better go," he said.

"The girls?" Savage asked.

"Always."

He hung up, leaving his phone on the drainer and opening his arms to his wife. She hugged him as gently as she could before stepping back. Her face was a Picasso, Evie's handiwork no doubt, with her little pack of felt-tips. The four-year-old was currently obsessed with makeup and she'd given Billie a set of sweeping black eyebrows that met in the middle. Her cheeks were bright orange and she wore a rather fetching shade of bright purple lipstick.

"Sorry," she said, resisting another yawn. "Knackered. Think I fell asleep."

Kett smiled.

"What?" she asked, putting a hand to her face.

"No wonder you're tired," he replied. "Walking the streets all night."

"*What*?" she said.

Kett used his phone to take a photograph of her, her new eyebrows almost catapulting off her head when she saw it.

"Evie!" she spluttered. "That bloody..."

"I think it suits you."

Kett tried to hold the laughter in his belly where it wouldn't hurt so much. Billie lifted a hand to bat him in the arm, remembering herself at the last minute. She pointed a finger at him instead, as if it was his fault.

"Those better not be Sharpies," she said.

Her purple lips were smiling, though, and it was good to see. Despite everything that had happened in the last few months, Billie seemed stronger than ever. She'd had to be, because he'd been so badly injured. Keefe may have let him live that night by Kett's Oak, but without Billie by his side, he never would have survived the days that followed.

She seemed to read the gratitude, leaning in and kissing him on his bearded cheek. She turned to go, then stopped.

"Who was on the phone?"

"Kate," he said.

She gave him a disapproving look, mouthing something under her breath:

Fresh. Start.

He nodded, watching her go. When he picked up his phone again he saw another message from Savage.

I mean it, I can leave you alone!

Don't, he wrote back. *Keep me posted.*

He thought of the boy on the rock, his heart gouged from his chest, his body a tapestry of wrack and ruin. And he typed another text:

I may have something.

CHAPTER SIX

DI PORTER WAS WAITING FOR HER WHEN SHE PULLED her Fiat around the corner, looking more like a bouncer than a policeman in his black overcoat and leather gloves. He leant against one of the oversized, wrought iron gateposts of the last house in the village, his phone to his ear, his words floating around his head in clouds of breath.

Savage pulled the car over by the side of the road, cutting the engine and feeling the cold creep into the fug of artificial heat. The last thing she wanted to do was open the door so she sat there until Porter sidled over, doing it for her with his free hand.

"Who's the princess now?" he said. He left his hand there to help her out but she ignored it, climbing into the freezing January afternoon. Porter slammed the door shut, still talking on his phone. "Nobody, Allie, you're my only princess. Look, Savage has finally shown up, I'd better go. But hey, don't be disappointed. It will happen."

"What will?" Savage asked as he hung up.

"None of your beeswax," Porter replied, stamping his feet to warm them up. He must have taken a cloth to his shoes because they were spotless. "Colder than a witch's tit."

"This the place, sir?"

"Yeah," Porter said, nodding at a slate sign on the wall that said *The Sawmill*. "According to the younger Masefield brother, Blake, this is the last place Chase was seen. Came here on Friday night for dinner with a new girlfriend and her family. His mum called us a couple of times when he didn't show up on Friday night or over the weekend, but nobody acted on it."

"Because it was less than forty-eight hours," said Savage.

"And because he was a teenage boy with a reputation for staying out. Nobody *here* has contacted the police."

"So they don't know he's missing?" Savage asked.

"Either that, or somebody here did it."

"One way to find out," Savage said.

She started walking, the long, gravelled driveway crunching beneath her boots. The house was deceptively big, the bulk of it a blocky new-build crouching behind a quaint, thatched front. Smoke rose from two of the four chimneys and further up the sweeping drive sat a Land Rover Defender and a pink Fiat 500—both 19 plates. To the left lay nothing but woods, the same gnarled, sickly trees that watched over Chase Masefield's mutilated body less than two miles away. There was nothing healthy about this woodland, the ground wet with mulch, the trunks soft with rot. Moss and algae had spread over the driveway and onto the walls of the house like it was an infectious disease. This place was stagnant, and it seemed to hang heavy on the damp air, making it hard to breathe.

"Grim," Porter remarked.

"Nice house, though. The brother say much else?"

"I'm not sure, he was cagey. Said all the kids know the

man who lives here, Greg Skinner, but he didn't want to tell me why, and it didn't seem like a good thing."

The gravel seemed deliberately designed to sound a warning, because as they were approaching the door a shadow appeared in the glass—a *big* shadow. It stood there, deathly still, until they were close enough to reach for the cast iron bell. Before they could touch it the door was ripped open hard enough for Savage to flinch. She went for her baton the way she always did, instinctively, even now after all these months out of uniform.

A man stood in the doorway. He *filled* the doorway, and then some, the top of his head hidden by the lintel and his shoulders in the wings. He was in his late forties, a walking *Country Living* advert in brown cords and a waxed Barbour jacket. His cheeks were mottled with veins and his nose was on the verge of turning an alcoholic's shade of purple. But there was a sharpness in his cold eyes that made Savage wary, and a smile that felt like it had been freshly made and stapled on.

He'd been waiting for them.

"Mr Skinner?" Porter said, rubbing his gloved hands together.

The man didn't speak, he just gave Porter the slightest of nods, staring down his nose at him with unfettered arrogance. There weren't many people that Porter had to look up to but Mr Skinner was one of them. He must have been six-four, six-five maybe, and he wasn't even wearing shoes.

"I'm DI Porter of the Norfolk Constabulary. This is DC Savage. Mind if we come in? It's cold out here."

Skinner shrugged but he didn't move out of the way. He stared past Porter, scanning the horizon, and Savage wondered what he was looking for.

"You were expecting more of us?" she asked, and he

turned those cold eyes down as if noticing her for the first time. He shrugged again, obviously bored. Savage stepped closer to the door, just a couple of feet away, forcing him to lean back. "There can be, if you like?"

He didn't react, although the corners of his mouth seemed to twitch up in a slight smile—the kind of smile that Kett might have put his knuckles through if he'd been here. Savage felt like doing the same but she stopped when a voice echoed down the flagstone hall from deeper inside the house.

"Who is it, dad?"

Footsteps, then a teenage girl peeked through the small gap between Skinner's arm and the door.

"Who are you?" she asked.

"Couple of Norfolk's finest," Skinner said, his voice low and somehow meaty, like he'd just been eating something sticky. "They're just leaving."

"No, we're not," Savage said. "We need to talk to you about Chase Masefield."

"Chase?" said the girl, but her father closed the gap, filling the doorway again.

"Lauren, get back in the kitchen."

She tutted, but Savage heard her walk away, calling for her mum. There was something in the man's voice that made it clear he wouldn't tolerate disobedience. He leaned out of the door, revealing a mottled pink head that was crowned by a poor display of wispy brown hair. He smiled again and this time Savage saw how yellow his teeth were.

"Whatever the little shit told you, he's lying," Skinner said, his voice low. "He's been after my daughter for weeks, and he's got no respect for the fact she told him to back off. Now he's taking it out on me, because I scared him off, so whatever he says, it's a lie."

"Actually," Porter started, but Savage interrupted.

"You scared him off?"

"It's what any good father would do," he said.

"How?" asked Porter, and Skinner's eyes slid over to look at him.

"Just made him aware of how unwelcome he was here, nothing else."

"You didn't touch him?" Savage asked, and Skinner licked his lips.

"I told you, whatever he said, it's bullshit. Now are you going to piss off, or do I have to call somebody?"

"Chase Masefield is dead," Savage said, locking eyes with the man the same way stags lock horns. She saw the way he flinched, the surprise, then a smile that creased his face for a fraction of a second before it turned to stone again.

"Dead," he said. "Wasn't expecting that."

"What were you expecting?" Porter asked. Skinner didn't answer. "We really do need to come in."

"Sure," he said after a second. He stood back so that he could pull the door open all the way. "Shoes off."

Savage took the lead, unlacing her boots and taking a moment to look around. The entrance hall was huge, twice the size as the living room in her flat and decked in expensive flagstones, a vast oak staircase rising to the top floor. Somewhere up there a little dog was yapping its head off. On the wall directly opposite the door was a professional studio shot of Greg Skinner and his wife and his daughter, big smiles and dead eyes. An archway led into a kitchen and Savage saw the daughter waiting there obediently, her mother standing next to her, kneading the girl's arm with both hands. The atmosphere in the house was as heavy as it had been in the woods, an air of promised violence, and she didn't have to look far to find the source.

"Kitchen," barked Skinner, following the echo of his voice, striding like the lord of the manor. There was plenty of room between the vast counters and the island but he made straight for his wife, forcing her to move out of his way. He filled a glass with water and chugged it down, slamming it in the sink as Savage and Porter entered the room.

"Tell them what you just told me," he said.

"It might be better if you take a seat," Porter said, looking at the two women. "I have some bad news."

"Your boyfriend is dead," Skinner said, and Lauren twisted around to look at him.

"What?" she said. "Chase? He can't be."

Porter fired Skinner a warning look before taking a couple of steps towards Lauren.

"I'm really sorry to have to tell you," he said. "But yes, he's dead."

Lauren had turned ashen but it was her mother who was in tears. The little woman's entire body seemed to shake with them and she had to let go of her daughter to wipe her eyes.

"Please, sit down for a moment," Savage said, and this time Lauren nodded, leading her mum to a cream sofa by the enormous bi-fold doors. Mrs Skinner dropped into the cushions, almost swallowed whole, but Lauren perched on the edge like a bird. She was an attractive girl, her big eyes gazing upwards like she could charm the world into changing its mind, into making everything okay.

"He's really gone?" she asked. "I don't understand, he was only here the other night."

"Lauren, I don't want you to worry yourself," Skinner said. "You lot can talk to me."

"He was here on Friday?" Savage asked, ignoring the big man.

"For dinner, right?" Porter added. Lauren nodded, glancing at her mum.

"We had a roast, then we went for a walk in the woods."

"Did you not hear me?" Skinner said, his voice louder now. "I said you can talk to me. Leave them alone."

"Tell me what happened," Porter went on. "You went for a walk? All of you? What time?"

"About seven?" Lauren replied. "I can't remember. We finished eating then dad showed Chase the guns, and—"

"The guns?" Savage asked.

"Shotguns, all licenced," Skinner said, walking to the sofa and standing over his wife like a bodyguard. "I thought he'd be interested, he wasn't. We went for a walk in the woods you passed a moment ago. It started raining so Chase went back to grab a couple of umbrellas, but he must have had enough of us because he never showed his face again. We waited a little while then walked on without him, maybe twenty minutes up the track and onto the road. We were out half an hour in all, and when we got home Chase's car was gone. End of story."

Savage wasn't watching him, she was watching Lauren, and she saw the frown that vanished almost as quickly as it appeared.

"Is that what happened?" she asked the girl.

"Uh," Lauren said, looking to her mum. Mrs Skinner was slumped into the sofa like a toddler, still sniffling.

"I just told you that's what happened," her husband said.

"You mind if I talk to you on your own?" Porter asked him.

"Yeah, I do," he said. "We're family, got nothing to hide from each other. So unless you've got any more pointless questions I'd like you to leave us alone and let my daughter grieve."

"Would you mind if we took a look around?" Porter asked, and Skinner actually laughed.

"What do you think?" he said.

Savage took her phone from her pocket, opening her texts and sending one to Kett.

Call me.

She slid it back, returning her attention to the conversation.

"One more thing," Porter was saying. "I hear you're friends with lots of kids from the village, Mr Skinner. Mostly teenage boys. Mind if I ask you what that friendship entails?"

It felt like the temperature in the room had plummeted by ten degrees. Skinner was staring at Porter like he meant to kill him. He was a big guy, and that was intimidating enough, but there was something else there, something Savage couldn't quite put her finger on. There was an unquestionable promise of brute violence and it made her hackles rise the same way they would if she was face to face with a big dog. She had to force herself to stand her ground.

"What are you saying?" the man growled. "I don't like your tone."

"Dad?" said Lauren in a voice made from glass.

Savage's phone began to ring but nobody was looking at her. She retrieved it, seeing Kett's number.

"I'm really sorry," she said. "I need to get this. I'll take it outside."

She answered it as she walked from the kitchen.

"Hey, boss."

"Boss?" said Kett. "Like I keep saying, not anymore. How's it going?"

"Sure, we'll head back to the station in a minute."

"Oh, right," Kett said. "You want me to pretend to be northern? And hairy?"

"No need for that, sir," Savage said as she pulled on her boots.

"I'm not very tossing happy about this, Savage," Kett went on in a pretty decent Colin Clare impression. "My nose hairs are all in a tizz!"

Savage had to force herself not to laugh. She laid the phone on the flagstones while she tied her laces then picked it up again, glancing back to see that Mr Skinner had sidled to the kitchen door to make sure she left.

"Thank you, sir," she said into the phone. "We'll be sure to do that."

She opened the front door and stepped into the brutal cold, slamming it shut behind her. Her teeth started chattering almost immediately.

"Fudge," she said. "It's bloody freezing."

"Where are you?" Kett asked.

"The Skinner house. Chase was here on Friday. They claim he got fed up and left but I don't know if I believe them. Dad's a real tyrant but there's something else, something I can't quite put my finger on."

"You like him for it?"

Savage bit her lip, staring across the driveway into the woods.

"I don't know," she said.

"You get my texts?"

"Oh, yeah, sorry. You've got something?"

"Maybe," said Kett, the reception fading. "Another case from another place. I just need to make some phone calls."

"What..."

And it took Savage a moment to work out why she was

feeling suddenly alert, her unconscious mind aware of it before the rest of her brain could catch up.

There was a kid staring at her from the trees up ahead, a teenage boy whose eyes almost popped out of his head when he realised he'd been spotted.

"I've got to go," Savage said, hanging up. "Hey, you!"

The kid vanished into the trees like a startled deer, branches cracking beneath his feet. Savage groaned.

"Don't do that, you fudging winker."

She pocketed the phone and started to run.

CHAPTER SEVEN

IT WAS LIKE THROWING HERSELF INTO THE FRONT LINE of a charging army, the woodland unexpectedly dense. Savage winced as a branch drew its sharpened tip down her cheek, another one jabbing at her eye like a bayonet. She put her head down, stumbling into a ditch that was hidden by long grass and landing hard on her left hand. Pain ratcheted up her wrist, her fingers going numb.

"Shit," she said, pushing herself up and crawling between two trunks, only getting to her feet again when the trees let her. It was dark in here, even with the leaves gone from the branches, and for a moment she was night blind.

A crack to her right, a rustle.

"Police!" she yelled. "Stop!"

She set off, the treacherous terrain hidden by a carpet of mulch, every step threatening to turn her ankle. The kid was running away from the road, heading in the direction of the house. She caught brief flashes of him between the crooked trunks, strobing wildly as if she was watching him through a zoetrope. He really wasn't cut out for stealth, his bright white puffer jacket had to have been visible from space and his panicked breaths were the loudest thing in the woods, louder even than the drum of his feet as he ran.

"I'm not going to hurt you," Savage called after him, grabbing at a branch as her foot caught on a root or a stone. "I just want to talk."

He obviously didn't. He shot a look back, nothing in his face except terror. It was a mistake because his legs tangled with each other and he fell, doing a full somersault and kicking up a storm of wet leaves. Savage upped her pace, just a dozen yards away, but he was on his feet again in a heartbeat and limping hard. They were parallel with the bulk of the Skinner farmhouse now, close enough surely for anyone inside to hear them. Behind it sat a cluster of outbuildings, including an enormous black barn that lurked like a predator amongst the trees.

"Stop," Savage ordered. "You're going to hurt yourself."

The kid must have been winded because he was slowing down, his arms wheeling. His breaths were hoarse and he was fumbling for something in his tracksuit trousers. Savage braced herself for a weapon but he pulled out a blue inhaler. It pinged from his fingers as he lifted it to his lips.

"Fuck!" he wheezed, abandoning it.

"Enough!" Savage yelled, this time a solid roar. "Stop!"

The kid knew when he'd been beaten. He staggered to a tree and put a hand to it, clawing in big, desperate breaths that might have come from an accordion. Savage slowed to a walk, collecting the inhaler from the ground and holding it out.

"You'd better take this back," she said.

The kid turned around, looking more like a frightened deer than ever. He was sixteen at a push, maybe younger, his hair razor short at the sides and curly on top just like Chase Masefield's. He tugged at the collar of his puffer jacket, trying to pull it away from his neck. He looked half-frozen, as if he'd been standing out in the cold all day. Savage took a few more steps towards him until he was close enough to snatch the inhaler.

"I'm not here for you," she said. "So calm down."

The kid sucked a couple of shots from the inhaler, his hand trembling. He didn't put it away, he just held onto it like it was a lifebuoy at sea. He was filthy, his jacket covered with leaves and his trousers green where they'd rubbed against the trees. There was fresh blood on his knuckles.

"You hurt?" Savage said, nodding at his hand. He stared at it like he'd never seen it before.

"No?" he said, the word more of a question than an answer.

"You're freezing," she said.

"I'm..." he stuttered, his teeth playing a tune. "I'm fine?"

"Why did you run?"

The boy glanced over his shoulder like he meant to do it again, then stared at the ground, shrugging.

"What's your name?"

"Devon," he said to the fallen leaves.

"First or last or both?" Savage said

"Both?" he asked, confused. She offered him a smile.

"Honestly, if you tell me your name is Devon Devon I'm straight up going to let you go. Nobody deserves that."

It took him a moment to catch up, but he seemed to relax a little.

"It's Devon Parris."

"That's somehow worse," Savage said. "You're here to see Lauren?"

He frowned, glancing at the house that was visible through the trees.

"Lauren?" he said. "Oh, right, yeah. Lauren. I wanted to see how she was doing."

"How she's doing? Is something wrong?"

"No?" he said, another question. "I mean, I don't think so."

"You're friends with her?"

He shrugged again, trembling in the cold.

"We go to the same school. Not friends, really."

"You know Chase Masefield?" Savage asked, and the kid nodded. "He's at your school too?"

"He's a couple of years above me."

"When was the last time you saw him?"

"Uh..." the kid stared into the branches overhead, his mouth open like he was performing advanced trigonometry. "Friday, I think. He was on the bus after school."

"About three?"

"Half past," Devon said. "Maybe a little later, it's never on time no more."

"He say anything to you?"

Devon shook his head. Savage studied him, seeing the sweat that was gathering in the hollow of his throat despite the fact he looked like he'd been pulled out of the freezer to defrost. He glanced at the house again, swallowing hard, working down whatever it was he wanted to hide.

"You want me to get Lauren for you?" Savage asked. "I was just with her. I'm sure she'd be happy to see you."

"No," Devon shot back, a little too quickly. "No, I'd better leave her to it. She's probably busy and stuff."

He seemed to see Savage for the first time.

"Wait, did you say you were police?"

"Yeah," Savage said.

"You here for her dad?"

"Greg Skinner?" Savage asked. "Why would you say that?"

The kid's mouth fell open, nothing but misty breath coming out of it.

"Is that who *you're* here to see?" Savage asked, taking another look at his coat, his shoes, trying to find the crack that would open up the truth. "That's some fancy gear for a, what, fifteen-year-old?"

He tugged at the collar of his coat, this time like he meant to pull it off and hide it. Savage kept hammering.

"I heard Mr Skinner was popular with the kids around here, the teenage boys especially. Bit weird that, don't you think?"

"It's not..." he stuttered. "I don't..."

"What is it?" she pressed, taking another step towards him. "Drugs? You sell for him?"

"No," the kid replied, nodding. "I mean, no?"

He glanced through the trees again, towards the barn.

"Worse than drugs, then?" Savage said, frowning. "I've met Mr Skinner, he's an intimidating man. He ever make you do anything you didn't want to do?"

There, in the way Devon's face contorted into an expression of misery. She'd hit the nail right on the head. The boy squirmed, on the edge of tears.

"What happened?" Savage asked. "Whatever it is, you can tell me and it won't go any further. Whatever it is, you haven't done anything wrong."

Devon was still staring through the trees, his bottom lip wobbling.

"Can I just go home?" he asked, not meeting her eye. "I won't never come back."

"You keep looking at the barn," Savage said. "What am I going to find in there?"

"Nothing," he squeaked, desperate now.

"You sure? If you tell me there's something worth looking at, something urgent, somebody in danger, then maybe I won't need you."

"Please, I just want to go."

He was squirming like he needed the toilet, and Savage simply waited.

"Might be somebody in there," he said, unsure. "Somebody in danger."

"You live in the village?" she asked, and he nodded hard. "So you know that I can find you when I need you?"

He finally looked at her, his eyes wide and wet.

"I can go?"

"You can go," Savage said. "Just be careful, okay?"

He was off like a flash, buggering over again after five steps and honking like a goose as he faceplanted in the leaves. Savage watched him with no small amount of pity as he pulled himself back to his feet and bolted, finally vanishing between the trees.

Only then did she turn to the barn.

"What are you hiding?" she asked, setting off towards it. She wasn't sure if the woodland was part of the Skinner estate or not, because there was no sign of a fence between the last line of trees and the black-painted back wall. Savage hesitated, aware that although she might not be crossing a boundary she was certainly crossing a line.

What would Robbie Kett do?

"Don't ask," she told herself, asking instead, "What would you do, granddad?"

The answer was pretty much the same, and she saw Chase Masefield's butchered body in the quiet darkness of her mind, his savaged throat, the space where his heart had been. She left the woods and made her way quietly down the side of the barn. It was huge, thirty feet long and two thirds as tall, not a single window in sight. The back of the farmhouse watched her, although the kitchen must have been on the other side of the property because there was no sign here of the big bifold doors.

She stopped at the corner and peeked around it to see a wide, short back garden shielded by immense hedges of what looked like willow, taller even than the barn. Other than a broken stone birdbath and a swing set without its swings there was nothing of note in the unmown lawn.

The barn door was shut, but when Savage turned the handle it opened easily enough. There were lights on inside, bare bulbs hanging from the huge oak roof beams, and Savage saw a home gym: a treadmill, a stationary bike, benches and a whole bunch of old-school free weights. A large flat-screen TV had been mounted on the wall opposite the door, and it was currently on—an episode of *Friends*, by the look of it.

She felt her phone vibrate, seeing Porter's name on the screen. She stepped inside before answering, speaking in a whisper.

"You're out of the house?"

"Yeah," said Porter. "Where'd you go?"

"Out the back, in the barn," she said. "Give me a minute, guv, can you keep Mr Skinner busy?"

"He's already gone," Porter said. "You should probably skedaddle."

"On it," she said, hanging up. She took another step into the barn, wondering what it was that had got Devon Parris so spooked. Steroids, maybe? Skinner was a big guy, he looked like he'd spent a good bit of time in the gym when he was younger. Maybe he was using the kids to sell them? That would explain why Devon had run. Maybe Chase had been working for Skinner too and had threatened to tell the police? It didn't seem like a good enough motive for murder, and certainly not the kind of violence that had been inflicted on the teenage boy.

Unless Greg Skinner was covering his tracks, making it look like something else.

Whatever it was, she didn't think she was going to find answers here. The barn was spotless, everything racked, everything in its place, the bare wooden floor freshly waxed. It was good enough to live in, and she wondered if that's what Skinner was doing because as she turned to go she saw a bed in the corner of the room, half-hidden by a Chinese-style screen. There were sheets and blankets piled on it and a pair of trainers tucked underneath. Sitting on top, like the cherry on a cake, was a camcorder, an old one.

Something turned in her thoughts, something deeply unpleasant.

You here for her dad? Devon had asked.

She thought about Greg Skinner, when he'd opened the door and heard Chase's name.

Whatever the little shit told you, he's lying.

"You'd better have a very fucking good reason for being in here."

The voice was right in her ear and it took every ounce of strength Savage possessed not to cry out. She turned as slowly as she could to find Skinner in the doorway not six feet behind her. He looked bigger than ever but he must have moved like a ninja to have made it across the garden without her hearing him. He closed the gap between them, a narrow smile splitting his face and his eyes colder than ever.

"This is called trespassing, police badge or not," he said. "You know what we do to intruders around here?"

"Step back," Savage said, hearing the tremor in her voice and hating it. She forced herself not to move away, squaring her stance instead, feeling herself reach instinctively for the baton that was no longer there. "I saw a kid in the woods, he said somebody was in danger."

"What kid?" Mr Skinner said. "I call bullshit. Nothing here but a gym, so kindly fuck off."

She couldn't have obeyed even if she'd wanted to because he was blocking the door. He knew it, too, his smile growing. His hands were bunched into fists as big as mallets and for the first time she noticed the smell of him—the odour of fear, of spent adrenaline.

"You want to tell me why the kids in the village like you so much?" she asked. "Why they'd want to come here?"

"They work out," he said. "I train them."

She glanced at the gym, at the equipment, at the bed, then back at the giant who stood in front of her.

"You train them."

"You a fucking parrot?" he said. "Yeah, I train them."

"So how come you give them money? Shouldn't it be the other way around?"

The smile left his face like a mouse that's seen a hawk's shadow.

"Who told you that?" he said. "They're full of shit. It was Devon, wasn't it? That little prick. Wouldn't know the truth if it bit him on the arse."

"So if I went over there and looked at that camcorder I wouldn't find anything dodgy?" Savage asked.

Mr Skinner licked his lips.

"I video them, to show them their technique," he said.

"Let me guess, it's better to show them when they're not wearing their shirts."

"You fucking bitch. I'm telling you one last time, get the fuck out of here."

"Good idea," she said. "And I'm taking you with me. Mr Skinner, I'm—"

The big man lunged, finger first. There was no way of knowing whether he was moving in for an attack or if he just wanted to make a point, and Savage didn't wait to find out. She grabbed his finger and twisted it hard to the side. It was like it was the controller for a video game, Skinner's entire body tilting with it, his feet beating out a tap dance as he tried to stay up.

"You fucki—"

She twisted it some more, only seeing his big left fist swing towards her at the last minute. She hopped back, Skinner's knuckles scraping her chin—still hard enough to jar her. The adrenaline was a grenade going off in her stomach, the world fizzing. Skinner pulled his finger free and ran at her like a rugby player, lifting her body off the ground as if she was stuffed with straw. He was foaming at the mouth, his eyes apoplectic with rage.

Savage drove her elbow down into the soft flesh of his neck and he grunted, losing his footing. She hit the ground first, the wind punched out of her lungs, Skinner landing hard on top of her. His fist rose and fell and she twisted her head out of the way, hearing his knuckles crack on the polished wood and his grunting cry of pain. She bucked hard, sending the big man rolling off her.

"Porter!" she yelled as she bounced back up, the word barely louder than a breath. She pointed a finger at Skinner. "Stay down."

But Skinner was past the point of listening. He was grunting like a bull as he used a weight bench to haul himself to his knees. There was a rack of dumbbells beside it and he hefted one from its slot, no uncertainty in his expression, no doubt about what he was capable of.

"Get away from him!" shouted a voice from the door, and Savage looked over to see Matilda Skinner there, everything jiggling as she trotted into the barn. "Leave him alone!"

Her husband was back on his feet now, swaying a little as he tried to claw in enough air.

"Don't," Savage told him.

"Fuck you," he replied, lumbering towards her, his weapon raised like a club. Savage bunched her fist, ready to drop him.

"Put it down!" came Porter's voice.

The DI was a blur, running into the barn so fast that he sent Matilda Skinner flying. He vaulted the bench, hitting Skinner with a flying tackle that sent them both rolling over the wooden floor. The big DI ended up on top, grabbing the lapels of Skinner's jacket and bunching his gloved fist.

"You're a big man, but you're in bad shape," Porter said. "For me, it's a full-time job. Now behave yourself."

He grinned at Savage like he was sharing a secret joke with her, but whatever it was, it was lost in the churning chaos of her thoughts. Matilda was trying to get to her feet, looking like a turtle that had been left on its shell. Behind her, silhouetted in the barn door, was their daughter.

"What's happening?" Lauren said, her hands covering her mouth. "Dad?"

"These pricks just bought themselves a lawsuit," Skinner replied, wiping blood and foam from his lips. "Get my phone, find the number for Dennis Pruitt. He'll do what I tell him, he'll have your fucking arses. Trespassing, search without a warrant, assault, am I missing anything?"

"Yeah," said Savage. "You're missing the bit where we arrest you."

"For what?" he spat back.

"For being an arsehole," Porter said, pulling a set of handcuffs from the pocket of his overcoat. He looked at Savage. "And assaulting a police officer. Anything else?"

"Coercion of a minor," Savage replied. "Maybe more than one."

Skinner looked like he was going to object but instead he rested his head on the floor, staring at the roof of the barn, his jaw flexing like he was chewing something unpleasant. Porter snapped the cuffs around one wrist, Skinner lifting his other in compliance.

"Dad?" Lauren said again. "What's she talking about?"

Matilda Skinner was sitting on her backside against the wall, her head buried in her hands, her sobs making every part of her shake.

"Mum?" Lauren said.

"That it?" said Porter. "You heard the lady. I'm arresting you for assaulting a police officer and for the coercion of a minor. You do not have to say anything, but it may harm your defence if you do not mention when questioned something which you later rely on in court. Anything you do say..."

Savage sat on the bench, Porter's words numbed by the burn of adrenaline, drowned out by the sobs of the mother and the daughter, and muted by the knowledge that Porter probably should have added a third charge to the list:

The murder of Chase Masefield.

CHAPTER EIGHT

"I COULD HAVE TAKEN HIM."

Savage angled her neck, wincing as the pain lanced through it all the way from her collarbone to her left ear. Her entire body had started to stiffen, caught unawares by the sudden burst of violence. She was fitter than she'd ever been, but there was a big difference between pounding the heavy bag in her garage and wrestling with a six-foot-four brute who had seemed pretty determined to kill her. She'd got off lightly, she knew. Other than the pulled muscle in her neck and the tender spot on the end of her chin she was unscathed.

"Huh?" Porter said, sliding his phone into his pocket and pushing himself away from the wall to take the seat next to her. They were inside the Norwich nick waiting for Greg Skinner to be processed, and it felt colder in here than it did outside. Or maybe it was the adrenaline run-off that was making her bones rattle—possibly even shock.

"I said I could have taken him, sir," Savage repeated. "Skinner. You didn't have to step in."

Porter lifted his hands in surrender.

"I know, I know. You looked like you were doing just fine down there on the floor."

"I wasn't on the floor," she said. "I was back on my feet by the time you arrived."

"About to be charged by a bull with a dumbbell," he said.

"I could have taken him!"

"I know!" Porter said, grinning. "Believe me, I've seen you in action."

They sat there for a moment before Savage managed a smile.

"You took care of Matilda Skinner just fine, though. I don't think I've ever actually seen somebody fly through the air before."

"I didn't even see her," Porter said. "She's so short. I hope she's okay."

"I'm more worried about the wall she flew into."

The door at the end of the corridor opened and a familiar face peered through, the anger lines etched even deeper than normal.

"There you are," said Superintendent Clare, stomping down the corridor with such determination that his coattails billowed out behind him. "Let me have a look at you."

"I'm fine, sir," Savage said. "He barely—"

"You misunderstand," Clare bellowed when he was standing above her. "I need to look at you to make sure of something."

He leant down ridiculously close, his nose hairs seeming to reach for her. His eyes darted back and forth over her face.

"Sir?" Savage said.

"I can't see a beard, I can't see the scars, I can't see the rugged good looks or the salt and pepper hair or that infuriating puppy-dog, '*Oh sorry sir it wasn't me I couldn't help myself*' expression that I've come to loathe so much."

Porter barked out a laugh that echoed off the walls, but the joke was lost on Savage until Clare jabbed her in the forehead and stood back.

"I'm trying to work out whether it's you in there, Savage, or whether somehow Robbie Kett has taken control of your body. Because that's the only reason I can think of that you'd end up in a fistfight with a suspect."

"Oh, right," Savage said. "I can—"

"I know you can explain," Clare interrupted. "I've already explained your tossing explanation to everyone who needs it explained to them, because my explanation doesn't involve what appears to be an illegal search of private property. You were told somebody was in danger, you went to help them, right?"

"Close enough," Savage said. "There was a kid in the woods. Devon Parris. I think he'd been out there for some time, he was frozen solid. He was there to see Greg Skinner in the barn but he'd been holding back for some reason. Probably scared. I think Skinner was grooming him, probably a whole load of other teenage boys as well."

Clare grimaced.

"We've confiscated several videotapes containing footage of boys," he said. "Seven individuals so far, none of them Chase Masefield. Some with no shirts, some in their underwear. As of now, that's all we've found."

"That's not enough, guv?" said Porter.

"We'll see. You think he might have had something to do with our murder?"

"Hard to say, sir," Savage said. "Based on first appearances I'd say he was more than capable of bullying, intimidation, coercion, and physical violence. But he doesn't seem the sort to cut out a boy's heart."

"Well, we're about to find out," Clare said. "He's in three and lawyered up. Porter, you're LIO, you're in charge of the interview. Savage, try not to hit him this time."

"I'll try," she said. "Anything else on the boy, sir?"

"Franklin's looking at him now, she should have her report ready by the time you two are done. Go on, time's ticking."

Savage stood, bracing a hand on the chair to stop a rush of vertigo. Porter was already walking down the corridor, oblivious, but Clare gave her a look.

"You okay?"

"I'm fine," she said. "He barely touched me."

"Well in my book the fact he touched you at all makes him a prime tossbag. So whatever happens in there, give him hell."

———

THE INTERVIEW ROOM stank of anger and wax. Greg Skinner sat in one chair in his Barbour jacket and a flat cap. His cheeks were flushed and there was an ugly yellow bruise spreading beneath his eye socket and over the bridge of his nose. Next to him sat a man about the same age, dressed in a suit and an obscenely ugly, tasselled leather coat that looked like it belonged in the 1980s. His thinning hair hung down to his shoulders and his bushy eyebrows gave even Clare's a run for their money. Both were eyeballing Savage and Porter hard as they entered.

Savage shut the door and followed Porter to the table in silence, everyone waiting for him to switch on the recorder and give the date.

"DI Porter and DC Savage conducting," he said. "Alongside..."

"Dennis Pruitt," said the solicitor, his voice deep and slow. He shot Greg Skinner a dirty look, like he was angry with him, gritting teeth that looked like yellow tombstones. "I think you'll find—"

"How's your face?" Porter interrupted, talking to Skinner.

The big man leaned over the table, but only for the second or two it took his solicitor to rest a hand on his arm and draw him back—a little more firmly than was needed.

"For the record, we intend to press charges against you both for assault," Pruitt said. "My client was harassed and beaten in his own home, during a search without a warrant. It's obscene, even for you lot."

Skinner cleared his throat and the solicitor carried on.

"Greg Skinner is an upstanding member of our vibrant little community, the very best of men, and you have no right to treat him this way."

"Don't you think the big question is why your client was recording footage of naked children in his barn?" Porter said. He turned to Skinner. "I mean that's what people will really want to know."

"They're hardly children," growled Skinner, his solicitor's hand landing on his arm again, squeezing hard.

"No comment," Pruitt said. "We won't be answering any questions until the matter of the attack on my client is addressed."

"You're right," said Porter, his chair creaking as he sat back. "They're not children, not really. Fourteen, fifteen, sixteen, old enough to make up their own minds, right?"

Skinner shrugged, licking his lips.

"No comment," said Pruitt. "You won't goad him, I'm afraid. He's proven himself to be very stubborn."

Pruitt gave Skinner a look that the bigger man ignored.

"Did your solicitor tell you that's what all the guilty people say?" asked Porter. "*No comment.* It's the criminal's favourite mantra."

"I'm not a criminal," Skinner said, folding his arms over his barrel chest. "I've never been in trouble with the police in my life. Right, Dennis?"

"My client is an upstanding member of both the village and the county," said Pruitt, his cheeks mottled. He ran a hand through his long hair, pulling it away from his face. "He's a village councillor, a volunteer firefighter, a school governor."

"Governor, eh?" Porter said. "Bet that post comes with a few extra perks. Is that how you met Devon Parris?"

"Devon who?" said Mr Skinner, sneering.

"Greg," warned Pruitt. "Don't."

"Sorry," said Porter. "I forgot, no comment. It's fine, because we've got your videotapes, we can ask the children all about it, we can get everything we need from them. We don't even need you, to be honest, so if you like you can just go."

"Whatever they tell you, it's bullshit," said Skinner. "Lying pack of pricks."

Pruitt reached for his arm again, the tassels on his coat jiggling, but Skinner shook him away. He leaned over the table and jabbed the same fat finger at Porter that he'd shown Savage. It looked swollen.

"I was helping them out, the ungrateful little shits. I was training them. Used to box, you know? Back in school. Bunch of pussies. I was toughening them up."

"Free weights," said Porter, flexing his enormous arms

beneath his suit. "I know a bit about them myself. I had a personal trainer for years, I don't remember him ever asking me to take my clothes off."

Skinner licked his lips again, his dark eyes studying Porter like he would happily stamp on his head until he was dead. The more time Savage spent around him, the more convinced she was that he was capable of doing something terrible.

"If you want to see somebody's correct form," the man said eventually, stumbling over the words. "They can't be hidden by clothing. Dennis? You going to join in any fucking time soon?"

"Mr Skinner was simply doing his bit to help the health and fitness of the villagers," Pruitt said, swallowing hard. "There is absolutely no evidence whatsoever that anything else was going on."

"Which is why Dennis is going to get me out of here," Skinner said, turning to the other man. "Right now. Or he'll regret it."

"So why pay them?" Savage asked.

Skinner hadn't looked at her once the whole time they'd been in the room, but now he turned his head slowly to her, his dark eyes drinking her in. There was something in his expression that made her want to curl up into a ball, something intensely ugly, but she'd been around worse people —way worse—and she made a show of leaning across the table, not even blinking. He held her eye, the pressure between them like a demolition charge about to blow.

"What?" he said eventually.

"You pay the children to take their clothes off, don't you?"

Pruitt glanced at his client, his mouth a grim line and his eyes full of quiet anger. They knew each other, that was clear, and there didn't seem to be much love lost between them.

"No comment," the lawyer said when he turned back to the table.

"They're not children," Skinner growled.

"What else do you pay the *children* for?" Savage asked. Her eyes were burning but she had no intention of looking away.

"They're not fucking *children*," he said again.

"Because those trainers aren't cheap," she pressed. "Those puffer jackets. Seems like a lot of money to pay a child just to get naked. Surely you'd want a bigger return on your investment."

"I just watch," Skinner said. "I don't touch."

"Greg!" Pruitt barked, turning an even more violent shade of red.

Savage turned away, allowing herself a smile.

"You know that dumbbell would have left a pretty little crater in that ugly face of yours," Skinner said. "Bitch."

"My client needs a little time," Pruitt blustered, pretending to search for something in his notes. "I'd like the chance to continue—"

"Did you leave a pretty little crater in Chase Mase-field?" Porter said.

"What?" Skinner and Pruitt said together, in perfect unison.

"What I didn't mention earlier was that Chase was murdered. Butchered is a better word for it. And whoever killed him cut out the boy's heart."

Mr Skinner laughed, but it was the sound of somebody in shock. The colour was draining from his face like he was the one whose arteries had been cut, and when his mouth opened nothing came out. He looked at Pruitt, who was just as paralysed as he was. The solicitor's cheeks were burning so fiercely Savage could have warmed her hands on them.

"His heart?" Skinner said.

"Maybe it's time you told the truth," said Pruitt, staring at his notes like there was an escape hatch there. "Before it catches up with you."

"Right," Skinner replied, staring at the table. All the fight had left him. He looked at Pruitt again but there was no help to be found there.

"Was Chase one of yours?" Savage asked.

"No."

"You never took him to the barn?"

"The first time I met him was Friday," he said. "Met him properly. I'd seen him outside the school. Lauren was dating him. I thought he was a little prick but I didn't kill him. Surely you don't think..."

"I think you were filming children, Mr Skinner," Savage said. "I think you were buying their silence and then bullying them when they started to make a fuss. I wonder if Chase was going to go public, tell the world what you were doing. You were showing him your guns. Why? Threatening him to keep his mouth shut?"

"That's called motive," said Porter, ignoring Skinner's shaking head, his trembling jowls. "Next we have opportunity. A dark night, a storm, a kid lost in the woods. What happened on Friday?"

"We went out together, just the four of us," Skinner said, looking back and forth between them. "It was pissing it down but I thought a walk would toughen him up and he was getting a little too close to Lauren, if you know what I mean. You a dad?"

He directed this question to Porter and the DI shook his head.

"You'll see when you are, you don't want their greasy little erections anywhere near your children. Yeah, I wanted to scare him off, but it had nothing to do with the barn."

"You told us Chase went back to the house to get umbrellas. Whose idea was that?" Porter asked.

"His," said Skinner, sniffing. "He didn't want Lauren getting soaked."

"And you didn't go after him?" Savage said.

"I..." he swallowed, scratching a fingernail on the surface of the table. He glanced at Pruitt but the solicitor may as well have been a statue carved from stone.

"He didn't show, he didn't come back. So I went to look for him. Only for a minute, but it was dark out there and he didn't have his torch, didn't have his phone. I walked out of the woods and saw his car going down the drive, figured he'd buggered off."

"Anyone else with you when you saw this?" Porter said.

"No, Tilly and Lauren were in the woods. I saw him go and we walked through the woods, back down the road. Maybe half an hour in all, that's it. Lauren was furious that he'd gone, blamed me."

"What happened after that?" Savage said.

"We dried off, Tilly went to bed, Lauren did whatever teenage girls do and I... I was in the barn."

"Alone?"

Mr Skinner licked his lips.

"Were you alone?" Savage pressed.

"No," he said, sighing. "Devon was there. He... we did some training."

"What time?" said Savage.

"He showed up after ten."

"How much did you owe him?"

"Fifty quid," Skinner said. "He was supposed to come back for it today."

"Right," said Porter, resting a clenched fist on the table.

"I had nothing to do with Chase," Skinner said, looking at Pruitt. "I'm not sick in the head like that. I wouldn't have touched him because I wouldn't do that to Lauren. I didn't like him but *she* did. I wouldn't have gone near him."

"*Wouldn't have* is a weird way to say it, don't you think?" Porter said. "It's a long way from *didn't.*"

"I think that's enough for now," said Pruitt. "If you're going to charge my client, do it."

"No," said Porter. "We're going to wait. You'd better get comfortable, Mr Skinner, you've got about twenty-two hours in a cell to look forward to."

He stood up, rapping his knuckles twice on the desk the same way Kett always did. He reached for the recorder but Savage stopped him with another question.

"You said Chase didn't have his phone, why not?"

"We don't like them at the table," Skinner said. "He obviously didn't think to pick it up on the way out."

"So where is it, then?"

"I... uh..." Skinner looked at Pruitt, who was long past caring. "I threw it in the bin."

"Why?" Savage said, and all Skinner could manage was a shrug.

Porter looked at Savage and she nodded.

"Interview terminated at 16:08," he said, ending the recording before grinning down at the beaten man. "And somebody had better get Mr Skinner some new pants because he just shat all over himself."

CHAPTER NINE

"I don't think he did it," said Porter.

He clipped in his seatbelt and started the Mondeo's engine, chewing on his thoughts. He was surprised at how much his body ached after the fight, his muscles protesting. Greg Skinner hadn't touched him, but there was a bruise on his hip where he'd collided with the man's wife.

"I mean, don't get me wrong, the guy's a premier league arsehole. Even his solicitor hated him, which isn't exactly surprising, given the way Skinner was talking to him."

"Yeah, I noticed," said Savage from the passenger seat. "Who talks to their brief like that? I'm amazed the guy didn't walk out of the room. You *don't* think he's guilty?"

"No, he's guilty of a lot of shit, and he's going to prison. But that wasn't the face of somebody who'd happily slice a kid open and take his heart. Besides, he's got an alibi in Devon Parris, if it checks out."

"I don't know. Even if it does, Chase vanished just after seven, Devon didn't show up until ten. That's more than enough time."

Savage sighed, resting a muddy foot on the dash.

"Disgusting," Porter said.

"It is," she replied. "God only knows what else he forced those kids to do."

"No, Kate," he said, backhanding her gently on the leg. "It's disgusting that you'd sully my car with your boots. Look!"

He brushed the mud from the fake leather, scowling at her.

"You don't see me putting my feet up in your shitty little Fiat, do you?"

"You'd have to be sitting in the boot to get your feet up in my car," Savage said. "Sorry, guv."

He tutted at her as he put the Mondeo in gear and pulled away from the police station. It was just past five and the traffic was snarled up all through town, everyone with somewhere to go. The rain had moved in again, cold and hard enough to feel like handfuls of chipped ice. The car's heater was booming but there was a chill in Porter's bones that felt like it would be there forever.

"So maybe Chase did head back to the house for the umbrellas," said Savage. "He went by himself, in the dark, but decided he couldn't deal with Skinner anymore and got into his car and drove away. If that's true, it makes things more difficult because there's no way of knowing where he went or where he was attacked."

"And there's no sign of the car," Porter said, easing forward.

"What if Greg Skinner wasn't working alone?" Savage put her foot up again, leaving it there for half a second before she remembered. She shuffled in her seat instead. "We've seen it so many times. These guys have a network, they share their trophies. Skinner might not have killed Chase but one of his friends might have."

"We'll know more when they've gone through Skinner's videos," Porter said, the traffic lights finally releasing them. He swung around the roundabout, heading downhill past the shadowy bulk of the Roman Catholic Cathedral. "And when we've had a chance to speak to the boys."

"Yeah," said Savage, frowning. "Where are you going, sir? HQ is the other way."

"Is it?" Porter said, feigning shock. "I had no idea, I've only been a Norwich copper for a couple of years. Thank god you're here, Kate, I wouldn't be able to tie my shoelaces without you."

"Sarcasm is the tool of the witless."

"You're a tool," he muttered. "There's somebody I want to check in on. Chase's brother. I spoke with him earlier."

"You can't call him?"

"He was in a bad way, and he knew about Skinner. I just want to make sure he's okay."

"You have a heart of gold, Peter Porter."

"My heart's one hundred percent muscle, thank you. Just like the rest of me. I can drop you off?"

"I'll tag along."

They drove in relative silence, the world outside picked out in blurred bursts of colour from the other cars. The only interruption was a phone call just as they were approaching Lyng, Allie's name on the display. Porter cancelled it.

"Don't mind me," Savage said. "Talk to your wife, might be important."

"It's nothing. I'll call her back later."

Savage left it, but Porter's heart was swimming somewhere in his stomach. Allie had been in a bad place lately too, and she wouldn't be calling with good news. He didn't want to talk to her at all, truth be told, and especially not with Savage listening in. Luckily, she didn't call back, and a short while later he pulled the Mondeo over to the side of the pencil-thin street in Lesser Lyng, leaving the hazard lights flashing.

"You coming?" he asked.

"I'll stay here," Savage said. "Need to call Robbie anyway and fill him in."

"Say hi from me." Porter opened the door to a fist of cold wind. "Bloody Nora, if I'm not back in ten send out a search party."

He slammed the door, pulling his heavy coat around himself and hunkering down to stop himself blowing away. The Masefield house was two dozen yards up the narrow street but it felt like climbing Everest, and he was panting for breath by the time he knocked on the door. The wind whipped and howled around him, furious at his intrusion, but even over the noise of it, he could hear shouts from inside. He knocked again and a second or so later the door swung open to reveal a tall woman in her late forties wearing pyjamas and a pink dressing gown. Porter saw the greying blonde hair and the drawn face and thought, for a second, that it was Cathy Masefield, only realising his mistake when she spoke.

"What do you want?" she said, her accent definitely not local. He thought it might be Geordie.

"I'm DI Pete Porter," he said, the wind making his hair dance. "I'm looking into Chase's death. May I come in for a second?"

She chewed on the question for a moment then stood back. Porter ducked under the low lintel, cracking his head on the ceiling again when he stood straight. The kitchen door was open and Cathy Masefield sat at the table, barely visible through a cloud of cigarette smoke. She turned her dark eyes to him but only for a fraction of a second. From here she looked like she too was formed of smoke, as if a single breath might unravel her.

"What do you want?" the other woman said again. Definitely a Newcastle accent. She lowered her voice. "You found out who killed our Chase?"

"You're his aunt?" Porter asked, although he didn't need to phrase it as a question. The two women were too similar for them not to be sisters. She nodded anyway, scratching her face with yellow-tipped fingers, her gold nail polish chipped to oblivion.

"Audrey," she said. "Cathy's wee sister. You caught him yet?"

"Not yet. But we're doing everything we can. Can I talk to Cathy for a moment?"

Audrey glanced back, then shook her head.

"I mean, you can try, but she's not said a thing to me since I got here, not said a thing to Blake *an'all*."

"He's here?"

He didn't really need to ask this, either, because he could hear the sounds of the PlayStation drifting out of the living room.

"How's he doing?"

"How do you think? He loved his brother. They were inseparable, not like me and Cath. We couldn't stand each other when we were kids. Blake's not said much to me either, he's putting on a brave face."

She sniffed, her eyes red raw.

"I don't get it. I don't get why anyone would do this to these boys. They're good kids. Can I ask how it happened? How did he die?"

"I can't say," Porter said. "Not yet. Do you mind?"

He motioned to the living room and she nodded, stepping out of his way. Porter practically had to do the limbo to get through the door, seeing Blake sitting alone on the sofa staring intently at the TV. He looked somehow transparent, as if he was in danger of fading away, and when he saw Porter he curled his legs up and hunched his back like he wanted to make himself invisible.

There was no sign of the cat.

"Hey," Porter said. Behind him, Audrey returned to the kitchen, speaking softly, and Porter took a few steps into the room before perching on the arm of the sofa. On-screen a soldier was running through a war-torn city, a sniper rifle in his hands. He was halfway to a shelled house when blood exploded from his head and he fell. Blake sucked in air through his teeth.

"Fuuuuuck," he said quietly.

"The trick is to not get shot," Porter said.

"Thanks. I'll try to remember that."

His character respawned and he started playing again, his fingers a blur on the controller. Porter watched him.

"How are you holding up?" he asked. The kid shrugged, his eyes locked on the screen. "I think you should know, we arrested Greg Skinner."

This time the boy looked over.

"Did he kill Chase?"

"We don't know," Porter said. "That's not why we arrested him. He was doing something else. I think you know what it was."

Blake's eyes dropped to the controller in his hands, his throat working hard like he was trying to swallow. He looked ashamed and Porter felt the anger detonate inside him.

"You have nothing to be sorry about," Porter said. "Greg Skinner is a monster. He's going to prison. Nobody needs to know except us. Did he ever approach you? Solicit you in any way?"

The boy shook his head, too fast. On-screen, the solder fell again, but Blake made no attempt to respawn.

"Blake," Porter said. "It's important. If Mr Skinner had anything to do with Chase's death then we need to know everything."

"It wasn't me," Blake said. "I mean, I went to his place, to the barn, but nothing happened. It was... I felt weird, you know?"

He looked up, struggling.

"It was Devon's idea, this kid in my class. He said we'd get some money, that Mr Skinner was loaded and he'd pay us to train in his gym. Devon was doing it, a couple of other guys too. They all said he was a perve, a paedo or whatever, but that he never touched you or anything, he just liked to watch you lift weights. So I thought about it, but I didn't go in, not for more than a second, and nothing happened."

"Did you tell your brother about it?" Porter asked.

"No," said Blake. "He'd have done something, called the police or something, and nothing happened, I swear."

"You haven't done anything wrong," Porter said again. "Not one thing. Has anyone ever reported Mr Skinner? Anyone accused him of anything?"

Blake shook his head, looking like a lost rabbit.

"He doesn't do nothing bad, I don't think. And besides, he's always at the school, knows all the teachers and stuff, enough to make life hard for you, I reckon. You met him?"

Porter nodded.

"He's scary, right? Maybe not for you, but he's a big man, and he's got a lot of guns."

"He ever threaten to use them?"

Blake shrugged.

"One kid said he had. Guy called Gary Redpath told Chase once that he'd threatened him with a shotty, told him to keep his mouth shut. But I only heard that from Chase and he only heard it from somebody else. Everyone at school knows Mr Skinner, everyone knows what you can get out of him, everyone knows what he'll do if you try to fuck him over."

"And you never thought that was a little weird?" Porter asked.

"It's the village, *innit*?" Blake said, like it was the stupidest question in the world.

He turned back to his game, his face so drawn it looked skeletal. His soldier only lasted a second or two before he fell and Blake threw the controller to the floor in disgust. Porter picked it up and pressed the button to respawn. He hadn't been lying, he'd played *Call of Duty* for years, and with a deft click of the trigger he took out an enemy on a distant rooftop.

"Pow," he said.

Blake craned forward, watching intently as Porter ran into a barn and knifed another player in the back.

"Brutal," he said. "You weren't kidding, were you?"

"Tenth level prestige, and that's just on *Black Ops*," Porter said, easing himself around a corner. There was somebody running at him and he took them out almost instantly, earning a gasp from the kid on the sofa.

"How do you do that?" he asked.

"Quickscope. Keep the crosshair at chest height at all times and learn to lead your shots. Aim where they're going, not where they are."

"Sweet," said Blake.

He took another shot, staring so intently at the screen that he didn't notice Cathy Masefield standing in the living room door until she cleared her throat. She seemed angry, although it only lasted a second before her expression softened.

"Sorry," Porter said, handing the controller back to Blake and scrambling off the arm of the sofa.

She sniffed, wiped her nose, and nodded.

"You want something to drink?" she said. "Kettle's on."

"Stay for a game, if you like," Blake added.

"I can't," said Porter. "Thank you. I just had a couple of questions, that's all. I'll be in touch."

"One game?" Blake said, gazing up at him. "Die and swap out?"

Porter thought of Savage in the car, freezing her arse off. Then he thought of Chase Masefield, draped over a rock with his heart removed, enshrined in frost. He thought of the young brother who would have to live with that image forever, when the truth hit the headlines.

He took the controller with a gentle smile.

"Sure," he said. "Why not."

CHAPTER TEN

"At last! The royal couple has deigned to bless us with its presence." Superintendent Clare's voice prowled around the morgue like an angry bear. "Quick, fill the crystal goblets with champagne and fetch the satin cushions for their majestic posteriors in case their lazy, late, irresponsible arseholes get tired and need a tossing rest. Move it, you two, *move!*"

Porter hesitated by the door, letting Savage go first.

"You really are a gentleman," she muttered as she walked through.

"Hardly," he replied, quietly. "I just want to be behind you in case he throws anything."

The boss stood at the head of the stainless-steel autopsy table, looking every inch an undertaker even though it was Emily Franklin who waited beside him with the tools of the trade in her hand. The young pathologist nodded at Savage and Savage smiled back, offering a wave.

"Sorry, sir," she said to the Superintendent. "Porter was in a gunfight, we got held up."

"A *gunfight?*" said DI Dunst from where he sat at the back of the room, his injured hand cradled in his lap.

"Video game," Porter said. "Long story."

"It's really not," Savage said.

"Do I look like I care?" Clare said. "Now shut your toss-holes, the pair of you."

Savage took a shallow breath, steeling herself as she walked to the table. She knew who lay there, she'd seen him just a few hours ago, but there was something worse about the fact that Chase Masefield was now lying beneath the buzzing lights for all of them to see. He was more exposed than ever, the skin of his butchered chest pulled back like an opened present. His face was so pale it might have been a mask and Savage was gripped by the horrific notion that underneath it the boy was screaming. She had to look away, taking a deep breath of chemical-scented air as the room cartwheeled around her.

"How are you doing, *Unusual* Emily Franklin?" said Porter. His voice was light, but he was evidently feeling the same way as Savage because he swallowed hard, staring at the clock, then at his shoes, then back at the clock.

"Same as always, *Irritating* Peter Porter," she replied. "Did your mother ever explain why she gave you such a ridiculous name?"

"You can shut your tosshole too, Miss Franklin," Clare said. "Unless you plan on telling us anything interesting."

"I can assure you, Superintendent, having studied under my father since I was a child, and having two degrees in biological sciences and a doctorate in pathology, that this thing on my face is not my *tosshole*."

She turned her attention to the young man in front of her, pointing a slim metal ruler at his face.

"Chase Masefield, seventeen years old, although very

shortly due to turn eighteen—close enough, I fear, that his folks might already have bought presents for him. He never made it. Anyone want to take a guess at what actually killed him?"

Nobody answered, and she looked up.

"Anyone? Pete?"

"Uh, I mean, I know you want me to say the heart, right? But I'm not going to fall into that trap."

"Are you sure?" she said, and Porter squirmed.

"Okay, the heart."

"Wrong," answered Franklin. "Idiot. It was actually the injuries to his throat."

She pressed her gloved hand to the skin there, using the ruler to peel open one side of the wound. It had been cleaned, and it was so huge that it looked almost like a lipless mouth.

"That's really horrible," Porter said, his throat gulping like he was drinking an invisible bottle of water.

"Indeed. Something punched its way into his throat just below his right ear, here, before literally ripping through his carotid artery and the top of his trachea on the way out."

"A knife?" Savage asked.

"I'm not sure yet, but I don't think so. You would need an immense amount of strength to do this much damage with a knife. I think that whatever this was, it was something longer, possibly a spear, maybe even a scythe."

"A scythe?" Clare said. "Christ, that's the last thing I need, the Grim Reaper."

Franklin took a step back, imitating somebody sweeping a scythe through the air.

"The angle fits, as well as the force of entry and exit. A longer weapon like this allows for greater speed and power. Fortunately for Chase, it would have been remarkably quick. Unfortunately, he'd already been through hell. See these."

She moved her gloved finger down his marbled skin, over the tapestry of cuts and bruises that decorated his body.

"Fourteen contusions, seventeen cuts of one kind or another. Most are on his front, although some can be seen on his back and his buttocks. They're all fresh. Look at his hands."

Savage did, seeing that the palm of his left hand was lacerated beyond recognition. His right palm looked untouched, although it was here that all four fingers had almost been amputated between the first and second joints.

"What does it look like to you?" Franklin asked. "Porter?"

"Stop picking on me," he said, pouting. "I don't know. Defensive wounds, right?"

He held up his left hand, flinching as if under attack.

"Would that explain the injuries to his fingers on the other hand?" asked Dunst.

"Maybe he was tied up," Porter said, angling his right hand behind his back. "Maybe he got one hand loose while he was being assaulted? An attack this frenzied may have severed the ropes or tape around his wrists."

"And the fingers?" Franklin asked.

"He was holding something," said Savage, seeing it in her head. "He was holding something in his right hand and using his left to defend himself."

"That's what I think too," Franklin said, giving Savage a nod of approval. She illustrated, wielding her steel ruler like a weapon. "He's being beaten senseless, sliced and diced, and he gets hold of something to defend himself with. His left hand's a shield, his right is a sword. Look at the cuts on his right arm, all the way up to the bicep."

She extended the ruler in slow motion, exposing her arm and her fingers.

"By this time he was badly hurt. He would have lost a lot of blood. He'd be dizzy, weak, half-blind, the adrenaline a hurricane, and death right there in the night, watching him. He'd have felt it, for sure. But he had heart, he kept fighting. Whoever his opponent was, he was expecting it. Every time Chase lunged, the attacker took another chunk out of him."

"And he struck his hand," said Savage. "The injuries to his fingers. The attacker wanted him to drop his weapon."

"Good," said Franklin. "Smack, the hand is almost cleaved in two. Another lunge and the attacker's blade punctures Chase's throat and kills him."

"He must have been terrified," said Porter, shaking his head.

Franklin looked as if she was about to fire another volley of sarcasm in his direction but she must have seen the expression on his face, the liquid sheen in his eyes, because she hesitated.

"Yes," she said after a moment. "I imagine he was."

"What about the heart?" asked Clare, shifting his weight, his brogues scuffing the floor.

"Definitely post-mortem," Franklin said. "The killer waited until Chase was dead then he cut open the chest, snapped the ribs, and pulled out the heart."

"Cut it out?" Savage said.

"No, they pulled it. There are no cuts, the connective tissue snapped. They literally ripped out his heart."

"Jesus," said Porter, one hand clenched in his hair.

For a moment, nobody else spoke. It didn't seem as if there was a word in all the world that could make this better. Savage looked at the boy, at the ruin of his body, and wondered what he'd be doing right now if he wasn't here. Playing video games with his brother. Or holding hands with his girlfriend. Or driving his car through the darkening day. All things he'd never get the chance to do again.

I'm so sorry, she thought, closing her eyes for a moment to give her mind a rest. When she opened them again, Franklin was looking at her with an expression of sympathy.

"Anything else?" Clare asked.

"Ligature marks around the wrists," the young pathologist said. "He was tied up. Wire. The absence of blood on his face, plus tape residue in his hair and a slight allergic reaction to the glue on his cheek, makes me think he was wearing some kind of mask, duct taped to his head."

"Would he have been able to see his attacker?" Savage asked, and Franklin shrugged.

"The post-mortem abrasions on his buttocks and back are consistent with him being moved," she said. "I think somebody dragged him for a while through the woods, holding his ankles. I found splinters in the skin, and plenty of mud."

"Any good news?" Dunst asked.

"No sign of any kind of sexual assault," the pathologist went on. "Small mercies. Oh, there was one other thing, and it's pretty important."

Everyone waited, as still as stone statues.

"There was a lot of blood on the victim and I ran it for blood type. It's not all his. In fact, the samples I took suggest that whoever killed him bled quite heavily."

"The attacker was injured," said Porter. "Chase must have managed to land a strike, right?"

"Theory is your job, mate. I just handle the facts."

"Run it against the database," said Clare. "This is good, this gives us a shot at finding him."

"Not to mention the fact that he may have needed medical treatment, sir," Savage said. "We'll check hospitals, vets, chemists, anywhere he might have gone."

Clare nodded.

"Better hop to it, then," he said.

Savage took one last look at the kid before turning and walking out of the room, feeling like she was taking her first-ever breath as she escaped into the corridor. She leaned against the wall until a rush of vertigo faded, then she pulled out her phone.

"Never gets any easier," Porter said as he joined her. "Who you calling?"

"Robbie, guv. I said I'd keep him in the loop."

"Really?" Porter said. "I'd leave him be, he's probably having a rest."

CHAPTER ELEVEN

He probably shouldn't have attempted the push-up.

Kett lay face-down in the living room, wedged between the sofa and the armchair on the floor—the same place he'd been for going on ten minutes now. It wasn't his chest that was preventing him from getting up, although the pain there was bad enough. It was his back that had gone, making a sound like a giant cracking his knuckles as he'd lowered himself into the first dip, before exploding like somebody had strapped dynamite to it. Every time he moved he thought he could feel his vertebrae grinding together.

And to make matters worse, the carpet smelled of chinchilla piss.

He angled his head to the side, grimacing. From down here he could see under the sofa, which was so thick with dust and cobwebs that it looked like Mirkwood Forest. He was pretty sure he could make out a little collection of fish fingers down there, which explained why Evie had suddenly got so good at clearing her plate at dinner time.

From the kitchen, his phone started to ring, the house

full of the ridiculously loud rendition of the *Mexican Hat Dance* that Alice had installed last year. He tried to roll onto his side but the gremlins in his back resisted, going to work on him with what felt like a collection of pitchforks.

"Ow," he said, capable of little more than a whisper. "Little help? Anyone?"

"Robbie, your phone," yelled Billie from upstairs.

"I know," he croaked. "I'm stuck."

It was coming up for seven and the kids were all in the bath. He could hear them jumping and splashing like a bloat of hippos. It's why he'd thought now would be a good time to try to exercise, because the doctors had told him how important it was to stay strong. In retrospect, though, a push-up had been a spectacularly bad idea.

His phone fell silent, then immediately started ringing again.

"Robbie!" shouted Billie.

"I'm stuck!" he called back, not much louder.

A house spider snuck out from beneath the sofa, looking hungry.

"You can fuck right off, mate," Kett said, and the spider must have heard his DCI's growl because it turned around and scuttled back the way it had come.

Upstairs there was an extra loud splash, then the thunder of tiny feet.

"Daddy!" Moira called out. "Dry me!"

"I can't," he muttered, as much to himself as to her. "I can't bloody move."

He heard her coming down the stairs on her backside before running into the kitchen. The phone stopped ringing and he wondered if she'd answered it, but then it started again.

"Daddy?" Moira said. She ran along the hallway and

into the living room—he couldn't see her, but he could hear her breathing.

"Can you get daddy's phone, sweetie?" he said.

"Yeah," she replied, and promptly walked across the room and sat on him. His back screamed, and he almost did too.

"Moira," he said, just a whisper. "Don't sit on daddy."

"Daddy a chair," she said, bouncing.

"Robbie, for god's sake get your bloody phone!" Billie yelled, although he could barely hear her over that insanely irritating ringtone.

"Please, Moira, get daddy's phone."

Another splash, another drumroll of feet running down the stairs.

"Is Mr Marshmallow down here?" Evie called out, genuinely worried. He heard her creep into the room, then she was laughing her head off. "You're sitting on daddy!"

Kett opened his mouth to tell her that she was, under no circumstances, allowed to sit on him, but before he could say it she'd perched herself right on the back of his ribs.

"Daddy a chair!" Moira said, giggling hard.

"He's a horse," Evie said, rocking back and forth. "Giddy up!"

"Evie!" Kett coughed.

His phone cut off and stayed quiet. Kett groaned into the carpet, in too much pain to shake his children off his back. He heard Alice walking down the stairs but mercifully she ran into the kitchen. Billie followed, and he waited for her to enter the room.

"Help," he squawked, but even as he said it he heard his phone again, Billie making for the kitchen instead. He cursed into the carpet for as long as it took his wife to carry the phone into the living room. By the time she'd seen him, it had fallen silent again.

"Robbie? What on earth are you doing?" she said. "Girls, get off him."

They moaned their disappointment and Kett moaned with relief as the weight shifted from his aching spine. He tried again to roll over but it was like he was locked in a barbed wire straitjacket.

"Are you okay down there?" Billie asked, and he could hear the smile in her voice.

"I'm great," he said. "Just thought it might be a nice place to lie down and die."

"You were trying to do push-ups, weren't you?"

"Push-*up*," he said. "Singular. I got halfway through it."

"You want a hand?"

"Just my phone, if you don't mind," he said. "I'm pretty sure I'll be living down here for the rest of time."

"I'll chuck a blanket over you when we go to bed," she said.

"Can I feed daddy a biscuit?" Evie added. "And some milk?"

There was a scream of delight from the door as Alice finally joined the party.

"Don't even think about it, missus," said Billie, and Kett heard her grab hold of their oldest daughter before she was able to throw herself on him.

"Can we do his makeup while he's down there?" Alice said. "I'll get the pens."

"No!" Kett and Billie said together.

Billie laid the phone down beside him and he managed to work his arm around to hold it. The missed calls were from a number he didn't recognise.

"You sure you don't want some help?" Billie said.

"Maybe in a minute," he replied. "I think I need a tea first."

"I think you do," she said, ducking down so that she could place a gentle, reassuring hand on his back. She stood again, herding the girls out of the room with promises of hot chocolate.

Kett unlocked the phone and called the unfamiliar number.

"Grimm," growled a voice as the phone connected, a mix of boulders rolling down a hill and a distant west country twang. Kett recognised it immediately, DCI Harry Grimm of the North Yorkshire Police.

"You certainly are," Kett said.

For a moment there was no reply.

"That silence is me laughing," Grimm said. "Feel free to fill it with your name so that I know who you are next time you call. I won't be answering it."

Kett laughed, then grunted in pain.

"It's Robbie Kett," he managed.

"Kett?" Grimm said, a smile riding the rubble in his voice. "I thought you were dead."

"Not quite."

"Pity," Grimm said.

"Thanks, Harry. How's what's left of your face?"

"Oh, it's a picture," Grimm said. "Feel free to have a run-in with an IED sometime and try it out for yourself."

It was a low joke and Kett knew it. Grimm had served in the Paras, been in theatre enough times to still be carrying some of it around with him, the scars of war not just on the surface, but underneath as well.

"I'll put it on my bucket list."

"How's Norwich?" Grimm said. "Enough sheep for you?"

"Says the copper working in *Wensleydale*. I thought you hated cheese."

"They eat it with cake up here," Grimm replied.

"Piss off."

"Don't knock it till you try it."

Grimm was laughing. It was good to hear from him. They'd never worked the same force but Grimm, who had until recently been based in Bristol, had spent a little time on a case in London when Kett had been a DI. They'd hit it off—mainly because they'd taken turns making fun of Porter.

"I'm actually calling because of a case," Kett said. "You got my message?"

"The boy with the missing heart," Grimm said. "Yeah, it rang a bell. Very similar to a case back in the southwest, what, six years ago? Feels like forever. What do you need to know?"

"Everything you do," he said.

"No one needs to know that," Grimm replied.

"Good point."

Down the line Kett heard the rustle of papers.

"Right then. Somerset, 2014. First dead lad's name was Ryan Fardell, thirteen years old. Had a shitty life right from the start, mother died young, dad didn't give a toss, in and out of foster homes. Fell in with a bad crowd, although we never found out who." Grimm breathed out a hefty sigh, the sound of it edged with that latent, righteous anger that Kett had noticed the man constantly carried around with him. "A couple of drug offences, nothing too serious. Went missing from his last foster home tail end of 2013. We had a look for him but to be honest he had a history of disappearing for weeks at a time so everyone just thought he'd upped and left for the city. It wasn't until some tourists found him on a stone at Stanton Drew just after New Year that we realised he hadn't upped and left at all."

"His heart was cut out, wasn't it?" Kett said.

"Hacked is the word I'd use. And not all the way. It had been partially torn out but they'd made a mess of it. Throat looked like someone had been at it with a saw and he'd been tortured, too, the poor little sod."

"They catch who did it?"

Kett tried to roll onto his side to get a little more air in his lungs, but once again his back refused.

"Yeah," Grimm said. "But not until another lad had died. Four days later. Hang on... Phillip Munser. A little older, he was sixteen. Completely different background. Good home, nice parents, both of them coppers, actually."

"Shit, *really*?"

"It's how they found him so quickly, the whole of Avon and Somerset Police mobilised. Kid was still alive when they got to him, and the killer... Shit, I can't for the life of me remember his name. It was a shit name for a serial killer, though. Flowerybollocks or something."

"*What?*"

"Flower*dew*. Kevin Flowerdew, that was it. Eighteen years old. He was slicing the kid up when the police found them, knife actually in the lad's chest. They were at another sacred spot, apparently, Somerset is full of stones. Munser was in intensive care for a week before he finally just gave up and slipped away."

"You know if he was wearing a mask?" Kett said.

"They both were. Hang on." He flicked through his papers. "Yeah, both were wearing a round mask with eyeholes cut into it, looks like a paper plate."

"Did Flowerdew ever say why he'd done it?" Kett asked.

"Did he bollocks, like," Grimm said. "I didn't actually work the case but it's pretty legendary in the southwest. They grilled him for three days, right up until he killed himself."

"Shit," said Kett.

"Didn't make sense, because this kid—Flowerdew—had no history of violence or mental health problems. He was as straight as they come, good grades at school, a girlfriend who had no idea why he'd killed some random kid in the woods in the middle of winter. He was a musician, had a great career ahead of him if he'd wanted to go there. His dad had died but his mum was a saint. Campaigned for years to clear his name. She still is, I think, even though he was literally caught red-handed."

"And he didn't say anything?" Kett said, his words muffled by the floor.

"You eating something?" Grimm asked.

"Carpet," Kett said.

"Best I don't ask any more, then. Anyway, as far as the reports go, Flowerdew only said a handful of words after he'd been arrested, and all of those were under a serious amount of sedation. He claimed that he was the Hateful Thing. Something like that."

"The Hateful Thing?" Kett said. "Doesn't ring a bell."

"It was total bollocks," Grimm said. "He'd lost his mind."

Kett sighed, instantly regretting it as his back cramped.

"Does that help?" Grimm asked.

"I don't know. We found a kid up here on a sacred stone —if you can call it that, looked like a boulder to me, nothing like Stanton Drew. Tortured, heart removed, severe injuries to his throat. We think he might have been wearing a mask. It all just sounded very familiar."

"I'll send over what I have."

"Not to me," Kett said. "I'm not on the case."

"I didn't want to ask. Even all the way up here in the Dales we occasionally get the news. That Pig Man stuff was rotten."

Kett nodded.

"I'd have done exactly the same thing," Grimm said. "Only I'd have skinned the bastard, too, and made a pair of trousers out of him just so he had to spend the rest of eternity kissing my arse."

"Wow," said Kett. "That's... worrying. But thanks. Send it over to Norfolk, would you?"

"I'll do it today," Grimm said. "And you look after yourself. No more gallivanting around like Clint Eastwood."

"My gallivanting days are over," said Kett, trying and failing to move his head. "Thanks, Harry."

"No problem," he said. "And if you see Porter, tell him I still haven't forgiven him for the fact his tea gave me the shits for a week."

Kett laughed, then cried out in pain, but Grimm had already hung up. He manoeuvred the phone around to his other ear, his entire body aching, and somehow managed to dial Porter.

"Hey," the big DI said, his voice faint like he was driving. "What's up?"

"Not me, that's for sure," Kett said. "Listen, an old friend of ours is sending some stuff over, take a look at it and let me know what you think. Might be nothing, might be important."

"Will do," Porter said. "But give me the skinny, I'm just on my way home."

Kett didn't answer straightaway, watching the spider trot out for another attack.

"Robbie?" Porter said.

Two masked boys, their hearts cleaved from their chests, both left on sacred stones.

"I'm pretty sure somebody else is going to die."

CHAPTER TWELVE

"Where are you?"

The man pushed out of the trees, bathed in moonlight so bright it might have made his bones glow. It burned the naked skin of his chest, his back, his stomach, made him shine like an angel. The rain had stopped falling but the cold was bitter. It made him brittle and slow, made him feel like he could shatter. The wound in his forearm stung, but not as much as it should have considering it was deep enough for him to see the layers there, the skin, the muscle, the fat. His right hand was crimson, and he couldn't feel his fingers at all.

His left, though, held firm onto the shaft of the scythe. He was using it as a walking stick, but the bladed end was sharp, and it had already drawn blood.

"Where are you?" he called out again, his words hot against the mask that covered his face. It itched, pressing uncomfortably on the bridge of his nose, but he didn't dare take it off.

Ahead of him, through the eye holes, he saw a rolling meadow, the grass knee-height all the way down the hill to where another band of dark woodland sat against the night.

The boy he was chasing had left a furrow in it, wide enough to remind him of the story about the Red Sea parting. Moses, wasn't it? He couldn't remember, because his religion was altogether different from any other. The water had come crashing down on Moses' enemies when they'd tried to cross it, and he wondered if that would happen now? If he'd step into the grass and the world would rise up and swallow him.

He laughed, a guttural, dog-like noise that scared him.

What the fuck are you doing? he said to himself. This is fucking insane.

But what choice did he have?

"The Hateful Thing," he said in a whisper. Then he opened his mouth and hollered something that was half shout and half song. "Here's your chance, take it or leave it, lambs to the slaughter or you're in the shit, in the shit!"

Ahead, floating out of the utter silence of the night, an animal's whine.

"Found you," the man said.

He set off at a pace—not running, because he'd lost a lot of blood and he didn't want to pass out—but jogging, his body working like a machine. The scythe rattled in his grip, the blade so sharp it seemed to sing as it cut through the cold air. The end of the shaft kept catching on the ground and he lifted it a little higher, his shoulder burning with the effort. The kid had built up a lead but it was only a small one, and his path through the grass was easy to see.

That, and the trail of blood he'd left, almost black.

The man ran for almost a full minute before he saw him. The boy was on his hands and knees now, a few yards from the treeline, in nothing but his underwear and his mask. He had slowed to a crawl and even that looked like it was almost too much for him. He looked back, his face rendered invisible by the grinning white moon that had been taped to his head, and loosed another feeble cry. The breath left his body as a cloud, as if his soul had abandoned him.

"Please," he said, his voice muffled.

His arms gave way and he tumbled onto his face. The man kept up his pace until he reached him, his exposed skin utterly numb. He could feel his body starting to shut down, the hypothermia setting in, but he wouldn't need much more time. The kid had curled into a ball, the injuries in his skin like angry mouths, like they might all open up as one and start screaming. The boy buried his head in the long grass and spoke again, just a whisper.

"Please, you don't have to do this."

"Why do people always say that?" the man replied, his teeth chattering. "Surely you know better by now."

He did have to do this. So much depended on it.

"When it's your turn don't fight it, don't flee," he sang. "Give yourself up for them, for me."

He used his other hand to nudge the mask back into position.

"Just be still. Just be quiet."

The kid rolled onto his back, his mask reflecting the sky. It wasn't white anymore, it was filthy, stained brown and green and red. It had been knocked so that one of the eyeholes revealed the boy's cheek. But his eye blinked through the other, wet with terror. The man was surprised to see that the boy still held the knife that he'd taken from him. It was clutched against his naked stomach, so close that he seemed to have cut himself. It was hard to tell, with all the blood. The kid remembered it, thrusting it into the air with both hands.

"Fuck... off," he said, clawing in a wet breath between the words.

"Soon," the man replied. He tried to hold the scythe in

both hands but his injured right arm wouldn't let him. It didn't matter. It wouldn't take much to finish this. "Just—"

He stopped, because he heard a noise from the woods.

A shout.

The kid must have heard it too, angling his head back, both of them holding their breath.

Another shout, then the bark of a dog.

Fuck.

The man lunged, swinging the scythe downwards as best he could. The blade twisted, slapping the kid with its flat side and wrenching itself from the man's frozen hand.

"Shit," he said, grabbing for the boy. But the kid was kicking out, pushing himself back. His heel caught the man's mask, knocking it, blinding him.

"Here!" the boy was calling, his voice not strong but not weak either, loud enough to slide its way into the trees. "Help! Help me!"

The man fixed the mask and reached out, grabbing the boy's ankle. He was writhing like an alligator, so much stronger than he had any right to be.

"Please!" he screamed.

"Shut up!"

"You don't have to do this anymore, you don't have to hurt me, look!"

A light in the trees, a voice.

"Who's out there?"

The man knelt on the ground, grabbing the kid's leg and hauling him close, reeling him in. The fingers on his right hand resisted, like they wanted nothing to do with this, but his left was strong enough. The kid screamed again, one hand fumbling at the mask which now covered both of his eyes.

"You don't have to do it!"

"The Hateful Thing," he said. "I have no choice."

The kid lifted the knife, one last gesture of blind defiance.

"I'm sorry," the man said.

He put his hands on top of the boy's, twisting the point of the knife downwards. Then he threw himself on it, using all of his weight, driving the blade through the shell of his sternum into the softness beneath. The kid gasped beneath his mask. He pulled a hand free, feeling the man's mask, his hair, reaching for the moon for the second or two until the strength left him.

"Who's there?" came the voice from the woods, closer now.

The man lay on the boy, feeling the blood bubble from him, the heat of it keeping the deadly cold at bay.

"Hello?" the voice shouted. But this time it had slipped away, deeper into the trees. A dog barked again, too far away to worry.

The man lay there for what felt like forever, until the voice had gone and the footsteps had faded and the night had fallen into silent mourning.

Only then did he push himself up, pull the knife from its fleshy sheath, and start to work.

CHAPTER THIRTEEN

Monday

SAVAGE DUCKED THEN STRAIGHTENED, DRIVING HER gloved fist into the heavy bag. It bounced noisily on its chain, hitting the side of the small garage before coming back for another attack. Colin danced around it on her back legs, growling playfully. Savage stepped around the dog, jabbing her left fist at the bag a couple of times, picturing Greg Skinner's flushed, angry face there as she swung a powerful roundhouse. It landed badly, pain lancing through the wrist she'd hurt in her tussle with the big man yesterday. She pulled it to her chest, wincing.

"Fudging winker," she said to the bag.

It didn't reply.

She shook the pain away and unwrapped the boxing gloves, pulling them off with her teeth. Colin sat on her haunches and yawned, her big tongue flopping out. The garage door was open and the morning air was brutally cold but Savage was sweating with the effort of the workout. It was just past six and still dark out. She hadn't been able to sleep at all last night. Every time she'd come close she'd had visions of Chase Masefield on the autopsy table, peeling off his face and grinning at her. She'd climbed out of bed at four and gone for a run with the dog, and when that wasn't enough to chase the horror away she'd come out here to kick seven bells out of the bag.

It creaked on its chain, protesting, and she rested a hand there to quieten it. The silence that followed lasted a second or two before her phone called out from where she'd left it by the garage door. She walked over, slinging a towel around her shoulders. It would almost certainly be her grandmother. She often called first thing in the morning because she, too, had trouble sleeping and was up and about long before dawn. Savage hated the fact that she was still out in Hemsby, still in the draughty little chalet she'd shared with her husband for all those years before he'd died. Savage had spoken to her a hundred times about moving to Norwich, and she'd probably do it a hundred more, but the old woman was notoriously stubborn.

It ran in the family.

When Savage lifted the phone it was Porter's name on the screen.

"You up?" he said when she answered.

"Yeah."

"Really? It's like six in the morning."

"I'm up," she said. "What is it?"

But she didn't really have to ask, did she? Porter had called her yesterday evening to pass on Kett's information about the Somerset murders, and she'd spent much of the hours that followed looking through Harry Grimm's files. Two dead boys, one with his heart cut out, the other about to meet the same fate when they'd discovered him.

Murders this awful never happened alone.

"They've found another one, haven't they?" she said before Porter could reply. Even over the phone she could see him nodding.

"They've found another one."

IT WAS light by the time she'd made her way west again, although only just. The skies, which had been clear overnight, had regrouped, armies of dark clouds trying to push the sun back below the horizon. She'd expected to have to trek through the woods again, just like at Lyng, but to her surprise she rounded a corner on the main road and saw an encampment of police right in front of her, the world a sea of flashing blues.

She pulled the Fiat over by the verge, behind an IRV, and climbed out. Her hair was still wet from the shower she'd taken before she left and the frozen morning leeched every scrap of heat from her body. It was positively Arctic, the grass and the trees bright with frost. If she put her foot down too hard, she thought, the whole frozen world might just snap in two.

A cluster of constables had gathered on a small, triangular green by the side of the road, looking every bit like a conspiracy of ravens. There was no sign of Porter yet, which was a surprise given that he'd had a head start. She nodded to the only person she recognised, a bear of a man with a bushy black beard.

"Alright, Duke," she said. "Cold enough for you?"

"Don't really feel it," PC Aaron Duke said, shrugging in his giant yellow jacket.

"Course you don't. Where is it?"

Duke nodded to the centre of the green, where a screen had been clumsily erected.

"*Here*?" said Savage, looking back at the road, then to a white-rendered house that peeked up over a monstrous hedge. She made her way over the green, the grass crunching beneath her boots. Sure enough, there was a body there, mounted on a small, square boulder. The rush of *déjà vu* she felt almost knocked her over.

"Fudge," she said, putting a hand to her mouth.

It could have been Chase Masefield, because the kid was so similar to the corpse they'd found yesterday. When she walked a little closer, though, she saw that this man was older, nineteen or twenty maybe, a scraggy blond beard on his chin. His eyes were open, one grey with frost, the other missing.

"Crows," said Duke. "They were all over him when we arrived."

The eye wasn't the only thing that had been taken. The boy's chest was wide open, whatever was left inside shielded by a pool of frozen blood. Whorls of frost and dirt marked his bare torso, something almost beautiful in their design. All Savage wanted to do was cover him up.

"He must have been out here a while," she said, every word appearing in front of her as a cloud of breath. "How did we find him?"

Duke nodded at the road.

"Spotted by a driver at about five this morning. She called it in, said she'd driven past it and halfway to Dereham before she turned around and came back. Apparently, dozens of cars passed him, but she was the only one who thought to check to see if he was okay."

"He was obviously *not* okay," Savage said, looking at the

pattern of cuts and bruises on his skin. "Ballsy move, leaving a body here. Anyone could have witnessed it."

She scanned the green, looking for more blood, but it was spotless.

"He was killed somewhere else," she said. "Like Masefield. You know anything about the stone?"

She ducked down to get a better look at it. It was a little smaller than the last one, wedged between the road sign and a wooden post that pointed down the track towards a public right of way. There was no moss on it, no markings of any kind, nothing making it special except for the dead boy draped over it.

A VW rumbled past, slowing down, the driver's expression of shock visible through the window. Duke eyeballed them until they'd turned the corner.

"Bloody rubberneckers," he said, pulling out a notebook. "A couple of people have actually got out of their cars to take a look, can you believe that?"

"You get their registrations?" Savage asked. "The killer might come back."

Duke answered her by jotting down the licence plate of the car that had just passed.

"Good man," she said. "Anything from the house?"

"We knocked, nobody answered."

"Maybe you didn't knock hard enough."

She set off towards it, stopping when she saw Porter's black Mondeo pull up behind her car. He got out, clapping his gloved hands together and stamping his feet.

"Jesus Christ, how is it this bloody cold?"

"Good *afternoon*, sir," Savage said. "Nice of you to join us."

"How did you get here so fast in that snot-coloured

bucket?" Porter said as he jogged over. "Oh, wait, I remember. Because you drive like an idiot."

"At least I don't drive like I'm driving Miss Daisy," she replied.

"Your driving would give Miss Daisy a heart attack."

"Well if *you* were driving, Miss Daisy would get out and push."

"Oh shit," Porter said when he'd walked around the screen. "*Groundhog Day*. No forensics?"

"On their way, sir," Duke said. "With Miss Daisy."

Porter and Savage both threw the constable a look, neither of them breaking into a smile. Duke looked down at his notepad, evidently disappointed in himself at the quality of his joke.

"Right," Porter said, looking around. "The house?"

"Was just on my way," said Savage, taking the lead. They crossed a small track and stamped down a driveway towards the farmhouse. There were no cars here, no signs of life at all. It seemed to be getting colder. Savage was numb beneath her jacket, her fingers unresponsive. When they reached the door and she rapped her knuckles against it she was worried they might shatter. Still, the knock echoed back up the driveway, the loudest sound in the morning.

"Weird," said Savage as they waited. "No birds."

Porter cocked his head, listening, but she was right. Nothing had scattered from the trees when she'd pounded on the door, and nothing sang there now. It wasn't exactly unusual, given the time of year, but it made Savage think of that clearing in the woods she'd been in yesterday, the feeling that something wasn't right amongst the mouldering trees and ancient rocks.

"They're not home, or they don't want to speak with us," Porter said.

Savage knocked again, even louder this time.

"You realise half the houses in the village will be answering their doors right now," he added.

Savage ignored him, walking along the front of the house to the nearest window. She cupped her hand to the frost-dappled glass and tried to make sense of the darkness inside. There were no curtains and very little furniture— just a sofa against the far wall. She passed Porter and tried the window on the other side of the front door, seeing a dining table but no chairs. Porter joined her, peering over her shoulder.

"Place looks deserted."

"I'm not so sure, guv," she said, making out a sideboard behind the table. On it was a stack of books and what looked like a spider plant, its sprouts almost on the floor. "Plant."

"Huh?"

"Plant," she said, tapping on the glass.

"Person?" Porter said.

"No, *plant*. How can you—"

"*Person*," Porter said, pushing his finger against the window. "Look at the door."

She did, seeing a shadow move in the gloom.

"Hey," Porter called out. "Police, we need to talk to you."

The shadow vanished to the left and Savage moved in the same direction, reaching the corner of the house and running down the side. There was a low gate here and she didn't stop to see if it was bolted, vaulting it with ease into a large garden.

The farmhouse's back door was there.

And it was propped open by a corpse.

"Porter!" she yelled, before realising that he was right behind her.

"Duke!" Porter roared. "Get back here, we've got another body."

Savage ran to the door. A woman lay there, her bare, blue-tinged feet stretching outside, all the way to the knees. The rest of her was sprawled face down in the entrance to the kitchen like she was swimming in the pool of blood that had spilled beneath her. Savage couldn't see her face past the mass of clotted silver hair that covered it, but it was clear from the liver spots on her hands and the wrinkles in her skin that she was in her seventies or eighties.

It was also clear that she hadn't been dead long.

"Duke!" Porter yelled again. Then, to Savage, "Stay sharp."

Savage took a step away from the door, bouncing on her heels to try to keep her cold body warmed up. Her right hand twitched, desperate for the baton.

"If somebody's in there, you need to make yourself known immediately," she shouted, hating the fact that her teeth were chattering. "The house is surrounded."

She heard a copper calling out from the other side of the house, and the sound of footsteps, pounding fast.

Then a scream.

"Hello?" she said, the drum of footsteps getting louder.

Not from outside, but from the *kitchen*.

"Oh shi—" was all she had time to say as a man leapt over the dead woman and thumped through the open door, still screaming.

CHAPTER FOURTEEN

PORTER SAW THE MAN FLY OUT OF THE HOUSE LIKE A cannonball, thumping into Savage so hard that they both hit the ground in a tangle of limbs. Her head cracked against the path, audible even from where Porter was standing twenty yards away.

"Hey!" he yelled, already on the move.

The guy pushed himself up, fighting to get away. He wasn't tall but he was stout, one foot landing on Savage's chest. She grabbed at him, her fingers slipping as he wrenched his leg away. The man staggered, lost his footing, falling into a sprinter's start. Then he was running again.

"Don't you fucking dare!" Porter yelled

He was ten yards away and closing fast, the other man struggling on the wet grass. He was wearing black suit trousers and a blue shirt, tucked in, his stomach bulging over his belt. He looked back, his glasses slipping from his face and landing in the grass.

"Stop!" Porter commanded.

The man screamed, nowhere to go. The garden was surrounded on three sides by dense hedging, no sign of a gate or a fence. He wasn't slowing down, though. If anything he was speeding up, lowering his head as if he meant to charge his way to freedom.

"Stop!"

The man leapt at the hedge like he was diving into a pool, his arms outstretched, his hands forming a point. He entered it headfirst and literally stuck there—the top of his body hidden and his legs off the ground, kicking hard. Porter slowed to a halt, his lungs working like bellows as they tried to suck oxygen from the frigid air.

"You okay?" PC Duke said as he ran around the back of the house.

"Check on Savage," Porter called back.

"I'm fine, sir," Savage replied, back on her feet and nursing her chest. She was sipping air like she'd been winded. "Which is a lot better than this arsehole is going to be when I'm done with him."

The man was wriggling and jiggling so much that the entire hedgerow was shaking, one of his cheap black shoes already on the ground. But he'd wedged himself in there pretty tight, and after a handful of seconds he fell still. From deep inside the laurel, Porter heard him sigh.

"That didn't work out too well for you, did it mate?" Porter said. "Do you want to tell me your name, and what you're doing hanging out with two dead bodies?"

The man replied, his voice too muffled to hear.

"You gonna behave if we pull you out of there?" Porter said. Duke was by his side now, baton in one hand. Porter was a big guy but the bearded PC looked like some kind of Viking berserker squeezed into a police uniform.

Another reply from the hedge that made absolutely no sense.

Porter nodded at Duke and Duke nodded back. They

grabbed one leg each and pulled hard, the man sliding out of the laurel and landing face-first on the grass. Duke moved in fast, planting a knee on his back, the baton raised high. Porter took the PC's handcuffs and clicked them onto the suspect's wrist, snapping the arm around hard enough to force a scream. He folded his other arm back and secured him, then stood.

"Let's see him," said Savage as she approached.

Porter grabbed the man's elbow and rolled him onto his back. He squawked in pain, staring up at the three coppers like a mouse cornered by cats. He was in his late thirties, maybe early forties, completely bald on the top with a memory of dark fuzz around the sides and back. His smooth face was round, his cheeks rosy, and there was a mark on the bridge of his nose where his glasses had been. His skin was decorated with a handful of fresh scratches which he'd probably got from the hedge.

"I didn't do it," he said in a trembling, nasal voice. "I swear to god."

"Didn't do what?" Porter growled.

"Kill her, kill any of them."

"Is there anyone else inside the house?" asked Savage.

"Just the woman," he said, stuttering from fear or from the cold. "The dead one. I didn't touch her."

"What about the kid on the stone?" Porter said.

"I didn't touch him either. I wouldn't. I just..."

He stalled, gulping air. Porter, Savage and Duke leaned in, glaring.

"I just needed to see," he squealed. "I had nothing to do with it. I just wanted to see it for myself."

"See what?" Porter said.

The man swallowed again, looking between them, the expression on his face less terror now than excitement.

"I wanted to see if the stories were true," he said. "I wanted to see if the Hateful Thing was coming."

PORTER TOOK another look at the driving licence in his hand, frowning. Then he peered over it at the man who sat in the back of the IRV.

"Norman Balls?" he said. "That can't be real."

Balls stared at his feet, pretty close to vomiting if the colour of his face was anything to go by. His hands were still cuffed and he had to lean forward awkwardly, resting his head against the back of the driver's seat.

"That can't be your name," Porter went on.

"Why not?" Balls replied, wincing as he tried to twist his head around.

"The name your parents gave you?"

"What's wrong with it?"

Porter glanced around for somebody to share the news with, but he and Balls were alone by the side of the road. A few of the coppers had moved into the house opposite, first to search it and then to shepherd the forensic team when they'd turned up fifteen minutes ago. The rest had gathered on the triangular green to examine the dead kid. Savage was nowhere to be seen.

"Nothing," said Porter, sliding the driving licence back into the man's wallet and throwing the wallet into the car. "Norman Balls. Now that we're comfortable, let's get to know each other. Let me ask you again, what were you doing in the house?"

Balls grimaced with pain as he tried to sit back, sliding down the seat until he was lying flat and staring at the ceiling. Porter had given him his glasses back, and in the darkness of the IRV his chubby face made him look like he was twelve years old.

"I didn't kill her," he said.

"I didn't ask you if you did."

"Shouldn't I have a lawyer or something?"

"Only if you did something illegal."

"I didn't!" Balls looked like he was about to start crying. "I just heard about the body, I wanted to see it for myself."

"How?" asked Porter.

"I've got a scanner," he said. "But I don't use it for anything illegal. I run a website, about folklore and myth and conspiracy. All local stuff. *Ballsknowsitalls.net.* I'm sure you've heard of it."

"No."

"Oh, well, I heard police talking about the boy on the stone yesterday, about his heart being missing, and I thought there would be another one. So I waited, and when I heard the call I came out here."

He paused, but Porter didn't say anything.

"I, uh... I only live over the way, in Dereham. I knew I could get here before any of you. So I came and I saw him but I didn't have time to do anything other than take a couple of photos because the police showed up."

"Photos?"

Balls muttered a curse beneath his breath. Porter patted the man's pocket and pulled out an ancient Nokia, holding it up.

"On here?"

The little man nodded as best he could.

"That doesn't explain the house," said Porter, sliding the phone into his trouser pocket. "The dead woman."

"I thought the driver of the police car had seen me," Balls said. "I ran for the nearest cover, the house. My car's parked up the lane, it's a Rover. I thought I'd cut through the garden and over the fields. But then the torches were out, and when I ran around the house there was nowhere to go and I saw the woman and she was dead and I thought..."

He actually whimpered, like a puppy.

"I thought you'd think I did it."

"Let me get this straight," said Porter. "You were worried that we'd think you were the killer, so you actually stepped over the body of a dead woman and entered a murder house to try to escape?"

Balls blinked up at him.

"What was your plan for after that?" he asked. "Evaporate?"

"I thought you might all go away," he said.

"Right."

Porter glanced up, studying the white-suited technicians who circled the dead boy like a flock of seagulls.

"Is your friend okay?" Balls asked. "I think I stood on her."

"She'll be fine. Just be grateful she's not here, and that she didn't have Old Betsy with her when you came flying out of that house." He peered into the darkness of the car. "Tell me why you were so interested. Tell me about the Angry Thing."

"Not angry," said Balls. "Hateful. It's a lot worse."

"Hateful, then. I've never heard of it."

"You're not local, are you?" said Balls, shuffling on the seat to try to get comfortable. Once again his face had lit up, his teeth small and white. "It's kind of a Norfolk legend, although you'll hear about it in a few places around the country."

"Somerset?" Porter asked, thinking of Kett's phone call. Balls nodded.

"Devon, Yorkshire, all the way over in Wales too. It's a migratory myth, it's travelled around a lot, and the details always change but the heart of it..." He pulled a face. "Sorry, bad choice of phrase. The *core* of the myth stays the same."

When he didn't continue, Porter shrugged.

"Oh, right. Well, the locals tell the story of a creature that haunts the countryside around here."

"A creature?" Porter interrupted, holding up a hand. "If you tell me it's a black dog called Shuck then I'm going to throw you back in the hedge."

"No, it's more of a shadow, a spectre. There have been a few sightings over the years, for centuries. You'd know all about it if you'd visited my website. One woman saw it when she was walking with her daughter and her young suitor, a dark shape that changed size and tried to run after them."

"Did they report it to the police?" Porter asked.

"No, I don't think so. This was a hundred years ago."

"Right," Porter said again, drawing the word out. "Anything more recent?"

Balls looked from side to side like he was about to offer Porter some illegal wares. Then he craned up.

"The talk was that the Hateful Thing was a man, a criminal who had been wrongfully accused of some heinous crime and he was tied to a stone, his heart ripped out of his chest. He was so furious at his death that he came back for revenge."

"This is all incredibly *not* useful," said Porter.

"No, bear with me. I don't know about all the other stuff but one thing I know for sure is this. It's happened before, and more than once. Why did you ask about Somerset before? You know, don't you?"

"About the dead boys, yeah."

"With their hearts cut out, or close enough. That was six years ago, 2014."

"Two of them, right?" Porter asked, and Balls shook his head.

"Two made the news because of what happened to them, but there was another kid murdered that winter too. Buried out near Stone Allerton. They didn't find him for a few years because he'd been buried, and nobody ever really connected it. But he was found with a mask on his face, and somebody had torn into him pretty bad."

"A mask," Porter said.

"That's not all," Balls went on, almost gleefully. "Go back to 2008 and you'll find the same crimes in a place called Neath. Two young men tied to sacred stones and *de-hearted*. And they weren't alone, because there were over a dozen more murders in that community inside of a month, all brutal, and all committed by the same killer."

"Neath," said Porter. "I remember the deaths, but not the missing hearts. They never caught the killer."

"They never will."

"They did, though," Porter said. "In Somerset, they collared the murderer as he was carving out his victim's chest. Kevin Flowerdew. He died a week later."

"Did he?" Balls asked, and Porter thought for a moment that the man was winking at him.

"This is *balls*, Balls." Porter threw his arms up in disgust. "It might be good for a shitty website but it's of bugger all use to me. And it doesn't explain why you were in the house, not really."

"I'm telling the truth," Balls said. "You mark my words, these dead kids are the work of the same psychopathic killer, the Hateful Thing. Is he real? Is he a ghost? I don't know!

But there were other cases too. 2002, Rudston. 1996, too. Look deeper, my friend, because the only thing I know for a fact is that these deaths are just the beginning. The dead boys are merely a harbinger of what's to come."

"A harbinger?" Porter said.

"A harbinger!" Balls repeated with no small amount of drama. "Dark days will follow."

"Sure," said Porter. He stood straight, rubbing the small of his back with both hands.

"Little help?" Balls said. "I can't get up."

Porter reached through the door, grabbing the man's arm and hauling him upright. Balls winced at Porter's touch.

"What?" Porter asked.

"It's nothing," he said.

Porter leaned in a little further, pulling back the sleeve of Balls' suit jacket.

"It's nothing," he said again, trying to wriggle away.

Porter held firm, seeing the gash across his right wrist, ugly and deep. The blood wasn't flowing anymore but it still looked sticky. It was a recent injury.

"How'd you do this?" he asked.

"I don't remember," Balls said, panicked. "Probably in the house. I was in such a state I never noticed. I'm fine."

"Sure you are," said Porter.

He slammed the car door, looking over the top of the IRV to see Savage crunching down the driveway of the house. She looked miserable, and she was still massaging her chest.

"How you feeling?" Porter said when she was in earshot.

"Like I've been kicked by a mule," she said.

"Kicked by a donkey, you mean," Porter said. "This

guy's full of shit. But he seems to know about the Somerset murders, and he's got a few other things that might be useful."

"You want me to take him back and interview him?" she asked, and Porter nodded. He opened the driver's door for her, stopping her as she was about to climb in.

"One thing," he whispered. "What the fuck is a harbinger?"

CHAPTER FIFTEEN

KETT HADN'T REALLY KNOWN WHERE HE WAS GOING until he arrived, and when he pulled the car into an empty spot and looked up at the sprawling headquarters of Norfolk Constabulary he almost turned around and drove straight home again.

He didn't, though. He switched off the Volvo's engine and sat for a moment in perfect silence, looking out at the grey morning as if he was waking from a deep sleep. In some ways it was like coming home, and he felt a yearning inside him that was almost painful. But this wasn't home, he knew. And it never would be again. He'd been banished, and the agony of that was so much worse.

He straightened as slowly as he dared, testing his back. Everything still ached but the agony he'd experienced last night had all but gone. It had taken him a good half an hour to get up off the living room floor after his conversation with Grimm, and he'd needed Billie and Alice's help to physically manoeuvre him onto the sofa. He'd stayed there all night, and by some miracle the battered old couch seemed to have realigned his vertebrae.

Of course, the girls had stampeded down the stairs at the arse end of six and almost scuppered the whole thing, but he'd managed to hobble out of the room before they could do too much damage. One hot shower and four cups of tea later and he'd been good to go.

He hadn't even been planning to leave the house, but Billie had suggested it.

"If you feel up to it, it will be good for you," she'd said. "You're going to become a hermit, otherwise. Go for a drive, see if the world is still there."

The world was still here, much to his relief. And nothing had changed, not really. The skies were dark, the rain was falling, and people roamed the streets like the walking dead. He'd driven through the dark and then driven through the dawn, through a city that had once been his and which had adopted him again—past its ancient churches and along its cobbled streets, past the house he'd grown up in over in Mile Cross, and his old high school, past the gates of the cathedral in Tombland, the last place he'd seen his mother before they'd stopped talking altogether, past Maisie Malone's house, where all the lights were blazing, and then Mike Walker's shop where he'd almost died, *twice*. He'd spent more of his life in London than Norwich, but this city was written in his blood.

And now he found himself here.

"Why?" he asked himself, tapping the wheel.

Because of the case, the dead boy.

Boys.

Savage had called to share the news about the second victim, but it hadn't shocked him. After what Grimm had told him about the murders in Somerset, he'd been ready for more death.

He just hadn't expected it to be so soon.

His back was starting to stiffen so he opened the door, exiting into the freezing drizzle. The shrapnel in his chest started to sing and he massaged his ribs, keeping his breaths shallow. He hadn't even thought to bring a coat, the water beading on his grey knitted jumper, soaking through his jeans. The cold was cruel, numbing his face even through the beard.

Still, it was good to be out.

He spotted an IRV pulling into the car park, recognising Savage as she drove towards the front of the building. She must have seen him because she passed the doors and looped all the way around, pulling up behind his car. She left the engine running and climbed out, beaming.

"Welcome back," she said. "It's good to see you here, sir."

"I'm not back," he said, his voice still hoarse, betraying how weak he felt. "I just needed to get away for a bit."

"Away from the house? You've been cooped up for a while now."

"Away from the kids," he admitted. "As much as I love them."

"They still giving you a hard time?"

"Always. Evie told Moira to use me as a pencil pot and she's been trying to stick crayons up my nose for a week now."

Savage laughed and Kett did his best to scowl. He couldn't manage it for long.

"It's nice to be here. Hard, you know? But good. Reminds me that even after all the shit, I did some good."

"You did," Savage said.

"Hey!" came a voice from inside the IRV. A meaty fist thumped on the glass and Kett leaned in to see a squirrel-like man there, staring at him through a pair of wire-frame glasses. "Hey, you're Robert Kett."

"Who have you got there?" Kett asked.

"Balls," said Savage.

"Balls?"

"Norman Balls."

"Norman Balls," Kett echoed. "That's his real name?"

"There's nothing wrong with it," said the man, trying to push forward in his seat to see through the open front door. "Can I speak with you? For my website? An interview, maybe? I want to know the truth about the Pig Man, about his followers. I—"

Savage pushed the door shut, muting him.

"Found him in a house next to the second dead kid," she said. "There was another woman there, her throat cut. No other injuries."

"That doesn't fit our killer's MO," said Kett. "How close was the house?"

"Literally next to the body. If anyone inside was looking out of the window they'd have seen the killer dumping the body."

"Which is probably what happened, right?"

"Right," said Savage. "We know our suspect kills his victims somewhere else then dumps the body on a sacred stone of some kind."

The man in the car yelled something and Savage rolled her eyes.

"Right. Balls tells me this stone is the fabled Stone of Hoe, supposed to be the very centre of Norfolk. Ley lines and beasties and all sorts of bullplop. Anyway, our killer turns up in the middle of the night and deposits the body on the stone, but he's being watched. He sees the woman and goes after her, cuts her throat and leaves her there."

"You know who she is?" Kett asked.

"Theresa Carson-Cooke," said another voice. Kett looked back to see DI Dunst walking across the car park, a sheaf of papers held over his head to defend him from the drizzle. "Seventy-nine. She lived there alone, mostly. Husband dead, kids not interested, but she has two adult grandchildren who come to stay a couple of times a year. They're not local. One's in London, the other's down in the southwest, Glastonbury way."

"Somerset," said Kett, and Dunst nodded.

"We haven't managed to reach either of them. She was clean as a whistle, her family's lived in the house for nearly two centuries."

"Just unlucky," Savage said. "Heard a noise, looked out the window, and that's that."

"What about the boy?" Kett asked.

"The dead one?" Savage sighed. "No ID, sir. Spalding's looking into missing persons to see if we can find a match. He's a carbon copy of the first. Badly beaten, tortured really. Cuts all over his body, his hands, abrasions on his back where he was dragged. No sign of blood on his face so he was probably wearing a mask. His chest was cut open and his heart was removed. Hard to see how because the blood was frozen solid."

"We'll have to defrost him," said Dunst, laughing quietly to himself before remembering what he was laughing about. He cleared his throat. "Time of death?"

"Forensics estimate he died around midnight," Savage said. "But the weather doesn't help pin that down."

"What's going on here?" came a mumbled voice. Everybody looked around to see DS Alison Spalding squeeze between two cars, her keys in her mouth as she tied back her hair.

"I'm not really sure," said Dunst.

"You can't be here, Kett," she said as she put her keys in her pocket. She spoke his last name like she was trying to dislodge a lump of old meat from the back of her throat.

"I'm not," he said, lifting his hands.

"The woman who called in the murder was Yasmin Bisset," Dunst continued. "Local all the way, she works in the Toftwood Garden Centre, a plant specialist apparently. Nothing suspicious there at all."

"Except she drove past the body a few times, didn't she?" Savage said.

"Drove past it, saw the body, thought it was a prank or a Halloween decoration or an art installation, but couldn't get it out of her head. Yeah, she turned around to check, then called it in. She's late forties, a grandmother, looks like she wouldn't say boo to a goose."

"Any *mis-per* matches for the dead boy, sarge?" Savage asked, looking at Spalding. The DS shot Kett a suspicious look, rubbing rainwater from her face.

"Doesn't match anything we've got on record here," she said. "But we've got a hit from Suffolk Con, a kid who went missing a week ago. Night fishing. Never came back, boat and gear found in the middle of the lake. They've dredged it, but no luck. We're waiting on photographs. His name's Frederick Sabbe. Freddie. Nineteen years old."

She spat out a rueful laugh.

"Nineteen years *young*."

Kett heard the grumble of a big engine as Colin Clare's monstrous old Mercedes purred into the car park. Even past the glare on the windscreen Kett could see his bug-eyed rage, and he braced himself as the car came right for them. It stopped in front of the IRV, the door opening.

"What the tossing hell is going on here?" Clare said as

he unfolded his lanky frame. "What kind of incompetent tosspot decides to have a meeting in the rain?"

He spotted Kett, growling.

"Oh," he said. "*That* tosspot."

"I wasn't even planning on coming here, sir," Kett said, raising his hands even higher, like he was being held at gunpoint. "I just wanted to get away from the kids."

"They've been sticking crayons up his nose," Savage explained.

"He'll be getting crayons shoved right up his tosshole if he's not careful," Clare said, and everyone winced. The boss took a breath, the rainwater gathering in his knitted eyebrows. "So, what are you all blethering about? A lead?"

"Not as such," said Savage. "We think—"

"I'm not having a bloody briefing out here, Savage," Clare said, shaking himself like a wet dog.

"My point exactly, sir," Spalding said, glaring at Kett. "It's highly unprofessional to be having a meeting at all with a former—"

"Everyone get in Kett's car," Clare ordered.

The Superintendent opened the passenger door of the Volvo hard enough to ding the car next to them, clambering inside and shutting it behind him.

"It's not really designed for meetings," Kett said. "There are car seats."

Dunst made a break for it, opening the back door and climbing into the middle where Alice's booster seat sat.

"Don't you dare," said Spalding, looking at the bright orange car seats on either side. "Sir, this is—"

"Get in here," Clare roared.

Spalding muttered darkly to herself as she climbed into Evie's seat, pulling her legs to her chest so that she could close the door. Savage managed to squeeze into Moira's space, laughing to herself. Kett got into the driver's seat and closed the door. Only now was he aware of how much the car smelled of Fruit Shoots and rotting cheese strings.

"Leads," barked Clare, far too loud for the car's muted interior. "We need something. Two dead boys, two missing hearts. Tell me what you have."

"Our latest victim died around midnight," Savage said. "The dead woman in the house, Mrs Carson-Cooke, died around three hours later, which is when we think the body was dumped on the stone. Forensics are studying soil samples on the body to see if they can pinpoint a location for the actual murder."

"They did the same with Chase Masefield," Clare said. "The results came through last night. Traces of gypsum."

"Gypsum?" said Kett. "Like the stuff in plaster?"

"Traces were found on his face and in his hair."

"The mask," Kett said. "Plaster of Paris, maybe?"

Clare nodded.

"What else?"

"They're almost certainly ritual murders," Savage said. "Or designed to look like them. There's a distinct pattern. Torture, exsanguination, the removal of the heart, then the positioning on a stone."

"What are these stones?" Clare asked. "I've never even heard of them."

"Glacial erratics, sir," Savage said. "Rocks that were carried in the ice and deposited millions of years ago. People have always attributed meaning to them, especially here where we don't really have any standing stones. There are hundreds of stories about how they were used for sacrifices or for executions, how they bleed if you prick them, that kind of thing."

"And you know all this *how*?" Clare asked.

"Because I had to ride here with Norman Balls," she said. "And yes, that's his real name."

"I know it's his real name," said Clare. "Norman Balls. I'm familiar with his website. *Balls Knows it Alls*. It's quite informative, if you're into folklore and urban legends and all that stuff. Why is he in your car?"

"He was found at the crime scene this morning, in the house with the murdered woman who we believe was a witness. He attacked me."

"Normal Balls *attacked* you?" Clare said, one eyebrow reaching for the sky. "I highly doubt it. I've seen him. He couldn't attack a peanut butter sandwich if he hadn't been fed for a week."

"You'd be surprised, guv," Savage muttered, rubbing her chest. "He has a theory that these crimes are being committed by somebody who calls himself the Hateful Thing. These killings certainly seem familiar. They follow a pattern."

"Two murders down in Somerset, six years ago," Kett said. "Teenage boys with their hearts removed."

"Maybe a third victim too," Savage said. "Balls was telling me about it. They found a dead boy who'd been buried, he was wearing a mask."

"Three dead kids?" Clare said. "That's all we need."

"I was doing some research last night and it happened again twelve years ago, in Wales," Kett said. "A town called Neath. Two dead teenagers were found tied to the Maen Bredwan Standing Stone, their hearts cut out. Both boys."

"I remember," said Clare. "That was a dark time. The village fell into chaos, a lot of people died in the days that followed. I don't remember ever hearing about a Hateful Man before?"

"Hateful *Thing*," Kett said. "I don't think the name was

mentioned publicly in Neath, because nobody thought an old wives' tale was any help. But it was mentioned in Somerset, because the guy they collared for it, Kevin Flowerdew, mentioned the Hateful Thing. And there's more. Back in 2002 three people were killed in East Yorkshire, their hearts removed, their corpses dumped next to the Rudston Monolith. All under twenty years of age. If this is the same person then he likes to kill in threes."

"But it can't be the same person," Savage said. "Flowerdew was a kid. A teenager himself. He would have been too young for the Yorkshire crimes and he died in custody, he couldn't have killed again."

"Maybe he was a copycat," said Spalding, struggling to get comfortable.

"Or maybe he wasn't working alone," said Kett. "We know better than most that killers sometimes work in packs. That fucker Schofield trained his own nephew to take over for him as the Pig Man."

"Maybe," said Clare. "But we need to find out who it is, and we need to find out now. Because if our suspect is following a pattern, and it seems he is, then he's got one more victim to kill. Has anyone got anything else? Any hint of a lead? Any microscopic nugget of information that they might want to remove from their arseholes and show the class?"

Nobody replied. In the back, Dunst and Spalding batted each other with their hands as they fought for leg space.

"That's enough!" roared Clare, making them both jump.

"She started it," said Dunst, pouting.

"Well at least we know one thing," said Savage. "It wasn't Greg Skinner. He was locked up all night."

Clare cleared his throat, looking uncomfortable.

"Yes, well... We didn't have any evidence of anything other than some topless footage of boys in a gym, and nothing material to tie him to the Chase Masefield murder—we haven't had DNA back yet but the blood we found on the boy isn't the same type as Skinner's. Not to mention the Devon Parris alibi came through. Skinner's solicitor, that tosser Pruitt, knows his stuff. I've never seen anyone come at us with as much as he did, and so aggressively. He even called in a favour from a judge. It was almost embarrassing, I don't think Skinner actually wanted to go home by the end of it. Anyway, we had to charge him or release him, so we let him go."

"When?" Savage asked, leaning forward.

"Last night," said Clare. "About four hours before our second victim was murdered."

CHAPTER SIXTEEN

"He did *what*?"

Porter studied the overcast skies, massaging his head with his free hand. He hadn't slept well last night, partly because of the case but partly because Allie had been upset. She'd greeted him at the front door when he'd arrived home, already in tears, and nothing he'd said to her had made the slightest bit of difference.

"It's not going to happen," she'd said, over and over. "I don't deserve it. I'm not good enough."

And he'd whispered all the kindnesses he could think of, all the reassurances, wrapping her in his arms until—with a little help from some Diazepam and half a bottle of Pinot Grigio—she'd fallen asleep on the black sheets of their king-size bed.

She was right, though. It was never going to happen. And the thought of it broke his heart.

"They let Skinner go?" he said, pushing Allie out of his head. "Why? He practically confessed to taking videos of minors."

"Topless videos of boys in the gym," said Savage, her

voice broken into pieces by the crappy reception. "The search team didn't find anything else. It's my fault, sir. His solicitor was right, I was in there without a warrant. It was stupid."

"Yeah, it was a bit of a Kett move," said Porter.

"We're conducting interviews this morning with some of the kids, he might be back in before the end of the day."

"But he was out last night," Porter said, turning his attention to the small triangular green. The dead boy had been taken away but the stone still sat there, painted with his blood. The patterns were random, Porter knew, but he could still see shapes in them, Rorschach blots that said far more about his own state of mind than the killer's. "He could have done this."

"I don't know," Savage said. "Clare left a car outside his house, just in case, and nobody came or went. Skinner is a douchebag but I don't think he's stupid. He wouldn't risk it. Besides, we know it wasn't his blood on Masefield's body. He's B negative, the killer's AB Neg."

"Doesn't mean he wasn't involved," Porter said. "So what's the plan now?"

"Dunst and I are trying to ID the second victim but he's proving elusive. Might be a young man called Frederick Sabbe but it's not confirmed, we're struggling to find a good photo. You?"

Porter glanced up again as the forensic team walked out of the driveway, heading back to their vehicles.

"Just finishing up here," he said. "I'll head back to the Masefield house and see if the mother is in a better place. Didn't get much out of her yesterday."

"Good luck," said Savage.

"You too."

He hung up, cutting across the green to head off the

technicians. Most ignored him, but Cara Hay, the lead forensic advisor, slowed to a halt. Her overalls were almost perfectly white, the brightest thing in the day if you ignored the dirt on the knees. She was in her fifties, her greying hair a buzz-cut that was even shorter than Porter's had been when he'd first joined the police. She had sharp eyes—*bird* eyes, Porter had always thought, like they could see for miles.

"Anything new?" he asked.

"No," she said, her accent pure Trinidad. "There's no evidence of intrusion. It looks like the killer arrived at the back door just as the victim was leaving. I'll leave the autopsy to Franklin but there's only the wound to the throat, nothing else. It's brutal, would have killed an old dear like that within seconds. There's a trace of blood in the house, but not much, and it doesn't correspond with the crime scene at the back door."

"Yeah?"

"Yes, broken plate on the dining room table, somebody cut themselves on the shards."

"That might explain Balls' injury."

Hay's expression hardened.

"The only footprints we can find belong to Mr Balls. I don't know what that idiot was doing in there but he could have fucked it up entirely. He must have been like a headless chicken, running from one room to the next. Oh, I did find one thing."

"Yeah?" said Porter.

"Somebody threw up in Mrs Carson-Cooke's cookie jar."

"*What?*"

"Judging by the mess he made on his way into the kitchen, it was almost certainly Balls. He ran in, threw up in the jar, then ran out again. Probably right before you lot arrived."

"What a dick," Porter said.

"Indeed. We have a few fingerprints, a few swabs from the victim, but I don't think we're going to find much. Whoever did this knew what they were doing. They came here to drop off one dead body, they seemed to have no trouble at all making another."

"Thanks, Cara," Porter said, and she waved a hand at him as she walked away, giving the stone a wide berth.

Porter looked at it. If it was a sacred stone, there was nothing special at all in its size or shape. It was just a rock, not particularly square, no markings or features that would make it stand out from any other piece of stone in the county.

"Why here?" he asked himself.

He glanced at the house, its top windows peeking over the hedge as if waiting for him to leave. The killer would have been here for minutes, just long enough to take the body from their vehicle, position him on the stone, and run. All the woman in the house had needed to do was stay in her bed and keep the curtains closed.

But she'd looked outside, and what she'd seen had killed her.

"Why here?" he asked again, popping his lips.

This stone wasn't like the ones in Somerset where the two boys had been found six years ago, or the ones in Neath and Yorkshire. Those had been proper standing stones, monuments to a forgotten age. They'd meant something, they had a history. He returned his attention to the rock, studying it so hard he thought he might give himself an aneurism.

And when no answers presented themselves, he made his way back to the car.

———

THERE WAS no answer at the Masefield place either.

Porter pounded on the door again, the cold making his hand feel like it might split in two even inside his lambskin glove. He shoved it into the pocket of his overcoat, stamping his feet as he waited for a response. The curtains of the small living room were pulled shut and only now did he realise how dirty the glass was—inside and out. They hadn't been cleaned for years.

"Mrs Masefield?" he called out, his words deafening in the silence of the street. "Blake?"

He knocked one more time, stepping back when he heard the sound of a bolt being drawn. It was the next door along the row that opened, though, a short, elderly man in a wrinkled pair of striped pyjamas that looked more like prison overalls. He was wearing a West Ham hat that was as long as a nightcap, as if he was Ebenezer Scrooge, and he threw Porter a filthy look.

"You mind?" he said, squinting like he'd forgotten to put his glasses on. His face looked like it was made of elastic.

Porter checked his watch.

"It's after ten," he said.

"Do I come to your house and tell you when to sleep?" he shot back, gurning. "What do you think you're doing, hammering on a door like that?"

"I'm police," Porter said.

The man's mouth moved like he was trying to chew a slab of toffee.

"If they're not in, they'll be over at the club," he said, pointing a yellow-nailed finger down the street."

"When—" Porter asked, but the door slammed shut.

He muttered a reply beneath his breath and wandered off in the direction of the man's finger, leaving his car. He'd driven through Lesser Lyng enough times now to have seen the little social club that sat next to the church, although it had looked so neglected that he'd assumed it was no longer used. It took him longer to get there than he'd thought it would, the cold making every step feel like torture. There weren't many folk out, and those who roamed the frozen streets gave him even colder looks. He was fairly sure one woman made the gesture of the cross on her chest, like he was a vampire.

"Bloody country folk," he said beneath his clouded breath.

The club was housed in a building that might once have been a village hall, squat and single-storied, big glass windows at the front shielded by net curtains. There must have been a sign over the door when it was built, but now there was only a rectangle of clean paint in the weathered cladding. Porter rapped his knuckles on the door and pushed it open without waiting for a reply.

"Hello?" he said, stepping into the bright interior.

It was a small space, one corner of which was a kitchenette. Beyond it, visible through more giant windows, was an enormous grassy area that had been given over to a football pitch. Blake Masefield was there, dressed in a tracksuit and bright orange trainers, kicking a football at the stone wall of the church next door. His mother stood a little distance away, staring at the sky and smoking a cigarette.

Porter had taken a couple of steps towards the back door before he noticed the rumble of the kettle as it came to boil.

It snapped off just as Blake's Auntie Audrey walked out of a door at the back of the kitchenette, dressed in jeans and a bright yellow crocheted jumper. She was holding a bottle of milk and she almost dropped it when she saw Porter standing there.

"Haddaway, man," she said in her thick Geordie accent. "You ought to know better than to creep up on folk at a time like this."

"Sorry," Porter said. "I did call out."

"Mustn't've called loud enough," she said, pulling a couple of cups from the cupboard then adding a third. "You want a brew?"

"Sure," he said. "I'm happy to make it."

"You southerners never make it strong enough."

She dumped a bag into each cup, adding the water. Porter half thought about reminding her that the milk was supposed to go in *before* the teabag but he didn't want to upset her any more than he already had. He walked to the window instead, watching the boy.

"How's he doing?"

"How do you expect?" Audrey said. "He's broken, plain and simple. His brother meant the world to him. You have brothers growing up? Sisters?"

"Just me," said Porter, his words steaming up the glass. He wiped the window clear with the sleeve of his jacket and Blake must have sensed the movement because he looked around, offering a sad smile and a wave. Porter waved back.

"It's different to losing your mum or dad," Audrey said, the spoon clinking as she stirred in the milk. "It's worse. You expect your folks to die, but losing a sibling's like losing a child. They're part of you."

"You sound like you know what you're talking about," Porter said, looking back.

"I don't. Not really. Cath and I hated each other growing up, but we always had each other's backs. I can't imagine what it would have been like if she'd died. If she'd been *murdered*."

She picked up all three teas in one hand, carrying them to the table beside Porter and wincing as she put them down. She kissed her knuckles where they'd been burned.

"You grew up around here, didn't you?" he asked.

"Dereham, aye. Nice place, really, good for raising kids. It's a little more remote out here but Chase and Blake liked it. Cath says they used to come up here together all the time, to the club."

"They played for the team?" Porter asked, looking at the dusty squad photos on the walls.

"On and off. Chase tore the tendon in his knee when he was little, made it hard for him to play, especially when the weather's like this. He was more into his cars, motorbikes, that sort of thing. But there weren't much else to do in the village proper, so yeah, they messed about. He's quite good, so I hear."

"Blake?"

"Yeah. The coach wanted him to try-out for the Norwich City youth team but he never did. Doesn't have much confidence, that one."

Blake kicked the ball again, moving swiftly in order to trap it when it bounced back.

"Who's the coach?" Porter asked. "Do I need to be worried about him?"

"I don't think so," she said. "Wee fella, very weird but harmless. Lives next door to Cath and the lads."

"West Ham supporter? Rubber face?"

Audrey laughed.

"That's the one, aye. He used to play for some big team,

I don't know who. You'll have to ask Cath about him, I don't live here."

"I can tell," Porter said. "The accent. You've been up north a while."

"*Wey aye,*" she said with a smile, laying it on thick. "Since I was sixteen. Married young, couldn't wait to leave home. Turns out he could barely wait to leave *me*, but I stayed up north. Good water there."

"Must have been hard leaving your sister, though, even if you didn't get on."

Porter watched her as she watched Cathy through the window, her expression unreadable.

"Yes and no. Like I said, losing a sibling is the hardest thing there is, other than losing a child. Better off if you die with them, maybe. I'm not sure I'll ever forgive myself."

"For leaving?"

"Aye," she said. "Cath hated me for it. She said I abandoned her. But I couldn't stay here. Town gets small after a while, and everyone knows your business. You coming out?"

She went to pick up the teas but Porter waved her away, scooping them up in his gloved hands. By the time he'd taken a couple of steps, though, Blake and his mum were heading in. Audrey held the door open for them as they stamped and shivered inside. They seemed to carry the cold in their clothes, in their faces too. It radiated from them, making Porter draw his heavy coat around himself.

"Hey," he said to Blake. "Looking good out there."

Blake looked down, but there was a sheepish smile on his face. He slumped into a chair and pulled out his phone, scrolling through it. His eyes were glazed, his mind elsewhere. Porter turned to Cathy Masefield instead, nodding a welcome. She looked as if her weight had halved overnight, like she'd withered. It was frightening, seeing what losing a child did to a person, the way it seemed to cut them clean in half, and for a moment Porter was relieved he didn't have any to lose.

Only for a moment, though.

"Sorry for intruding," he said. "I just came to see how you were all doing, and to ask a couple of questions."

"You found the man who did it yet?" Cathy asked, her dark eyes on the floor. She took a fresh cigarette from the pack and put it in her mouth, taking it out again straightaway.

"We're following every lead we have," Porter said. "But it's essential that we know everything. Can I ask, Mrs Masefield, did—"

"It's Miss," she said, still not looking up. "Never married their joke of a father."

Porter saw Blake flinch, his face a mask of misery.

"Sorry. *Miss* Masefield. I take it the father is out of the picture?"

"Could be dead as far as I'm concerned," she said. "Useless prick never gave a shit about his kids. Only wanted a bit of fun."

"Cath," said Audrey, tilting her head towards Blake.

"What? He knows, don't you, Blake? Not like Jimmy ever showed up with armfuls of presents or anything. We haven't seen him in years, not since Chase was in nursery and Blake was in nappies."

Porter watched Blake, seeing the way his head dropped even further, as if he was trying to hide behind his phone.

"Jimmy what?" Porter asked.

"Preston," said Cathy. "James Preston. He lives on the other side of Dereham, not that you'd know it."

"Does he know about Chase?"

Cathy glanced at Audrey and they both frowned as if they hadn't even considered that he would need to know.

"Would you like me to do it?" Porter asked, and Cathy shrugged.

He picked up a mug from the table and passed it to Audrey, handing another to her sister. He frowned at his as he picked it up. There were none of the little oily dark patches that he always found on his tea, but when he took a sip it tasted fine. He held onto it, enjoying the warmth.

"Did Chase mention meeting any new people? Had he made new friends, or was he out at strange hours? Any unexplained money, gifts?"

"Chase?" Cathy spluttered a laugh, cradling her mug against her chest. "No. He was a good lad, always helped out. He had friends at school but they hung out on that game more than they did in real life."

"He had his new girlfriend," said Audrey. "Lauren."

"What the fuck do you know about it?" Cathy said, glaring at her sister. "You show up after thirty years and you're a fucking expert on my son? You only ever met him once, and he was too young to remember it."

Audrey's face tightened and she took a sip of her tea.

"He ever talk about Lauren's dad?" Porter asked. "Greg Skinner."

Cathy shook her head.

"Just that he was a prick. But we all knew that. Chase was a normal kid with normal friends and a nice girl on his arm. He was good, he was kind, I couldn't have asked for any more. He was the best son..."

She caught herself, but it was too late. Blake shrank even deeper into himself, as if her words had been fists.

"And now he's dead," Cathy said, finally meeting Porter's eye. "He's fucking dead."

She hurled her mug at the wall so hard that Porter flinched. It hit hard but didn't break, recoiling with a peacock tail of tea. Only when it struck the wooden floor did it give up, shattering.

"Cath!" Audrey said, shocked.

"I'll get it," Blake said, grateful for the chance to get out of his seat.

The boy ran to the side of the room, down on his knees as he picked up the pieces. Porter muttered an excuse and went to help him, his joints popping as he dropped by Blake's side. Behind them, Cathy was running for the exit, making a noise that was half sob and half laugh and entirely terrifying. Audrey chased after her, calling her sister's name.

"Watch yourself," Porter said as Blake piled the shards in the palm of his hand. "Let me, I've got gloves."

"I'm sorry about mum," Blake said. "She's not been right."

"You never have to be sorry," Porter replied, scooping up the smaller shards. "This isn't your fault, and it's not hers either. I can't imagine what either of you are going through."

Blake shrugged, sitting back on his haunches.

"It's not just that, she's not been right for ages now. Chase said she was depressed but mums shouldn't get depressed, not when they've got kids to look after. It's not fair."

"Nobody can stop themselves feeling bad," Porter said. "It's like the weather. The clouds roll in sometimes, things get dark. Nothing you can do except look after yourself and wait for the sun."

"I don't think it's ever going to stop raining," the kid said, looking at the broken pieces of the cup.

Porter chewed on something.

"Your dad. He's back, isn't he?"

Blake's head jerked up like he'd had an electric shock, and it was all the confirmation Porter needed.

"Was it him who got in touch, or was it you?"

"It was me," Blake said, looking nervously towards the door. "I didn't know what to do about mum, and Chase wasn't helping. I thought..."

He swallowed like he was trying to work down a brick.

"He must have made her happy once upon a time, right? He must have. I just thought he might be able to cheer her up, make her normal again, make her *mum* again."

"You met with him?"

"Just once. Last week." The way his face creased reminded Porter of submarines in the depths crushed by the pressure. All he wanted to do was reach out to him, to give him some kind of comfort, but he held back. "I met him in Dereham, at Jack's. Skipped school and just went."

"How was it?"

"It was shit. *He* was shit. He was this arrogant prick, so full of himself. Didn't ask about mum once, or about me, just sat there and talked about himself for forty minutes till he said he had to go. Then he just fu... he just *pissed* off. Rubbed my head like I was some dog and didn't even pay for my food."

"I'm sorry that happened," Porter said. "He sounds like a loser. You're better than him, you know?"

Blake shrugged again, staring at those little pieces of broken china like he could will them into reforming, into no longer being broken.

"It got worse," he said after a moment, taking a shuddering breath. "Chase found out what I'd done and he called dad. He was so angry, I've never seen him that furious. He said he was going to kill him if he ever found out he'd spoken to me again."

"He said that?" Porter asked. Blake nodded. "Why didn't you mention this to me yesterday?"

Blake opened his mouth, hesitating.

"I didn't think," he said. "I'm sorry. Dad was angry too, when he spoke to Chase. I could hear him. I could hear him screaming down the phone. Then Chase was crying, and so was I."

He sniffed, his eyes glassy.

"Fucking arsehole."

"Can you tell me anything else about him?" Porter asked. "Your dad. Has he ever been in trouble?"

"Like with the police? No, I don't think so. He's not that kind of guy, he's just a prick. He's an artist, if you can believe that."

"An artist?" Porter said. "Paints?"

"Sculptures and shit," he said. "Makes stuff out of that powdery stuff kids use at school, not even stone or anything, just that Play-Doh shit."

"Plaster of Paris?" Porter asked.

The kid looked up, nodding.

"Blake," said Porter. "Do you know where I can find your dad *right now*?"

CHAPTER SEVENTEEN

"THANKS," SAVAGE SAID, PUTTING DOWN THE PHONE. "For absolutely nothing."

She rocked back in her chair, sliding a well-chewed pencil between her teeth. She'd been speaking to DS Helen Stuart at Suffolk Constabulary—after being on hold for the better part of half an hour—who had given her absolutely nothing useful when she'd asked about Frederick Sabbe. All Stuart had done was confirm what they already knew: Sabbe had gone missing a week ago while fishing and nobody had seen him since.

"We'll do it the old-fashioned way, then," she said, leaning forwards again and pulling her computer keyboard closer.

"Who are you talking to, Kate?"

Savage looked over her shoulder to see Superintendent Clare standing at the back of the Incident Room exploring his nose with an ugly brown handkerchief. It was right up one nostril, his expression deadly serious as he fished around for something he'd obviously lost in there. There was a spot of blood on the bandage wrapped around his head, the wound refusing to heal.

"Myself, sir," she said. "Sorry. I didn't think anyone else was here."

He waved her apology away and walked up behind her, depositing the hankie in his pocket.

"Did SuffCon have anything interesting?"

"They're going to fax over what they have, but they said it might take a while."

"Fax?" said Clare. "Christ, what happened? Did their carrier pigeon have a heart attack?"

Savage laughed as she loaded up Google, typing Frederick Sabbe into the search bar. The usual list of results came back, Facebook at the top. She clicked through, finding a private profile with only a handful of photos. One showed a boy on a motorcycle, a helmet obscuring his face. The other was a shot from behind, of Frederick on his fishing boat, the sun setting in the background.

"I'd have to be friends with him to see more," she said, clicking back.

"Sabbe has been missing for a week," said Clare. "I doubt this is our dead boy. Any other missing persons cases that match?"

"None of a boy his age and his description," Savage said. "We're still waiting for a few other forces to get back to us."

Clare pulled his hankie out, using it to sheath his finger before jamming it up his nose again.

"We need to find him," he said, his voice nasal.

"You're not going to find him in there," Savage muttered, grimacing.

"What?"

On the other side of the Incident Room the fax machine clicked and grunted, making a noise like an old man trying to climb out of an armchair. Savage jogged over to it, waiting what seemed like an eternity for the papers to appear. They were hot, and she examined the photograph of Frederick Sabbe as she carried them back. This kid looked older, in his early twenties, close-cropped dark hair and an angular face. He had a scar between his mouth and his nose that looked as if it had been left after cleft lip surgery.

"Sabbe isn't our victim," she said, handing the first sheet to Clare.

"Definitely not," Clare said. "That's good for Sabbe, bad for us. What else did they send?"

"Traffic cam shot," Savage said, reading the notes and studying the photograph of a clunky silver Jaguar X-Type. It was being driven without plates, which was suspicious enough in itself. There was a face behind the windscreen, concealed by a cap. "This was on the northbound A11 six days ago. They're not sure if it's Sabbe or not. Parents say the car is theirs, it was SORN, in storage. They don't know how he got it started. It was the last anyone saw of him."

"Heading towards Norwich?" Clare said. "Weird."

Savage scanned the final sheet.

"Never in trouble with the police, although his mum said he's been acting a little weird lately. Hang on... 'Unusual behaviour, spending more time than usual online, sullen and snappy.' But no history of violence or anything like that. There's nothing else. But he's not our dead boy."

She handed Clare the sheet of paper. He glanced at it then dropped it onto her desk.

"Toss me right off!" he said, his face creasing with annoyance.

"Uh..."

Savage was saved from any further reaction when her phone rang.

"Porter," she said to Clare as she pulled it out of her pocket. She put it on speaker.

"Chase Masefield's dad is an artist," said Porter before she could say hello. "Works with Plaster of Paris. He's back on the scene after a long absence, Blake said he fell out with Chase, threatened him."

"What's his name?" asked Clare.

"Jesus, Savage, what's wrong with your voice? You sound like you've tried to inhale a toad."

"It's me, Porter," said Clare. "You're on speaker. His name."

"James Preston. Blake doesn't know his address. Can you run him?"

"Sure thing, guv," said Savage, resting the phone on the table and accessing the system. She entered Preston's name, chewing her pencil as she waited for the results to filter through. "No arrest record, he has an address in Dereham, just outside the town."

"Local," Clare said. "You said he was an artist? That might explain the gypsum we found in Chase's hair."

"I'm heading there now," said Porter. "He doesn't know about Chase yet, I don't think. You want me to bring him in, sir?"

"Talk to him. I'll send some backup just in case. Wait for them to get there before you knock on the door, okay?"

"Yes, sir," Porter said.

"I mean it," boomed Clare. "Don't *Kett* this up. You *wait*."

Porter laughed, then hung up.

"That's a little unfair, isn't it?" Savage said. "Using Kett's name as a verb."

"You've *Ketted* up once already on this case, Savage, so

zip it. Get me anything you can on Preston. He's looking like a good fit for this."

Savage clicked back to the browser and typed the man's name into the search engine. The first hit was a website and when Savage clicked through to it her jaw dropped.

"Oh shoot," she said.

"Oh shoot indeed," said Clare, leaning in.

Blake was right, his father was an artist. On the front page of his website was a collection of sculptures, impressively realistic. They were all different, but they all had one thing in common.

They were all sculptures of people, some limbless, others faceless, their bodies contorted in agony.

"Look at that, sir," said Savage, pointing to one. It showed a sculpted stone the size of a bedside cabinet, and fashioned on top was the image of a man in agony, his stomach open to reveal the painted mess of his insides. A beautifully detailed eagle perched on his ribs, its beak crimson.

"Prometheus," said Clare. "He stole the fire of the gods and they punished him by tying him to a rock for the rest of eternity, an eagle tearing him open to devour his liver every single day."

"That's no coincidence, right sir?" Savage said, and Clare shook his head.

"Call Porter, tell him to be careful," the Super said as he walked away. "I'll prep a tactical team, just in case."

Savage nodded, clicking back to the search engine and onto the Images tab. She was greeted by more sculptures, some paintings too, but it was the photos of Preston himself that made her call Clare's name.

"What is it?" he said, marching back.

She tapped her finger on the monitor hard enough to

make it wobble, both of them craning in to get a better look at the grainy photograph displayed there. It showed a group of men standing around a large, abstract sculpture in what looked like an office lobby or maybe a school reception. In the middle of the group, beaming like a madman, was James Preston, most of his blond hair missing and the rest hanging like strands of seaweed past his shoulders. He didn't look like Chase Masefield at all, his skin pulled tight over his high cheekbones and his strong jaw.

Next to him, tall and broad and stone-faced, was another man.

"That's Greg Skinner," said Savage. "This is from six months ago. They know each other."

"That utter bastard," Clare said, stamping one enormous brogue on the floor. "Go get him."

———

PC AARON DUKE may have been a big man, but right now he was squealing like a baby.

Savage put her foot down, the IRV's siren parting traffic on the A47 with ease. Duke clung to the handle over the door with both hands, his big chest puffing as Savage hit seventy.

"You okay?" she asked.

"I'm fine," he coughed. "Nothing to see here. Just focus on the—"

He sucked the last word back in as Savage overtook a bus, then spluttered it out again when she slowed down to take the slip road. Savage laughed. She couldn't help it. Not laughter at Duke's expense, just at the sheer joy of driving, the rush of adrenaline. When she was moving, nothing bad could happen to her.

It was only when she stopped that she needed to worry.

It took another twenty minutes to reach Lesser Lyng, and by that time the rain had started to fall again. Savage saw the flashing lights outside the Skinner house, a couple of local constables waiting for her. She pulled up behind them, switching off the engine. Duke fumbled with the handle and threw himself out of the car like he was expecting her to take off again. Only when he was outside, his hat back on his shaved head, did he regain any sense of composure. He shot Savage a look as she climbed out of the car, but she ignored him, turning to the other Uniforms.

"You been in?" she asked.

"Not yet," said the woman. She was young, but she had an alertness about her that was reassuring. "Control asked us to hang back. Haven't seen anyone, but the door's open."

She was right. The front door was wide open, the driveway deserted.

"Weird, on a day like this," Savage said. "No cars, either."

"What do you want us to do?" asked the other constable, fiddling with his belt. He was young too, and he looked nervous.

"Nothing yet. I'll handle it. But stay sharp. I don't think Greg Skinner will try anything, but he's got guns in there and he's a big fan of intimidation. Duke, with me."

Duke grumbled something but he fell in beside her as she walked onto the long, wide driveway. To her left, in the woods, the trees whispered to each other as they watched her pass, and overhead a storm of crows wheeled through the overcast skies, screaming their hoarse cry like a warning.

It felt like a bad omen.

"Hello?" Savage called out as she approached the door. The wind whipped the word away, carrying it into the sky.

"Mr Skinner? Mrs Skinner? It's DC Kate Savage. Is anybody home?"

Only the crows replied, the snap of their wings overhead like thunder. Savage reached the door and stared down the dark hallway into the kitchen beyond. It felt empty, but she couldn't be sure.

"Is anybody home?" she called out. "It's the police."

No answer.

"What do you want to do?" Duke asked quietly, one hand resting on his baton.

Savage wasn't sure. She'd already messed up once by entering the Skinner barn without a warrant, and she didn't want to make the same mistake again. She knocked on the door, the sound of it chasing more birds from the trees, their spiralling bodies making the skies even darker.

"Mr Skinner? I just want to ask you a couple of questions. If you're in, can you come to the door?"

The house gaped at her, utterly silent.

"Check the back," Savage said. "Make sure he's not in the barn."

Duke nodded, breaking into a jog as he made his way around the side of the house. Savage didn't think he was going to find anything. No car, the door wide open. She wondered if Skinner had packed his bags and his family and legged it.

And she wondered if he'd murdered another boy before he'd left.

"Nobody here," Duke shouted from the garden, his voice almost lost beneath the cries of the crows. "You want me to—?"

And he never had the chance to finish as the bark of a shotgun lit up the day.

CHAPTER EIGHTEEN

Savage broke into a run, seeing the two constables on the road start to move towards her and waving them back.

"Call it in," she yelled. "Get an armed response unit, now!"

She ran down the side of the house, her fingertips skimming the bricks to steady herself. Overhead the crows seemed to scream.

"Duke?" she shouted.

She was answered by a scream, wet and desperate.

"Aaron?"

She kept moving, reaching the end of the house just as Duke skidded around the corner, his equipment belt rattling. He was scared but he was in control, his hand on his radio.

"Yeah, the Skinner place," he said. "One shot, I think somebody's hurt."

"I thought it was *you*," said Savage when he'd finished. She turned to the trees. "The woods."

"Wait," Duke said when she started moving.

She didn't stop—she *couldn't*, because whoever had screamed before was doing it again now, the sound of it awful. She pushed through the first line of branches, her boots slipping on the wet leaves, the trees groping at her face, her throat. She heard Duke curse, the sound of him crashing after her.

"Police!" she yelled, ducking beneath a branch.

The ground was treacherous beneath its skin of leaves, as if there were mouths there. It seemed to want to open up and swallow her, and twice she spilled onto her hands and knees, growling with the pain of it. The same voice called to her, a guttural scream that was growing weaker by the second.

"You see anything?" she called back.

"No," said Duke, pointing deeper into the shadows. "Coming from over there I think."

She couldn't tell and she forced herself to stop running, trying to listen past the storm of blood in her skull. Duke stopped too, hands on his knees as he clawed in a breath. There were leaves stuck in his beard and somewhere on the run he'd lost his hat. He opened his mouth to ask something but Savage held up a hand to silence him.

The noise came again, not so much a scream now as a gargle. Savage squinted into the spaces between the trees, scanning the gloom and seeing it.

A leg, sticking out from the base of a tree. One bare foot.

"There," she said, running again.

The closer she got, the worse it became. The leg was naked and it was drenched in blood. The foot pushed feebly at the soil, filth gathering between the toes. Savage motioned for Duke to break left, around the other side of the tree. She went right, more of the injured man coming into view—a pair of dirty underpants, a bulging stomach with a sheen of crimson blood, a broad chest. By the time the face had come into view she already knew who it was.

Greg Skinner.

And it was just as well, because there wasn't much of his face left.

"Oh god," Savage said, putting her hand to her mouth. She turned away. She *had* to, because the sight of the dying man was almost too much to bear. The side of Skinner's face looked as if it had been removed, flashes of teeth in the ruin of his cheek. His right eye wasn't there at all, and the other roved wildly, *blindly*. His hands dug in the soil like he was trying to find something, his fingers clenching and unclenching, over and over.

"Fuck," said Duke when he rounded the tree. "Oh, fucking hell."

He doubled over, and Savage thought he was throwing up until she realised what he was looking at. A double-barrelled shotgun lay by Skinner's foot, still smoking. Her first instinct was to move it but she decided not to. It wasn't like Skinner was capable of picking it up again. He wasn't even going to survive long enough for an ambulance to arrive.

That knowledge came at her like a wave, impossibly dark and unbearably loud. She gritted her teeth, balled her fists so hard she could feel her nails digging into the flesh of her palms. The tears were in her eyes before she could do anything about it. They *burned*.

"Call for help," Savage said, just a whisper.

She dropped to her knees beside Skinner, and when she looked up and saw that Duke wasn't responding she almost screamed at him.

"An ambulance, Aaron, now."

"But he's—"

"Now!"

He nodded at her as he backed off, speaking into his radio. Savage turned to Skinner, forcing herself to look at him, to see him. The man had been an arsehole, there was no doubt about it, but he was still a man. He tried to turn his head to her but he couldn't seem to make it work. His mouth opened and nothing but blood came out, great gouts of it. His eye found her, lost her, found her again. His breaths were slowing, too much damage to his face, to his throat.

Savage took his hand, she held it, feeling his blood-slick fingers grasping at her, doing everything they could not to let go.

"It's okay," she said, holding tight. "It's okay."

His other hand swung up, hanging there, his fingers pointing at the trees, then at the sky, then crumpling by his side. His body bucked like somebody had run an electric charge through it and his hand gripped her own with such force that she gasped.

Then, just like that, he let out one final breath and fell still.

SAVAGE SAT with Skinner until the ambulance arrived. She didn't let go of his hand.

Nobody deserved to die like this, nobody deserved to be on their own.

"Leave him," Duke said more than once as he paced back and forth. "You do realise he did it because he knew we were going to get him for that kid's death? Leave him, he doesn't deserve it."

We don't know that, Savage thought, but she couldn't bring herself to say it. She knelt on the wet ground, in the filth and the blood, feeling Greg Skinner settle into a still-ness that was absolute and terrifying. Seeing the dead was part of the job. Seeing the *dying* was so much worse. She didn't have the words for it, she couldn't quite accept that what had happened was real, and there was a panic deep inside her that roared. She wasn't crying, and yet she had to keep scrubbing the tears from her face. They wouldn't stop falling.

Only when she saw the paramedics struggling through the woods did she finally pull her hand free. It was far too early for rigor mortis, and yet Skinner seemed to hold onto her, his fingers tight. When she stood up she almost fell, her legs numb, but she waved Duke away when he went to help her.

"Sorry," she said, holding up her bloody hands as an explanation. She met the paramedics with a grim nod. "There's nothing we could do."

"Shit a brick," said the first, an overweight man who looked like he smoked way too many cigarettes. "Suicide?"

Savage shrugged.

"We didn't see anyone else."

The man dutifully checked Skinner's pulse, even though there wasn't a hope in hell of finding anything. Savage took the opportunity to study the ground. There was no evidence of any kind of struggle, the ferns and the bram-bles largely undisturbed. The shotgun lay to Skinner's left, the stock by his foot, the barrel no longer smoking. The tree behind him was drenched in blood and matter, and the shot had ripped chunks from the bark.

"Must have pulled the trigger with his toe," said the paramedic. "Cobain-style."

Savage blew out a breath and the man turned to look at her—at her red eyes, at the streaks on her cheeks.

"Did you know him?" he asked.

"No," she said.

She walked away, her feet catching on the stubborn roots. The world seemed to tilt and sway beneath her like it wanted to shake her off, and when the woods finally released her back onto the Skinner driveway the sky seemed too bright.

Come on, Kate, just breathe.

She took her own advice, sucking down air, grateful for a moment of peace before she heard the screams coming from the road—not a soundtrack of pain, this time, but one of grief. Matilda Skinner was there, being held back by the two young constables as she tried to make a break for the woods.

"Fudge," Savage said, jogging the length of the drive-way. Matilda was tiny but she was fighting hard, and she'd already given one of the coppers a bloody nose. They didn't know what to do with her. "Hey, it's okay, let her go."

They did as she asked and Savage planted herself in the little woman's path before she could run.

"Mrs Skinner. Matilda. Stop."

She said it with enough authority for the woman to hear her. Matilda looked up, her eyes wild and full of fear. She huffed and puffed, her fists clenched beside her chest.

"Where is he?" she said. "Where's my Greg?"

She knew, though. She knew. It was there in her eyes, in the lines of her face, and in the way she seemed to suddenly deflate. She fell into Savage and Savage held her with the same bloodied hands she'd used to hold her dying husband, feeling her sobs, hearing her speak.

"He never asks me to go out," she said. "He never does. He never does."

She remembered herself, pulling away and using both hands to smudge her eyes.

"Mrs Skinner, did Greg ask you to leave the house?" Savage asked.

"An hour ago," she said, pointing back up the street to where her little Fiat 500 blocked the road. "He said we needed milk but I knew we didn't. We had eight pints in the fridge. But then I looked and we didn't, it was gone, and he said he was busy and he asked me to go and he never does that. He never does it."

She looked at Savage, seeing the blood on her hands, and her face seemed to dissolve even further.

"He used the gun, didn't he? Oh god, that stupid man, that stupid, stupid man. What am I going to tell Lauren? Her daddy's dead, he's gone."

"I'm..." Savage started, but she stopped when she heard the growl of an engine. There was another car behind Matilda Skinner's, a giant black Range Rover that loosed a startling blast of its horn. Realising he couldn't pass, the driver opened the door and hopped down. It was Dennis Pruitt, Savage saw, the solicitor, still decked in his awful leather jacket. He was furious.

"Oi!" he yelled, pointing a finger at Savage. "Get away from her."

He marched past the ambulance, his footsteps echoing back from the distant house. One of the constables moved to intercept him but Savage waved her off.

"You have no right to be here," Pruitt went on, sweeping his hands through the air as if he could waft her away. His hair flowed behind him like a cape, and chunky gold jewellery caught the light. "Tilly called me and told me you'd showed up again. It's harassment. If you want to talk to my client then you do it through me, or I swear to god—"

"He's dead," Savage said when the big man was close enough for her to speak quietly.

Pruitt's feet stopped moving but his head craned forward like it hadn't got the same command. He studied her for a moment, as if trying to work out whether she was telling the truth.

"What?" he said.

"Greg Skinner is dead, and it might have been a suicide."

"He would never..." Pruitt said, fumbling the words. "Why would he do that?"

"You tell me," Savage said.

If he knew, he had no intention of saying anything. He spotted Matilda and barged towards her, calling her name. She ran to him and they embraced, both of them looking into the trees, imagining the horrors there.

Savage left them to it, walking back to the house. Her throat was bone dry and the blood on her hands was starting to itch, the feel of it maddening. She returned to the open front door—it could have been a million years since she'd stood here last—and struggled out of her boots. Stepping inside felt like entering a tomb. The air was still and heavy, impossibly quiet. Something caught in her nose, acrid and unpleasant.

Something burning.

It was coming from deeper in the house and she tried the kitchen first, putting her hand to the AGA. A door was ajar at the back of the room and she used her elbow to pry it open, seeing a small room and a massive metal safe. Whatever state of mind Greg Skinner had been in, he'd had enough sense to lock the guns up behind him.

She retreated, stepping over a couple of clumps of mud on the tiles as she moved out of the kitchen. She took a right and found a cosy living room at the back of the house. Big windows showed the garden and the enormous barn and she wondered if this was where Greg Skinner had spotted her from yesterday when she'd investigated it.

It's my fault, she said. If she'd left the barn alone then they never would have brought Skinner in, and none of this would have happened.

Then she caught herself.

This was *his* doing, not hers.

Besides, there was a log burner in the corner of the room, a modern one with a big, black cylinder. The window had been charred with use but Savage could still see the flames inside. She ran to it, taking the thick oven gloves from the floor and twisting the handle. The door opened, heat and smoke pouring out and forcing her back.

Not before she'd seen the photos, though. Or what was left of them.

"Shit," she said, running back to the kitchen, her socks slipping on the tiles as she skidded to the sink. There was a teapot in the rack and she filled it up, water slopping everywhere as she ran back.

It did the job, the fire replaced by a curtain of steam and smoke. Reaching in, she grabbed handfuls of ash and sludge, shards of broken DVDs scratching her skin as she deposited the mess on the brick hearth. She tried to make sense of the scraps of detail that remained and quickly wished she hadn't.

Naked bodies and eyes that gleamed with terror.

There was more there too, letters full of spidery hand-writing. She brushed the dust from one, trying to read it.

I know what you did. I know about the boys.

The same line, over and over again.

Why would he do that? Pruitt had asked.

The answer lay right here, still smoking.

CHAPTER NINETEEN

"OH JESUS, KATE," PORTER SAID, TILTING HIS HEAD back and closing his eyes. "You okay?"

He heard Savage sigh down the phone, and everything he needed to know was in that stuttered breath.

"I will be. But I'll see his face forever, you know?"

"You want me to come back?" Porter said, blowing out a sigh of his own when he heard how useless his words were. What was he supposed to do to make it better? What *could* he do? Savage was one of the strongest people he knew, and she certainly didn't need his shoulder to cry on.

"Sure, Pete," she said. "Come back and make me a cuppa. That will take my mind off it, at least."

He wasn't sure if she was being serious or not until she whispered a sad laugh.

"I'll be okay. You there yet?"

Porter looked over the steering wheel towards the squat little cottage that sat at the arse end of Dereham. It was the last known address of James Preston, Chase Masefield's father, and it was pretty evident that he still lived here. The garden was a junkyard of statues that were either half-finished or half-rotted, twisted figures that looked almost human but not quite right, with too many limbs or none at all, their faces split wide by smiles or sobs. They were carved from a white stone of some kind—or moulded in Plaster of Paris, perhaps, Porter couldn't be sure—dull and yellow with age, and they were all drowning in the long grass and overgrown hedges.

The cottage itself was pretty much derelict, one of the two ground-floor windows boarded up and the other shielded by a curtain so thick it might have been sculpted from the same stone. Ivy had claimed the building as its own, a great blanket of dark veins that gripped the walls and the sagging roof. The car that sat on the side of the road was almost as bad, a shitty Morris Traveller with wooden panels. The rain was doing its best to wash the whole sorry scene away, as if it was a stubborn stain.

The last thing Porter wanted to do was get out of the Ford, but this wasn't something that could wait.

He reached for the handle, glancing through the window to see a man staring back at him through the rain-streaked glass, so close that his nose was almost pressed against it. The shock of it loosed a bolt of adrenaline and Porter's knees cracked off the bottom of the wheel.

"Fuck," he said, his head roaring. He waved his hand. "Back off."

The man retreated, grinning like the village idiot. Porter opened the door and got out, the freezing rain pissing him off even more than the dickhead who stood in front of him. He was a short, wiry guy wearing cut-off jeans that ended just above his ankles. On his feet was a pair of sandals that would already have been out of fashion when the Romans had settled here. His feet were filthy. Despite the rain, all he wore on his top half was a faded *Metallica* T-shirt that was covered in paint. He had barely any hair on the top of his head and yet somehow he'd worked what was left into a rat-tail that perfectly matched the one on his chin.

Porter hated him immediately.

The guy poked a finger in his direction, sneering. His face belonged to a man about fifty years old but the eyes seemed younger. They were too blue, out here in the grey world.

"You thought you were watching me but I was watching you," he said, his voice surprisingly deep for such a small guy. His laugh was the sound of heavy machinery starting, and he hawked air in through his nose like he was about to spit. "You never even saw me, and I was right there for five whole minutes."

"Good for you," Porter said. "James Preston?"

"Yeah," he said. "That's me. You were gonna nick one, weren't you?"

"Nick what?" Porter said, looking at the cottage. "One of *those*?"

"You wouldn't be able to sell it. I'm too well known. Walk into a gallery with one of them and they'd tell you to get lost, because only James Preston can sell a James Preston."

"They'd tell me to get lost, for sure," Porter said. "Not sure if that's the reason. I'm police, Mr Preston. DI Peter Porter, Norfolk Constabulary."

He pulled out his warrant card but Preston didn't even look at it.

"I don't believe in the police," Preston said.

"We're not ghosts, Mr Preston. We're here whether you believe in us or not. Can we go inside?"

"Not until you tell me what this is about."

Porter sighed, wiping the rain from his eyes.

"It's about your son," he said.

And just like that, the smile vanished. Preston's tongue darted out, flicking across his bad teeth. He studied Porter like he might be lying, then nodded. He pushed past him, stepping over the low gate rather than opening it and weaving through the carnival of freaks who cowered in the tall grass. They had no eyes and yet something about them made Porter feel watched, as if they were silently screaming. He half-remembered a story his mother had told him where the children were turned into statues by a witch. *Hansel and Gretel*, maybe? He couldn't remember, but he hadn't thought about it for thirty-odd years and it unsettled him more than it should have now that it was back in his head.

"If they've done something, I'm the wrong person to talk to," Preston said as he unlocked the door with a huge key that hung around his neck on a length of rope. "They live with their bitch mother."

"Watch your tongue," Porter said.

Unless you want to lose it, he didn't add.

Preston pretended not to hear him, ducking through the door and flicking a switch that looked damp with rainwater. The lintel was as low here as it was at the Masefield place and Porter crouched underneath it, cursing the short-arses who'd built the houses in this part of the world.

If the garden was a museum of weirdness then the cottage itself was a shrine. Almost all of the interior walls had been removed, the ceiling joists supported by industrial metal strongboys—four or five giant Acrow props that belonged on a building site. Everywhere Porter looked there were sculptures in various stages of completion, and the floor was inch-deep in white dust. Sketches hung on the damp walls, tortured images that belonged in a madhouse.

"Careful where you walk," Preston said over his shoulder. "Some of these are selling for a fortune. Can't have a bellend like you costing me money now, can we?"

"Don't you worry about that," Porter said as he stepped past a painted bust that sat delicately on a plinth. His elbow grazed it hard enough to make it rock and when he reached out to steady it he almost knocked the whole bloody thing off.

"I said be careful, you klutz," Preston said, and Porter wondered how hard he'd have to hit him with the nearest statue for it to break.

When the wiry man turned away, Porter bent down and scooped up a pinch of the dust on the floor, pocketing it. Preston squatted by a wooden chest that sat by the far wall and pulled out a bottle of Bells. He used his teeth to unscrew the cap, spitting it to the floor, then he stood and necked a good half dozen swallows. When he looked at Porter again his eyes were watering.

"Want some?" he wheezed, holding it out.

"Not even with your mouth," Porter muttered.

"What?"

"These all your pieces?" Porter studied the sculptures, their faces either missing or distorted, their limbs stumps. "What is *wrong* with you?"

"You would say that, you're police. You don't have the slightest inkling of what makes something art, why certain shapes move us, repel us, excite us. You need an imagination for that, my friend, and I can tell just by looking at you that you don't have one. I bet you never had one. You were shit at art in school, weren't you?"

"Drew a pretty cool penguin once," Porter said. "My mum still has it."

Preston scoffed, nodding to the piece that had wobbled on its plinth.

"Commission," he said. "Theatre Royal asked me for it. Ophelia, from *Hamlet*. I don't think you'll know who that is. Fourteen grand is what they're paying."

He grinned, and Porter saw from the looseness of the expression that this wasn't the first drink he'd had that day.

"That's more than I'd pay," he said. "By about fifteen grand. Look, Mr Preston, I appreciate that you like to mess around with Play-Doh, but that's not why I'm here. You've recently got in touch with your sons again, is that right? After well over a decade."

"They got bored of waiting for their cunt mother—"

"I told you, watch your mouth," Porter growled, and there was no chance of a third warning in his tone. Preston sniffed again, moving from foot to foot, restless.

"You haven't met her, she's a nightmare. Was happy enough to see me when she wanted her hole filled but the moment those boys fell out of her she decided I wasn't good enough. She kept them from me, told them all sorts of lies, and they must have seen she was full of shit, they must have decided they didn't want to wait anymore. Everyone's on Facebook these days so they found me, reached out. No crime in that, and if she's sent you here to tell me otherwise then—"

"That's not why I'm here," Porter said. "I have bad news about Chase."

Preston took another sip of whisky, his brow furrowing.

"I'm very sorry to have to tell you that your son was found dead yesterday morning, in the woods a few miles from here."

The man licked his lips, then he shrugged.

"The other one?"

"The other one?" Porter said. "You mean Blake?"

"Yeah, what about him?"

"He's fine." Porter took a step towards the man. "But Chase was murdered."

"From what I could see he liked pissing people off," Preston said. "He probably had it coming."

"*What*?" Porter said. "This is your son. He was killed."

Preston shrugged again, whisky slopping out of the bottle.

"Never knew him," he said. "Got more kids out there than I can count. Sowed a lot of oats in my time."

"Did Chase piss *you* off?" Porter asked. "I heard you had an argument with him shortly before he died. You want to tell me what that was about?"

"Blake's a little snitch, isn't he?" Preston said. "It was nothing. He told me he didn't want me anywhere near his brother and I told him that wouldn't be a problem. I told them both I was too busy to see them."

"That's it?" Porter said.

"He gave me the Billy Big Bollocks, told me he'd 'ave me if he saw me again. I figured he was just gearing up to black-mail me, get some money. Turned out he must have just been a pussy."

Porter's leather glove squeaked as he balled a fist, and he had to force himself to relax it. For once he was glad Kett wasn't here, because right now Robbie would be force-feeding the man one of his own statues.

"Chase threatened to kill you," Porter said. "Blake says he thought you'd done the same."

"He wasn't worth it," Preston said. "I didn't even know him, why would I waste the rest of my life by killing him? He's better off dead, his brother would be too, then they wouldn't have to hang out with *her* anymore."

Porter took a breath and counted to five, never taking his eyes from Preston's. Even when he breathed out again the anger was almost overwhelming.

"Where were you on Friday night?" he asked, trying to keep his voice level.

"Right here," Preston said.

"Alone?"

"No," he said, that smile reappearing. "But I can't remember her name."

"Well start remembering," Porter said. "Because the autopsy showed that your son had traces of gypsum on him when he died."

"Gypsum?"

"Yeah, like Plaster of Paris." Porter swung his arm around to the statues that littered the cottage. "Like all this shit. We think somebody made him wear a mask before he was tortured to death."

Preston shook his head, some of the colour leaving him.

"A mask?" he said.

"You make masks?" Porter went on.

"No. Not for a long time."

"Since when?"

"Since I was a fucking kid, an art student."

"What about last night. Did you have company then?"

Preston nodded.

"Was down the Lion," he said. "Till closing time."

"After that?"

"Closing time's around four in the morning. Lock-in. Check with Rita, she'll tell you."

"Greg Skinner? You know him?"

"Skinny, sure," Preston said. "Why? What's that bald prick got to do with this?"

"He's dead too," Porter said. "Shot himself in the face less than an hour ago."

For the first time since Porter had arrived, Preston's stone exterior seemed to crack. He licked his lips again, taking another long swallow from the bottle.

"He shot *himself*?" he said.

"You think somebody else did it?"

Preston gulped, as if he still had the bottle to his lips. His eyes darted to the door, then back to Porter.

"Don't know anything about it," he said, recovering. "If I was that cunt I'd have shot myself too, a long time ago."

"How did you know each other?"

"School," he said. "Fucking years ago. We played in a band for a while but he was a prick, he'd fuck anyone over if he got the chance."

"You seen him recently?" Porter went on, drilling deeper.

"No, not for years. Why would—"

"There's a photo of the two of you together, just a few months ago. It was in the paper."

"That?" Preston was reeling. "That was just parish council shit, they bought one of my sculptures because I was local. He was there, we barely even—"

"Did you know he liked taking pictures of little boys?"

Preston shook his head, dancing from foot to foot like a monkey.

"No, but he always struck me as—"

"You ever take photographs of people, James?" he said, not relenting. "Boys? You must need models for all this stuff."

Preston opened his mouth but this time nothing came out.

"Chase was at Skinner's house the night he died," Porter said.

Still nothing, but anger had carved lines into Preston's face.

"Did you know they knew each other, him and Skinner? Did you tell Greg about your two boys? Did you offer them to him?"

"You... you *what*?"

Porter could see the man's grip on the bottle tighten, like he was planning to use it as a weapon. The DI stepped even closer, looming over him.

"Did you two like to share?"

"Fuck off," Preston said, something dangerous in his voice, in his face. "He wouldn't have dared."

"You just said you don't give a shit about your sons. What do you care what happened?"

"Because they're *mine*. I made them, so I fucking own them, don't I?"

"Is that why Skinner is dead?" Porter said. "Because you found out, threatened him, threatened to *tell*? You ever write him any letters, James?"

"Letters? No. If I'd known he was anywhere near Chase, I'd have..."

He caught himself, licking his lips again.

"Killed him yourself?" Porter guessed. "I'm thinking maybe you should come into the station."

"You arresting me?"

That arrogant smile was back, and Porter bit his tongue while he thought about it. In the end, he shook his head. There just wasn't enough to hold him, especially if his alibis came through.

"We're going to speak to you again very soon," he said. "And we'll be watching you. Don't go anywhere."

Preston hawked up a ball of phlegm again, launching it to the floor halfway to Porter's shoes. He took another long drink, the whisky a quarter-bottle lighter. The way his red, raw eyes scuttled over the room made him look like a spider, a bug, and Porter would happily have squashed him. He thought of Blake, and even though he didn't want to, he could see the boy in his father, in the shape of his eyes, the furrowed brow. He thought about what it must have been like for him, sitting with his dad in a café. He must have had such hope of finding in his father a good man, a kind man, a man who could make up for all those years of absence.

And he got this, he got James Preston.

"You don't deserve those boys," Porter said, his voice low. "And you know something? You think you're happy now, but when you're old and alone, probably still infesting this shithole, nobody in the world to give a fuck about you, you'll look back and realise just how much you fucked up. You had two good sons, but you don't deserve them."

Preston exhaled like he'd been punched in the gut, but he quickly recovered. He leaned in, his breath toxic even from where Porter was standing.

"Sounds like Greg isn't the only one who likes the company of teenage boys," he said, laughing.

Porter might have killed him there and then. Instead, he turned around and walked away.

"I mean it," he said. "Don't leave town."

He passed the statue of Ophelia on the plinth and rammed his shoulder into it, sending it toppling to the floor. The bust exploded in a storm of powder, James Preston's howls of outrage filling the cottage.

"Sorry mate," Porter said, looking back. "I can be such a fucking klutz sometimes."

CHAPTER TWENTY

Porter's head was swimming as he walked back to his car, the adrenaline runoff worse than it was after a fight. He hesitated before he got in, finding his phone and Googling the Lion Freehouse and finding it just a mile or so away. He called them, giving his name and rank and asking to speak to Rita.

"I'm going to ask you one question," he said when she arrived on the other end of the line, already breathless. "Tell me the truth and I'll pretend I don't give a shit about the lock-ins. Agreed?"

No reply, but he thought he heard her swallow.

"Last night, who was in, and when did they leave?"

"Just four of us," she said, her voice ancient. "Me and Ruthy, she works the bar. Her cousin Anthony and her boyfriend, James."

"James who?"

"Preston. Jimmy Preston, we call him. They were here all night, left together about four, half four maybe, pissed as farts."

"You know if James was with Ruth on Friday night too?"

"They were here together, left together, don't know much else. We've got a camera behind the bar if you need to see it? Just had it installed this year, fancy little thing it is."

"I'll send somebody for it," he said. "Thank you."

He hung up, calling Clare.

"You think Preston did it?" the Superintendent asked, right off the bat.

"I'm not sure, his alibis seem solid. Even if he did, I don't think we have enough to hold him. He definitely works with gypsum, though, I nabbed some from the floor, looks identical to the stuff we found on Masefield's face. I can bring him in?"

"Don't. I'll send a car to keep an eye on him. I need you to head to the school, see if they know our second dead boy."

"Will do." Porter opened the door. "How's Kate?"

"I don't know," Clare said, hanging up.

He waited twenty minutes for the IRV to arrive, a young constable from Dereham at the wheel.

"If he leaves, you follow him," Porter said, passing his card through the open window. "If he so much as shits in a bush you call me."

"He's going to shit in a bush?" the young man said, horrified.

Porter pulled away, doing a clumsy seven-point turn in the narrow road before accelerating hard. Despite the lunchtime traffic it didn't take long to get back into the centre of Dereham, and when he drove into the car park of the Nelson Academy he was surprised to see Savage's shitty green Fiat in the visitors' car park. He swung in next to her, checked that it was empty, then ran through the rain to reception.

Savage was sitting on a chair in the waiting area, flicking through a brochure, and she glanced up when he walked through the door. She looked hollow. Her hands were still trembling, and she put the brochure back on the table and tucked them between her legs. She'd changed her clothes, he noticed, and her hair was wet.

"What are you doing here?" she asked, just as Porter was asking the exact same thing. This, at least, brought a smile to her face.

"Clare asked me to come," Porter went on.

"I told him I'd do it," she said.

"I don't mind, Kate."

"We'll do it together then, guv," she said, patting the seat next to her.

Porter walked over, but before he could sit down a man in a suit leant around the partition next to the reception desk and smiled at them. He was so young that at first Porter thought he was a Sixth Form student, then he shook Porter's hand with a grip that could only belong to a headmaster. He did the same to Savage when she bounced out of the low chair.

"Ben Enthoven," he said. "Principal. I wasn't expecting two of you."

"Neither was I," said Savage. "I'm DC Kate Savage, this is DI Peter Porter. Can we step inside your office?"

"Uh, no, I'm very sorry, they're using it for a revision session. I think the library's free, follow me."

It was a short walk across the hall, the library decked out in an impressive display of witch's hats, tissue paper masks and *papier mâché* cats.

"Miss Finch," Enthoven said, nodding to the bright-eyed woman who sat behind the desk.

The librarian gave them a cheerful wave as the principal led them up a set of stairs to a mezzanine level that looked down over the stacks of books. Two kids sat on a sofa in the half-light engaged in what Porter's mum had always called heavy petting. Enthoven cleared his throat and they snapped apart like a firecracker had gone off on their lips, the boy almost screaming.

"Didn't you two have enough to eat at lunch?" the principal said. "Go on, get to your classes."

They scarpered, almost tumbling down the stairs in their bid to escape. Enthoven offered Savage the sofa but she shook her head. Porter stayed standing too, barely room for him beneath the low ceiling.

"This is about Chase?" Enthoven said. "Do you know any more?"

"How much have you been told?" Savage asked.

"Enough. Chase's aunt called this morning and told us that Blake wouldn't be in. She said that Chase had passed away. I can't tell you how sorry I was to hear it. How did he, uh...?"

"He was murdered," said Savage. There was a tightness to her voice that Porter hadn't heard before, and she paced the small space like a caged tiger. "Friday night, we think. Somebody killed him, then dragged his body into the woods."

Enthoven put a hand to his mouth, shaking his head.

"Can you tell us if he had any enemies?" Porter asked. "Or friendships that might have gone wrong. Did he ever get in trouble?"

"Chase? Never. He was a good student—not a great one, not a model one, but he put his head down. He wasn't academic but he loved his cars, he was going to pursue a vocational qualification after he left sixth form. I..." He moved his hand to his forehead, looking like a Rodin statue as he concentrated. "I can't think of anything he might have done that would have led to this. He had a small group of friends, not a troublemaker amongst them, and he was hanging around with Lauren Skinner, do you know her?"

Porter nodded.

"Now *she's* a model student. Great things ahead of her. Her dad's a governor here, nice guy, if a little imposing. Greg Skinner."

Savage flinched, her hands bunched by her sides. She opened her mouth but nothing came out. Porter stepped gently in front of her, although he had no idea why. Enthoven didn't seem to notice. He turned to the sofa as if there was somebody still sitting on it.

"I'm not sure how this will affect her. Or Blake, for that matter." He turned back. "How is he? That poor kid, he's been through some bad times."

"Blake?" Porter said. "How so?"

"Oh, you know, his dad isn't particularly nice."

"I'm aware," Porter said. "But he's not been around much, right?"

"No, as far as I know. His mum's not well, MS I think. Early stages, but the boys were finding it hard. Blake isn't like his big brother, he's not as strong. He was bullied here for quite a while."

"Chase never tried to stop it?" Porter asked.

"I'm sure he did, but there's only so much one can do in these situations. Blake always felt, I don't know, *breakable* somehow. He was one of the students we felt was vulnerable, one we made an effort to look out for."

He shook his head.

"Born under an unlucky star, I feel."

"Yeah," Porter said.

Savage stepped out from behind him, her phone in her hand.

"Mr Enthoven, I'm afraid that this isn't the only thing we need to discuss. What I'm about to tell you must remain confidential, for now. Chase isn't the only boy who has been murdered. Last night another young man was killed. We haven't managed to identify him. Would you mind taking a look? It's not easy, I'm afraid, but we'd appreciate your help."

"I... I can do that for you," the man said, holding out a hand. His big eyes blinked in the gloom, uncertain. Savage passed him the phone and Porter saw the boy's face, thankfully unmarked by injury or blood. His eyes were closed, but there was no mistaking it for sleep. This was death, quiet and unforgettable. Enthoven swallowed hard, then again, then he shook his head. "I'm very sorry, he isn't one of ours."

Savage took the phone back and tucked it into her pocket.

"Can you tell me about Greg Skinner?" Savage said. "You must know him well."

"I do," said Enthoven. "My father went to school with him, right here. So did Miss Finch downstairs, for that matter. He's an upstanding member of our vibrant little community."

"You're not the first person to use those words," Porter said. "Those *exact* words."

"Well, it's true," the principal said. "He's been a governor here for longer than I've been a teacher, and you won't find many people who speak ill of him. He provides abundant opportunities for students to find their passion in life, their voice. Troubled students especially. We have three on placement with him right now."

"Boys?" Savage said.

"Yes, why?"

"Because we have reason to believe Skinner was abusing teenage boys. We're not certain exactly how."

"What?" Enthoven spluttered. "No, that's preposterous. It's *untrue*. Let me speak with him, there's been some misunderstanding here."

"I'm afraid that's impossible," Porter said. "Greg Skinner is dead."

Enthoven's mouth gaped like a fish, the quiet in the library suddenly unbearable, like it meant to crush them.

"Did Skinner ever take Chase on as an apprentice? Or Blake?" Porter asked.

"No, never," said Enthoven, just a whisper.

"We'll need a list of boys who did," Savage added. "Now, if you can."

"Uh, of course," he said. "Come with me, I'll get you everything you need."

He squeezed delicately between them, heading for the stairs.

"You say your dad knew Greg when they went to school," Porter said as they followed. "Did he know James Preston too?"

"Sure. They weren't friends or anything, but he knew them."

"Did he say what they were like?"

They reached the bottom of the stairs, the library deserted now, and Enthoven stopped, chewing on something. He was stooped, as if somewhere between Porter and Savage arriving and this moment in time his back had been broken. He looked at the chair where the librarian had been sitting, then at Porter, something wanting out.

"Whatever it is, you can tell us," Porter said.

Enthoven shook his head, laughing uncomfortably. He set off and Porter met Savage's eyes again.

"Mr Enthoven," the DI said.

"It's nothing," the man went on. "I was just remembering something my dad told me. Greg Skinner and James Preston, they were in a band together. Heavy metal, I think. Not for long, because they got banned from performing."

They'd reached the reception desk and Enthoven leant on it like he was about to keel over.

"Dad said they performed as part of the school's Christmas concert, an original song. Bear in mind the whole school was there, Year Eight and up. I can't remember exactly, but I think they said the C-word half a dozen times before the power was cut. Dad said it was the best thing that ever happened at school, other than meeting mum."

He laughed.

"I'm not sure why I'm telling you this, sorry. I think it's to do with the way Greg is—sorry, *was*. Preston too, although I never met him. They thought they were rock stars when they were younger. They entered some battle of the bands in Norwich a few weeks later and for a little while it looked like they might have gone somewhere. Then the whole thing collapsed. Preston got expelled or something. I can't remember."

"Would your dad mind if we spoke to him about it?" Savage said.

"He would have loved it, but sadly we lost him a couple of years back. Mum's not been herself since either, I don't think she'd be much help. Oh, I do have something, though. Bear with me."

He trotted off around the partition and Porter heard a knock, then muffled voices. He returned a minute or so later with a large scrapbook, thumping it onto the reception desk hard enough to release a cloud of dust.

"Hang on," he said. "It'll be in here somewhere."

He flicked through yellowing newspaper clippings of sports victories and fashion shows, ribbon-cuttings and charity car washes, before opening the book fully and tapping on a badly clipped article from the local newspaper. A photograph almost too dark to decipher showed James Preston on stage playing the guitar, his face partially concealed by his long hair. Next to him was Greg Skinner, taller and skinnier and with a full head of hair but instantly recognisable. His hands gripped the microphone like he was wringing the life out of it, his mouth twisted open mid-song, his face full of anger. If there was anyone else in the band they were out of sight in the shadows of the stage, but Porter wasn't looking for them, he was reading the article.

"Holy shit," he said quietly.

He watched Savage as she caught up, seeing her expression change.

"That's what they were called?" she asked, pointing at the article.

Enthoven leaned in and nodded.

"Like I said, it was heavy metal. It always sounded angry, cruel. I couldn't think of a better name for a band like that than the *Heartless Boys*."

CHAPTER TWENTY-ONE

SAVAGE DIDN'T THINK SHE'D EVER BEEN SO HAPPY TO step out into the freezing rain. As soon as the automatic doors slid shut behind her she heaved in an almighty breath, planting her hands on her hips to centre herself. For a second back there, when Principle Enthoven had been talking about Greg Skinner, she'd thought she was going to vomit. The words had picked her up and carried her back to the man in the woods, his blood-throttled final breath, his mad, wild, roving eye.

The world moved in like it meant to swallow her whole. Then, just as she was about to fall, Porter was there, one big hand on her arm. The touch anchored her, it made the horizon level out again, and even when the vertigo had passed she didn't shake him off.

"Go home," he said. "Nobody expects you to be here, Kate, not after what happened."

"I'm fine, sir," she said, struggling to find oxygen in the scraps of air she was pulling in. She forced herself to slow down, taking a big breath through her nose and holding it. She released it gently through her lips. "I'm fine."

"Then—" Porter started, but he was cut off by a voice.

"Excuse me?"

Savage looked past Porter's barn-door of a chest to see a woman emerge from the school doors. It was the librarian, Miss Finch, pulling her striped woollen cardigan tight against the cold. She had to be closing in on fifty, and she moved with a pronounced limp that made her slow down well before she reached them.

"I'm sorry," she said. "I overheard some of what you were saying. You can hear everything in the mezzanine when you're downstairs. Did you say that Chase Masefield had been..."

She lunged the last few yards, her chin thrust out like she was crossing a finish line. Glancing left, then right, she continued to speak in a whisper.

"That he'd been *murdered*?"

"I'm afraid so," said Porter. "On Friday. Did you know him? Miss Finch, wasn't it?"

"Phoebe," she said. "Not well enough. He wasn't a book lover, him or his little brother. It's shocking. You say there were two boys?"

Porter nodded, looking at Savage. She took the hint, pulling out her phone and accessing the photograph she'd taken of the second victim.

"It's not easy to see," she said, holding back.

"I know death," said Phoebe. "We've had more than our fair share of it in my family."

She took the phone, studying it for the better part of a minute before handing it back.

"What did Mr Enthoven say?" she asked.

"That he wasn't one of yours," Savage replied. "Was he?"

Miss Finch hesitated, evidently torn. She glanced back

at the school before leaning in, speaking so quietly that Savage and Porter both had to huddle in too, their faces almost touching.

"He's not," she said. "But he was once. Bartley Hearn. Came from a community of, uh, what's the right term, Travellers? Not Gypsies, I know that much."

"How long ago was this?" Savage asked, and the librarian sucked her teeth.

"I'd say three years ago now. Bart and his big sister attended the school for a few months, never took to it. Left without any kind of warning or notice."

"Why wouldn't Mr Enthoven tell us this?" Porter said, glaring at the doors like he was about to march back through them.

"I don't know. I really don't. Ben's a good man but he's a stickler for the rules, and he's as straight as they come in every sense of the word. Norfolk born and bred. He never liked those kids, made things very difficult for them. I'm not saying he threatened them or anything but he didn't have much love for their way of life and I never once saw him take their side in an argument, even when they weren't at fault."

"You're sure this is Bart?" Savage asked.

"I am. He doesn't look a day older than he did when I last saw him. I always tried to get him into the library, you know? Thought I was winning him around until he upped and left. Never did hear what happened to the family, and I can't say my heart isn't broken knowing that he died like this."

She wiped the back of her hand over her eyes, her face full of grief.

"He deserves, at the very least, to be reunited with his family. Do you know who did it?"

"Not yet," said Savage. "But we will."

"I hope you catch him. I hope you make him pay."

"Me too," said Porter. "Do you know the names of Bart's parents, by any chance?"

"No, sorry." She sighed, then suddenly brightened. "But I do remember the sister. Chloe, her name was. Chloe Hearn. She'd be, what? Twenty-one by now? Twenty-two at a pinch."

"Thank you," said Savage. "That's been very helpful."

"You were at this school, right?" Porter asked. "You don't happen to remember Greg Skinner and James Preston, do you?"

The librarian nodded, managing a smile.

"They were in the year above me but everyone remembers them."

"Because of the band?"

She laughed, lost in a memory.

"That stupid band, yes. People talked about it for years. They still do."

"*Heartless Boys*," said Savage. "Weird name, don't you think?"

"No weirder than the first name they had. Uh, I think it was the *Pumpkin Heads*. Or *Turnip Heads* maybe, this being Norfolk. And afterwards they were the *Heartless Boys*, then they were the *Church of the Heartless Boys*, or something ridiculously pretentious like that. They had more names for the band than they had weeks actually in it."

"They ever get in any other trouble?"

"No." Miss Finch laughed. "Jimmy and Greg weren't bad kids, just mischievous."

"Do you remember the other members of the band, by any chance?" Savage asked.

The librarian looked up at the sky, lost in the dark clouds.

"Let me think," she said after a moment. "The guy on the bass was called Pete Little, which everyone thought was hilarious because he was actually huge. Tallest kid in the school by a long shot. The drummer was, uh... I think he was French. I remember everyone called him Michelle, but of course it would have been Michael. I don't remember his surname."

"Thank you," Porter said, making a note of it. He reached for a card and realised he didn't have any left. Savage took the hint, handing over one of hers.

"Let us know if you think of anything else," she said.

Miss Finch stood there expectantly, and when nobody else spoke she muttered a quiet "oh" and turned around, limping back to the doors.

"Why the fuck wouldn't the principal tell us that?" Porter said.

"Maybe he didn't recognise him. A lot of kids must pass through here. Maybe he didn't look."

"Maybe."

Porter huffed a breath.

"This case is getting to me," he said. "I honestly haven't got a clue what's going on."

"Let's head back to base, guv. Get it all on the wall, see if we can make some sense of it."

Porter nodded, pulling his keys from his pocket.

"Race you," he said.

"You'll lose."

Porter laughed as he made for his Mondeo. Savage took a look at the school, scanning the cloud-drenched first-floor windows and seeing Ben Enthoven staring back at her, his face carved from stone. After a second or two, he turned away and disappeared into the dark.

———

SAVAGE TOOK the pen from her mouth and wrote Bartley Hearn on the whiteboard, trying not to inhale the fumes. She stood back, seeing her careless scribbles and smudging them out with her sleeve.

Bart deserved more than that.

She wrote his name again with greater care, and this time when she'd finished she turned back to see Colin Clare watching her from the Incident Room door.

"Bartley Hearn," he said. "We're sure about that?"

Savage nodded, picking up a printout from the desk. On it was a photograph of the boy, very much alive, that she'd pulled from Google. Hearn hadn't had a social media presence, not one that she could find, anyway, but he'd cropped up in a search because he'd been part of a boxing club down in Thetford. The photo was dated eighteen months ago, and in it Hearn stood with three other boys, all of them posing with their shirts off and their gloves on, a trainer standing behind them. He was a handsome kid, with thick, curly blonde hair all the way down past his shoulders. The hair had gone by the time he'd been killed, but there was no doubt at all that this was the same boy they'd found on the stone.

"He was nineteen," she said. "Family left Dereham three years ago and moved south, to Thetford. Dunst is trying to put together a timeline but I don't think he enrolled in another school. No arrest record. Not much on him at all, to be honest. The dad died last year, mum migrated overseas when the kids were little."

"Kids?"

"Yes, sir. He has a sister, Chloe. We're trying to find her too."

Clare nodded, leaning out of the door and bellowing into the bullpen. He walked to the front of the room with a collection of papers clutched to his chest. One slipped free and when he bent down to collect it the rest followed. The Super swore beneath his breath as he tried to scoop them up, looking like a scarecrow blowing in a hurricane.

"You need a hand, boss?" Porter asked as he walked through the door.

"Thank you, Pete," Clare barked, and Porter was halfway to him before he stood straight and carried on. "Thirty years in the police, achieved the rank of Superintendent, a number of commendations, shot, stabbed and a multitude of other injuries. I *definitely* need your help picking up a piece of paper."

He shot Porter a look that sent the big DI scuttling off to the nearest desk. DI Dunst walked in, yawning, and DS Alison Spalding followed.

"Kett's car not available this afternoon?" she asked, earning a scowl from Clare.

"Where are we, people?" the Super said. "I have a press conference in fifteen minutes and it would be nice to have some tossing news to give them."

"I wouldn't give them that," Porter muttered.

"Two victims, three days apart," Clare said, pointing to the photographs tacked onto the wall behind him. "Chase Masefield, seventeen, and now we have Bartley Hearn, nineteen. Both tortured, both with their throats slit, and both with their hearts removed."

"Has Emily done the autopsy on Hearn yet, sir?" Savage asked.

"He's on her table as we speak," said Clare. "She'll call when she's done. Who are our suspects?"

"Chase's dad, James Preston, was looking like a good fit," Porter said. "Absolute arsehole, doesn't give a shit about his sons. Didn't even bat an eyelid when I told him about Chase. He says he has an alibi for both deaths, a woman. They were at the pub until four in the morning, but we'll need the video footage to make sure he didn't slip out."

"Skinner?" Clare asked.

Savage closed her eyes, forcing herself not to see the man's face and seeing it anyway, his single eye rolling in its bloody socket.

"His family is adamant that he walked back to the house with them after Chase left on Friday," said Dunst. "Matilda said he was with her all night."

"I think she'd say anything to protect her husband," Clare said. "I wouldn't take her word as gospel."

"Yeah, but Lauren backs her up. She didn't sleep on Friday night, she was worried about Chase, thought she'd upset him, and she says she would have heard her father if he'd left the house. She strikes me as an honest kid who doesn't necessarily have all that much love for her dad."

"And last night Matilda picked Skinner up from the nick and drove him home," said Spalding. "Claims he never left."

"I had a car on the house all night," Clare said. "No sign of anyone leaving. Who else?"

"What if Skinner and Preston were working together?" Savage said. "They went to school at the same time, in Dereham. The principal told us they were in a band together. You want to hazard a guess at the name?"

Clare answered the question with an impatient glare.

"The *Heartless Boys*," she went on. "That's some coincidence."

"Or not," Clare said.

"We've seen it before, sir. Two criminals working together. James Preston and Greg Skinner start a metal band together back in the late seventies. Maybe they got carried away?"

Even as she said it, Savage realised how crazy it sounded.

"I checked the other two band members," Porter said, studying his notes. "The librarian at Nelson gave us their names. Pete Little died of a traumatic aortic rupture in '06. The French kid had to have been Michel Debussy. He's lived in Montreal for the last twenty years, never been back."

"If it's Skinner and Preston then they would have been behind the Somerset killings too," Clare asked. "Plausible?"

"Preston's never left Norfolk," Porter said. "I mean, he's never lived anywhere else. Local boy through and through."

"Skinner too," said Spalding. "But I'll double-check."

Clare's phone rang from his pocket, loud enough to shatter glass. He pulled it out, answered it, then laid it on the desk in front of him.

"You're on speaker, Emily."

"Then I'd best behave," said the young pathologist. "I've finished with the kid, the second one. Want to take a guess at how he died? Porter, you there? Do you want to guess?"

"No," said Porter, pouting.

"Are you sure?"

"I'm not going to say the heart," Porter said. "I'm not falling for that again. It was his throat."

"Idiot," Franklin said. "He died from the injury to his heart. Somebody drove a blade between his ribs, straight into the left atrium. He would have bled out in seconds, and he would have felt every one of them. The killer used the same knife to carve out the organ, no ripping this time. It wasn't a neat job, though, he was hacking hard and fast—sixty-three separate thrusts to sever it."

Porter grimaced.

"The kid's throat was cut almost as an afterthought. There was absolutely no chance of him being alive at this point. Oh, and he was riddled with injuries, just like the last one. No drag marks this time, though. The killer moved him more carefully, he might have lifted him."

"Good work," said Clare. "Anything else?"

"That's not enough for you?" she replied, and Savage heard her take a sip of a drink. "He had dust on his face as well, gypsum. Tape residue in his hair. He was wearing a mask, no doubt about it. But the killer must have learned from his mistakes because as far as I can see the only blood on this victim's body is his own, there's no secondary bleeding source. There is something, though. I found lip marks."

"You found *what*?" Porter asked.

"A kiss," she said. "Imagine lipstick, only this was with blood."

"You're saying the killer kissed him?" Savage asked.

"He did. It was on the side of his chest, almost on the armpit. There's a perfect imprint of his lips. One kiss, he must have had blood all over him. I've sent it to the lab but I don't think it will help you."

"Thank you," Clare said, ending the call. The Super paced back and forth, one hand rubbing the wound in his head. He winced, checking his fingertips for blood, then turned to the room.

"The dust you found on Preston's floor, what was it?"

"I gave it to Spalding," Porter said, looking at her.

"Plaster of Paris," she said. "Gypsum. Lab said it was similar to the stuff they found on Masefield, but not identical."

"Right," Clare said. "It's close enough. Bring Preston in, just for questioning. But if he resists, arrest him. If nothing else, we can at least try to match the print of his lips."

"I'll do it," Porter said, grinning as he pushed himself up. "I think he likes me."

He walked out of the room and Savage leaned back in her chair, exhausted.

"Tell me," said Clare. "From what you've all seen, is this over?"

"There were two dead boys in Somerset with their hearts torn out," Savage said. "But maybe a third that was killed at the same time and found later."

"And there were three kids in the Rudston case in Yorkshire, right?" Spalding said. "All with their hearts removed."

"And two in Neath," said Dunst. "Followed by a lot more killing. I don't think our man is done."

"Me neither," said Savage. "My instincts say he's going to kill again. And soon."

"Then we go public. We issue a warning." Clare hung his head for a second before looking up again. "The Hateful Thing is here."

CHAPTER TWENTY-TWO

Porter saw the smoke before he saw the fire.

"Fuck," he said as he steered the Mondeo around the corner, loose gravel making the car slide. He pumped the brakes, shuddering to a stop. It was just as well because there was a fire engine in the middle of the street, the fire-fighters already out and wrestling with the hose. The constable from earlier was there, looking mightily sheepish.

Behind them, James Preston's cottage was a pyre. The whole building was engulfed in flames, the inferno singeing Porter's skin even from fifty yards away as he climbed out of the car. A roiling wall of smoke joined the black clouds, turning the overcast afternoon into night. He coughed, then fished out his warrant card as one of the firemen ran his way.

"Police," he said, spluttering.

"I don't care if you're the Queen," the man said through his mask. "Stay back."

"I was here this afternoon, there was a man inside, James Preston."

"Thanks," said the firefighter as he ran back to the engine.

"Do I look like the bloody Queen?" Porter muttered, turning to the constable and making a gesture with his arms that clearly said *What the fuck happened here?*

"Uh," said the young PC, his hat clenched in both hands. "I honestly don't know. I was watching the cottage, I didn't see anyone. Then I saw the flames in the window and called it in." He checked his watch. "Thirty-eight minutes ago."

"You're sure nobody left?" Porter said.

"Not out the front door," the PC replied.

"So what happened to his fucking car?"

The Morris Traveller had gone, and the young PC's mouth fell open.

"Uh... That must have happened when I was calling it in," he said eventually. "Sorry."

"Right. Well, you sharted that one up royally. Get out there, try and find him."

The PC nodded, relieved to be let go. Porter watched the firefighters work but there wasn't much they could do. In less than a minute the cottage gave up the ghost, the battered roof crumbling into ash and blasting out another wave of heat as it collapsed. The fire was spreading into the garden, tongues of flame exploring the statues there. The building groaned like a dying animal, the sulphuric smell of it unbearable. The hose was out, but it wasn't on. The lead firefighter motioned for everyone to move back. They were going to let it burn out.

It didn't take long, the flames guttering, burning vivid shades of blue and green as they fought for the last few scraps of life. The air was damp and the rain was still falling, and there couldn't have been much fuel in the cottage's mould-blackened walls. Only when the flames were on their last legs did the hose spring to life, the hiss of steam replacing the roar of smoke until all that remained was a quagmire.

Shapes remained in the filth, almost unbearably human, hints of bone and charred flesh. Porter heard a cry of alarm from one of the firefighters before they worked out what they were looking at. Statues, dozens of them. The fire had rejected them.

Porter coughed the acrid dust from his lungs and watched the men and women move in, combing the sludge for survivors. It was a small space and it didn't take long.

"Nobody there?" Porter asked.

"It's clear," said the man he'd spoken to before, pulling off his helmet to reveal a hard but kind face, the soot-filled wrinkles etched into his skin like pencil marks. "You were expecting somebody?"

"Wasn't sure, to be honest," Porter said. "I was here earlier, spoke to the man who owns the place. Came back to arrest him."

"Came too late," the firefighter said. "Hang around if you like, see what we pull up?"

"No, but if you find anything give us a call, yeah?"

The man nodded and they both turned to the scene, to the statues that stuck up from the ground like the stumps of rotting teeth.

"What's all that about?" the firefighter asked.

"Art. If you can call it that. So shit even the fire didn't want them."

"Plaster of Paris," the firefighter said. "Gypsum. Doesn't burn."

"Gypsum. You know if it's used for anything else? We

found some in the hair of a murder victim, just dust. We can't figure out why."

The man shrugged.

"Can't tell you, I'm afraid. They use it in plaster, though, don't they? For the walls? My other half's old man was a plasterer, covered in dust he was, all day and all night. Used to call it spear stone."

"Spear stone?" Porter said, frowning. "Why?"

The man shrugged.

"No idea."

One of the firefighters called out and the man put on his helmet, patting it down.

"I'll call you if we find anything," he said. "Good luck with the murder."

Porter nodded to the man's back before walking to the car. His mind was wheeling, and it was only partly to do with the toxic fumes in the air. That was twice, now, that they'd spoken to somebody about the dead boys only for something bad to follow. For Greg Skinner, it had been fatal, the actions of a guilty man. The same might be said for Preston if they found his body.

Once was weird. Twice was suspicious.

Porter didn't think they'd find Preston's body, though. This felt like a diversion. If Preston had killed his son and Bartley Hearn then he'd be on the run, and setting fire to his house was one way of slowing down the police.

He climbed into the car, rainwater dripping down his face like he was being tortured. He started the engine before making a call on his phone, so that it would feed through the speakers. As it rang, he performed the world's longest three-point turn, losing a fair bit of paintwork on the high verge.

"What?" barked Clare's voice.

"Nice to speak to you too, sir," Porter said.

"It's not nice though, is it? I hear your voice and I'm instantly annoyed. *It's Porter*, I think, *what's he screwed up this time? The suspect shot himself, a dog bit my arsehole, the house burned down*, it's always something. What is it this time?"

"Uh," Porter said. "I'm at Preston's house. It, uh, burned down."

"See!" Clare said. "I knew it. Where is he? Dead?"

"I don't know. They're looking for him. I think he's probably done a runner."

"That's great!" said Clare, positively hysterical. "Another suspect down the drain. Go find him, Pete."

"I'm going—"

The speakers clicked as the Superintendent hung up. Porter threw his middle finger up in the vague direction of the console, slowing to a crawl as he checked for traffic on the main road. He indicated right, for Norwich, but turned left instead, some instinct calling him back towards Lesser Lyng, towards the Masefield house.

I made them, so I own them, Preston had said, his twisted idea of fatherhood.

It was a short drive, the night moving in so fast it was like the whole world was sinking into a muddy pit. Somebody else was parked at the corner of the narrow road where he usually left his car, so he had to drive past Blake's house and around the next bend, leaving the Mondeo right up against a hedge so that traffic could squeeze past. He hopped out, stretching his back as he walked back along the street. The curtains were drawn and the house had a stillness that felt too much like death. When Porter knocked on the door it seemed to swallow the sound.

Still, after a moment or two, he heard the key in the lock. It was Audrey Masefield who answered, and she looked like she'd been crying. She blinked up at him through swollen eyes, then stepped out into the street in her bare feet, pulling the door shut behind her.

"You've got news?" she said quietly. "I don't think Cathy's in any place to hear it. She's in a bad way."

"Sorry," Porter said, keeping his voice down. "I just wanted to make sure you were okay, that Blake was okay. I visited with his father earlier."

"What did that piece of shit have to say for himself?"

"Not much. And piece of shit is right. I spoke with him and left him. Just went back and he's set his bloody house on fire."

Audrey didn't seem surprised.

"I just wanted to make sure he hasn't turned up here," Porter said.

"If he does, I'll fucking castrate him," she said.

"Well keep your door locked, okay? Windows too. If you see him, don't speak to him, don't even engage with him. Just call 999."

"You think he killed Chase?" she said, full of fury. "I fucking knew it. I hope he burned to death."

"We don't know that," said Porter. "Just watch out for him, okay? Is Blake in?"

"He is, but he's having some quiet time. I gave him one of my pills, just a Valium. It's probably best he doesn't see you here."

"Fair enough," Porter said. "Listen, you said you went to school around here, didn't you? In Dereham?"

She nodded.

"Same school as Preston? And Greg Skinner?"

"No, Cath and I were across town, the grammar school. We weren't complete fuck-ups. Why?"

"Did you know them, back then? Preston and Skinner

were tight, they were in a band."

Audrey bit her lip, thinking for a moment before shaking her head.

"I mean, maybe," she said. "Wasn't everyone in a band back in the Eighties?"

"They called themselves..." he hesitated, not sure if he should say it. "The *Heartless Boys*. That was their name."

She took a step back, shivering hard.

"I'm really sorry, I can't remember."

"I do," came a voice from the house. The door opened and Porter saw Cathy there, dressed in thick pyjamas and a dressing gown. If Audrey's face showed signs of grief then Cathy's was infinitely worse. It was so puffy that it looked like overcooked meat ready to slide right off the bone.

"Hey," Porter said, and she tried and failed to smile at him.

"Why are you asking about the band?" she said.

"Because Greg Skinner and James Preston seem to have something to do with this. I don't know what. I don't know if the band is relevant. I'm just trying to put the pieces together in my head. You remember?"

"Of course," Cathy said. "I met Jimmy at one of his gigs. It's how we got together. They were so awful. I stood right by the speakers and I think my ears still ring sometimes because of it. He was handsome back then, before I worked out he was a worthless prick."

"They were in it with another couple of lads, right?" Porter asked. Cathy shrugged.

"Couple of kids from the year above," she said. "I can't remember the other guitar player's name, the bassist. Wait, wasn't it Pete? Tall Pete?"

"Pete Little," said Audrey. "That's right."

"I think he died," Cathy went on. "Poor thing. He had

three kids. Who was the drummer?"

"That French guy," said Audrey. "The cute one. Michelle, wasn't it? But the French version. *Michel*."

Cathy frowned as she tried to remember.

"His surname was Deschanel or something weird," Audrey went on. "Debussy. Debassy. I don't know."

"Michel Debussy," Porter said, and Audrey nodded.

"French?" said Cathy, frowning. "My memory is shot."

"You know what happened to them?" Porter asked.

"This was thirty years ago," Audrey said. "And they had that band for about three months."

"Fair enough."

Porter stood there for a moment, the rain running off the end of his nose.

"I just wanted to check," he said. "Remember, lock your doors."

"You want to come in?" Cathy said.

"You shouldn't," Audrey replied, giving her sister a look. "Blake needs his rest, I don't think it's good for—"

"It's fine," said a voice from the dark, and Porter had to duck down to see Blake Masefield standing in the living room door. He was holding his controller, and even though there was no sign of tears it was obvious he was holding them in with every ounce of strength he had. His face was a dam, ready to crack. "I'm about to prestige, wanna watch?"

Porter looked down the street, seeing nothing but the settling dark. He looked the other way, wondering if Preston was staring back from the shadows. He thought of Allie, his wife, waiting for him in a house that seemed far too big, and far too empty. He thought of the cold looks, the accusations, the tears.

"Sure," he said, ducking down to step beneath the low lintel. "Just for a minute."

CHAPTER TWENTY-THREE

IT WAS THE DOORBELL THAT WOKE HIM.

Kett opened his eyes, feeling for a moment like he was underwater. He sat up sharply, crying out as the pain remembered what it was supposed to be doing. Clamping a hand to his chest, he took a couple of shallow breaths until the panic had passed.

By that time, he'd noticed that he wasn't alone in the living room. Evie sat to his left, looking fearfully up at him—as if it wasn't her dad who had spluttered awake beside her but a monster. She was holding a pen in her hand like she might be about to whack him with it. On his other side sat Moira, oblivious, her big blue eyes locked on the TV where *Bing* was moaning about something like only that miserable-arsed bunny could. Kett turned back to Evie, trying to fashion his face into a smile. It was like wrestling with a leather boot.

"Hey," he croaked. "You okay?"

"Yeah," she said, although she didn't look it. She looked scared.

"Mr Marshmallow?" he asked.

She didn't have a chance to reply before the doorbell went again. It was dark outside, the curtains wide open and the rain battering the windows like fists. Kett felt ridiculously exposed sitting here on the sofa with the lights blazing.

"Where's mummy?" he asked, trying to sit up. The pain was worse than ever, like a knife worrying its way into his heart, and he tried to remember the last time he'd taken painkillers. He didn't even remember falling asleep. It was his own fault he was so exhausted. He'd pushed himself way too far today.

"Having a poo," Evie said.

"Bath!" Moira countered, without taking her eyes from the TV.

"She's having a poo in the bath?" Kett said, attempting a joke.

"Yeah," Evie replied, a smile finding its way to her face.

The doorbell went again, followed by the hammering of a fist. Kett heard water upstairs, followed by Billie's voice.

"Robbie?"

"I'll get it," he said, just a whisper. He cleared his throat and tried again. "I'll get it."

"Sorry," she called back.

More hammering, urgent this time. Kett struggled to his feet, shuffling across the room like an old man. There was a figure at the door, the patterned glass turning it into a pig-faced monster that made Kett's blood run cold. It loomed in, one dark eye blinking as it tried to see inside. Kett leaned on the doorframe, aware of how weak he was, how vulnerable. He had visions of opening the door and seeing Schofield there, vast and terrifying, those giant hands pulling him to pieces before starting work on his wife, on his daughters. He wouldn't be able to do a damned thing about it.

"Who is it?" he shouted.

"I need to speak to you," came the reply, high and muffled.

"About what?" Kett said, taking a step towards the door.

"The Hateful Thing."

"Who is it, dad?" Alice shouted from upstairs. She appeared on the landing, the chinchilla cradled in her arms. Alice was very much a child of the day. If it had been light outside she'd have charged down like the Secret Service, ripping the door open and throwing herself at whoever was outside. But as soon as night fell all of that confidence vanished and the smoke-filled nightmares rolled back into her thoughts.

Kett was the same, now. He knew what lived out there in the dark.

"I'm not part of the case," he said. "You need to call DI Porter, or DC Savage. If you wait there I'll get their numbers for you."

"I don't want to talk to them," the man said. "I want to talk to you. You'll listen to me."

Kett sighed.

"You want to start by telling me your name?" he said.

"Norman," the man said. "Norman Balls."

"That's not a name. That's an insult."

"It's my name," the man protested, and Kett remembered hearing it earlier. Balls had been in the back of Savage's IRV when they'd had the meeting in the Volvo. "Please," he went on. "I've found something."

"Who is it?" Billie called from upstairs, a note of worry in her voice.

"It's fine," Kett said. "It's the... neighbours."

He slid the safety chain into its socket then wrenched the stubborn door open a crack. Norman Balls peered up at him through his wire-frame glasses, his brow creasing into an expression of puzzlement. His face was round and covered in little scratches—presumably from the hedge incident that Savage had told him about. There was something mole-like about him, something that reminded Kett of Penfold from the old cartoon—especially given the brown anorak that was zipped tight beneath his double chin. There was absolutely nothing about him that seemed dangerous, but even so, Kett kept the chain on.

"Robert Kett," said Balls. He slid a damp hand through the crack as if he expected Kett to shake it. He was disappointed. "I've wanted to meet you for a while now, ever since the whole Pig thing. I've got so many questions."

"I've got zero answers. Why are you here?"

Balls studied Kett's face like he was looking for something.

"Um..." he said.

"The Hateful Thing," Kett prompted.

"Oh, right." Balls shivered, looking through the door the same way a dog might if it had been locked outside. Kett thought he could hear him whimpering. "I know you're not police anymore, but I saw you at headquarters earlier—"

"Hush," Kett said, glancing back. He hadn't told Billie where he'd been that morning, but only because she hadn't asked.

"Sorry," Balls whispered, leaning in. Water dripped off his nose and his teeth chattered. "You're familiar with the other crimes he's associated with? Somerset, East Yorkshire, Neath, those ones?"

Kett glanced back to make sure nobody was listening. Alice and the chinchilla had gone, and Evie was whispering conspiratorially to Moira on the sofa.

"All young adults with their hearts removed. Yeah, we know."

"Do you know about Skegness?" he said. "1996."

Kett waited, and Balls leaned in even further, like he was trying to push his face through the gap.

"Six teenagers dead over the course of three days, their bodies burned."

"That doesn't sound anything like what we're dealing with now," Kett said.

"That's what I thought. But I checked the medical reports and—"

"How?" Kett asked, and Balls seemed to wink with both eyes.

"I have my sources. Six dead, and all but one of them were missing their hearts. I was looking into it, for my website. *Ballsknowsitalls.net*. Are you familiar with it?"

"I can't say that I am," Kett said.

Balls frowned.

"Well, it's worth a look, especially for a man like your-self. Plenty of stuff on there that can help your active cases."

"I'm not a copper anymore," Kett said.

"Sure," said Balls. "Not on paper. But anyway, they never caught the killer in Skegness, but those missing hearts, it has to be connected, right?

Kett shrugged, but Balls was undeterred.

"And I was looking into the Neath files again, because something didn't fit right with me. Two victims, right? Two young men with their throats cut and their hearts removed. I know it was him, the Hateful Thing, same guy who's out there right now killing kids. But what I couldn't figure out is why he only killed two people that time."

"He didn't just kill two in Neath," Kett said. "He killed a lot more. Fourteen, wasn't it?"

"Yeah, but they're different. The heartless victims are ritual killings, they have to be. It's so specific. The victims are tortured, their throats are cut, their hearts removed. It's his signature. But why sometimes two victims and sometimes three?"

"Maybe he can't count," said Kett. The cold pushing into his chest, it was making his ribs scream, but he wasn't about to let Balls inside because he had the feeling he would never leave.

"No, that's not it," said Balls, taking Kett literally. "I think he always *tries* for three. It's like a challenge, or a test. But he can't always do it."

"So why do you think Skegness has anything to do with it, if he killed six people there?"

"Look at the dates. Skegness, Wales, Somerset, Yorkshire, and now here, all with a six-year gap between them, more or less. Always in the winter. I think there's meaning in those numbers, for him at least."

"That's it?" Kett said when Balls stopped.

"Uh, yes, that's what I wanted to tell you. It's good intel, right?"

"Nope," Kett said, shivering. "Look, I'm going to close my door now. I'll pass it on to the team."

"But—"

"The door is closing," Kett said, pushing it shut. "Goodnight, Normal Balls."

"*Norman*, and—"

The door clicked shut, Balls' smudged outline hanging in the glass for a good minute before the letterbox opened and a business card fell through.

"I'm available day or night," he shouted as he walked away. "And not just for this, Robbie. There are other things I can help with. Other things I can tell you."

Kett almost opened the door again, but Billie was walking down the stairs, wrapping her dressing gown around her.

"Who was that?" she asked.

"Just Frank from up the road," Kett said, lifting the business card from the mat and tucking it into his pocket. "Bloody weirdo, if you ask me."

Billie grinned.

"I'm sure he thought the same about you," she said. "Tea?"

"Sure. You didn't have to come out."

"I was in danger of dissolving," she said. "I didn't think you were going to fall asleep."

"What makes you think I was asleep?"

She laughed, leaning in and kissing him on the nose.

"I wasn't asleep," he protested as she walked away.

"You say that."

Mystified, Kett walked back into the living room, picking up his phone from the windowsill before drawing the curtains. Balls had melted into the night but he'd left Kett with an unpleasant feeling in his gut. How had he worked out his address? There was no way in hell that anyone from the department would have told him, and it wasn't a matter of public record. Balls would have had to be pretty resourceful to find him.

Resourceful, or dangerous.

It was always the ones you didn't suspect, after all. The quiet ones. People like Raymond Figg with his goatee beard and his tank tops. People like Joseph Bains and his chinchilla.

Are you the Hateful Thing, Balls? he asked. Then he scoffed. Balls would lose a fight to Maggie the chinchilla, he wouldn't have stood a chance against two fit and healthy teenage boys like Chase and Hearn—especially given that Hearn was a boxer.

"Daddy, can you play with us?" Evie asked.

"Play!" Moira demanded, sliding off the sofa and running to him. She was holding a couple of *Playmobil* people and she thrust one at him—a pink-cheeked princess. "Be this one."

"It's not long until bedtime," he said, wishing more than anything in the world that he could pick his youngest daughter up. She pushed the figure at him for a moment before giving up, sitting on the floor by his feet.

"I don't want to go to bed," Evie said. "Mr Marshmallow might be in the toilet."

He opened his mouth to tell her, for the millionth time, that Mr Marshmallow didn't exist. It was pointless, though, so he settled on a different tactic.

"Nothing can get you in this house, okay? This place is monster-proof."

She nodded, but she wasn't convinced. Kett limped to her and eased himself onto the sofa. Evie was still clutching her felt-tip and he held out his hand for it.

"Let me show you a secret," he said. "Give me the pen for a sec."

She passed it over and he pulled the lid off, drawing a wiggly line on the back of his hand.

"You know what this is?"

"Pen!" said Moira, waddling over.

"It's a secret," he said. "This is a very powerful mark that we use in the police. The Mark of... uh... Clare's Nostrils."

"The *what*?" Evie said, leaning over and studying it. "It looks like a worm."

"It's not a worm, it's a powerful mark. A rune."

"What's a rune?"

"A symbol that keeps you safe," he said. "If you have a mark like this, nothing can hurt you."

Evie frowned up at him.

"Really?"

"I promise," he said. "But only brave people can have it. That's why we use it in the Force. Are you brave?"

"My do it," Moira said, holding out her hand. Kett drew a squiggly line on it and she laughed as the pen tickled her.

"Now you're protected," Kett said. "Even from something like Mr Marshmallow. Evie?"

The four-year-old nodded, holding out her palm. Kett took his time, drawing the biggest wavy line he could between the base of her thumb and the base of her pinkie.

"Wow," he said, putting the cap back on. "You must be fearless."

Evie grinned, holding her hand up like *Iron Man*.

"Monsters be gone!" she yelled, leaping off the sofa. "Super Evie is here!"

She ran from the room, giggling like a lunatic, and Moira ran after her making *pow pow* noises. They clattered down the corridor like a herd of cattle, Billie yelping from the kitchen. Kett sat back as slowly as he dared, the pain in his chest like a welding iron. It made him think of the boys they'd found, about the agony they'd endured.

And he thought about Balls, about what the strange little man had asked.

Why sometimes two victims and sometimes three?

He was right, it didn't make sense.

He lifted his phone, firing a message to Savage.

The Hateful Thing. Were there definitely only two victims in Neath?

"That better not be work," said Billie as she walked into the living room, a mug of tea in each hand.

"It's definitely not," he said. "It's, uh, online gambling. I think I'm addicted."

"You're a *dick*, alright," Billie said, sitting next to him and putting the mugs on the floor. "But my name's not Ted."

Kett laughed, instantly regretting it. Billie laughed too, a laughter that she seemed to give herself to completely, that she seemed to lose herself in. It was laughter he hadn't seen since they'd first been courting, all those years ago when London hadn't seemed so frightening and when creatures like the Pig Man belonged only in fairy tales. It was so good to see, because in that beautiful act the horror that she'd been through shrank deeper into the shadows, and her scars faded further. She wiped a tear from her eye and rested her hand on his, her palm still hot from the tea.

"Do me a favour and use your phone for something useful," she said. "Like a mirror."

"A mirror?"

He flicked the iPhone back on and opened the camera. To be fair, Evie had done a pretty good job at colouring in his eyebrows and highlighting his freckles with the green felt-tip, but the lipstick was all over the place.

"Oh god," he said, remembering the puzzled look that Balls had given him when he'd opened the door, and his daughter's fear when he'd woken up. "Evie!"

The little girl screamed with frightened laughter as she thumped her way up the stairs.

"It was Moira!" she yelled from the top.

And even though he was annoyed, Kett didn't mind at all, not really, not when his wife was sitting next to him laughing. Not when things felt so close to being okay.

CHAPTER TWENTY-FOUR

IT WAS WAY TOO LATE FOR THIS, AND SHE WAS FAR TOO exhausted.

But some things couldn't wait.

Savage checked the clock on the dashboard, seeing that it was just after nine. The news was on the local radio, Clare's brash northern tones playing on repeat as he warned the county about the killer. He'd never actually mentioned a name, but somehow it was out there, riding the wind. It would be all over the papers tomorrow, all anyone was talking about.

The Hateful Thing.

It had taken her the better part of an hour to get to Thetford, an accident on the A11 slowing her down. She hadn't managed to find an address for Chloe Hearn, the second victim's sister, but the young woman was on Facebook and under *Employment* she'd listed a BP garage on the edge of the town. It was a long shot, but it had been worth it because even from where she'd parked on the forecourt, through the rain and the still-sweeping wipers, she could see Bartley's sister behind the counter. She was talking to a man in a fluorescent yellow jacket as he paid for his fuel, tucking a strand of hair behind her ear and laughing. He looked back more than once before he'd reached the door.

Savage waited for him to climb into his van and pull away before getting out of the Fiat and running through the blistering chill of the night. The heating in the garage was on full blast, like stepping into a warm bath, and she was shivering hard with the relief of it as the door closed behind her.

"Nasty out there," Chloe said, offering a smile from behind the counter. She was an attractive girl, there was no doubt about it, and she was every inch a member of the Hearn clan—the same fair hair and jutting cheekbones that her brother had, the same grey eyes. A badge on her green shirt confirmed her identity. "Fuel?"

"No," Savage said, pulling her warrant card out of her pocket as she walked to the counter. "I'm police. DC Kate Savage. Is there anywhere we can talk?"

The smile dropped from Chloe's face like it had been shot dead, replaced by fear and something else, something worse—a kind of awful, inevitable acceptance.

"It's just me here," she said, her long nails scratching mindlessly at the counter. "Is it about... is he *dead*?"

Savage opened her mouth, taken aback. Behind her, the door opened and a woman walked in, shaking herself like a wet dog as she made for the newspapers. Chloe didn't even notice, her eyes locked on Savage.

"Is he dead?" she said again.

"Your brother?" Savage asked. "Bartley?"

It was all the confirmation the girl needed. She swallowed hard, her fingers still scratching, scratching, scratching until Savage laid a cold hand on hers and stopped them.

"I'm so sorry," she said. "It happened last night."

"I knew it," Chloe said. "I knew it, I knew it. I tried calling him, I had such a bad feeling."

Savage felt the woman walk up behind her and she turned to her.

"Police," she said. "Take it, I'll pay."

"Oh," she said, looking at Chloe and nodding. "Of course."

She walked to the door and Savage followed her, turning the lock and flicking the sign to *Closed*. By the time she'd returned to the counter Chloe had managed to compose herself, but her whole body was trembling like it was about to explode.

"Would you like to sit down?" Savage asked, and she shook her head.

"Can't," she said. "People."

"I'll call somebody to take over."

"Can't," Chloe said and left it at that.

"I know how hard this is," Savage said. "It's going to get harder. But can you tell me why you were worried about your brother? Do you know where he was yesterday, who he was with?"

Chloe sniffed, groaning.

"I just... we're close, you know? But not like we used to be."

"When you were kids? In Dereham, right?"

She looked surprised.

"Yeah, for a bit anyways. We used to move around a lot but it all changed when da died. Settled down, you know?" She frowned. "Not proper though. I live on a mate's sofa bed at the moment. Shit credit."

"When was the last time you saw him?"

"Yesterday," she said. "He told me he had work, something out of town. He wouldn't tell me what it was so I figured it was something..."

"Naughty?" Savage prompted.

"He never did nothing too bad, just courier work sometimes."

"Drugs?"

"I don't know." She sniffed. "I don't want to talk bad about him, not now he's not here. He had a good heart, a big heart. Big enough for both of us, da always used to say. If he had money he'd always share it, always had big plans to..."

She groaned again, this time like she might vomit.

"I'm sorry," Savage said again. "Are you sure you don't want to—"

"I can't," she said, shaking her head, strands of hair pulling free.

The door rattled and Savage looked back to see an elderly man trying to open it.

"Wait," she said to him, turning back to the girl. "I don't care what he was doing. I don't care if it was something illegal, I promise you. I just want to find out who did this to him. Whoever it was, they didn't just kill your brother, they killed another boy too. You're going to hear about it tomorrow so you might as well know now. We're looking for a killer known as the Hateful Thing. Have you heard of him?"

"What?" Chloe said, wiping her eyes. "No, never."

"Where did you see Bart?"

"Here," she said. "I was working."

The door was still rattling, the man trying to pry it open with his fingers.

"We're closed!" Savage shouted. "He came here?"

"Yeah, he said he was going up to Norfolk. Some fella wanted him to help with some work. Like I said, I had a weird feeling when I saw this guy, I thought he was well shifty. I—"

She frowned, shaking her head.

"Bart asked to borrow some money, about three this was. Just for a sandwich. Like I say, we always helped each other out. I ended up giving him a tenner *and* a sandwich. He told me what he was doing and I didn't think nothing of it until I watched him go, and there was this other man with him and there was just something about him that made me feel bad, made me feel like bad things were going to happen."

"You'd never seen the other man before?"

She shook her head.

"Never. And it wasn't like he was nasty or anything, it was just something about the way he was standing, watching. He got out of his car to make sure Bart came in, and that he came out again. It was his aura, it looked desperate. He looked hungry. There was something wild about him. That make sense?"

"Did Bart seem threatened? Did he give you any sign that anything was wrong?"

More rattling, the man trying to shunt the door open with his shoulder. Savage did her best to ignore him.

"Nothing," said Chloe. "But Bart was simple like that, he trusted folks. He was good with strangers, always made friends when he worked the gigs, the festivals. He told me not to worry when I said how I felt. He told me Freddie was a top bloke."

"Freddie?" Savage said. "He give you a surname?"

"Nope," Chloe said, shaking her head.

"Can you describe him?"

"Like, same height as Bart, probably, five-ten, something like that. Dark hair, looked fit. Good looking. It's what got me, fella like that, I would have looked twice, you know? But there was something wrong with him."

"Did he have a scar?"

"No, not wrong like that," she said. "I don't mind a scar, just wrong in—"

"No, I'm asking if you saw a scar on his face, about here."

Savage touched her top lip.

"Maybe," Chloe said. "Yeah, maybe he did, red line. I thought it was pen or something."

"Frederick Sabbe, does that mean anything to you?"

She shook her head again, sniffing hard.

"Hello?" said the man from outside, his voice muffled. "I think the door's stuck."

"We're closed!" Savage roared, making a mental note to wallop the guy when she passed him. Amazingly, when she looked back at Chloe the girl had pulled on a smile—the expression so fragile it might have been made of glass.

"I should get back to it," she said.

"You should get somebody to cover you," Savage replied. "News like this can put you in shock. Let me call somebody."

"You don't have to. People like me and Bart, we're always destined to go out fast and hard, same as our mum, same as our dad. It's written into us. Been expecting it for a while now, with my brother. I was ready for it. And one day you'll hear about me as well, young, tragic. But know that I was ready for that too."

There was something so resolute in the way she said it that Savage felt her heart break a little. She put her hand back on Chloe's and squeezed hard, then she pulled out her wallet.

"How much for the newspaper?"

"Leave it," Chloe said.

Savage pulled a contact card from the wallet instead and laid it on the counter.

"Any time, day or night," she said.

"I've told you what I—"

"Not that, just to talk. Nothing's written into us, Chloe. We write it ourselves, every last word."

Chloe frowned, picking up the card with both hands and reading it.

"Savage," she said. "I've known a few folk by that name, always been good souls but true to it, untamed, you know? You like that? Untamed?"

Savage didn't have an answer.

"Any time," she repeated, and she was about to leave when she realised there was a question she hadn't asked. "Chloe, the car that your brother and Freddie drove off in, was it Bart's?"

"He never had a car," she said. "I mean he drove all the time, but never had his licence. No, this was the other fella's car, big silver thing."

"Jaguar?"

She nodded.

"You didn't happen to see the number plate?"

"Wasn't one," she said. "But this is Bart, like I said. He wasn't always on the level."

"Thank you," Savage said. "Call me, please. You shouldn't have to go through this alone."

She walked to the door. The man was still trying to pick at the handle with his fingernails.

"Get yourself a bloody car wash token while you're in there," she said to him when she'd opened it. "Clean your ears out."

He stared at her in shock, his mouth hanging open. She

left him to it, locking herself in her car and pulling out her phone. Porter answered after the third ring.

"Yeah," he said. "This is Porter's answerphone, he's currently enjoying some quiet time and a glass of vino and can't be arsed to deal with any of your nonsense."

"Funny, sir," Savage said. "I've just spoken to the sister, Chloe Hearn."

Porter groaned and she heard him getting up.

"I thought you'd gone home," he said.

"I'm not a quitter, guv. She says that Bart left Thetford yesterday to head up to Norwich, around three in the afternoon. Want to guess who he was with?"

She could almost hear him shrug.

"Frederick Sabbe. The kid who went missing a week ago."

"The fisherman? From Ipswich, right?"

"Right. Chloe said he was shifty, nervous. He was driving a silver estate by the sounds of it. Jaguar X-Type. No plates. I think it's the one that belonged to his parents. We should check cameras, we might be able to establish a timeline, figure out where they went."

"Sure," Porter said. "Anything else?"

Savage started the engine, closing her eyes for a moment and feeling like she could sleep right here, in the garage forecourt, for a year.

"Yeah," she said. "Lay off the *vino*, sir. Today was bad. I think tomorrow is going to be a whole lot worse."

CHAPTER TWENTY-FIVE

IT WAS NEARLY OVER. IT WAS NEARLY TIME.

Just one more death stood between him and ecstasy, between him and his calling.

The man closed the car door behind him, embracing the rain that fell from the lightless sky. He couldn't remember ever seeing a night as dark as this one, where even the stars seemed to hide. Were they hiding from him? He couldn't be sure, but he didn't blame them if they were.

He was about to do something horrific.

He was about to unleash hell.

He'd had the sense to bring a torch with him and he used both thumbs to press the stubborn button. It slipped from his grip, the rubber wet and his hands aching from the cold. It hit the grass and rolled, casting spectres in the trees that crowded the edge of the road. It seemed, for a moment, like devils were standing there in the shadows between the trunks, an audience of spectral, serious faces.

"You can't stop me," he told them. "Not this time."

He laughed at the volume of his voice against the quiet

night, at the lunacy of his words. For some reason he felt like leaving the torch on the ground and dancing in its unkind light, stripping naked and baying to the wolves.

But he didn't. He had work to do.

He scooped up the torch and aimed it down the road. It was a cheap one that he'd bought online and it did little to penetrate the night. But it would do.

It wasn't like he had far to go.

He set off, his feet crunching on the road. He hadn't intended to come here, to this familiar place. He hadn't wanted to. But his hand had been forced, and his hand was Hateful. The slope was rising and he pushed on, the relentless cold making him breathless. It would snow tonight, he thought. A blessing of some kind, perhaps. The torchlight swept across something dark on the tarmac and the man stopped for a moment to examine the rabbit which had met its end there, nesting in a loop of organs that looked almost deliberate.

Another sign, he thought as he started moving again. A harbinger of what would follow.

"Life is fragile, but the force is strong," he said to himself as he crested the hill. "The strength was in it all along. Be good, dear boy, be good, be smart. Take the goodness of the heart."

Ahead of him sat the lights of a village, braver than the stars. Or stupider, perhaps. We are here, they seemed to say. We are waiting for you. Come knock on the door and carry us away.

All of us.

He grinned, and his shivers were nothing to do with the cold.

He made his way towards the village, hot now despite the

weather, despite the fact that his clothes had already surrendered themselves to the rain. He wondered if this, too, was a sign that he was somehow holy, somehow divine. He was immune to the cold. He was immune to the worries of mortal life.

Lights, and the growl of an engine. The man walked slowly off the road into the arms of the trees and they held him tight as a car drove past, its wipers going ten to the dozen. It was heading into the village but the driver wouldn't linger, not in this weather. The man waited for the sound of it to fade before stumbling back onto the road, the beam of torchlight swinging wildly.

He clicked it off, swallowed whole by the dark. He didn't need it now because the first houses were appearing, throwing out shields of yellow light. It was late, but people were still about, and even those that had gone to bed had left their lights on tonight. They'd all heard about him by now, their heads full of the Hateful Thing. They would be restless but they wouldn't look outside. They wouldn't dare, in case they saw his face staring back at them through the glass.

In case they saw the knife that he carried in his pocket.

He kept walking, his skin numb but his bones like cut glass. He was past the grander houses now, heading for the middle of the village. Rounding a corner he saw the church rise up like a guardian, as if it might challenge him, but it quickly shrank back into the shadows when he threw a grin its way, as mad as the moon.

"Hate is all there is," he said quietly. "Hate is all there will ever be. But hate isn't why I'm killing you. My love will set you free."

Somewhere close by, a door slammed shut and the man's heart shifted in his chest, as nervous as a mouse in its cage.

He put a hand there, calming it, wondering what it would feel like to have somebody slide a knife through his ribs and sever the meat from the bone, to hack and claw and chew the organ from its home. He wondered if it would hurt as much if people knew why it was happening, if they knew what their sacrifice would prevent. Such a simple act, but it would hold back the night, and all the horrors of hell.

He rounded the corner onto a narrow street, the houses here standing shoulder to shoulder, so small that they almost looked like miniatures. He moved into the shadows of a tall hedge, holding his face up to the rain, to the ageless abyss of the starless sky. Anybody else would freeze out here. They would die. But not him.

He couldn't die.

The sound of a key in a lock, right on time.

The man peeked from his shelter, scanning the houses until he saw a door open—a gift being unwrapped. A woman leaned out, staring sadly at the sky. She turned and said something too quiet for him to hear, then she stepped into the street.

The victim followed, as clear as day, a teenage boy whose beating heart the man could almost hear even from across the street.

A teenage boy who was all that stood between the world and the devil.

The woman said something again, zipping the boy's coat up for him then resting a hand on his shoulder, leaning in. A smile landed on the boy's lips, as fragile as a butterfly and taking flight just as quickly. He glanced up the street, his chest rising and falling in a sigh, as if he knew what was about to happen to him, what he was about to give.

They started walking and the Hateful Thing shrank back

into the hedge, holding his breath. They passed, close enough for him to reach out and touch if he needed to.

He didn't. He couldn't. Not yet.

He wasn't allowed.

All he could do was wait.

And then, when enough time had passed, follow.

CHAPTER TWENTY-SIX

Tuesday

PORTER COULDN'T SLEEP.

That in itself wasn't unusual. He'd never been a big sleeper, not even as a kid. It was something his mum constantly reminded him of, whenever he spoke to her. *Some folk burrow deep when they sleep,* he'd heard her say once to a friend. *Others just pull the thinnest quilt of night over themselves and they'll wake at the drop of a pin.*

It wasn't a pin that was stopping him from sleeping this time. He wasn't even sure it was the case—although the two dead boys had been spinning through his thoughts for hours. No, it was Allie, lying next to him, snoring gently the way she only really did when she'd been crying. The Diazepam had knocked her out long before midnight, and it was just as well because the wine she'd had before that had made her almost hysterical. He hadn't known what to do with her, with the tears.

Something had changed in her during the last few months. Or maybe everything had changed, Porter wasn't sure. He knew what had triggered it, of course. Robbie bloody Kett and his adorable bloody children.

When Porter had first got with Allie they'd had no time for dreams of kids, no time for anything other than each other. They'd been besotted for so long, utterly consumed by the relationship. There simply hadn't been room for anything else until suddenly, just like that, it had been their careers that they were lost in—he in the Met, Allie racing her way to the top at Kelmscott High School. She'd hit Head of English in a heartbeat, then Head of Year before an academy chain offered her the deputy leadership role in a place down in Cornwall, all in the time it had taken him to shuffle up from Detective Sergeant to Detective Inspector.

And it had seemed so perfect. Wherever they were in life, it was the right size for them. The right-sized jobs, the right-sized house. They had fit perfectly together, and perfectly into the slots that had been carved for them.

And then one day they hadn't.

Because the night that he and Allie had babysat for Robbie so that he could investigate the Morton scrapyard, the night that little Moira had fallen asleep on his wife, her chubby, sweaty face positively angelic, something had changed in Allie. Something deep, something tectonic and world-altering. That's why Porter had done it, of course. He'd wanted her to change her mind about children, he'd wanted her to see the miracle there, the joy.

He just hadn't expected it to go to shit so quickly.

Allie stirred, whispering something in her sleep. She was still so beautiful, he thought as he pulled the satin duvet up around her neck to keep out the chill. He'd heard it said too many times that she had a hard kind of beauty, an unfriendly and unapproachable glamour. But only to begin with, only if she didn't trust you. Allie had a big heart, she just didn't like people to see it. She'd make a great mum, Porter thought, gritting his teeth as the panic crept in, the uncertainty, the guilt.

Fuck this.

He climbed out of the bed as quietly as he could, although there wasn't a hope in hell of waking her. The house sat silently around him. It had changed too. Where once the five-bed new build in Wymondham—almost literally a stone's throw from HQ—had been perfect for them, its enormous kitchen diner designed for parties, its extra rooms perfect for Allie's office and his gaming den, now it felt far too big, and far too empty. All it seemed to do was remind his wife of how alone she was. How *lonely.*

All it seemed to do was make it clear how much they were missing.

Porter checked his phone—nearly four—and left the room, the cold wrapping itself around his naked torso. He walked into the bathroom, clicking on the light and seeing himself in the mirror. He pumped a bicep to cheer himself up, brushing his teeth and washing his face before clattering down the stairs. His suit was where he'd left it, hanging on the back of one of their velvet dining chairs with a fresh shirt on top. He shivered uncontrollably as he dressed.

"Right," he said, drumming his fingers on the table, turning his thoughts to the dead boys. He checked his phone again before plucking his keys from the peg in the kitchen and walking through to the integral double garage. He didn't need to leave a note for Allie, she was used to his work, and to his sleepless nights. Starting the car, he called control as he waited for the garage door to open, giving his name when a woman answered.

"Hey, Pete," she said, "It's Tracey. Bit early, isn't it?"

"Bit late," he said. "Never actually went to sleep."

"Need something to do?" she asked.

"Anything weird overnight? Anything related to the two dead boys?"

"Not that I can think of," she said. "Few domestics, couple of D and Ds, lost cat—that last one was a 999 call. One RTI, fatal but nothing suspicious."

"Nothing out Dereham way?" he asked. "Out in the sticks?"

He heard the sound of a keyboard clacking.

"There have been a couple of break-ins, uh, one report of screaming in the woods, another missing cat—and yes, that was a 999 call too, believe it or not."

"Go back," Porter said. "Screaming in the woods?"

"Not last night, the night before. Sunday night, Monday morning. A man was walking his dog in the woods near Weston, heard somebody scream."

"Weston," he said. "That's not a million miles from our first dead boy. Nobody checked?"

"They did. Had a constable go out to talk with him in the early hours of yesterday morning, but by that time the man was convinced it was an owl. Barn Owls, you hear them all the time out there. Says here the man was obviously intoxicated. They went back the next morning, did a sweep, didn't find anything."

Screams in the woods. It was probably nothing, but what else was he going to do?

"Where was this?" he asked. "Exactly."

———

HE TOOK it slow because it was minus four and the roads were treacherous. The gritters had been out, but by the time he left the city he could feel the shifting movement of the

Mondeo when it hit pockets of black ice. The wind had risen and it was doing its best to punch the big car into the verges and the woods and the fields, relentless in its attacks. Porter hunkered down, the heating on full blast, and tried not to look away from the road—not because he was worried about his driving but because the countryside felt like a solid black mass that was closing in on all sides. It was bad enough out here in the day but at night he felt as if he was being swallowed alive.

Still, *Kenny G* gave him a little comfort, the saxophone melting through the cold. How Savage could prefer thrashing guitars and murderous drums to smooth jazz was beyond him.

Tracey at control had given him the approximate address for the woods where the man had been walking his dog, but the satnav was determined to keep him away, redirecting him to the main road so many times that he ended up ignoring it and hunting for weed-littered street signs. It was well after five by the time it announced he had reached his destination—as if congratulating itself—and there was still no sign of the sun.

He cut the engine, looking through the windows to see absolutely nothing at all. No stars, no moon, no trees, no road. It was like he'd driven himself out of existence completely. He felt his skin prickle into goosebumps.

"I hate this fucking place," he muttered, pulling his phone from his pocket. Despite the hour, he chanced it, calling Savage. She answered almost immediately, and it sounded like she was out of breath.

"Sir?" she said, and he heard the pounding of feet on the pavement.

"Are you *running*?" he said. "It's like five o'clock in the morning, Kate, what the hell's wrong with you?"

"Couldn't sleep," she said.

"Join the club. I'm back in the sticks."

"Yeah?" There was a bark. "Colin says hello."

"Uh, say hi."

"Pete says hi."

Another bark.

"You don't want to know what she called you, sir. What're you looking for?"

The footsteps stopped and he could picture her bracing a hand on a wall while she drew breath.

"Somebody reported a scream in the woods a couple of nights ago," he said. "Weston. Probably nothing, just wanted to check it out."

"And you're telling me because..."

Porter looked out of the window again, seeing nothing but his own face reflected back at him.

"Because it's dark out," he said. "And the countryside is scary."

Savage laughed.

"Send me the address, guv, I'll be right there."

He hung up, opening the door and then pulling it shut again immediately when the wind howled its way inside.

"Christ," he said.

Bracing himself, he tried again, hopping into the brutal, unforgiving morning. There were three Maglites in the boot and he took two, sliding one into his pocket and firing up the other. It pierced the dark like a giant's finger, fearless. He'd parked the car beside a junction on a winding, single-carriageway road that had split from the A1067. A track entered the woods here, and according to the report, this is where the man had been walking his dogs when he'd heard the scream.

Porter set off, feeling like screaming himself every

time he heard something rustle in the spreading branches overhead. The powerful torch chased away the night but it created freakish, dancing shadows between the gnarled trunks, lunging figures who seemed to reach out for him. He shuddered again, wondering whether he should wait in the car until Savage arrived. He growled like a bear to try to make himself braver, tensing his arms and his chest.

"You are Pete Porter," he said, as loudly as he dared. "You are not afraid."

Then he aimed the torch skyward and found a dinosaur in the trees.

"Fuck!" he squeaked, realising pretty quickly that it wasn't a real one, just a plastic replica that stared over the top of a wire fence. There was a dinosaur park out here, he remembered, a play area for kids. He scowled at it. "Bet you thought that was funny, you lanky bastard."

He pushed on, the cold making his legs numb through the thin fabric of his suit, making his face feel like it was made of rubber.

Like he was wearing a *mask*.

Half a mile from the road the track split, one end heading towards what might have been fields, the other vanishing into the woods. He took the latter, suddenly surrounded by trees that seemed to stand perfectly still despite the breeze. Like statues, he thought, thinking of James Preston's eyeless, mouthless creations, their twisted limbs.

A shudder ripped through him so powerfully that he dropped the torch.

"Fuck!" he said, picking it up, noticing that for the first time that morning he could see a little further than the trees. There was a soft red glow to the east as the sun woke—light but no fire, because it was still freezing. "Took you long enough," he muttered to it.

This was pointless. Even if there had been somebody screaming in the woods, the chances of it having anything to do with this case were minuscule. And even if by some miracle it had been the killer chasing his victim, they would be long gone. Whoever had come out here yesterday hadn't found anything, so what the hell was he even looking for?

The cold was maddening, it actually felt dangerous. He stamped his feet, thought again about turning back before pressing on. He'd walked for another twenty minutes before the woods opened up onto a wide, grassy meadow, a hill rising towards more woodland a hundred yards or so away. Day was here, bleak and unfriendly, the heavy red skies promising snow. There was something alien about the light, something thick and dreamlike, and as he edged his way along the meadow he wondered if maybe he'd fallen asleep after all, if none of this was real.

His phone buzzed and he pulled it out.

"You part of this nightmare, Savage?" he asked.

"What?" He heard a door slam. "*Shoot*, guv, it's absolutely bloody freezing out here. Where are you?"

"Follow the track, take a right where it splits, I'm in the woods. There's a..."

He stopped, because something had caught his eye. A dozen or so yards from where he stood there was a splash of colour against the wet grass, so dark it might have been ink.

"There's a what?" Savage said, walking. "A café? Please say there's a café."

"Hang on."

He approached with caution, aiming the Maglite at the ground. The stains there switched from black to red almost immediately.

"Blood," he said, sweeping the light into the under-growth, then into the trees. He couldn't see any more so he turned around and looked up the hill. From here he could see the line in the grass where somebody had walked, the stems trampled.

"How much, sir?" Savage asked.

"Not much. Listen, can you stay there? Call forensics just in case, bring them out here when they arrive."

Again he thought about how unlikely it was that this had anything to do with the man they were looking for. It had probably been a fox feeding on a rabbit. Maybe a hawk or an owl.

But what if it wasn't?

"Sure," Savage said. "I'll wait in the car. The nice, warm car."

"Ha bloody ha," Porter said, hanging up.

He set off up the hill, walking parallel with the channel that had been cut into the long grass. It was steeper than it looked, the ground frozen and slippy, and by the time he got to the top, he was out of breath. Light flooded the meadow, and looking back he saw over the tops of the trees, cars glinting like fish in water as they travelled along the main road.

He left them to it, pushing into the woods. The meadow of parted grass had ended but it didn't take long for him to see the splashes of blood on the leaves, on the moss-covered stones. Somebody had run this way, and they'd been badly injured. He followed the trail, twigs cracking beneath his feet as he fought his way through the grasping branches. The brambles clawed at his suit trousers, at his jacket, doing their best to unstitch him, to pull him apart before he stumbled onto whatever horrors lay ahead.

There. A break in the trees. Porter sniffed the air,

smelling smoke, and when he cleared the woods he found himself in the back garden of a small farmhouse. A fire pit sat in the middle of the space, still smouldering, a couple of cheap garden chairs on their backs beside it, like he'd caught them mid-nap.

Past them, propped up against the wall of the house like it had every right in the world to be there, was a scythe.

Porter pulled out his phone again, calling Savage. She answered after a single ring.

"It's—" she started, but he rode over her.

"Call in the troops. I'm at a farmhouse on the northern edge of the woods, at the top of the hill. There's a scythe here, a fire, a trail of blood heading south. See if you can find your way to it in the car."

"Will do," she said, starting the engine. "North, right?"

"Right."

"Wait for me, sir, don't go in."

"Don't *Kett* this up, you mean?" he said. "I won't. Just hurry."

He returned the phone to his pocket and walked into the garden, doing his best to stay low. He skirted around the fire, keeping his eyes on the small windows of the farmhouse. None of them were masked by curtains, and there was no sign of life behind the dark glass. The scythe stood next to the back door, its blade orange with rust, the shaft rotten and one of the handles missing. It was hard to tell whether it was bloodied or not.

Porter reached the back door, trying the handle and finding it locked. He eased himself along the farmhouse and peeked around the corner, seeing a small gravel driveway with the house on one side and a huge wooden carport on the other. Both seemed to lean into each other like weary travellers. He skipped onto the rotting grass of the verge to avoid making any sound, his shoes slipping in the mulch.

The front of the farmhouse was deserted, the door boarded up with plyboard sheets, two of the four windows smashed. But there was a silver Jaguar Estate in the carport that looked spotless, the plates missing

It was Freddie Sabbe's car.

And it wasn't alone. Parked behind it, crowned in shadows, was a little red Golf that had almost certainly belonged to Chase Masefield.

Porter pulled out his phone again, his thumb hitting Savage's name just as he saw the shadow rise up behind the wheel of the Jaguar.

"Hey!" he yelled, his heart revving. "Police, stay where you are!"

The car spluttered to life, the big engine roaring, its high beams burning their way into Porter's skull.

"Stop!" he said again, lifting a hand to block the glare— the only thing he had time to do as the car lurched towards him.

CHAPTER TWENTY-SEVEN

PORTER MOVED FAST, BUT NOT FAST ENOUGH. HE DIVED to the side, his feet slipping on the shingle, the Jaguar's bonnet cracking into the knuckles of his left hand and sending the phone flying. The world exploded, too bright, the pain taking a second or two to catch up. He staggered away, the car's tyres spraying shrapnel into his face as it passed.

There was nowhere for it to go, the front of the house shielded by hawthorn hedges.

"Fucker," Porter wheezed, cradling his hand.

The Jag skidded to a halt and Porter heard the crunch of gears as the driver fought to find reverse. This time he moved back, pushing himself into the doorway of the house as the car whined its way across the driveway. Its rear end hit the bricks beside him in an explosion of dust.

"Stop!"

The driver wasn't going to. Through the window Porter saw him wrestling the gear stick, a frightened look back. A man, but he couldn't make out any more details in the dark. He chanced it anyway.

"Freddie! This is the police, stop the fucking car."

The silver beast gunned away, facing the right way this time and skidding onto the street. The front end hit the verge, lurching up and slamming down again. Porter was already on the move, scooping up his phone as he went. His left hand radiated agony like it was being held over a grill, the tips of his fingers numb. From the street he heard the car pull away, then another crunch.

He ran onto the road, one shoe sliding on the loose gravel and almost sending him flying. They were in the middle of the countryside here, not a straight road in sight, and the Jag had mounted another grassy verge. The driver was reversing but he was panicked, the back of the car swinging too far and hitting dirt.

"Stop!" Porter yelled, catching up fast. He slammed his good hand on the top of the car, almost losing the phone again, then reached for the handle. Inside, a young man who couldn't be anybody other than Freddie Sabbe looked up at him with eyes like pickled eggs. It was locked, and Porter pointed at him through the glass. "Stop the fucking car."

Sabbe floored it, riding the verge. Porter tried to hang on to the handle but he didn't stand a chance, the rear end of the car thumping past him. The Jag accelerated fast and hard, a junction ahead.

Porter saw the top of the little green car too late.

Savage's Fiat.

The two cars collided hard, the sound of it louder than the world breaking. Porter was running again, the phone forgotten, the road suddenly impossibly long. He rounded a corner to see the Jag maybe fifty yards ahead, its bonnet halfway through Savage's Punto. Through the smoke he could see that her windscreen had been sheared in two, no sign of anyone there.

"Kate!" he yelled, almost a scream.

The Jag's door opened a crack, the window shattering. A foot appeared, kicking hard, then the rest of Freddie Sabbe followed. He was winded, but one look back down the road and he was running. Porter ignored him, sprinting the last thirty yards and skidding past the Jag. It was a big car and it had piledrived its way into the little Fiat like a metal fist, crumpling the bonnet beyond recognition.

"Kate?" Porter said, scrambling onto the verge, slipping and crying out as he landed on his left hand.

Savage was in the driver's seat, motionless.

"No."

There was no way of getting the driver's door open so he staggered along the verge beside the car, trying to work his way around to the other side. The road was so narrow it was almost impossible. He remembered his phone, dialling 999 and resting it on the top of the Fiat so that he could tug on the passenger side handle with both hands. The door opened reluctantly, like a steel trap that didn't want to let go of its prey.

Savage frowned up at him through the blood and the white powder from the airbag.

"Fudge," she said. "That hurt."

Porter let out a breath he didn't even realise he'd been holding. He leant inside the car, reaching for Savage's buckle, but she waved him away.

"Go, sir," she said. "Go get him."

"You sure?" he said, coughing out smoke. Savage nodded as she unclipped her belt, scrambling over the seat.

"Go!"

Porter snatched his phone, ignoring the man who was speaking.

"I'm DI Pete Porter, Norfolk Constabulary," he said,

breathless. "I'm in Weston, uh Morton Road I think. In pursuit of a suspect, there's been an RTI, one officer injured. We need an ambulance and backup."

He lowered the phone, scanning the field beside the road. There was no sign of Freddie Sabbe so he scampered back down and ran up the other verge.

There, halfway to the woods, a figure in a white T-shirt and jeans.

Porter glanced back at Savage. She was out of the car now, limping to the side of the road.

"Pete, go!"

Pocketing the phone, he scrambled onto a field of stubbled earth, the ridges frozen solid and almost impossible to walk on. He had to slow to a jog to avoid breaking an ankle, still cradling his swollen hand. Ahead, Freddie Sabbe slipped and fell, crying out. He was up again in a heartbeat but he was running more slowly now and there was a definite limp. He looked back, seeing Porter steaming after him, and his expression became a mask of misery.

Porter didn't waste his energy on words, driving forwards. Sabbe had reached the treeline but it wouldn't be hard to see him in his bright white T-shirt. There was nowhere for him to go.

It took another minute to reach the woods. The trees seemed to have held in the cold and dark of the night, the temperature brutal. If Sabbe didn't stop running soon then there was every chance he'd freeze to death out here. Porter pushed through the bare branches, seeing no sign of life.

"You're out of luck, Freddie," he shouted, his breath billowing. "Why don't you just give yourself up and we can get out of this fucking cold?"

There was a reply from nearby, but it was less a word

than a scream. There was something almost animalistic about it, something feral that made the hair on the back of Porter's neck stand on end. He kept walking, slower now, the ground a gauntlet of moss and broken branches. There was no noise here at all, he realised, other than the bellows of his own breath and that same snarling voice from somewhere ahead.

"Stay where you are," Porter said, a shout that should have scattered birds from the trees but which seemed to fall dead. "Try anything stupid, mate, and I'll finish you."

He stumbled up a tall bank, grabbing hold of a low branch with his good hand to steady himself. The ground ahead sloped down and from here he could see the glow of Freddie Sabbe's T-shirt, just a sleeve poking out from behind a tree. He hesitated, knowing that it wouldn't take long before the woods were swarming with coppers. As long as Freddie didn't move, Porter could wait.

But what was the kid doing down there? Hiding? He was utterly motionless, and the noises had stopped. All Porter could hear was the thrashing beat of his own heart and—

There, to the right, a cracking branch. He swung his head around to see Freddie running towards him, almost on him. He was naked from the waist up and in his hand he held a knife. The kid loosed a cry that was half wolf's howl, half scream, his face scarred with hatred.

Porter stepped back, letting go of the branch he was holding. It swept through the air and cracked against Freddie's naked chest as he pounced, making a sound like a gunshot. The kid yelped and Porter threw both hands out, shoving him with every ounce of strength he had. His injured hand burned but Freddie practically came off the ground, skittering down the slope then losing his balance and landing on his backside. His legs cartwheeled over his head in a hail of leaves, the knife pinging into the moss.

Porter went after him, losing his footing on the hill and sliding down on the seat of his trousers. Freddie was trying to get up but he was struggling, his skin so pale it was almost blue.

"Stay the fuck down," Porter said.

Sabbe rolled away, pushing himself to his feet just as Porter reached the bottom of the hill. The kid searched the ground, desperate to find his knife, then balled his fists and took a couple of steps back.

"Last chance," Porter said, bunching his own fist.

"It's *your* last chance," Sabbe said, every word broken into pieces by his chattering teeth. His whole body was trembling.

"My last chance?" Porter said. "Fuck you on about? You gonna come quietly or not?"

Sabbe hawked up a ball of spit but when he let it go it clung to his quivering bottom lip, hanging there. He wiped it away with the back of his skinny arm, never breaking eye contact.

"You have no idea what you've done," he said. "No idea what will happen if you try to stop me."

"I'm not going to *try*," Porter said. "I *am* going to stop you."

Sirens, rising from the dawn as if trying to make up for the silence of the birds. If Sabbe heard them he made no sign of it. He was tensing up, his body a tightly wound coil, his teeth bared like an animal. He was going to attack.

Porter angled his body, shifting his weight onto his back foot, ready for him. Sabbe took a couple of shallow breaths and charged, his fists by his face, letting the right one loose when he was two feet away. Porter dodged it easily then threw out his own hand—not a punch but a grapple. He hooked it under Sabbe's armpit and around his neck and pulled tight, the kid's arm trapped between them. Then he kicked his leg and pushed hard. Sabbe crumpled like a sapling, face first, and Porter pushed him to the wet ground. He pinned him with a knee, the kid practically vibrating beneath him. Sabbe's right arm was a mess, a deep wound that was still oozing blood.

"Frederick Sabbe, I am arresting you for the murders of Chase Masefield, Bartley Hearn and Theresa Carson-Cooke, not to mention a whole heap of other nasty shit. You do not have to say anything, but it may harm your defence if you do not mention when questioned something which you later rely on in court. Anything you do say may be given in evidence. Got that?"

The kid was shivering hard enough to break bones, his skin cold to the touch even through Porter's thick gloves. Porter pulled out his phone to call Savage but stopped when he heard shouts from the field nearby.

"Over here," he called back. "I got him."

Sabbe was speaking into the mulch, a stream of fast, breathless words that made no sense.

"Save it for the interview room," Porter said, seeing a uniformed copper appear through the trees. "Hey, mate, down here."

The PC ran towards them and Savage took his place, still wearing a mask of powder and blood. She made her way carefully down the slope, grabbing the constable's elbow when she started to slip and almost bringing them both down.

"You okay, guv?" she asked, and Porter nodded.

"You?"

"I'm better for seeing him in the dirt," she said, eyeballing Sabbe.

Porter leaned back so that the constable could snap a set of handcuffs around the kid's wrists. Sabbe was talking so fast now there was foam coming out of his mouth, and his eyes looked like they were starting to roll up in their sockets.

"You got him," Savage said.

"I got him," Porter replied. "I got the Hateful Thing."

Hearing this, Sabbe opened his mouth and screamed. And this time, finally, a murder of crows scattered from the trees.

CHAPTER TWENTY-EIGHT

SAVAGE SAT ON THE EDGE OF HER CHAIR IN THE Incident Room, cradling her head in her hands. She'd been checked out by the paramedics in Weston but all they'd found was a cut to her forehead which they'd quickly patched up. She had a hell of a headache, though, and every time she closed her eyes she felt like she was moving, like she was still in the car, tearing towards the junction as the big silver Jag pulled out of it.

Like she was still in the car.

Her beautiful Fiat. *Little Jeff*. It had been the first thing she'd bought when she joined the force, her pride and joy, and Sabbe had almost torn it in two.

Still, better the car than her.

"Savage?" said Clare as he marched into the room. "How's it going?"

She looked up, wincing into the unforgiving light of HQ. The Super was in full headmaster mode, complete with a length of bamboo cane in his right hand which he pointed at her.

"Oh, right sir, the case. It's going well. Sabbe is almost

certainly our man. He was found near the site of an attack, there was a scythe on the property, and he ran. It doesn't look good for him."

"I meant how's the head?" Clare asked, tapping the cane against his own bandaged brow.

"It's fine, sir," she said. "Just a graze."

Clare nodded, looking around the room. Porter sat on the next desk along, his bruised left hand held against his chest. Savage had seen him turn down a ride to the hospital for an X-ray, and it couldn't have been bad because he'd driven them both back here without moaning too much.

"How about you, Porter?" Clare asked. "How's it going?"

"It's nothing, boss. A little painful but—"

"I was talking about the case," Clare said, slapping the end of the bamboo on Porter's desk.

There was a rumble of gentle laughter across the room, most of it coming from Spalding who sat near the door. Dunst was there too, and there was a collection of Uniforms scattered between them. PC Aaron Duke was amongst them and when he caught Savage's eye he snapped his head up to study the ceiling instead, his lips forming a silent whistle.

Weirdo, she thought.

"Did anyone manage to get hold of Kett?" Clare asked. "He may have some insight."

"He's there, I think," Savage said, prodding her phone. "Robbie?"

Somebody breathed into the line, the sound of it amplified by the speakers. Everyone in the incident room craned in, trying to make sense of it.

"Kett?" Clare said.

"Are you Mr Marshmallow?" came a quiet voice.

"Uh, no. Evie," Savage said. "Can you put your dad on?"

"He's having a poo on the floor," the little girl said, and the laughter in the Incident Room was louder. There was a hammering of feet and then Kett's voice.

"Thank you, Evie. I wasn't having a poo, I was making a cuppa. Go play with your sisters."

There was the sound of a muffled argument. Savage caught the word 'Smarties' and Kett was back.

"Sorry," he said. "Where were we? You got Sabbe?"

"And he's our man, I'm sure of it," Clare said. "Freddie Sabbe left Ipswich six days ago in the same silver Jaguar that he was driving today, heading towards Norwich. Judging by the state of his car, he's been living in it all this time in the carport where you found him, Porter. We're still waiting for traffic cams but we think he drove down to Thetford yesterday where he picked up our second victim, Bartley Hearn, as witnessed by Bartley's sister, and by garage CCTV, am I right?"

"Right," Dunst said. "Footage is clear as day."

"And the other car we found there belonged to Chase Masefield. There's blood along the back seat. Either he intercepted Chase when our young victim was driving home on Friday, or he attacked him in the woods by the Skinner house."

"Not looking good for Freddie," said Porter.

"So, the house, whose is it?" Clare asked.

Spalding flicked through a collection of papers until she found the one she needed.

"Owned by a Margaret Grange, sir, but she's long dead. It passed to her son but he lives overseas, absolutely no interest in it apparently. It's been rotting for years. A few of the windows have been smashed but there's no sign Sabbe spent any time inside."

"How did he not freeze to death in that car?" Porter asked.

"Forensics is still working the blood they found in the woods but they also found the remains of a fire nearby. Somebody tried to burn some clothes and they did a shit job of it. Bartley's wallet was there, pretty much untouched."

"Tell me about the scythe," said Clare.

"Clean, sir, as far as we can tell," Savage said. "Blade's blunt, pitted with age, no sign of blood. The fact there was a scythe there at all is a weird coincidence. It's not a working farm but there is plenty of rusted equipment in the outbuildings, it's not implausible that Sabbe found another weapon onsite and used it against his victims."

"He had a wound on his arm, too," Porter said. "A bad one, already infected. Paramedics said it was a few days old, he could have got it as far back as Friday."

"When Masefield died," Clare said, swishing the bamboo cane through the air. "Good. Is there any connection between the men?"

"None that we could find," said Dunst. "Complete strangers, no overlaps at all on social media. The only connection between Masefield and Hearn is that they attended the same school for a while, but Sabbe was a complete stranger. Different city, different life."

"That's what doesn't make any sense," said Spalding. "Sabbe was a normal kid from a good home, no priors. There's no reason for him to do this."

"But when his folks reported him missing they said he'd been acting weird for a while," Savage said. "He'd been online a lot, withdrawn."

"We'll check his socials," Clare said.

"It's like in Somerset," Kett said on the phone, slurping tea. "Flowerdew. The kid who was arrested for murder down there, the one who was caught in the act of cutting his victim's heart out and talking about the Hateful Thing, he'd never been in trouble before. He just snapped. Nobody could figure out why, and he killed himself before they could get it out of him."

"Speaking of which," said Savage. "How's Sabbe doing? He's on suicide watch, right? He was in a bad way out there."

"Because he knew it was over, we'd got him," Clare said. "But yes, he is. They're keeping him sedated. He hasn't said a word. Did he say anything to either of you?"

Savage shook her head but Porter cleared his throat, frowning.

"Just the usual fucked up stuff that these people always come out with. You'll regret this, that kind of thing."

"What did he say exactly?" Kett asked.

"Well, it's hard to remember, *exactly*, because I was rolling around in the mud with him and he was doing a lot of screaming. But it was like, '*You have no idea what will happen if you try to stop me.*' I think that was it."

The room fell silent, except for the sound of Kett's girls. They were chanting something together, the sound of it getting louder as they walked into the room.

"Smell my butt. Smell my butt."

Savage heard the former DCI sigh and couldn't keep the smile off her face.

"There's a pattern here," Kett said when the chorus had faded. "I haven't figured it out yet but it has to be connected to Somerset, Neath, Yorkshire."

"But Sabbe's too young to have been anywhere near those cases," Savage replied, picturing the kid. "He'd have been a baby when the Yorkshire killings happened. Flowerdew too."

"And that's the crux of it, isn't it?" Clare said. "The same crimes but committed years apart and miles away from each other, and by different people."

"Like a cult," said Savage. "A religion. Maybe that's why Sabbe has been acting withdrawn. Maybe he fell in with a bad crowd online."

"Does it matter?" said Dunst, chewing on a nail, obviously bored. "We've got him."

Porter's phone rang and the DI answered it.

"Yeah, he's on another call," he said, laying the phone on the desk. "It's Unusual Emily Franklin. You're on speaker."

"Thank you for the warning, Pete," Franklin said. "I was about to call you a ridiculously over-muscled, under-brained boggart but I won't now that I know everyone is listening."

Porter's face fell.

"Cara Hay is here too."

"Hey," Porter said.

"Yes, *Hay*, you dolt."

Savage could almost picture Franklin rolling her eyes. Cara's lilting voice replaced that of the young pathologist.

"DNA won't be back for a while, but I thought you should know that Freddie Sabbe's an AB Negative blood type, same kind we found splashed all over Chase Masefield."

"That's good news," said Clare.

"Doctors let me have a quick peek at Sabbe," Franklin butted in. "Even though he's not dead. Injury to his arm is a knife wound, he's got two or three of them and they're probably defensive."

"So Chase did get a few hits in," PC Duke said from the back of the room. "That's something, I guess."

"It gets better," said Hay. "We took samples of the blood you found on the weapons in the car. It matches Chase's. It's B positive, so a little more common, but there are still fewer than one in ten people with it."

"You think the DNA will match?" Clare asked.

"It will," Hay said. "But even if it doesn't, I've got something almost as good for you. We've dusted Sabbe's car. Most of the prints are his, and there are a fair few of Bartley Hearn's too. There's also a partial thumbprint on one weapon that matches Chase."

"Holy shit," said Porter.

"I could tossing kiss you," Clare said.

"Please don't," replied Hay. "I'll report back as and when we get confirmation on the DNA."

"And I'll sit tight," added Franklin. "Because I don't think we're going to see any more heartless boys."

She hung up. Or at least that's what Savage thought until Franklin's voice came through again, soft and muffled.

"Hey, Cara, what do you get when you mix DI Porter with a teabag?"

The entire incident room leaned in waiting for the answer, but all that came was a muttered curse, a fizz of static, then the bleep of the call ending.

"What?" said Dunst. "What do you get?"

"Enough," Clare said, but there was no anger in his voice. He almost looked like he might be smiling—although it was always hard to tell with him. "This is all good. We can tie Sabbe to Bartley Hearn and Chase Masefield. DNA or no DNA, he's finished."

Porter punched his good fist into the air in celebration. Clare slapped the bamboo cane onto the nearest desk.

"Right, paperwork the lot of you, this has to be absolutely watertight. And there are still a lot of loose ends that need chasing up, not least the whereabouts of James Preston."

He marched from the room, Spalding and Dunst following. Porter started to crack his knuckles then yelped, shaking his injured left hand.

"I'm gonna put the kettle on," he said. "You in?"

"Sure," Savage said, more out of pity than thirst.

He walked from the room, leaving only Savage and Aaron Duke. The giant PC hovered by the door, his hat in his hands, looking like he needed permission to use the toilet.

"You okay?" Savage asked him.

"Yeah, I was just..." he spluttered air through his lips like a horse. "It's, like, you're okay? Like, after yesterday?"

"Oh, right, yeah. Thanks, Aaron."

She wasn't okay, not at all. She didn't think her time in the woods with Greg Skinner was something she'd ever be able to forget. But there was no point talking about it, not now, certainly not to Duke. He nodded, studying his hat like he was looking for clues.

"There something else?" she asked.

"I was just wondering if you'd like to dinner one day?" he said, the words running together. "Like, not dinner, I mean *go* to dinner one day. Or night. Probably night. Or evening. Dinner."

His face cringed with embarrassment and expectation.

"Oh," Savage said. "Uh... dinner?"

"Like, a date?" Duke said, suddenly two foot smaller than he had been when the conversation started.

"Oh," Savage said again. "I can't. I mean it's not like I don't want to but... you know... I'm... married?"

"Oh, god, sorry," Duke said, banging his shoulder as he backed out of the door.

"Not, like, *married* married," Savage blustered. "I mean to my dog."

"Uh..."

"Job," she said. "I mean my job."

"It's fine, it's cool," Duke squeaked, turning tail and crossing the bullpen like his clothes were on fire.

"Duke!" Savage shouted after him, then she put a hand to her mouth as a wave of nervous laughter spilled out of her.

"Smooth," said Kett from where she'd left her phone on the desk. Savage laughed even harder, wondering if the bump to the head had been worse than the paramedics had let on.

"Sorry," she said. "I have no idea where that came from."

"The laughter or Duke?"

"Both."

She perched on the edge of the desk, rubbing her temples with both hands.

"What do you make of it all, sir?"

"He's a good-looking guy, a little too serious for me. His beard makes mine look bad."

"The case," she said.

"Oh, right." He breathed out slowly. "I think Sabbe is guilty. I just can't figure out why, and what it has to do with the other cases across the country."

"Maybe nothing. Maybe a copycat. Maybe this is about something else, a deal gone wrong, a broken friendship, a bad relationship. There's always the chance that Sabbe could have heard about the Hateful Thing and made his murders look like the other ones to cover his real motives."

"Maybe," said Kett. "Good theory. I was going to go and

speak with Balls later today, he claims he's got some new intel."

"Balls," Savage said and left it at that.

"There's something there," Kett said. "Something in the pattern of killings, in the six-year gaps. It might have started as far back as '96, those dead kids in Skegness. The missing hearts there are too much to ignore. Then three dead in Yorkshire in '02, two dead in Neath in '08, followed by the other killings. Three in Somerset six years ago, and now two. I just can't work it out. What's your next move?"

"I don't know," she said, rubbing her temples again. "Head's banging."

"Go home. You can't just shake off a head injury."

There was a moment of silence while they both chewed on their thoughts. It was Kett who spoke next.

"What does your gut tell you, Kate? Is it over?"

Savage hesitated, using a finger to spin the phone in circles. She thought about Sabbe, his face a Halloween mask of panic through the windscreen as he rounded the corner in the Jag, the animal-like noises he'd made in the woods when Porter had collared him. All the evidence pointed to him, to this sad, desperate, broken young man.

So why was her stomach still churning?

"No, sir," she said eventually. "I'm honestly not sure that it is."

CHAPTER TWENTY-NINE

Loose ends. Clare was right, this case was absolutely full of them.

Porter parked the car in the same place he had before, just across the road from the Preston cottage. The only difference this time was that the cottage had all but gone. The fire had reduced it to ash and rubble, and the water from the hoses had done a pretty good job of washing it all away. The statues in the garden had avoided the flames but the smoke had turned them coal black. They looked like rotting teeth sticking out of the mud. They looked like *Preston's* teeth.

The firefighters had gone—the young PC too—a notice on the gate warning people not to enter the remains of the property. Porter put the car in first and cut the engine, wincing as the pain started another fire between his knuckles. His left hand was purple but he was pretty sure it wasn't broken. He stepped out into the day, bracing himself for the cold only to find that the air still held some of the heat of the inferno. Nobody had called him, which meant that they hadn't found a body anywhere nearby. Preston had legged it.

The question was *why*? If Sabbe really was the Hateful Thing then Preston had no reason to run.

Unless he was guilty of something else, of course.

Porter ignored the sign, stepping over the low gate. The wind roared in his ears, scooping up great handfuls of wet ash and throwing it at him as if all of this was his fault. He navigated the graveyard of tortured sculptures, almost buggering over twice before he'd reached the remains of the little building. The roof had gone, the metal props jutting up towards the dark sky like stone columns in a ruined church, no idea what to do with themselves.

There was nothing here. Nothing in the ash, in the filth. Porter scanned it anyway, seeing what might have been furniture, a wire bed frame, a guitar burned to its shell. He half-heartedly kicked a few clumps of filth away but he knew he wouldn't find anything.

"What are you doing, Pete?" he asked himself.

A pigeon answered him from a nearby tree, fat and curious.

"You see what happened?" he asked, and it took off with a clap of its wings, vanishing into the woods behind the cottage. "Thanks a lot, mate," Porter grumbled as he watched it go.

He took a deep breath of smoke-heavy air, puffing it out slowly as he turned and made his way back to the car. He'd put out an alert for Preston's crappy wooden Morris, it wouldn't be hard to spot. All he could do now was wait.

He checked his watch, surprised to find it was almost midday. It felt more like mid*night*, the lack of sleep last night catching up with him, making him feel like a balloon that had been partially deflated. He climbed into the

Mondeo and started the engine, taking more than a minute to turn the big car around in the narrow road and bringing half of the verge with him as he drove off.

There wasn't much else to do out here, but he wasn't ready to head back yet. He knew the route to Lesser Lyng by heart now, humming along to Kenny G's *Forever in Love* as he navigated the narrow roads. The bleak countryside seemed to watch him go, fields of black-eyed cattle studying him as he passed.

"Evil bloody cows," he muttered, turning the music up.

By the time he'd parked the car in his usual spot, hail was drumming on the windscreen, the wipers in a frenzy. He waited a few minutes for it to calm down, and when it didn't he opened the door and ran into it, both hands over his head until he reached the house. He used his good hand to knock, wondering if they'd hear it over the hammer-blows of the hail.

Then, just like that, the icy downpour stopped, leaving the street white and Porter's skin glowing. The door opened a crack, Audrey Masefield's face appearing. She looked up at Porter and smiled, pulling the door the rest of the way.

"You look frozen, pal," she said. "But I'm frightened to let you in in case you drip."

"It's fine," he said, doing everything he could not to shiver and shivering twice as hard as a result. "I just wanted to update you on the case. We've made an arrest."

Audrey's brow creased with disbelief and she opened her mouth to say something, only for her sister to beat her to it.

"God, let him in Aud, he'll catch his death out there."

Cathy appeared from the shadows of the dark house, scrubbing red eyes with tight fists. Even in the short time since Porter had last seen her she'd faded further, brittle and broken. She had to brace one hand on the wall to stop herself from falling over.

"Come on," she said.

Porter ducked into the house, cracking his head on the ceiling for a third time. Cathy didn't notice. She walked into the living room, the cord of her dressing gown sweeping behind her. Audrey waited for Porter to step out of the way before closing the door behind them. There were no lights on, and even with the windows open the house felt as dark and as airless as a coffin.

"How's Blake doing?" he asked.

"You say you've arrested someone?" Audrey answered, ignoring the question. "Chase's killer?"

The words seemed to knock Cathy backwards onto the sofa where she curled into herself, her chin practically resting on her knees. She stared at the wall like she could will the entire world into oblivion. Porter walked into the minuscule room and stood awkwardly by the wall while Audrey boxed him in.

"We've, uh, arrested a man we believe to be the killer," he said, feeling like the house was shrinking around him. "I wanted to run the name past you to see if you recognised it."

Audrey stood in the doorway, her face in shadow.

"Go on then," she said. "What are you waiting for?"

"Freddie Sabbe," Porter stuttered. "Frederick. He's nineteen, from Ipswich. He drove up to Norwich a few days ago and he's been living locally."

Audrey breathed slowly through pursed lips, like she'd been smoking.

"He's who killed my boy?" Cathy said, still not looking up.

"We don't know for sure, but it looks likely. There's a lot

of evidence, and we picked him up nearby. Does the name mean anything to either of you?"

"Where is he now?" Audrey said.

"You mind answering my question first?"

"Sorry," she said. "No, I've never heard of him. Cath?"

Cathy shook her head.

"You mind if I ask Blake?" Porter said.

"I don't care," Cathy said, curling up even tighter. "He's in his room."

"He's resting," added Audrey. "He's been through so much."

"I'll make it quick," said Porter.

He tried to move past her but she held her ground, shouting through the door loud enough to make him jump.

"Blake. Your police friend is here. He wants to talk."

"Police friend," Porter said. "That's a first."

"Where is he now, this man?" Audrey asked, turning back. "This *prick*."

"In hospital," Porter said. "But he's in custody. He's not going anywhere."

There was no sound of anyone upstairs and Audrey walked into the hallway, bellowing Blake's name. Cathy didn't move, as motionless as one of her ex-boyfriend's statues. Porter studied his nails, not quite sure what to do with himself. He heard Audrey stomping up the steps, the joists over his head trembling as she went.

"Blake," she said, as clearly as if she was in the same room. "Blake?"

More footsteps, and this time Cathy glanced up—not at Porter but at the door. She was wreathed in shadow but her eyes were bright.

"Blake?" Audrey called, then she was clattering down

the stairs and leaning through the living room door. "Did he go out?"

"No," Cathy said, clawing herself out of the sofa. "He's not allowed. He's in his room, isn't he?"

She pushed past Porter, running up the stairs so fast she tripped and fell. He heard her cry out Blake's name, her voice drenched in horror. Porter followed her up the creaking steps, the house even smaller up here than downstairs—just two bedrooms. Cathy was in one, screaming her son's name.

"Where is he?" she said, almost falling out of the door. Audrey had followed Pete and the three of them stood there, no room, no air. Porter held up a hand to try to calm them, everything swimming.

"He didn't say he was going out," Audrey said. "He'll just be down the club or something, that's what it'll be."

Cathy tried to push past but there wasn't enough space between Porter and the wall. He stood back and she somehow made it, a cloud of sweat and sorrow chasing her as she thumped down the stairs.

"He'll just be at the club," Audrey said again. "Right? He'll just be getting some scran. He knows not to go anywhere without us."

"When was the last time you saw him?" Porter said, speaking to her back as they returned to the ground floor.

"I've not seen him," Cathy said, grabbing a coat from the hook in the hall. "I've been asleep."

"I took him a cuppa a wee while ago, he was fine," said Audrey, the first notes of concern in her own voice. "He was fine, said he just wanted to rest."

"Call the police," Cathy said, looking at Porter. "Please, call them, *everyone*."

"Don't panic," Porter said. "He's almost certainly fine.

We'll check the club. Is there anywhere else he might have gone?"

"He knows not to go anywhere," Cathy said. "I don't even know how he got out, I locked the door, I've got my keys."

She patted her dressing gown pocket, nothing but silence.

"He took them," she said. "Oh fucking hell, Aud, he took the keys."

"The door was unlocked just now when I let you in," Audrey said. "I didn't even think."

She took her own coat from the peg, struggling to pull it on. Cathy was already out of the door in her slippers, skidding on the carpet of hail as she screamed Blake's name down the street. Audrey ran after her, Porter following, both of them trying to call the desperate woman back. Neighbours were at their windows but the doors stayed shut. Nobody wanted any part of this.

Porter put his head down and ran, catching up with Cathy and touching her arm. She shook him off, glaring at him like he was the one who'd taken her son. She was sprinting now, surprisingly fast, her smoker's lungs struggling. They rounded the corner, the church appearing up ahead, its stunted steeple seeming to cower behind the leafless trees. Porter sped up, overtaking Cathy, the first to arrive at the church hall. The door was open.

"Blake!" Cathy shrieked as she pushed past him, loud enough to make his ears ring. "Blake, where are you?"

There was nobody here, but the building wasn't empty.

A small, blackened statue stood in the middle of the room, its face twisted like a pretzel, no eyes and no nose just a gaping mouth locked into an endless cry of horror.

Somebody had gouged a hole in the statue's chest.

And in that hole, they'd left a heart. Dead and grey and still, but unmistakable.

Cathy saw it and fell to her knees, punching out a scream that was surely loud enough to tear the roof off the building. Audrey wrapped herself around her sister like she meant to strangle her, her eyes wild.

Porter glanced at the heart—too old to be fresh, not Blake's—then ran to the windows along the back of the church hall, the football field deserted. He doubled back, checking the bathroom behind the kitchenette, then the cupboard, before running outside. There was music coming from the church and he made for it, pushing open the side door to see a handful of elderly women inside doing some kind of craftwork at folding tables. They all looked up, then turned as one to the only man in the room. Even though he wasn't in black, the white collar gave away the fact that he was the priest.

"Can I help you?" he asked.

"Police," Porter said, not bothering with his warrant card. "I'm looking for a young man, Blake Masefield, you know him?"

The priest nodded, as did most of the women.

"Has he been here?"

"No," the man said. "Not here. We're making decorations for the food parcels, all volunteers. They don't ask us, but it's nice, don't you think, when you're receiving a gift, to—"

"Have you seen him at all today?" Porter interrupted. "It's vital that we find him."

"Yes," the priest said. "Yes, I saw him a little while ago. He seemed fine."

"Was he alone?"

"No. I believe he was being picked up by somebody. He was getting into a car."

"What kind of car?" Porter asked.

"A car," the priest spluttered, lifting his hands in ignorance. He frowned, deep in thought. "Wait, I believe it was a van of some kind, it had wooden panels."

"Shit," Porter said, the word echoing back and forth in the church like a naughty child. One of the women gasped, putting her hand to her mouth. "It's his father's car. Did you see the driver?"

"No," the priest said, still frowning. "In fact, I honestly couldn't tell you for sure that it was Blake. I mean, I'm pretty certain because I recognised the hair, the clothes, those ludicrous orange trainers. But..."

He paused, like he couldn't quite believe what he was remembering.

"But?" Porter barked.

"But I couldn't see his face," the man said eventually. "He was wearing some kind of mask."

CHAPTER THIRTY

SAVAGE PULLED BACK HER ARM AND LAUNCHED THE stick into the air. It was a bad shot, striking a low branch and spinning into the bushes. Colin the dog looked up at her, her disdain writ clearly on her face.

There's no way I'm getting that.

"Sorry," Savage said, scooping another branch from the mud. She aimed a little better this time, hurling it down the path they were walking along. The dog scampered after it, foaming at the mouth, her little feet kicking up a spray of dirty water. Savage let her go, taking a deep breath of stagnant air and wondering what on earth she was doing returning to the Great Stone of Lyng.

It had been a spur of the moment decision, and only partly to do with her pounding head. She'd taken Kett's advice and headed home—with Clare's blessing and a borrowed police Audi A1—but her flat had seemed too small and too dark, and everywhere she'd turned she'd seen Greg Skinner's half-formed face, his mad, roving eye searching for her. She'd lifted Colin into the boot of the car and headed west again, not really sure why, just grateful to be moving, to feel the cold wind in her hair through the open window, that surge of adrenaline as she put her foot down and flew around the slower cars, as she took the racing line around the corners.

Now here she was, the skeletal trees dancing their wild gyre around her as the wind picked up, the sky heavy. The rain had turned to hail, falling like arrows. Ahead, Colin had given up on the stick and was investigating a mound of something that looked suspiciously like poop.

"Don't you dare," she warned the little dog. "If you eat that, you're walking home."

Colin barked, licking her lips as she trotted on, happy to be somewhere new. Savage felt the same sense of foreboding here that she'd sensed the first time, a dread born from the utter silence that gripped the woods. She felt for the whistle that hung around her neck, wondering whether to blow it as hard as she could just to startle some life back into the place. The dog wasn't bothered at all, her stubby tail wagging so hard that her entire backside was swaying from side to side. She crested the hill, releasing another gunshot bark as if telling Savage to hurry up.

"I'm coming," Savage said, grabbing a branch to help her climb the hill. "Quit your moaning."

Beneath her was the hollow, the great, green stone at the centre of it as if its sheer mass had caused the ground to sag. There was no sign that the police had ever been here, the forensic tags removed, the tent gone. The dead boy had left his mark, though, in the brown stain that decorated the top of the rock. Savage closed her eyes for a moment and saw him there, that alabaster face sitting pristine in the ruin of his body. She would see that face forever, she knew, just as she'd see Skinner and all the other dead. They were carved into her brain, as permanent as stone.

But it was worth it, because they'd got him. They'd caught the Hateful Thing.

Right?

Savage made her way carefully down the slope, trying to picture what had happened to Chase Masefield. It wasn't hard, because she'd seen how desperate Sabbe had been, how capable of mindless violence. Bartley Hearn had gone with his killer willingly, so it wasn't out of the question that Masefield had done the same. Then what? Sabbe had driven him to the farmhouse in the woods, tied him up, placed a mask over his face and tortured him. In the chaos Masefield had got loose, found a weapon, and fought back—his efforts valiant but futile. Sabbe had dragged him here and left him on the rock.

But why? Why here?

Savage made it to the bottom without falling, and only then did Colin fall quiet, suddenly aware of something in the air. The dog whimpered, falling to heel by Savage's leg even though she hadn't been called. The Great Stone of Lyng seemed larger than it had before, like it had grown.

Like it has been fed, she thought, remembering the stories her grandfather had told her. *The stone has gorged itself on the dead so many times that when you prick it with a needle, it bleeds.*

The shudder ripped through her and she crouched down, scratching the fur around Colin's ears, relieved that she wasn't alone here. The stone seemed to watch her, ancient and restless. She had the idea that it was waiting.

You have no idea what will happen if you try to stop me, Sabbe had said.

Two sacred stones. Two dead boys. Two missing hearts.

What were they stopping him from doing? Murdering a third victim? Just like in Somerset, in Yorkshire. Three dead boys, three hearts taken, and the killing stopped for six years.

Colin barked, uncertain, her big eyes pleading with Savage.

"He wanted to kill three people," Savage said, massaging her scalp as the headache started to creep back in. "Why three? What happens now?"

Colin whined, licking her lips.

"You're right. It doesn't matter. He can't do anything bad to anyone else."

And she almost had time to take comfort in the thought before her phone rang.

"Pete," she said as she answered it. "What's up, sir?"

"It's Blake," the DI said, his voice thick with emotion. "He's gone, and I think the Hateful Thing has him."

———

BY THE TIME she'd scrambled back to the Audi and driven it into the heart of Lesser Lyng, the village was crawling with police. She had to leave the car in the middle of the road behind an IRV, telling Colin she'd be right back before running the hundred yards or so to the Masefield house. Porter stood outside the front door between two constables, pointing at something on his phone. She called his name and he looked up. She'd known Porter for a long time but she couldn't remember him looking like this before. He looked *frightened.*

"It's a hard vehicle to miss," he told the PCs. "So don't miss it."

They walked away and Porter turned to her, both hands

in his hair. He looked scared, yes, but he was exhausted too, like he hadn't slept for a week.

"What happened, guv?" Savage asked.

"He was seen getting into a car." Porter checked his watch. "Three hours ago. Outside the church. It was his father's car, James Preston, a shitty wooden Morris Traveller. He was wearing a fucking mask, Kate. Round, whitish-yellow. The priest who saw him said it looked like the moon."

"He got into the car willingly?" Savage asked. Porter nodded, his arms slapping to his sides.

"No struggle. He got into the front passenger seat."

"Did he have the mask on before he was picked up?"

"I don't know. The witness only saw Blake getting into the car, nothing else. But it has to have been Preston, because he left one of his fucking statues in the church, with a heart inside it."

"A *heart*?" Savage said.

"Chase's, I think. Or Bartley Hearn's. Franklin is going to figure it out."

Porter's red eyes blinked at something only he could see, like he'd tranced out for a moment. He turned back to her.

"He's just a kid, and that fucker has taken him."

"You sure it's Preston?"

"Who else would it be? Prick torched his house then came to pick up Blake. He told me himself that his kids were his property, he thinks he can do whatever he wants to them."

"Maybe he's running from something else," Savage said. "We've got Sabbe, why would Preston take Blake now?"

She hesitated, then answered her own question.

"Because it needs to be three victims."

"He made his son wear a mask. The priest said it

looked like a carnival mask, like it was made of clay or something. Plaster of fucking Paris. He's going to kill him, Kate."

His face crumpled and Savage put a hand on his arm, squeezing. He nodded to her, grateful.

"We've got half of Norfolk Constabulary out looking for him," the big DI said, resolute. "We'll find him."

"We'll find him," Savage echoed. "I'll help, sir. Where do you need me?"

"I'm waiting for his mum, she's putting together a list of anywhere Preston might have gone."

He glanced through the open door into the house and Savage looked too, surprised at the darkness she found there, as if the Masefield family had learned how to bottle night.

"Cathy?" he called out.

"Hang on," came a reply. A shape peeled itself from the shadows at the end of the corridor, wreathed in smoke. It was a woman in her late forties, and Savage assumed it was Blake's mum until Porter spoke.

"Audrey Masefield, this is DC Kate Savage. Savage, this is Blake and Chase's aunt."

"Hiya," Audrey said, although she didn't meet Savage's eye. Her face was heavy with worry and lined with grief, and when she turned to the house she sniffed back a sob. The thickness of her accent was unexpected. "She's just coming. I don't think she should be out."

"She's our best shot at finding him," Porter said. "I'll send Savage along to keep an eye on her. I'll go with you."

Audrey nodded, then shook her head. She studied Savage for a moment then looked up at Porter.

"Can you go with Cath? She can get aggressive when she's like this. Well, you know, not aggressive but... She has these episodes." She shrugged, giving up. "I don't think your pal will be able to handle her if she kicks off."

"Sure," Porter said.

They turned to the door as another woman walked out of it, almost the spitting image of the first—although she seemed older. She was dressed in jeans and a jumper and she had a tatty old dressing gown over the top, white with pink spots. One cigarette was clamped in her thin lips and she had another in her hand, ready to be lit. She looked at Porter without any sign of emotion at all, and when her eyes crawled to Savage there was something lizard-like about them. Savage wondered if she'd been sedated, or if it was just the horror of losing two sons that had hollowed her out.

"Is that okay, Cath?" Audrey asked, putting a hand on her sister's arm. "You head out with Mr Porter here?"

"You know where we're going?" Porter asked. "Places James might have taken Blake when he was a kid. Anywhere James knew about that was quiet, hard to find."

"Jimmy had a place up near King's Lynn," Cathy said, so quietly that Savage had to lean in. "His nan's old house."

"We'll start there," Porter said, taking hold of Cathy's elbow and steering her away from the house a little more forcefully than he needed to. "Savage, go with Audrey, let me know if you see anything."

"Sure, guv," Savage said. She turned to the other woman. "Any ideas?"

Audrey shrugged.

"Blake loves the woods," she said with another shrug. "I don't know him all too well, I'm afraid. I was never here for them. But I remember he loved the woods, and so did Jimmy when he was younger. There's a place a few miles down the road from here where his dad took him for walks when he was a baby."

"Sounds good," Savage said. "My car's just over there."

They started walking, weaving through the growing collection of police and curious neighbours. It was only when the car came into sight, its windows cracked and a familiar goofy face staring over the dash, that Savage stopped.

"Oh," she said. "How do you feel about dogs?"

CHAPTER THIRTY-ONE

"WE'RE NEVER GOING TO FIND HIM, ARE WE?"

There was so much desperation in Cathy Masefield's voice, so much raw sorrow, that Porter couldn't bear to hear it. He flipped over a length of mouldering plywood with his shoe, as if there was a chance Blake Masefield might be hiding underneath it, then turned his attention back to the house that had once belonged to James Preston's grandmother.

What was left of it, anyway.

Whereas Preston's cottage had burned, this place had been left to rot. The thatched roof had all but gone, fallen into the crumbling shell of what would once have been a quaint little farmhouse. Two ugly new builds hemmed in the brick cadaver as if they were trying to hide it—one for sale and obviously empty. They shared a driveway, and Porter wondered if Preston had sold off the land at some point. Either way, all of the trees around the house had been cut down. There was nowhere to hide.

"He's gone," Cathy said, trying to light another cigarette with her trembling hands. Porter took pity on her, using his good hand to steady hers until the tip flared. He coughed away the smoke before answering.

"We'll find him. He can't have gone far."

And he had to turn away so that she wouldn't see the lie on his face, because the truth was that if the same person who'd killed Chase had taken Blake—if somehow Preston was at the centre of this—then the chances of seeing the boy alive again were next to nothing.

"Give me a minute," he said, doing his best to beat his face into a smile.

He crunched up the driveway to the door of the house on the left, hammering on it with his fist. It opened immediately, and the middle-aged man who stood there looked like he'd been rehearsing his greeting.

"Hello!" he said, far too loud. Behind him, inside the house, Porter heard the sounds of kids playing. "I saw you standing there. You're police, aren't you?"

"I am," said Porter, proving it with his warrant card. "I'm—"

"Here about the eyesore next door, I'm sure," the man continued. "I've filed so many complaints, it's about time somebody took me seriously."

"You've seen somebody there?"

"Yes, somebody suspicious," the man said, lowering his voice to a dramatic whisper. "*Teenagers.*"

Porter pulled out the photograph he'd taken from the Masefield house, Chase in a tracksuit, his arm around Blake, both of them beaming.

"Either of these two?"

"Um..." The man studied them for a moment then shook his head. "No, these ones are girls. They sit there all evening and drink and they're so... *screechy.*"

"You haven't seen this boy here today?" Porter asked,

pointing at Blake. "Would have been in the last four hours. He might have been wearing a mask, and he might have been driven here in a Morris Traveller, one of the ones with wooden panelling."

"No," said the man, shaking his head. "No, *he's* definitely a boy. I lodged a complaint about *girls*. You know they throw their rubbish over my fence."

"Have you seen anyone next door today?" Porter asked. "Anyone at all?"

"No," said the man, enunciating his words like he was talking to an idiot. "The girls sit there in the *evening*. The bit just after the day, and just before the night."

"Thanks," Porter said, turning to leave.

"What about the girls?" the man called after him. "The teenagers. What are you going to do about them?"

"It's above my paygrade, I'm afraid," he called back. "I'll have my Superintendent come and sort it out."

"Oh, that's brilliant, thank you!"

Porter heard the man calling for somebody, presumably to share the good news. Then the door slammed shut and there was just Cathy, leaning against the bonnet of the Mondeo and almost bent double with the weight of her grief. Behind her the sky was dark with sympathy, the day fast giving up hope. Crows wheeled through the sky, the sound of their taunts almost deafening.

A harbinger, he thought. *We're not going to find him.*

"Right," he said, clapping his gloved hands together. "Where next?"

Cathy didn't answer. She didn't move. Porter walked to her, resting his hand gently on her shoulder. Before he could speak, though, his phone rang. It was Superintendent Clare.

"Boss," he said when he answered it.

"You've found him?"

"No, sir," Porter said, walking away. "But we've only just started. Any news from your end?"

"We've had a couple of leads," he said. "DNA is back. It's Sabbe's blood on Chase Masefield, and Chase's blood on the weapons we found in Sabbe's car, Hearn's too. It's confirmed, Sabbe killed them. There's something else. Sabbe had an old phone in the car, a Motorola flip, probably stolen. Forensics found it. Nothing much on there, and only one number, a few calls and a handful of texts. Somebody he calls Ianthe. Ring any bells?"

"Ianthe?" Porter said. "No. Sorry. You tried calling it?"

"They're not answering."

Porter walked back to the car, the sound of his feet on the gravel like thunder.

"Ianthe. No last name?"

"Well I don't know, Porter," spat Clare. "Maybe there is and I just forgot to mention it to you."

Cathy looked up, the cold making her more ghostlike than ever.

"Ianthe?" she asked.

"Hang on, sir," Porter said to Clare, who was halfway through a sentence. "You know one?"

"Yes and no," she said. "Ianthe was my grandmother. My mum's mum. Died the same year my sister was born, which is why they gave it to her as a middle name. She always called herself that when she was a kid."

"Wait, your sister? Audrey?"

"Yeah," said Cathy. "Audrey Ianthe Masefield."

"Oh shit," said Porter, putting the phone back to his ear. "It's the aunt. Where the hell is Savage?"

"IT'S JUST IN THERE."

Audrey pointed a finger over the steering wheel to a road up ahead. Savage pumped the brake, slowing down and flicking on the indicator. Not that she needed to. She hadn't seen a single car in the thirty-minute drive east of Lesser Lyng, the roads utterly deserted. There might have been some kind of zombie apocalypse for all the people who were out in Norfolk today. Not that she blamed them. Even with the heaters roaring she could still feel the chill.

And there was nothing like news of a serial killer to keep people behind locked doors.

"Here?" Savage said, pulling into a track so narrow that the trees scraped their branches down both sides of the Audi. Colin barked, maybe because of the sound, maybe because she was still mad at being relegated to the boot. "Sorry," Savage said for the twentieth time.

"Honestly, it's fine," Audrey replied. "She's good company, especially today. There's a car park up ahead, from what I remember. It's been years since I was last here."

She was right, the track widening into a small, badly maintained square of fractured tarmac. There was no Morris Traveller here. No cars at all, in fact. The Audi rumbled forwards, everything rocking until it came to a halt.

"You've got a good memory," Savage said, switching off the engine.

From deep inside her coat, Audrey's phone rang. She pulled it out and studied the screen, her brow furrowed with worry.

"Might be news about Blake?" Savage said.

"It's not," Audrey replied, returning the phone to her pocket.

"You're sure this is the place Preston took his kids when they were little?"

"I'm certain."

A powerful gust of wind thumped into the car, shaking the trees that surrounded them. It was quiet here, unnervingly so. It made her think of the hollow with the butchered boy.

"No sign of Preston's car."

"He might have hidden it?" Audrey said.

"Let's take a look."

Savage braced herself before opening the door. The cold grabbed her like it had claws, the wind roaring. From inside, Colin let loose a volley of panicked barks.

"It's only the wind," she called back, looking at Audrey as she clambered out of the car. "Do you think we should bring her? She's not exactly a tracker dog but she might sniff him out."

Audrey shook her head.

"There are fields here," she said. "Cows. I wouldn't want her to scare them."

"The dog's the one who'd be scared," Savage said, slamming her door. "She bloody hates cows."

Audrey set off, heading for a break in the wild hedgerows that surrounded the car park. Back in the Audi Colin was barking her head off in a way she never did, her claws scrabbling at the glass. Savage glanced back, frowning.

"Blake?" Audrey called out, loud enough to make Savage jump. "Blake, it's your Auntie Audrey, are you here?"

They walked through the hedge, the path thick with mud. Savage grabbed Audrey before she could go any further, pointing down.

"No tracks," she said. "No car, no footprints. Nobody's been out here."

"Oh, good spot," Audrey said. "Damn it. I think we

should look anyway, right? What if he, I don't know." She opened her mouth a few times, her eyes darting to the trees, to the verges. "What if they walked on the grass, to save their shoes?"

"I don't think so," Savage said. "Where else might they have gone?"

"I think..." Audrey shook her head. "No. You're right. I'm being silly. I know another place."

"Hold up," Savage said, feeling her phone vibrate. She walked back through the opening in the hedge as she answered it, Colin still barking her head off in the Audi's boot. "Porter, sir, what've you got?"

"Kate, are you still with Audrey?" Porter said, his voice full of panic.

"Yeah, why?"

"It's her," he said. "Sabbe had a phone in his car, hidden. He was texting somebody called Ianthe. It's Audrey's middle name."

"Shit," said Savage.

Everyone has a secret, her granddad had warned her. *You just need to learn to see them.*

She turned back in time to see Audrey running towards her, a snapped branch held above her head like a club.

"Pete!" was all she had time to say.

Then the club hit home, and the world went dark.

CHAPTER THIRTY-TWO

Thump-thump. Thump-thump. Thump-thump.

It was the drums that woke her, so loud and so fast that she thought it might have been her pulse. Savage tilted her head, groaning as a wave of sickness rolled through her skull. The world cartwheeled as if gravity had been switched off and she put out a hand to ground herself only to find that she couldn't move. She swallowed, tasting copper.

Blood.

Her wrists had been bound behind her back—not by rope but by wire because she could feel the sharpness of it where it had bitten into her skin. She was sitting down, and she'd been this way for a while because everything from her lower back to her feet was completely numb. Although that might have been the cold, of course. It bit into her like a wild animal, utterly relentless.

Now that her vision was clearing she could see that there was something in front of her face, something that blocked all but a memory of daylight.

A mask.

"No," she said, the mask trapping the word and making it sound like somebody else was speaking. Her head was a mess of pain and static, it was impossible to think. She reached inside her memories, finding nothing but darkness. How had she got here? The last thing she could see was Colin, the little dog running down the hill towards the Great Stone of Lyng. Then there was Porter, standing outside of the Masefield house.

Blake, Savage thought, and as if a drain had been unclogged the horror sluiced through her: the woods, the phone call, and Audrey Masefield running at her with a branch held high.

The panic that had been sitting in her gut suddenly flared, a fire doused with petrol. All she could see was Chase, his chest cracked open and his heart torn out. Hearn, too, the second heartless boy. Their deaths had been a ritual, a dark ceremony.

They needed three victims. And here she was, bound and blindfolded, serenaded by drums.

She screwed her eyes shut, even though she couldn't see anything anyway. It was hard to pinpoint where the noise was coming from because it rolled around her like an ocean. Past it, she could hear the roar of the wind, the creak of branches, and another sound too.

Voices.

She angled her head to try to make sense of it, and when the wind died down she realised it wasn't a conversation, it was a song.

"... *down, down, down in the rushes he waits, he waits, he waits for our ashes...*"

Was it one voice or two she could hear? She couldn't be sure. The song rose and fell with the howl of the wind, with the dance of the trees. There was something sickeningly melodic about it, something in the tune that threatened to drive her mad. It was Audrey out there, it had to be. Did the woman know that Savage was awake?

She flexed her aching fingers, no sensation there at all. If she could just work her hands towards her pocket then her phone might be there—doubtful, of course, but it had to be worth a shot. She moved as slowly as she could, her back a block of frozen pain. Her fingers found her hip and paused there, looking for a pocket and finding only the thin fabric of her underwear.

That's why she was so cold, she realised. She was almost naked.

The panic shifted into dread, into the graveyard chill of knowing that her life hung by a thread. Savage swallowed again, her throat dry and sore, her jaw aching. She pushed her hands around to her side, searching, searching, because what else could she do? The wire chewed into her wrists, the blood a blessed relief from the frozen air. She could feel her bra digging into her as she moved, but the comforting weight of her granddad's whistle had gone.

Around her the song grew in volume, the wind howled, and even as she felt like opening her mouth to scream she heard another voice peel itself from the dark.

"Hello?"

A boy's voice, not quite deep enough to be a man. It rang with fear, as clear as a crystal glass struck with a spoon.

"Hello? Please, I don't know what's happening. I can't see."

If Audrey heard it, she didn't stop singing. It was more of a chant now, a chorus, the same words over and over.

"Give me your heart and I'll take you away, give me your heart and we'll keep death at bay."

"Please," the boy said. Was it Blake? It had to be. He

was sobbing, the sound of it worse than the song. She couldn't bear it.

"Blake," she said, her voice so hoarse that it was unrecognisable.

The sobbing quietened.

"Hello? Who is that?"

"I'm DC Kate Savage," she said. "I'm police."

"Get me out of here!" the kid screamed. "I don't want to be here!"

"Hush," Savage said, testing the wire around her wrists again. "Quiet, Blake. I'm tied up. I was attacked by your aunt, Audrey. Just stay calm, I'll get us out of here."

I promise, she thought, but she couldn't bring herself to say it.

The words of the song had dropped into a low, droning note, one that reminded Savage of the Buddhist monks she'd seen on the TV. Then, just like that, it stopped. There was something about the silence that followed that was infinitely worse.

Footsteps, closing in, branches cracking.

"Audrey," said Savage. "Listen to me, it's not too late. Let me go, let the boy go. This doesn't have to end in bloodshed."

"We celebrate our children, bring peace to them and say aye," Audrey said.

"Aye," came a reply—not one voice but several.

"Just as they bring peace to the world, their sacrifice keeps death away, and we say aye."

"Aye."

"Audrey," Savage said, the word barely fitting past the lump in her throat, past the tears.

She shook her head, trying to shift the mask so that she could see. To her surprise, she heard Audrey laugh, and suddenly there was a hand on her face. Savage jerked away but there was another hand rooted in her hair, twisting hard enough to make her cry out.

"Stay still, pet," Audrey said.

The mask shifted and the world rolled into view through the eyeholes. Audrey crouched in front of her, her face drawn, her eyes weeping from the cold. She was wearing a loose white dress that covered her arms and fell all the way to her bare feet. Her hair billowed around her in the wind, making it look like she was floating underwater, and the thought of it made Savage gasp for air that just didn't seem to be there.

"That's better," Audrey said. "These bloody things never stay on properly. Good lass."

She stood up and backed away, and behind her Savage saw the dense woods and the mad trees jittering beneath a sky that looked as heavy and as dark as stone. It wasn't night yet but two bonfires had been lit, each of them spluttering feebly, no match for the winter wind. Beside one was a table and a portable speaker, its lights flashing as it beat out the sound of drums.

Standing between the fires were two more women, each wearing the same style of dress as Audrey. Their faces were hidden by masks, round and moon-yellow, their eyes blinking wetly through the rough-cut holes.

One of them was holding a shotgun.

The other was holding a scythe.

"Audrey," Savage said, her voice sounding like it was coming from a million miles away. "You have to stop. You have to stop this *now*."

"I know," Audrey said, picking up her own mask from the ground and cradling it like it was a new-born baby. "But I can't. You don't understand what will happen if I stop."

"I understand what will happen if you don't stop," Savage said, trying to shift her body weight to ease the growing pain in her back. "If you kill us then it's all over, you'll go away for life."

"I think that ship has sailed," Audrey said. "You shouldn't even be here, Kate. It wasn't supposed to be you."

"Freddie Sabbe," Savage said. "It was supposed to be him, right?"

"It needs to be someone. It doesn't matter who. He has to have somebody to test him. We are not killers here. We are not monsters. We are angels, my dear, because our actions keep the world safe. We do not kill, we only watch."

Savage's thoughts reeled.

"It's Blake," she said. "Please, let him go. He's your nephew, he's a kid, he doesn't deserve this."

For the first time, a look of doubt appeared on Audrey's face, and she covered it with her mask.

"He doesn't have to die," Savage said.

"That's up to him," Audrey replied, her voice muffled. "And it's up to you. We watch, we do not kill."

"You only need one more victim," Savage said. "You can let him go. Keep me."

"The rules are not ours to change, I'm afraid," said Audrey. "The rules are his. But you can save the boy, if you choose."

"Please," Blake sobbed. "I don't want to be here. I want my mum."

Audrey sniffed, her trembling hands clasped together.

"Mum!" Blake shouted. "Mum, please!"

"The hour grows late, and I sense him here, I sense his hate. Let us lay him to rest in these sacred woods, let us lay him to rest on a bed of blood, on a stone of mercy."

"Aye!" said the other two women, the one with the

scythe thumping the shaft on the ground. "We lay you to rest on a bed of blood."

Blake was keening now, the sound of a trapped animal. Savage's thoughts were boiling over, a mess of foam that she couldn't make any sense of. She tugged at the binds around her wrists, screaming into her mask as the agony threatened to knock her back into unconsciousness. Past the roar of it, she heard Audrey speak.

"Blood must be spilled. A life must be taken. But it is not ours to take, it is yours. To leave this sacred place you must be the last one standing. Shed blood and save us all."

"What?" Savage said. The mask was slipping down her face again, the world fading into black. She felt a hand on hers, somebody working at the wire, then Audrey's voice in her ear.

"Kill him or be killed by him. Those are your options. Anything else and we'll shoot you like a dog."

The wire uncoiled and her hands were free, but before she could move, Audrey gave her a mighty shove. Savage spilled into the mud, the mask shifting again and blinding her. Her back shrieked as she pushed herself up but everything else was numb, her boneless legs collapsing beneath her. Past the roar of her pulse she heard Audrey talking to Blake, heard his cry of desperate, animal rage.

Then the sound of him running towards her.

She pushed up again, managing to stand. She wrestled with the mask, trying to pull it off, but it had to have been wrapped around her head with tape because it wouldn't budge.

"Blake," she said. "Wait!"

He was right there, she could sense him. She moved her hands in front of her only to feel something slice across her left palm, brutally cold even past the numbness.

"Blake!" she said again.

"I'm sorry," he grunted, right in her ear. "I'm sorry I'm sorry I'm—"

Savage jabbed her hands out, finding only air and stumbling into it. Blake's blade cut across her shoulder, the pain of it lost in the explosion of adrenaline. She kept moving, working at her mask, shifting it back into place and then turning to see Blake right behind her. He was naked apart from his underwear, his skin filthy, his moon-yellow mask mummified in black tape. His right hand was outstretched, a hunting knife pointed at her and already wet with her blood.

"Stop," Savage said. "You don't have to—"

He lunged and she sidestepped, giving him a shove. He lost his footing, collapsing to the mud. Savage left him there, backing away. Audrey had formed ranks with the other moon-faced women, all of them chanting that same infernal song. The one with the scythe stepped forward and threw it into the middle of the clearing, the blade clanging.

"I won't," Savage said, shaking her head.

The third woman simply levelled the shotgun, her finger on the trigger. Blake was grunting as he tried to get up, the knife gripped in his hand. He was mad with fear, his eyes wide and wet through the sockets in the mask. He panted hard, hyperventilating. Savage backed away.

"Blake," she said. "Listen to me, it's not too late. Your brother wouldn't want this, your mum wouldn't want this."

"I don't want to die," he said, sweeping the knife back and forth.

Savage's foot landed on the shaft of the scythe and she almost tripped. She bent down and snatched it up, the weapon far heavier than it had any right to be. Blake didn't even seem to see it.

"I don't want to die," he said again.

"Then don't," Savage said. "Just run."

He drew his arm back, ready to thrust the knife at her, only seeming to hear her when she said it again.

"Run, Blake."

She didn't want to turn her back on him, but what choice did she have? Savage wheeled around, holding the shaft of the scythe like a hammer throw and letting go of it with a cry of rage. It spun through the air, the blade humming, the women scattering as it clattered past them.

Savage put her head down and charged, her bare feet pounding the forest floor. She'd warmed up now, her muscles working, and she was *fast*, vaulting the nearest campfire and throwing herself at the woman with the gun just as she was lifting it.

She hit her hard and low, hearing the expulsion of breath as her shoulder connected with the woman's solar plexus. They crunched into the ground together, the shotgun discharging, shot kicking up mud. Savage bunched her fist and let fly but the woman moved her head and her knuckles cracked into the roots of a tree. Something crunched into her ribs and she rolled away, her feet in the flames of the campfire. Another of the women was right there, lining up for another kick, her eyes blisters of fury through the mask. It was Audrey, and she was screaming.

"No! You stupid fuck! You don't know what you're doing."

Savage kept rolling, managing to push herself up again. She was already breathless, no air here. Audrey pressed in, and behind her the woman with the shotgun was trying to get up, grunting like a bear.

There was no sign of Blake, though, or the third woman.

"You bitch," Audrey said. "There are rules for a reason. You have to follow them."

The woman with the gun was almost on her feet. Time was running out. Savage relaxed her body, forcing herself to take a breath. Audrey closed in, reaching for her.

Savage punched her in the throat as hard as she could, the wet snap of it louder than the shotgun had been. Audrey staggered back, her hands to her neck. Savage threw another punch, a powerful roundhouse that connected with her temple and dropped her like her strings had been cut.

The other woman was using the gun like a staff as she tried to push herself to her feet. She saw Audrey go down and lifted the weapon.

"Don't," Savage said.

Somewhere in the woods an engine growled and the woman looked away. Savage took her chance, running at her, blind to anything but the gun.

She didn't see the shape to her left until it was too late, the third woman stepping out from behind a tree with a heavy wooden stick in her hand. She swung high and Savage managed to lift her arms in time, the weapon glancing off her elbow. She lost her footing, falling at the feet of the woman with the gun.

"Stop her!" said Audrey, her voice just a whisper. "Hold her there."

One of the women dropped onto Savage's back, a hand on her head pushing her face into the mud. She tried to get up but the woman was too heavy.

"No!" she said, the word lost to the dirt, to the stagnant leaves.

"We can't do it like this," somebody said. "We need the other one."

"There's no time," said Audrey. "Just do it."

A blade against the back of her neck, pushing between the vertebrae.

"No!" Savage grunted, fighting with everything she had, feeling the bulk of the woman shift then settle again.

"Like this?"

"Just do it, Yasmin! For fuck's sake!"

The blade slid in and Savage's head exploded in a supernova of pain and panic. She screamed, and over the sound of it, past the horror of it, she heard something else.

A bark.

"Oh Christ!" said one of the women. "Oh Christ, what the—"

Another bark, then a snarl and a wet scream. The weight on Savage's back shifted and she pushed herself out of the mud, suddenly free.

The woman that had been on her back was now on the ground, Colin's jaws wrapped around her wrist. She howled beneath her mask, pulling away with a tearing sound. The woman with the gun was lifting it, trying to aim at the dog, and Savage roared—a noise she didn't even know she was capable of making. She hurled herself at her, hitting the woman just as the gun went off and sending them both crashing to the mud. She loosed a punch with everything she had and the mask shattered—something cracking underneath.

There was a glint of silver around the woman's neck, a chain. Savage reached into the top of the dress and pulled out her granddad's whistle.

"This is mine," she growled, wrenching it free.

She hit the woman again for good measure, then planted a hand on her face and pushed herself back to her feet. She tried to slide the whistle into her pocket with numb fingers before remembering she was dressed in her underwear. She tucked it into her bra instead.

The back of her neck stung, and there was blood, but she was still alive, still standing. The blade couldn't have gone deep.

The second woman was still down, wrapped around herself as she cradled her wounded hand. Colin stood beside her, her tail between her legs, her eyes wide with panic, with *guilt*.

"You're okay," Savage said, barely able to get the words out. She wrenched at the mask, feeling her hair tear from her scalp as she pulled it free. She gulped down air, an attack of vertigo almost flooring her again. "You did good."

She scanned the clearing, seeing a ghostly form sprinting through the trees.

Audrey was making a break for it.

Savage picked up the shotgun and forced herself to run, Colin falling into heel. Her body was a shell, utterly empty, but she was still a lot faster than Blake's aunt. In a few seconds she'd caught up to her, both of them breaking out of the trees into the little car park at the same time. The Audi was right there, the engine on and the headlights blazing. Its front half was beached on a steep verge, looking ready to roll onto its side, and the passenger door was open.

"Stop," Savage said. "Audrey, it's over."

Colin barked, spitting foam, and Audrey slowed to a halt, bracing her hands on her knees as she fought for breath. Savage didn't know if the shotgun was loaded but she kept hold of it anyway, aiming it at the ground. Her hand was slick with blood, the gun so heavy it felt like it might slip free.

"On your knees," she said.

Audrey reached up and pulled her mask away, not looking back.

"I knew this was a mistake," she said. "I knew it. I knew it."

"Knees," Savage said. "Or I swear to god..."

Colin barked again, one final warning. Audrey groaned as she lowered herself to the ground—not onto her knees but her backside, her legs crossed in front of her like a child. Savage circled her, never looking away as she backed towards the car. Only when she reached it did she look inside, seeing Blake in the driver's seat, his head resting against the wheel, sobs making his entire body rock.

"Hey, it's okay," she said, rapping on the glass. "It's over, Blake. Just don't move. Don't move."

She walked back to Audrey, cracking the shotgun open to see that both cartridges were spent. She snapped it back, hanging onto it in case the other two women appeared. She tilted her head back and tried to remember how to breathe. Flakes of snow landed on her skin, on her tongue, and she thought it was the most beautiful thing she'd ever felt.

Somewhere in the distance she could hear sirens, and she couldn't work out how they'd found her. Then she looked at the police issue Audi and remembered the AVLS. They'd tracked her.

Thank you, Pete, she thought.

She ducked onto her haunches and scratched Colin's neck. The little dog stood on her back legs and licked her face.

"Thank you too," she said.

Colin whined, her tail sweeping the asphalt and kicking up slush.

"Why?" Savage said. "Why would you do this?"

Audrey stared at the dirt, her eyes scrolling back and forth as if she was watching a film that only she could see.

"You wouldn't understand," she said. "You don't know what we've been through, what we've done. You don't know the lives we've saved."

"Saved?" Savage spat. "You're insane. And you're finished."

Colin whined again, staring into the growing darkness between the trees.

"Don't worry, it's over," Savage said. "It's over."

From where she sat slumped in the dirt, Audrey Masefield spat out a bitter laugh.

"It's never over," she said. "It's never fucking done."

CHAPTER THIRTY-THREE

From the outside, it was easily the most boring house that Kett had ever seen. The prefab box sat in a street of identical new builds at the end of a dreary *cul-de-sac* just west of Dereham. Not even the thin layer of snow that had fallen could make it look good. There was an ancient, boat-sized Rover in the driveway so Kett parked the Volvo right outside, accidentally bumping the curb.

"Ouch," said Evie from the back.

"Sorry," he replied.

He hadn't wanted to bring her with him, but there had been a full-blown, three-daughter meltdown right before he'd left and he didn't have the heart to leave Billie with all of them. It was weird how the maths worked with his girls. Any combination of two ran like a dream, but if you left all three in a room together then within minutes there wouldn't be much of the room left. He'd grabbed Evie and thrown her in the car before the others could ask where he was going—out of all of them, she was the easiest to control.

Usually.

"Where are we?" she asked. "I like that house. Can we move here? It's quiet."

"It's never quiet with you around," he said, giving her a smile. "Daddy just needs to talk with somebody, it won't take long. I brought some pens."

"For makeup?"

"No," Kett said, turning his attention to the mirror. He'd managed to get most of the felt-tip off but there were still faded lines of green and blue running through his eyebrows and in the nest of his beard. "Definitely not. Just for paper."

He opened the door and stepped into the freezing air, giant flakes of snow batting against his skin like insects. He wrestled Evie out of her seat, her hair billowing in his face. He wasn't strong enough to lift her yet, certainly not for long, and she moaned as she walked to the front door and continued to moan for the minute or so it took for the man on the other side to slide back what sounded like half a dozen bolts. It opened to reveal Norman Balls, wearing a dressing gown over his blue shirt and black trousers, and a deerstalker hat on his balding head. He was puffing on a pipe like somebody twice his age.

"Robbie," he said as if they were old friends. He frowned at Evie. "I didn't think you were bringing company."

"I didn't think I'd be coming at all," Kett said. "It's amazing how things change. You mind? It's cold out here."

Balls sucked on the pipe, which thankfully wasn't lit, and stood back and welcomed them in with a flourish.

"Shoes off, if you please."

"If you want me to take them off you'll have to do it for me," Kett said, trying to work the knots of pain out of his chest. "I can't really get to them."

Balls frowned, then shook his head.

"It's fine, I don't mind, just try not to make a mess. Mother doesn't like it."

Kett and Evie shared a look as they followed Balls down a short corridor and past a bright, open kitchen. The house was spotless, Kett noticed, not even a speck of dust caught in the light. Balls stopped at a door and turned back to them.

"I'm glad you're here, Robbie. Believe me, I've been following your adventures for some time. What happened to Billie, the Pig—"

"Don't," Kett snapped. "Don't say his name."

He glanced at Evie, who was mercifully studying some of the portraits on the walls. Although it was hard to tell with her, he knew. She heard more than she let on. Balls nodded, licking his lips.

"Of course, I can't imagine what it must have been like."

He turned the handle and opened the door.

"This is my private sanctum. My control centre. A harbour of knowledge in the vast ocean of ignorance that is humankind. I'll ask you to be respectful, and to only look at the things I allow you to look at. Nothing else."

"I'll try to restrain myself," Kett said, with a little more sarcasm than he'd intended. "Are you going to let us in, or do we need a password?"

"Butt," said Evie. "I bet that's the password."

"We don't say butt," Kett said sternly.

"No," said Balls, utterly serious. "That isn't it at all. That would be an awful password."

"*You're* an awful password," Evie muttered, but Balls had already moved on, leading the way into an enormous garage. He hadn't been lying, this place was a sanctum of the highest order, floor to ceiling shelving against almost every wall, leaving space for the door and for a green screen that hung in front of a camera. A desk stretched the full length of the room, six computer monitors watching them as they walked inside and a highly illegal police scanner perched on the edge. Hanging over the desk was a large framed photograph of Balls sitting on a lawn, dressed just as he was now, beaming his lopsided smile at the camera.

There was an immense square table in the middle of the garage, better suited to Churchill's war room. Papers were stacked so high on it that Kett couldn't see the top of them amongst the ceiling joists.

"This place is weird," Evie said. "And smelly. I don't like it."

"Well you weren't invited," Balls said. "So who cares what you think?"

"Just sit down there for a moment," Kett said, pointing to a clear space on the floor. "Draw me a picture of what you'd like it to look like."

Evie didn't seem as if she wanted to, but he pulled his secret weapon from his pocket and gave it a shake.

"Smarties!" Evie said, collapsing onto her backside and patting her lap.

"Don't eat them all," he said, knowing how pointless the command was.

Balls had made his way to the desk and was rotating from side to side in a plush office chair, his hands steepled under his substantial chin. He popped his lips around the pipe a few more times then took it out of his mouth and laid it on the desk.

"Consider me your oracle," he said as Kett walked over. "Ask me anything."

"Anything?" Kett asked, chancing it. "The name Hollenbeck mean anything to you?"

Balls swallowed, his eyes drifting to the far wall as he considered the question. After a moment he shook his head.

"Doesn't matter," Kett said. There was a chair beside the other man's but he didn't sit in it. He knew how painful it would be trying to stand up again. "You told me you had information about this case. We've got the killer known as the Hateful Thing behind bars, but if you have anything we can use against him then I'd like to hear it."

"You have a man behind bars," Balls said. "Frederick Sabbe, if I'm not mistaken. I don't know if he's the Hateful Thing."

"He tore the hearts out of two of his victims," said Kett in a whisper. "His DNA is all over the place. It's him."

"Maybe," said Balls. "I was doing some digging, speaking to some contacts of mine in Somerset. I wrote a whole article on the murders down there, on my website, did you read it?"

"Uh, no," said Kett. "I don't really do Google."

Balls looked disgusted.

"The boy they arrested for the crimes, his name was Flowerdew. He killed himself before he could talk."

"I know," said Kett, looking back to make sure Evie was still out of earshot.

"He was a good kid, never been in any trouble before," Balls went on.

"Yeah, I know all this."

"But did you know he was a musician?"

Kett spluttered out a breath.

"You brought me here to tell me he diddled on a clarinet?"

"You don't diddle a clarinet, Robbie," Balls said. "And no, he was a metal head. Played guitar in a local band. They scrutinised his web history after they arrested him, of course, but they dismissed the music stuff as irrelevant. I don't think it was. Look at this."

He clicked a file on his computer and a video loaded, grainy with age. A greasy-faced kid with a shaved head was headbanging in front of a band, screaming into a microphone. Kett couldn't work out a word he was saying.

"I've watched it a few times," Balls said, jabbing the screen with his finger. "'*Down, down, down in the rushes he waits, he waits, he waits for our ashes.*' And so on."

"Wait," said Kett, holding up a hand. "Avon and Somerset Police would have listened to this. They would have made a connection if he was singing about his crimes."

"This video wasn't easy to find," said Balls. "And yes, they would have taken his notebooks as evidence, his lyrics and whatever else, but I don't think they would have found *this* song when they confiscated his belongings."

"Why?" Kett asked.

"You'll see. Generally, Flowerdew doesn't sing about the Hateful Thing, or about the dead kids, anything like that. In fact, there's a pretty positive tone to his lyrics, they're about saving the world if you listen closely. But this song is different, what do you make of this, the chorus."

He upped the volume, the music pumped through a set of tinny speakers.

"*Give me your heart and I'll take you away, give me your heart and we'll keep death at bay,*" the boy sang. Then, even louder: "*Kill them to save them, kill them to save them,*"

"I don't get it," Kett said. "It doesn't explain why he did what he did."

"Only it does," said Balls. "It explains everything. Because this song isn't his."

"He didn't write it?" Kett asked, and Balls shook his head. He clicked the video closed and opened up another one. The quality was a million times worse, but Kett thought he could make out a band on stage. It was impossible to identify their faces. It didn't even look like they *had* faces.

"I don't just deal with conspiracy stuff, I'm an archivist for everything in this part of the country. Norfolk born and bred."

"You mean *Normal for Norfolk?*" Kett said.

Balls ignored the jibe.

"I've lived here my whole life, it's my world, so I make a note of everything important or interesting that's ever happened here." He gestured to the shelves that were groaning under the weight of the folders and box files. "And I've got the memory of an elephant. It's hard for me to forget something. I knew I'd heard that song before, so I went looking."

He played the video, the sound quality much worse, as if Kett was hearing it through somebody else's earphones. He leaned in and sure enough the lyrics were the same. Now that the video was moving he understood why he hadn't been able to make out the faces of the singers.

They were wearing masks, moon-yellow and mad.

"Who are they?" he asked.

"Want to guess?"

"It's Greg Skinner, isn't it? This is their band from high school."

"Right," said Balls, pointing to the lead guitarist. Kett could see the long hair that hung beneath the mask. "That one is James Preston, father of the murdered boy."

Kett nodded, feeling his Spidey sense start to wake for the first time on this bastard case, feeling the pieces begin to click together.

"This was 1992," Balls said.

"1992, they'd have been out of school. Skinner and Preston would have been, what, nineteen by then?"

"Right. They kept the music going for a little while, although they didn't tell many people. By this time they were going by the name *The Church of the Heartless Boys*. Bit of a mouthful if you ask me. This is a gig in Ipswich. They had the masks for a little while as a gimmick, long before *Slipknot* thought of it. They never amounted to much, but the song is theirs, word for word."

"Oh shit," Kett said.

"I think they're your Hateful Men," Balls said. "I think Skinner and Preston are the ones behind the killings. I'd stake my life on it. The song you're hearing is called *Stone Cold Dead*, it's the only one they ever really performed. Listen to the lyrics. It's all darkness versus light, evil versus good, devils versus common folk and death forced back by love. I think Skinner and Preston got carried away with their own lyrics, their own mythology. They are your killers."

Kett opened his mouth to ask a question and was cut off by his phone. He gave Balls an apologetic smile at the ear-shattering volume of the *Mexican Hat Dance*. It was Porter, and he sounded breathless.

"Don't worry," the DI said. "She's fine, they're both fine. We found them."

"Whoa, Pete. You're going to have to back up. Who's fine?"

"Oh, shit, sorry. Savage, they took her, tried to fucking kill her. Blake Masefield too."

"*What?*" Kett said, putting his free hand in his hair, ignoring the pain.

"It was Audrey, Blake's aunt. She must have stolen Preston's car, picked Blake up, and taken him to the woods. It's why he went with her so willingly, why he put on the mask. Then Audrey and Savage went to look for him and she knocked Kate out, tied her up. They were going to make her and Blake fight to the death, some kind of ritual. It's what they did to Chase and Bart, they made them both fight Freddie Sabbe. But Blake ran and Savage... well, she *Ketted* her way out of it."

"Ketted?" Kett said.

"Kicked seven shades of shit out of them, with a little help from Colin."

"*What?*"

"The little hairy one, that is. But she's okay, they're both okay. We tracked her car, found her in time. Audrey's in cuffs and so are the other two. You're not going to believe it, Robbie, one's a fucking librarian from the high school, the other's a grandmother. She's Yasmin Bisset, the woman who called in Bart's body. We know them all."

"*What?*" Kett said again, unable to stop himself. "I don't... you're telling me that those three women are the killers? They're the Hateful Thing?"

Norman Balls' eyes widened, his mouth falling open.

"Looks that way," Porter said.

"They talking?"

"Yeah, but they're a stuck record. '*You don't know what you've done, you don't know what you've unleashed.*' All that bollocks. Forget it, we caught them red-handed, they're not getting off."

"Nice work," Kett said. "This fudging job, eh?"

"This fudging job," Porter said. "I've got to go, I don't want to leave Blake on his own."

He hung up and Kett stood there for a moment, trying to digest what he'd heard.

"Three *women?*" Balls said. "I don't understand."

Neither did Kett. Something didn't feel right.

You don't know what you've done.

According to Savage, Sabbe had said exactly the same thing when they'd caught him.

You don't know what you've unleashed.

What were they talking about?

He looked at the video that was still playing, watching Greg Skinner grandstanding to the crowd, screaming from behind his mask. He was dead, but Preston was missing. Was he doing this?

"Who else was in the band?" Kett asked, trying to remember what the team had told him. "Pete Little, and some French kid?"

As if listening to him, the camera panned around to show the bassist, a ridiculously tall kid wearing a mask of his own.

"I don't think it was a French kid," said Balls. "That's Pete Little on bass. You can tell by the sheer size of him. He went on to present some local radio, died a few years ago. He was just too tall, something snapped in him."

The camera spun a little more, the masked drummer almost lost behind a massive cymbal. Greg Skinner was singing his heart out.

"*Here's your chance, take it or leave it, lambs to the slaughter or you're in the shit, in the shit.*"

"Daddy," came Evie's voice from the back of the room.

"Hang on," Kett said. "Just give me a minute, sweetie."

"I need a poo."

He ignored her, willing the camera to shift, to reveal the man who sat behind the drum set. But it didn't, and then the song ended, both Skinner and Preston hurling themselves off the stage into the crowd.

"That's it," Balls said, ready to close the window.

"Wait," Kett said.

The bassist pulled off his mask, revealing a goofy-looking young man grinning hard. Then the drummer stood up, hurling his sticks into the air. He was young and tall, his hair long behind his mask. He was built like a brick shit house, trunk-like arms sticking out of a sleeveless vest.

"Who is that?" Kett said. "Michel Debussy?"

Before Balls could answer, the drummer ripped off his mask. The face beneath was gripped by a frightening intensity, an almost religious fervour, made somehow worse as the video froze.

"Who is that?" Kett asked.

"Dennis Pruitt," Balls said. "Went to school with Skinner and Preston."

Kett used his phone to snap a photograph, texting it to Porter. He gave him ten seconds then called.

"You know this guy?" he asked.

"The drummer? Sure, I saw him yesterday. He's Skinner's solicitor."

"Pruitt?"

"Yeah," Porter said. "How do you know? Where is that?"

"It's Skinner's band," Kett said. "He was the drummer."

"*Seriously?*"

"Daddy *please*," Evie said.

"Hang on a minute," Kett answered, bracing his free hand against his forehead like he could physically manoeuvre the pieces of this case into the right place.

"The toilet is right across the hall," said Balls. "Please don't poo on my floor."

"I don't want to go on my own," Evie wailed. "Mr Marshmallow will be waiting for me."

"Mr *who?*"

"Robbie," said Porter. "We got Sabbe, we got Audrey Masefield and her coven. I think we're done."

You don't know what you've unleashed.

Evie walked to Kett, tugging at his jacket. He studied the green line on her hand, the one he'd drawn himself last night in felt-tip, the one that kept her safe from the monsters in her head.

And suddenly he saw it. Suddenly he understood.

A ritual, to keep the devil away.

"Oh no," he said. "It's a ceremony, just like in the song. *Lambs to the slaughter.* I don't think Audrey Masefield is doing this because she wants to hurt anyone, she's doing it to keep people *safe.*"

Balls stared up at him and Porter breathed down the phone, both of them waiting.

"Three people have to die," Kett said. "Christ, that's it, three lambs have to be sacrificed. It's right there in the song. *Stone Cold Dead.* If three kids die then it keeps the Hateful Thing away. It's the price they have to pay to stop him from killing indiscriminately. And if they don't do it, the devil's unleashed. He can do whatever the hell he wants."

"That's insane," said Porter.

"It is," Kett said. "It's madness. But it fits. Somerset, three dead. Yorkshire, three dead. But Neath, they only found two kids, then all hell broke loose. All those people died. They couldn't sacrifice three victims in time so the Hateful Thing was free to kill as many people as he liked. Men, women, children."

"Oh shit," Porter said. "Blake was supposed to fight Sabbe but they both survived. Chase Masefield and Bartley Hearn. We've only lost two."

"Then it isn't over," Kett said, taking Evie's hand, pulling her close. "Pruitt's the Hateful Thing, and he's about to go on the hunt."

CHAPTER THIRTY-FOUR

PORTER HUNG UP THE PHONE AND STARTED RUNNING, weaving his way through a sea of blue lights and a storm of falling snow until he saw Clare at the far end of the car park. The Superintendent looked exhausted, both hands resting on the bonnet of an IRV. He was watching an ambulance pull onto the road, its siren wailing as it accelerated. Blake Masefield was inside, hollowed out by hypothermia and shock.

But alive, thanks to Savage.

Two of the women who had attacked her had been carted away in ambulances too, under police guard. Phoebe Finch, the librarian at the Nelson Academy, had a lacerated wrist from Colin's teeth. The other woman was Yasmin Bisset, the same one who'd reported Bartley Hearn's body on the rock, and she still hadn't come around from the punch to the face. Audrey Masefield sat alone in the cell in the back of a police van, cuffed and broken.

Savage crouched by the open rear door of an IRV, dressed in a borrowed tracksuit that was three sizes too big for her and looking about twelve years old. She was holding onto her grandfather's police whistle with one bandaged hand like it was the only thing stopping her from sinking. Her other hand gently stroked Colin the wonderdog, who had fallen fast asleep on the back seat. The little dog had earned her rest.

"Hey, boss," Porter called out.

Clare turned to him.

"Porter," he said. "Whatever it is, I don't want to hear it. We've got them, let's leave it at that."

"I don't think we do, sir," Porter said. "I've just spoken to Kett."

Clare's face grew sour.

"He thinks there's somebody else involved, somebody else giving the orders."

Savage saw them talking and walked over. Her hands were filthy, and her hair was matted with mud. A large bandage covered the back of her neck, spotted with blood. She'd been offered medical treatment, of course, and a ride home. But it was Savage. She would be here until the end.

"It's Pruitt," Porter said when she was close enough to hear. "Dennis Pruitt."

"The solicitor?" Clare spat. "Toss off. Nonsense."

"He was in the same high school band as Preston and Skinner. He was the drummer."

"So?" Clare said. "I played the flute at school, it doesn't make me Jack the Ripper."

"But..." Porter hesitated. "The *flute*, sir?"

Clare waved the words away.

"Why did we never question the fact he was in the same band?" the Super asked. "That's a connection we should have made."

"We asked the wrong people. Phoebe Finch, the librarian, told me it was a French kid. She must have told Audrey we were asking because when I asked her she said the same thing. They were protecting Pruitt."

"Toss off," Clare said again.

"They had a few songs, but there was one in particular," Porter said. "One about a kind of battle between good and evil. *Stone Cold Dead*, it was called. I don't know the whole thing but I think it tells the story of a hateful demon who appears every six years and tries to kill as many people as it can."

"Like in Neath," Savage said, shivering.

"Exactly. There's only one way of stopping him, and that's by performing a ritual that involves killing three innocent people."

"That doesn't make any sense," Clare said. "In order to stop him from killing, you have to kill?"

"I don't think they care about it making sense to us, guv, but it makes perfect sense to *them*. According to Kett's sources, the guy they collared in Somerset was in a band too, there's footage of him singing that same song. Flowerdew, his name was. Avon and Somerset Police knew about the music, but they only confiscated *his* notebooks, they only saw the songs *he* wrote. They didn't know about this one, because he'd learned it from Pruitt. The only thing Flowerdew talked about before he killed himself was the Hateful Thing. I don't think he was claiming to *be* the Hateful Thing, I think he was warning them that the Hateful Thing was coming."

"Because he thought he'd only managed to kill two people," Savage said. "He killed himself before Phillip Munser passed away."

Clare frowned, then turned to her.

"Is your woman talking?"

"*My* woman? You mean Audrey? No."

"Then let's change that," he said, pushing between them and walking to the van. "Open it up," he ordered the uniformed officer who stood there, and the PC did as he was asked. Audrey sat in the cage, her head bowed, her hair hanging between her legs, hiding her face. She was still wearing the dress—more brown than white now—and she was shivering hard. "Miss Masefield, my name is Superintendent Colin Clare. We're going to ask you some questions and you're going to answer them. Is that clear?"

No reply. Porter stepped forward.

"It's Dennis Pruitt, isn't it? He's the Hateful Thing."

Audrey's head tilted up, her dark eyes studying him though tangled knots of hair.

"He made you do this," Porter went on. "And it's not just this time, is it? He's made you do it before. He made you kill."

Audrey didn't speak, but she didn't look away.

"He never made me do anything," she said.

"You've known him since high school," said Porter. "Did it start back then? With the music, the gigs? But it was more than that, wasn't it? Pruitt created... I don't know, some kind of mythology. He spun this story about a Hateful Thing, and then what? He started believing it himself?"

"You don't understand," Audrey said.

"I *don't* understand. So help me out. You're not a killer, right? You're a saviour. You're protecting people from him."

"You don't know what he's capable of," she said. "He's evil. He's monstrous. He always has been. Even in school. He..."

She took a deep breath, the words flowing.

"It was his idea for the band. Jimmy and Greg wanted to fuck around, they wanted the fame, but Dennis was different. He wrote the songs. They were horrid, when you listened to them. Brutal. Violent. But nobody cared because the band was going somewhere—at least until Preston messed it up by getting expelled. After we'd all left school they reformed, they managed to get gigs. There was one, in Skegness, in this awful, awful bar."

She put a hand to her mouth, her fingers trembling.

"1996," Porter said. "Six people died. All kids."

"It happened afterwards, at a party. I wasn't there, but I knew it was him. We all knew. Me and Phoebe and Yasmin, we followed the band everywhere because we were young. We liked the attention. But Dennis was getting worse, he was... I don't know. There was a darkness in him, a sickness, we all saw it."

"Why didn't you call the police?" asked Clare.

"We were too scared. You don't know him, you don't know what he's like. James and Greg didn't believe us, we were on our own. We were scared, but we asked him to stop. We did that much. Dennis was ill, he knew he was ill. He thought he was possessed. He said he would stop but he needed our help, he needed us to do something for him."

"You had to sacrifice three people," Porter said, shaking his head. "Just like the song."

Audrey nodded, her eyes dead.

"Every six years," she said. "If we did that, he'd leave folks alone. And he's always fair. He plays by the rules. If we do this, if we sacrifice the lambs, then he goes away."

"You have to kill for him?"

"Never," she said. "I've never killed anybody. They do it themselves, they're always willing."

"To fight to the death?" said Porter.

"To fight for *life*," she said. "To have the chance to walk away."

"What happens if you can't find enough people to sacrifice? He goes on a killing spree?"

"He's unleashed. All he brings is death. Nothing can stop him. It happened in Skegness, and it happened again in a place called Neath."

"Fourteen dead," said Savage.

"More," Audrey whispered. "So many more, over the next six years."

Clare's eyes had swollen, his jaw bulging.

"What the hell is wrong with you?" he said. "Did you never think of just calling the police?"

Audrey shook her head.

"You can't stop him."

"Where?" asked Savage. "Where is Pruitt now? Who is he going to kill?"

"I don't know," she said. "He can be anywhere. You can't see him, you can't stop him."

"And you believe that?" Porter said. "That he's some kind of demon?"

"I'm not stupid. I know what he is. But these are the rules he plays by."

"And you're okay with the fact he asked you to kill your own nephews? Your own blood?"

This time, her face fell.

"They're not my blood," she said. "I hardly know them."

"But why them?" Savage said. "It doesn't make sense, you could have picked anyone, right? Why your sister's boys?"

"Because Dennis asked for them," she said, groaning. "He never asks, he never cares, but this time he did."

"He wanted Preston's children dead," Savage said, speaking to Porter. "That's personal. Why?"

"And why here?" Clare asked. "He killed in Somerset,

in Neath, in Yorkshire and Skegness, never on home turf. Why come back to Norfolk?"

Savage frowned, her eyes scrolling back and forth.

"What is it?" Porter said.

"Back at Greg Skinner's house, after he... after he died. I found those photos in the fire, the letters."

"He was being blackmailed, wasn't he?" Clare said.

"That's what I thought, sir. Somebody knew about the photos he took and they were trying to get money from him. *'I know what you did. I know about the boys.'* That's what it said."

"The boys," Porter said. "Maybe they didn't mean the boys in the barn. Maybe they meant the ones that had been murdered. The *heartless* boys."

"Yeah," said Savage. "Skinner wasn't the one who was being blackmailed. *He* was the one doing the blackmailing."

"He was blackmailing Pruitt," Porter said, catching on. "I knew there was something weird going on in the interview, the way Skinner was speaking to him. I thought he was just being an arsehole, but... Shit, they worked it out, didn't they? Skinner and Preston met up last year for the first time in ages, for the sculpture thing. Maybe they were talking about old times, the band. Maybe they worked out that it was Pruitt who was killing those kids."

"Because of the song," Savage said, nodding. "They put two and two together, realised what he was doing, and tried to blackmail him."

"And it went seriously fucking wrong," Porter said. "This ringing any bells, Audrey?"

If it did, she didn't reply. She was done talking.

"So Pruitt came home and sent his disciples after Chase and Blake Masefield," Porter said. "To get his revenge on Preston."

"Oh," said Savage, flinching like she'd been given an electric shock. "Wait, Pruitt showed up just after Skinner shot himself. Right? Within minutes. I'll bet you anything that Greg Skinner asked to meet with Pruitt. He knew Pruitt had killed Chase, so he was going to weasel out of the blackmail plans, hand over the evidence. He must have been terrified."

"So Pruitt killed Skinner," Clare said. "Tossing hell."

"I bet he burned Preston's house down as well," Porter said. "But that's not enough for him. He was pissed enough to kill Preston's children, I think he'd do the same to Skinner. I think he'd go after Skinner's child too."

The snow fell hard, like it wanted to bury them all, like it wanted to hide the truth away forever. Porter looked at Clare.

"I know where he is."

CHAPTER THIRTY-FIVE

Savage drove, Porter up front and Clare sliding around in the back seat every time they hit a bend. Two more IRVs followed, packed with police.

They weren't going to take any chances.

It wasn't a long drive, just twenty minutes to the eastern edge of Lesser Lyng where Greg Skinner's monstrous house waited for them. Savage swung the car onto the driveway, shuddering to a halt behind the only vehicle that sat there.

Dennis Pruitt's immense black Range Rover.

"You were right," she said, cutting the engine and clambering out.

"Wait," said Clare, fighting with his child-locked door. "Somebody let me out!"

Porter climbed into the falling snow, surveying the house. The curtains were open but the glass was dark, no sign of anybody inside. He opened Clare's door and offered the Super his hand.

"I'm not an infant, Pete," Clare said, struggling out.

The other IRVs rounded the corner, lights blazing, and within seconds the driveway was swarming with police.

The driver of the first one climbed out, staring at Savage, one eyebrow raised.

"What did you learn to drive in?" he said. "A bloody RAF Tornado?"

"A dodgem," she replied with an apologetic shrug.

Duke appeared, and Porter saw him give Savage a nervous smile.

"How do you want to do this?" the big PC asked.

"How I want to do this is wait for an armed response unit," Clare said, his brows knitted together as he took in the house and the woodland next door. "Skinner had guns."

"Lots of them," Porter said. "But if Pruitt's in there right now, he knows we're here. He won't hesitate. He might have Lauren, her mum too."

As if answering, a shout broke free from the house, dragged away by the wind.

"Tossing hell," Clare said. "I can't send you in there, Pete."

"You don't have to. Just don't stand in my way."

The Super shook his head.

"Kett version 2.0. It's not worth it."

But it *was* worth it, Porter knew. He hadn't been there for Blake, but he was here now. He could put an end to it.

Another shout and Porter started moving. Savage was with him, flagging, and he waved her away.

"Make sure they cover the sides, the back," he said to her. "Make sure Pruitt doesn't go anywhere."

"I've got your back," Duke said, and Porter almost chased him off too before he decided not to. If he couldn't have Savage by his side in a fight, the big man was a good second choice. Duke flicked out his baton, the PR24 looking like a toy in his giant hand.

"Pruitt's a murderer," Porter said. "A psychopath. He's killed before, he won't hesitate."

"Neither will I, boss," said Duke.

They reached the front door and Porter grabbed the handle before realising he didn't need to. It was open, and a solid push revealed the entrance hall, heavy with shadows. He held his breath, listening past the howling wind. Were those voices he could hear, full of fear, full of *hate*?

"Police," he called out, his booming voice echoing down the corridor, bouncing up the stairs. "Dennis Pruitt, we know you're here. Make yourself known."

A scream, broken into words.

"Don't! Don't! Don't!"

"Ah fuck this," Porter said.

He nodded at Duke and the PC nodded back. They pushed into the house, Porter leading the way down the corridor, the sound of his shoes on the flagstones like gunfire. The kitchen was deserted, a pan of something smoking on the stove. The door on the other side of the room was open and Porter made his way to it, seeing a small room and a big safe. It was locked, but shotgun cartridges lay scattered over the floor like dead mice.

"Sir," Duke hissed from the other side of the kitchen. Porter looked back and saw the PC pointing to the ceiling with his baton. "They're upstairs."

Sure enough, he could hear the thump of footsteps up there. Somebody was running.

"No!" screamed the same voice.

Porter ran back into the hallway, Duke already at the base of the wide stairs. They climbed them together, halfway up before a woman literally launched herself from the top. It was Matilda Skinner, her face warped with fear, her hands wheeling as she tripped and fell. She bounced once, her legs spiralling over her head, then she thumped into Duke. He was ready for her, stopping her like a rugby player and holding her tight. The little woman opened her mouth and screamed in his face, raking her nails down his cheek. Duke wrapped his arms around her, doing his best not to go arse over tit down the stairs.

"Police," he said. "Calm down."

She seemed to see him, then Porter, spitting out a mangled cry of desperation.

"He's got her, he's got my baby, he's got her."

"Where?" Porter said.

"Her bedroom, he's got a knife, he's going to—"

Porter ignored her, climbing the stairs only for Duke to call him back.

"Here," he said, offering the baton.

Porter took it, the shape of it still so familiar in his hand even after so many years in a suit. He swung it back and forth a couple of times as he climbed the stairs onto a wide, bright landing. It wasn't hard to guess which room was Lauren's, and it had nothing to do with the hearts that had been painted on her open door.

Screams poured out of it, full of horror. The sound of them stoked a fire inside Porter's gut, a flare of rage that threatened to overwhelm him.

"Pruitt!" Porter yelled. "Last chance."

He walked to the door, angling his head around it— seeing Lauren Skinner on the bed, her wrists tied to the posts; seeing the man who stood over her, a wicked-looking blade in his hand. His hair hung to his shoulders in lank curls, and he was shirtless, his glistening torso decked with tattoos. He looked bigger than he had any right to.

"How the fuck did you work it out?" Pruitt said. "I'm pretty fucking pissed off, if you want to know the truth."

"Not as pissed off as you'll be in a minute when I wrap this baton around your head," Porter shouted, stepping through the door. "Drop the knife."

"You alone?" Pruitt asked.

"I've got the whole Force with me," Porter said. "But I don't need them. Drop the knife and get on your knees."

Pruitt sighed, Lauren's screams reduced to sobs. He lowered the knife to her throat and she tried to worm away, the bed creaking beneath her.

"Please," she said. "Oh please, I don't want to die, I don't—"

"Shut up," Pruitt said. "Just shut the fuck up and let me think."

The solicitor stood at the head of the bed, his face purple with anger. The knife was thin and curved, the handle made of what looked like bone. It was something from a horror movie, and Porter had no doubt it would be razor-sharp.

"Put it down," he said. "And let her go. It's over. We've picked up Audrey Masefield and the others, we've got Freddie Sabbe. We know about the deal you made with them. We know everything."

"And the Preston boy?" Pruitt asked. "What was his fate?"

"Blake's alive," Porter said, and Pruitt gritted his teeth.

"I wanted both of them," he said. "I wanted their father to know what I'd done."

"Believe me, their dad's as big a piece of shit as you are." Porter glanced at Lauren, who was looking back at him with wide, wet eyes. "It's over," he said when he returned his attention to Pruitt. "You either come now or you wait for the people with guns. It's all the same to me."

"This is my time," Pruitt said. "My *right*. I fucking earned it."

The stairs creaked, then Duke was breathing in Porter's ear.

"It's over," Porter said again.

"You're probably wondering why I did all this, aren't you?" Pruitt said.

"To be honest, mate, I really don't give a shit," Porter replied.

Pruitt shrugged, almost wistful.

"You know how easy it is to be a god?" He looked at Porter, his wet lips curling into a smile. "A god *or* a devil, take your pick, they're one and the same. You know how fucking easy it is to make people do what you want them to do? That's what you're looking at, you know. Something *holy*. I've taken so many lives. So many. I'm so much more than you could ever imagine."

"You're a prick," Porter said. "Put it down."

"I will," said Pruitt. "As soon as I finish this."

He flexed his grip on the knife, everything tensing, and Porter was running before he even knew it. The room was big but he crossed it in a heartbeat, lobbing the baton at Pruitt's face. It was a lucky shot, cracking into the bridge of the big man's nose. Pruitt opened his mouth to cry out then Porter slammed into him like a train, both of them crunching into the wall.

The knife pinged away and Pruitt squawked, one hand batting at Porter's face as he fought to find his balance. He was a big guy, but he couldn't get any force behind his attack and Porter slapped his arm away. He grabbed him by the hair and swung him around, hurling him across the room. Pruitt tripped on his own feet, falling back, his head ringing off the bare boards.

"I've got him," Duke said, entering the room.

"No," Porter growled. "He's mine."

Pruitt was trying to get up but Porter straddled him, one hand around his meaty throat, the other reaching for the baton. Pruitt groped at him with fat fingers but Porter didn't even feel it.

"How many kids?" he said. "How many kids like Blake died because of you?"

Pruitt was trying to speak but Porter was gripping his neck too hard. He found Duke's baton and lifted it.

"You don't deserve to walk out of here, you piece of shit."

"Porter, sir," said Duke, a warning.

But Porter wasn't listening. All that mattered was the filth beneath him, and the weapon in his hand. It wasn't an executioner's blade, but then neither was the hammer that Kett had sunk into the back of the Pig Man's head. This was no different, was it? This is what he deserved. This is what was needed.

Pruitt's eyes bulged, his giant tongue sliding out of his mouth.

One hit, and he'd never hurt another child.

"Fuck you," Porter said.

He slammed the baton down, hard enough to splinter the floorboard beside Pruitt's head. The man whimpered, choking on his own spit.

"Fuck you," Porter said again, letting go of Pruitt's throat. Rage was making the whole room spin, white spots flashing in his vision. He struggled up, sitting on the edge of the bed. "Cuff him."

Duke flashed Porter a wary glance as he flipped Pruitt over onto his belly and snapped the handcuffs around his wrists. A tattoo covered the man's broad back, a dead boy strung up against a menhir, his chest a ruin. Above it loomed a devil in a moon-bright mask, and below were four words.

Lamb to the slaughter.

Porter turned to Lauren. She was weeping, the tears rolling down her face.

"Please," she said, as if he might do anything other than free her.

He worked at the knots and she tugged herself loose, almost falling off the bed. She ran from the room, stopping only to launch a ball of spit at Pruitt. It fell short, landing on Duke's back, but the PC didn't seem to notice. Porter heard her calling her mum's name as she thumped down the stairs, then the sound of Superintendent Clare answering her.

"Fuck me," Duke said, wiping the sweat from his face. Pruitt had given up and was whispering sweet nothings to the floor. When Porter leaned in, it sounded almost like a song.

Footsteps on the stairs, then Clare lurched into the room. He looked at Porter, then at Pruitt, then at the baton which lay on the floor.

"Good job," Clare said. "From where I was standing it sounded like you were going to kill him."

Porter laughed.

"Never crossed my mind, sir," he said.

"And you're sure he's the last one?" Clare asked? "You're certain there are no more layers to this bloody case?"

"The buck stops with him," Porter said. "He's our Hateful Thing."

Not hateful, though, Porter thought, watching as Duke dragged Pruitt up and pushed him through the door. *Just pathetic, just lost, just finished.*

CHAPTER THIRTY-SIX

Thursday

"HEY, KATE, WAIT UP."

Savage turned around—gingerly, because of the pain in the back of her neck. Porter was running along the corridor towards her and she opened the door and held it for him.

"Morning, sir," she said, smiling. "Age before beauty."

"Thanks," he said as they made their way into HQ. "But to be honest you're looking a little rough around the edges today."

Savage put a hand to her face, to the cut that had split the skin of her cheek. A blood vessel had broken in her left eye, making her look like something from a zombie film. Her hand and shoulder had stitches, but they would heal.

She wasn't sure she could say the same about her mind.

"How're you doing?" Porter asked.

"I'm good," she said. "The whole thing feels like a... like a dream or something. A nightmare."

"Yeah," he said. "Colin okay? That dog's a little champ."

"She is," Savage said.

She walked into the bullpen, Porter right behind her. There were a dozen people at their desks and they all looked up. Somebody whistled, and a second later Clare popped his head out of his door.

"What tosser is whistling?" he said, then he spotted them. "Oh, right."

He lifted his big hands so dramatically that Savage couldn't figure out what he was doing with them. Then he brought them together in a mighty clap. Everyone else in the room joined in, a round of applause accompanied by whoops and cheers. Savage was laughing before she even knew it, one hand to her mouth until the room fell silent again. She turned to Porter, and even he was speechless.

"You earned that," Clare said. "Give me a minute, I'll be right out."

The Super's mouth warped into what might have been a grimaced grin, and he ducked back through his door.

"Was that a *smile*?" Porter asked. "I didn't even know he could."

"Probably wind," Savage said. "Like with babies."

She walked to Spalding's desk. The DS leaned back in her chair, a pencil clamped between her teeth.

"The Masefield mum's in there," she mumbled. "The boy too."

"Blake?" said Porter, perching on the desk.

Spalding took the pencil out of her mouth and held it up.

"Hey, Porter, have a guess at where this is going if you don't get off my desk."

"Sorry," he said, jumping back to his feet.

"Any news?" Savage asked. She hadn't been into work yesterday because Clare had forced her to go for a check-up —literally driving her to the hospital himself. After that, he had taken her home and told her that if he saw her again before the morning he was going to fire her.

Out of a tossing cannon, had been his exact words.

"I'm still trying to get my head around it," Spalding said. "But the whole thing makes a twisted kind of sense. They were kids when it started, teenagers. Both of the Masefield sisters were groupies. Cathy dated James Preston back then, and on and off over the years. Although she was never into the music. That's why she was never part of the secret they all shared. Audrey and Pruitt were together too, although they kept it a secret. They've been together ever since, in one way or another. Even when she was up north, they never stopped writing to each other."

"What about the other two women?" asked Porter.

"They all grew up with each other. Finch and Bisset were at the gig in Skegness. There was an after-party, and after that Pruitt murdered six kids on the beach—not much younger than him, to be honest. Drugs and drink were involved, but this was all on him. The police never worked out who did it because all the witnesses were dead. He bought into his own image as this devil figure, came up with the idea of the Hateful Thing after reading the legend. I guess Audrey and the others were looking for something to believe in and this was it."

Savage shook her head.

"So the women willingly went along with him?"

"Yes and no," said Spalding. "I think they believed that they were doing the right thing. I think he convinced them of that. Forensics are inside Finch and Bisset's houses as we speak and there's a lot of arcane stuff there. They were heavily into it. We found masks at Finch's place, and in the school. She was decorating the library with them. Same masks that Preston originally made for the band."

"They were lost in it," Savage said, remembering the faces she'd glimpsed behind the masks, that religious ecstasy. "I don't think there was any doubt in their minds." She laughed sadly, touching the whistle beneath her shirt, the one that rested against her heart. "Everyone has a secret."

"But I think they probably saved people," Spalding said. "As messed up as it was, the fact that they killed at all meant that Pruitt couldn't. I have no doubt that there are people walking around right now who owe their lives to those three women. And they wanted out, that was clear. They didn't want to do it anymore. Bisset was the one who called us about Bartley's body, and Phoebe Finch was the one who identified him. They wanted it to stop. Not that it makes it any better."

"People are nuts," said Porter.

Savage looked up and so did Spalding, seeing DI Dunst cross the room towards them, yawning.

"Anything new?" she asked him.

"Kinda," he replied. "Freddie Sabbe lived in Ipswich, but he was a member of some online groups that dealt in the occult. Guess who ran them?"

Nobody replied, and Dunst looked disappointed.

"Finch," he said. "The librarian, out of the school. You should see some of the messages she sent to these kids, proper cult stuff. I almost bought into it myself. Sabbe is a loner, likes fish more than people. Finch had been getting into his head for months now, grooming him as a weapon, promising him untold riches. He's still going on about it now, in hospital. His mind's a ruin. We'll find the same links between Finch and Kevin Flowerdew as well, I'm sure of it."

"What about Hearn?" Savage asked. "What's the connection there?"

"Apparently Audrey told Sabbe that he could pick the last victim himself. They knew they were going to kill the two Masefield boys, and Pruitt wanted Lauren Skinner for himself, but it was up to Sabbe to find a third. Turns out Bartley Hearn's dad ripped off Sabbe's parents, cheated them out of some money years ago."

"So he thought he'd kill him, even up the score," Savage said. "Jesus. How's James Preston doing, sir?"

"Still bawling like a baby," said Dunst.

Preston had been found in the woods east of his burnt-out cottage, camping in a tent. According to him, he'd seen somebody break into his car and he'd legged it, thinking it was Pruitt coming for revenge. It hadn't been Pruitt, of course, it had been Audrey. But Preston had confirmed the blackmail story in a flood of tears. Both he and Skinner had recognised Pruitt's crimes and tried to pry some money from him.

"Safe to say he regrets it," Savage said.

"Pruitt has confessed anyway," Dunst said. "Just heard, he's pleading guilty to all of them. There are dozens. Nearly a quarter of a century of death."

Savage heard a door opening and she looked back, surprised to see Kett limp into the bullpen. He was struggling, one hand massaging his chest as he crossed the floor.

"Are you supposed to be here?" asked Spalding.

"Someone else booked out the meeting room in my Volvo," he replied with half a smile. "Clare wants my contribution down on paper, for the record. I said I'd pop in on my way out of town."

"You going anywhere nice, sir?" Savage asked.

"No," he said. "How're you doing? I heard you both went through the wringer."

"All part of the job," Savage said. "And Colin did most of the fighting."

She laughed.

"I'm glad you rescued her, Robbie. She rescued me. I never would have made it without her."

Kett nodded, but Spalding tutted.

"You do realise it *shouldn't* be part of the job," she said, waving her pencil between them. "All this *Indiana Jones* shit."

"Indiana Jones was an archaeologist," Porter said, disgusted.

Spalding looked ready to make good on her promise of pencil insertion when the door to Clare's office opened again. He ushered out Blake and his mum, the pair of them standing there with broken backs, as if they carried an invisible weight between them. Cathy Masefield had a cane in one hand, her knuckles white around the handle.

"And we're here if you need us," Clare said. "Anything at all."

Porter walked over to them and Savage followed him.

"Hey, Blake," Porter said, his voice gentle. The kid looked like he'd been pulled up from the depths of a frozen ocean, but when he saw the big DI his face opened into a tired smile.

"Hey, Pete," he said.

"How you holding up? You quick-scoping yet?"

"I'm getting there," Blake said. "I'll get the hang of it one day."

"Well, you know my PlayStation tag. You ever want a wingman then just holler."

"*KennyGForce*, right?" Blake said. "Stupid name, but I'll be there."

"And you remember what I said. You're a good kid. The

best. You've just had some serious bad luck. You deserve more than your dad had to give you, and what *he* is plays no part in what *you* are. That all comes from here." He tapped his own chest. "You're going to do amazing things, Blake. And hey, there's always a place for you here in a few years, if you want to do some good."

Blake beamed at Porter.

"Thanks," he said.

His mum put her free arm around the boy's shoulder, squeezing.

"We should go," she said, her voice a husk.

Blake nodded, shaking Clare's hand, then shaking Savage's.

"I'm sorry," he said to her, looking at the bandages that covered her palm. "I really am."

"It's already forgotten," she said, smiling.

Porter held out his hand to the boy, but Blake moved in and wrapped his arms around his torso instead. Porter looked stunned for a second, then hugged him back, patting him hard until they parted.

Savage watched the big DI as he watched them go, and she could have sworn he had tears in his eyes.

"I need a cuppa," he said when the door closed behind them.

"Let me," said Kett, but Porter waved him away, heading for the department's little kitchen.

"Is anyone going to stop him?" Clare hissed, aghast. When nobody moved, he turned back to Kett. "Come on then, let's hear what you have to say about all this. Weird times, Robbie. We can't seem to catch a break at the moment."

"Weird times indeed, sir," Kett replied. "Something's

changed in the world. You feel it? Things are getting worse. *People* are getting worse."

Clare nodded, and so did Savage, her head full of wild women and heartless boys.

"You did great, Kate," Kett said, nursing his chest and looking at her bandaged neck, her bandaged hand. "But be careful. You don't want to end up like me."

He walked into Clare's office, the Super shutting the door behind them. By the time Savage had made her way to the kitchen the kettle was boiling. Porter stood with both hands on the counter, staring into space. His eyes were definitely puffy.

"How're you doing, sir?" she asked.

He looked up like he hadn't heard her enter, sniffing.

"Oh, I'm great. I'm fine. Honestly."

She walked up beside him and leaned against the fridge. She knew Porter well enough by now to understand that the best way to make him talk was to say nothing at all.

"I mean, it just makes me angry," he said after a moment. "Why do arseholes like James Preston get to have kids? They have them and then what? Ignore them for years, miss out on all those moments, all those amazing things. They shit all over them and they still get to call themselves dads."

The kettle snapped off and Porter grabbed a couple of cups, slamming them on the worktop. He fished some teabags from the box and dropped one in each.

"It's just..."

He hesitated, tapping a teaspoon against the rim of the nearest mug. He couldn't meet Savage's eye but there was something inside him that needed out, she could feel it. She waited, giving him the space he needed.

"It's just Allie wants a baby. She's wanted one for

months now. I do too, more than anything. And we've been trying."

He seemed to choke on his own words as he lifted the kettle and poured water into the cups. The smell of tea filled the little room, beautifully fragrant.

"I don't know why it's not working," he said quietly, shrugging his big shoulders. "Or maybe I do. I think that maybe I do, Kate. Because I always wondered why it *never* happened, not once, not even by accident."

He stirred, lost in the spiral of golden tea for what had to be a full minute.

"I don't think I can have them," he said. "I don't think I can have children."

He blinked, his eyes wet, and Savage's heart almost broke clean in two. He waved her away, opening the fridge and pulling out the milk. He added a dash and a half to both mugs, his hands shaking.

"I'm sorry," he said. "You don't want to hear it."

Savage leant over and rested her hand on his. He didn't pull away, he didn't look at her, he just let her be there for him.

"You can't call men like Preston fathers," she said. "They don't deserve the title. You're the best man I know, Pete. Look at the way you were with Blake. Look at the way *he* was with *you*. You were more of a dad to him in a week than Preston was in years. If you want to be a dad, you'll be a dad—biology or not. And whoever you end up being a father to, however it ends up happening, they're going to be the luckiest kid on the planet."

She squeezed his hand.

"And for what it's worth, these things happen a lot more easily when you stop thinking too hard about it, when you take the pressure off. Just look what happens when you take a step back, when you *trust* yourself."

"What do you mean?" he said.

Savage laughed, nodding at the mugs that sat on the counter.

"You just brewed a decent cup of tea, Pete Porter."

He looked at the drinks as if he couldn't remember making them, and then grinned.

"I just made a decent cup of tea," he said. "Holy shit."

He picked up the mugs.

"I gotta show Robbie before he goes."

He started to run, tea slopping everywhere, and then stopped, looking back.

"Thank you, Kate," he said.

Then he was gone.

"You're welcome, mate," Savage said, drumming her hands on the worktop and frowning. "Hey, wait up, that was my tea!"

ROBBIE KETT KNOCKED on the door then stood back, pulling his jacket around his chest against the brutal cold. It had started snowing again an hour ago and the weather reporters didn't seem to think it was going to quit anytime soon. If he wasn't careful he'd be stranded out here, even with the Volvo.

He couldn't think of anywhere he'd less like to spend the night.

He went to knock again, stopping when he heard the sound of bolts being drawn back. The door opened and Norman Balls looked out, his face even rounder and paler than Kett remembered. He grinned like he was a kid who'd opened the door to Santa Claus.

"I knew you'd be back," he said. "I just knew it."

"Then you know why I'm here," Kett said.

Balls retreated and Kett walked past him into the welcome fug of heat. Somebody had been baking bread, the smell of it making his mouth water. Balls shut the door and scampered down the hall, past the kitchen where a woman the exact same size and shape as him pulled something out of the oven.

"I've got a friend over, mother," Balls shouted to her. "Don't come into my control centre."

Balls opened the door to the garage and walked in, positively fizzing with excitement. Kett followed, seeing the walls of folders, the groaning weight of files on the table in the middle of the room. He remembered the last time he'd been here, the way Balls' eyes had strayed to the far side of the room when he'd asked him about that word.

Hollenbeck.

"You know something," Kett said, massaging his chest, feeling the shard of Keefe's bullet press against his heart.

They won't stop coming. They'll never let you go.

"I know lots of things," Balls said. "But are you willing to listen?"

Kett tipped some books from a chair and sat down, groaning as the steel trap of pain closed around his ribs.

"Tell me who they are."

Balls grinned.

"I don't know everything," he said. "But I know a little. I know that these are people you don't mess with. Can I ask you a question first, before we begin? What are you going to do if you find them? If you find the people who call themselves Hollenbeck?"

Kett smiled, although there was no warmth there, no humour. He thought of the Pig Man, of Stillwater and Figg, of the two ghosts that had been sent to frame him and murder him, and every wound in his body seemed to open up and roar.

"I'm going to end them," he said. "I'm going to end every last fucking one of them."

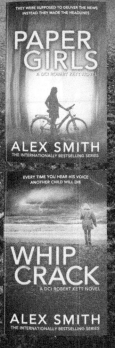

www.ballsknowsitalls.net

IT'S THE MOTHER OF ALL CRIMES

EVERY MOTHER'S SON

A DCI ROBERT KETT NOVEL

ALEX SMITH

THE INTERNATIONALLY BESTSELLING SERIES

EVERY MOTHER'S SON
THE SEVENTH DCI KETT CRIME THRILLER

It's the Mother of All Crimes.

DCI Robert Kett's efforts to return to a normal life are dashed after he receives a phone call from his mother, Mary —a woman he hasn't spoken to in almost a decade. When she invites him and the girls to visit her in the isolated community where she has been staying, Kett sees an opportunity to heal their fractured relationship.

But this is no family reunion. Mary Kett needs his help. A young couple have been brutally murdered, and their newborn son is missing—a note left in his crib saying that the baby will die if the police are called.

Forced to go undercover with Porter and Savage, Kett discovers that somebody here has everything to hide and nothing to lose. And with time running out fast, Kett must solve one of the most terrifying mysteries of his life.

A mystery that threatens to tear his own family apart.

ABOUT THE AUTHOR

Alex Smith wrote his first book when he was six. It wasn't particularly good, but it did have some supernatural monsters in it. His latest books, the DCI Robert Kett thrillers, have monsters in them too, although these monsters are very human, and all the more terrifying for it. In between, he has published twelve novels for children and teenagers under his full name, Alexander Gordon Smith—including the number one bestselling series Escape From Furnace, which is loved by millions of readers worldwide and which is soon to become a motion picture. He lives in Norwich with his wife and three young daughters.

Find out more at alexsmithbooks.com

Made in the USA
Coppell, TX
12 April 2021

52910815R00215